ALL THIS COULD BE YOURS

ALL
THIS
COULD
BE
YOURS

HANK PHILLIPPI RYAN

MINOTAUR BOOKS
NEW YORK

First published in the United States by Minotaur Books, an imprint of St. Martin's Publishing Group

EU Representative: Macmillan Publishers Ireland Ltd, 1st Floor, The Liffey Trust Centre, 117–126 Sheriff Street Upper, Dublin 1, DO1 YC43

www.minotaurbooks.com

Designed by Gabriel Guma

The Library of Congress Cataloging-in-Publication Data is available upon request.

ISBN 978-1-250-34999-6 (hardcover)
ISBN 978-1-250-35000-8 (ebook)

Our books may be purchased in bulk for specialty retail/wholesale, literacy, corporate/premium, educational, and subscription box use. Please contact MacmillanSpecialMarkets@macmillan.com.

First Edition: 2025

10 9 8 7 6 5 4 3 2 1

Choices are the hinges of destiny.
—Pythagoras

To Jonathan, of course. I am endlessly grateful
that we chose each other.

————————

Ye who believe in affection that hopes, and endures, and is patient,
Ye who believe in the beauty and strength of woman's devotion,
List to the mournful tradition still sung by the pines of the forest;
List to a Tale of Love in Acadie, home of the happy.

FROM *EVANGELINE* BY HENRY WADSWORTH LONGFELLOW

"I'm going live because I want you to witness this." Tessa swiveled her cell phone to show the carpeted corridor of Swain and Woodworth, then walked toward the company's mahogany-paneled elevator bank, the camera shot swaying a bit with each step. "See this, whoever's out there watching? I'm headed for the elevator. For the last time."

Funny way to get courage, she thought, *putting it on social media*. But it meant she couldn't change her mind. She hadn't even told Henry—though it was only his shiny new job that made today's radical decision financially possible. She was lucky, she knew that.

"I'm trying to remember how passionate I feel right now," she went on. "How powerful. I'm at the elevator. I'm pushing the down button." She turned the camera again, pointed it at herself. "I'm Tessa Calloway. You've seen my comments here on #MomsWithDreams. And now, I want you dreamers to be with me in person. Ready?"

One comment appeared. **Ready!** Then another. ***So ready!***

"I'm quitting my job. I've had it with the ridiculous stress. With the unnecessary pressure. With being absolutely invisible at every single moment. I've had it with the creeping horrendous reality that I'm wasting my one life—my *one* life . . ."

Tessa had to stop, surprised at the catch in her voice. At the tears spilling down her cheeks. "I'm sorry to cry—but no, honestly, I'm not sorry. I'm probably burning bridges, and I don't mean to be critical but—well, yes, I do." She paused, gathering her thoughts, imagining who might be watching. Strangers, all of them. She hoped.

But she wanted to share this. Needed to. She was steel and stone and immovable. "I've been a good, faithful, successful employee. But tonight I had to stay late to clean up someone else's mess. And you know? Not anymore. No. Why is *their* mismanagement *my* emergency? I've juggled my husband and my kids and my job and yes, I *can* do it. But I don't—*want* to. I simply—want my life to be my own."

The viewer numbers had ticked up, slowly, now in triple digits. Smiley faces and applauding hands flooded the screen. She drew power from them; from the support, the enthusiasm, the sisterhood.

"Look." She turned the camera again. "The elevator doors are opening. I'm about to take my first step. My first step into my new reality. It's risky, I know. But I swear I will figure it out. Because listen, you all. Hear me. I only have one life."

She stood a little straighter as she walked into the elevator. "And I, Tessa Calloway, right this very moment, am taking my one life back. I'm *doing* it. Are you with me?"

The screen exploded with emojis; hearts and flowers and bottles of champagne.

The elevator doors closed in front of her camera lens.

Through her welling tears, she saw the viewer comments now racing beneath her still-live video, scrolling almost faster than she could read them. Who was out there, watching? But she was Tessa Calloway now, and safe.

One life! one said. And the next and the next. ***One life!***

"Henry? Linny? Zack?" she said as the elevator descended. "I'll be home soon."

Three hundred comments now, four, blurring into a stream of digital approval. She paused, taking a moment as the potentially devastating consequences of her decision threatened to derail her. But no. Not this time.

"Thank you all," she said. "Thank you. I could not do this without you. And I'll keep you posted."

She clicked a button. The phone screen went to black. She was alone. Alone with another life-changing choice.

"Wish me luck," she whispered.

1

Tessa would never get used to this, not ever, and she would never cease being thrilled by it; the waves of affection as she strode by the rows of women, shoulder to shoulder and filling every beige folding chair the bookstore could hold. She felt their admiration, felt their sisterhood, felt their support—they knew who she was, and she knew them, because even as strangers they were her friends, her readers, those who understood that a book could open your life and open your heart. She tried to silence the warning voice in her head as she continued up the center aisle of the store's bookshelf-lined event space. She was Tessa Calloway now, best-selling author, and she had nothing to fear.

"Tessa, our book club loves you!" A woman in a periwinkle-blue cardigan reached out and touched Tessa's arm as she walked by. Tessa stopped and turned to her, smiling.

"I love you, too," she whispered, and now it seemed like every woman had a cell phone out, pointing it at Tessa, the tiny flashes popping like celebratory fireworks. *Capturing the moment*, Tessa thought, and she wished she could do the same thing, save up every morsel of this, wrap herself in it, reassure herself that dreams could indeed come true.

"And we love Annabelle! She's so kick-ass!"

Tessa's laughing response was drowned in applause, and the room became a sea of periwinkle-blue book covers, some held in readers' arms, some arrayed in a massive multibook display, backdropped by the oversized cover of *All This Could Be Yours* hanging behind the podium. The portrait of her protagonist, Annabelle Brown, on the cover, with her tortoiseshell glasses, periwinkle earrings, and signature attitude, seemed to watch over the whole event, amused and approving. Confident. Empowered. Never surprised.

All this could be yours, Tessa thought. Her husband had said that to her, joking, arms wide, the day they got engaged. The phrase had stayed with her, but the more she thought about it, the more sinister it sounded. How chilling the exact same words became in fiction when Annabelle's boss said them, offering her that life-changing choice. Tessa's editor had instantly loved it. "Double entendre," Olivette had pronounced. "Perfect."

Now Tessa sent a silent thank-you to the writing gods, and to Annabelle, too. Maybe all this, and more, already *was* hers. After all this time, and after all of her own life-changing choices. For worse, and for better.

"Come on, you all, let Tessa by!" An amplified voice came from the front of the event space. Lisa Mooney, chignoned and chic in black linen, clapped her hands to get the crowd's attention. "You want to hear her talk, don't you?"

Tessa's publicist had forewarned her that the savvy and influential Lisa was the doyenne of the women's fiction world—and that a successful event at Excelsior Books almost guaranteed another week on the bestseller lists. Tessa crossed her fingers, wishing, as she stepped onto the dais. Then paused as Lisa motioned her to wait.

The bookstore owner tipped the black gooseneck microphone closer, then quieted the audience with two palms.

"You don't need me to introduce Tessa Calloway," she began.

"One life!" someone in the audience called out.

"Moms with dreams!"

Tessa touched a hand to her heart, seeing the women's faces now, rapt and attentive, so many of them, like Tessa herself, wearing Annabelle's signature periwinkle-blue earrings.

Lisa went on with the familiar paragraph of the careful introduction publicist Djamila Parekh had crafted for booksellers and librarians and book clubs—recapping the viral moment when Tessa walked out on her corporate career to focus on husband and kids in Massachusetts, her late-in-life debut novel, her starred reviews, the instant *New York Times* bestsellerdom. Her devoted followers, and the almost cult of the life-empowering Annabelle.

Tessa had heard that intro, sometimes twice a day, for more than three weeks now, as her book tour, triumphant at every stop, took her to different cities and different bookstores and different audiences. Three weeks to go. *Aren't you exhausted?* Henry would ask. But she wasn't, not a bit, who needed sleep? She was flying on love and success and, she had to admit, financial necessity. Which Henry—and their brand-new mortgage—did not let her forget.

"So let's give a big Indianapolis welcome," Lisa was saying, "to our darling Tessa, who has introduced us to the instantly iconic Annabelle Brown."

Tessa took a step forward, but Lisa stopped her again.

"Wait. Let me ask you," Lisa said. "How many of you have had your lives changed by Annabelle? How many have learned from her sass, and her spirit, and her confidence? Let's see a show of hands as we welcome Tessa to the microphone. I am honored to present—Tessa Calloway."

Tessa opened her arms in gratitude as Lisa gestured her to the podium, the audience now a swell of waving hands, women cheering, some brandishing their periwinkle books in the air like prized trophies, or symbols of their sisterhood.

"I know you can't tell with this podium in front of me." Tessa patted the air with her palms to settle the crowd. "But my feet are not touching the ground. I am absolutely floating, floating with joy and appreciation, and with surprise, I must say, at all that's happened. And it has happened because of *you*. Thank you."

Her speech flew by; her desire to be a writer since she was a child, the love-at-first-sight meeting with her husband, Henry, her business career, her renunciation of corporate pressures, her devotion to her family, and then, at midlife, stepping into the world of fiction.

"And I loved being a mom, and still do, but when I had a good idea for a novel . . ." She went on, telling the familiar and reassuring story. Creating the confident and inspirational Annabelle, with her search for happiness and her search for justice, her insistence on equality, and her resistance to the patriarchy. It had been a lark when Tessa started the book, almost a personal rewriting of her own professional history, but then Annabelle had taken on a life of her own.

"Sometimes," she said, "and I've heard other authors say this, too, it feels as if I'm simply transcribing what Annabelle says. That it's not me, Tessa, writing it, but me channeling Annabelle onto the page. It's almost magic, there's no other way to explain it. So. Enough of me yammering. Who has a question?"

The hands shot up. Tessa pointed to a woman in the back, black jacket, long braided hair.

"Yes?"

The woman stood, clutching her book. "Do you, like, literally *hear* Annabelle's voice?"

Someone always asked this. And if they only knew how true it was. Annabelle did talk to her, like a supportive older sister. There was no actual magic to it, she knew it was simply her subconscious, her writer brain, the clear and present voice of her imagination.

"Yes, funnily enough, I do. Annabelle's voice was very distinct as I began to write the book, almost as if she had wanted her story to be told."

Got that right, Annabelle said.

Tessa paused, knowing the audience could never understand the depth of her connection to the character in her head. The voice of Annabelle. She'd heard it first when she was a child—and realized it was her own particular way of coping with stress and pressure. "Annabelle" offered guidance. Confidence. And grace. A way for Tessa to be her own best friend. She chose another raised hand. "Yes?"

"That's so cool about Annabelle's voice. I saw you, live, on Moms with Dreams, when you walked out on that job. How'd you have the courage to do it?"

"Oh, you've felt it, I'm sure, that inner voice saying you're doing the right thing?" Tessa nodded, remembering. "And thank you for being with me at that pivotal time. I was a corporate trainer, even before Kid One and Kid Two. I traveled constantly, taught classes in productivity and teamwork. It was—rewarding, sometimes, but the rest of the time it was soul-crushing. Still, it had health insurance. You all know about balancing *that* deal, right?"

"We sure do," someone said.

"But that day—I'm not sure it was as much courage as it was—well, one last straw. We'd been in a meeting, and I'd presented what I thought was a terrific idea. And not one person seemed to notice I had spoken. No one reacted. Until ten minutes later, when some guy presented exactly the same idea, and everyone applauded how genius he was. I felt—invisible. I remember thinking I could go rob a bank, and no one would notice, because I was *so* invisible. You know?"

"Totally!"

"Every day!"

"And then I was assigned to 'help' on the project. And fix his mistakes!"

"No way."

"Yup. But I was lucky," Tessa went on. "My husband had taken a new job, and I knew we could handle it financially, and I was missing the kids so much, and sometimes—you gotta do what you gotta do."

"One life!" someone called out.

"Exactly." Tessa pointed to her, emphasizing. "And I was lucky enough to be able to reclaim mine. And you know I'm still on Moms with Dreams, because you all are my sisters. We all have dreams. And only one life. So. Who else has a question?"

"Yes, you certainly have been lucky. So far. As an adult." The woman who stood was elegantly thin, her hair expensively casual. "But let me ask. Many successful authors say they had terrible childhoods. Traumatic. Did you? Were you 'lucky' as a teenager, too?"

Uh-oh, Annabelle said.

2

Tessa had worried about questions like that, even before the book was published. She'd hesitantly broached it with Sadie Bailey at one of their first meetings, asking her agent for advice on how to handle them.

"I don't like talking about my childhood," Tessa had explained. "Or my parents. Or being a teenager. My book is not about *me*. It's about inspiring *other* people—women—to stand up for themselves."

Sadie had commiserated, listening unjudgmentally, her years of babysitting needy authors revealed in her patient consideration of Tessa's concerns.

"There are ways to handle questions you don't want to answer," her agent said. "Try to finesse, give an answer that's question-adjacent, and then take another question. People are inquisitive, and they're attempting to get to know you, as they would a friend. But you don't need to *let* them. Not unless you want to." She'd paused, as if considering whether to go on. "And you probably don't want to."

Sadie had mistaken Tessa's silence for fear. "Don't worry, darling," she'd said. "Your only responsibility is to write fabulous books. But whatever you want to keep private, you keep private."

Her agent had swiveled in her black chair, eyeing Tessa up and down. Then she'd pushed the sleeves of her creamy cashmere sweater to her elbows and leaned forward, eyes narrowing.

"Except from me." Sadie had laced her fingers in front of her. "Look,

Tessa. Private is private, personal is personal. But . . ." She'd paused. "You and I have a contract. If there's something damaging or untoward that would materially affect this book or this agency or Waverly Publishing or anything connected with this book in any way, I'm not even going to say the specific words out loud, *that* I need to know."

"Oh, I—sure."

"But I'm going to say this, once, because it's in our contract—*your* contract—with Waverly Publishing. You guaranteed that there is nothing that you have ever done that could put the publisher in a bad light, put your book or yourself in a bad light, nor have you hidden anything that would be detrimental to sales. And that you would take responsibility—indemnify them—if anything unacceptable is revealed. It's called moral turpitude." Sadie had fiddled with a big black pen on her desk, spinning it on the glossy surface. "This is a business, darling, I don't need to tell you. Oh, everyone loves terrific books and talented authors and the joy of the craft, but there's one unavoidable bottom line. It's all about the money."

"Oh, I know. I—"

Sadie had stopped the pen, leaned forward, her eyes hardening.

"So if you *harm* their bottom line, *you'll* pay, not them. All that advance money, all those promises, everything you've dreamed of. Your career. Gone. With no possible recovery. And everyone might be sad, and disappointed, but it won't matter. When you signed on the dotted line to write two books, that was the deal. So." Sadie flipped a palm, as if to dismiss the annoying financial calculations. "It's my job to tell you. Now I have."

"Of course. Nothing to worry about." Tessa remembered answering, Annabelle-confident, as if it were true. "And as for the personal questions, I can handle them."

"Good." Her agent had given that Sadie Bailey nod, that single dismissive dip of her head that indicated the subject was closed.

Now, at the podium in Indianapolis, Tessa pretended to be pondering her answer about whether she had a traumatic childhood. Finally she smiled, as if rueful.

"It depends, doesn't it? On what you mean by traumatic. I was an only child, and I remember thinking it was terrible that my mother wouldn't let me wear lipstick when I was twelve, even when everyone else did. Nor would she let me thumbtack my Backstreet Boys poster to my bedroom wall." She paused, trying to look nostalgic. "It certainly felt traumatic then, but I assume that's not what you're talking about."

The silence felt infinite, the event on pause, as Tessa walked the tight-rope.

"Seriously," she went on, wanting to respect the questioner, not make her feel dismissed. "I agree that childhood drama, or trauma, has led to some spectacularly relatable novels, and we can feel authors almost heal on the page. But in my case, it's just not—relevant."

She gave her own version of the Sadie Bailey nod, then pointed to a woman near the front, flowered blouse and cabled cardigan. But the first woman kept talking.

"Even the deal with the devil Annabelle makes? Intercepting the memo, snaking the job from her male colleague? She says, 'Feeling guilty is simply another excuse for being weak.' Do you believe that?"

"Well, again, that's Annabelle talking." Tessa shrugged, embracing the impossibility. "I seem to have created a main character who makes her own decisions."

We make them together, Annabelle said.

The woman finally took her seat. Tessa pointed to Flowered Blouse again.

"I love your blue earrings," the woman said, fingering one of her own. "Where did you get the idea that Annabelle would always wear them?"

"Well, so funny. They were an anonymous gift from one of my first social media followers. She told me that the blue meant 'the sky's the limit.' And she was right. Now my head is in the clouds every day. On airplanes."

As the approving laughter subsided, Lisa Mooney edged to the podium and stood by Tessa, clipboard in hand.

"One last question." Lisa pointed to a woman in the back. "Yes, how about you?"

"Where is your hometown, and how did your life there inform your book?"

Careful, Annabelle said.

Tessa stared at the woman in black. Wondering if this was just an-other question from a curious reader, or if it was *the* question. The one her mother had warned would ruin her.

3

The polished marble lobby of the Indie Hotel bustled with comings and go-ings, roller bags rumbling over the shiny floors, pop music piped through some invisible sound system, a column of travelers shepherding their suitcases through the velvet-roped registration line. Tessa, with her own black roller bag and black carryall and carrying the biggest bouquet of frothy pink peonies she had ever seen, now stood one person away from check-in. The reader at Excelsior Books who brought the flowers had leaned in—almost too close—to whisper her story.

"I quit my job because you did," the woman said. "You are so brave, and Annabelle is so brave, and I wanted *my* one life, too." She'd laughed, pointing to her oversized canvas tote bag. "Yeah, I'm using a diaper bag. I know it's not very glam, but at least I'm with my kids and husband, and I use my study as an office for my *own* business, and I don't have to show up nine to five and drudge for some bozo anymore."

"And everything worked out?" Though Tessa was gratified by her readers' passionate reactions, she always worried that they'd make un-fortunate life decisions based on fiction. What was the balance between inspiration and folly?

"I've never been happier," the woman had said. "And it's all because of you."

Tessa had inhaled the flowers' lush fragrance; didn't have the heart to reveal she'd have to leave them in her hotel room. "Same," she said. "*I've never been happier, and it's all because of you.*"

Now she shifted her own tote bag to the other shoulder, the scent of the peonies as intoxicating as her memories of tonight's event. Lisa Mooney had told her the signing line was a record for Excelsior Books, with three women actually crying, two who'd brought their teenaged daughters, one of whom demanded Tessa sign her arm. Lisa had offered to adopt Tessa, keep her, never let her go.

"Sorry that the questions got personal," Lisa had apologized as she guided Tessa to the signing table. "That'll happen, but you handled it beautifully. You only have to answer what you feel comfortable answering."

"No problem," Tessa had said. "I know it comes out of love."

Now the woman at the registration desk—her dark hair pulled back with a black ribbon, and wearing a trim navy jacket—was beckoning Tessa forward.

"Gorgeous flowers," she said, as Tessa approached the registration desk. "I'm Graciela, welcome to the Indie Hotel. And your name?"

"Calloway." Tessa spelled it. "First name Tessa."

"Oh!" Graciela's eyes widened. "Of course. I should have recog—"

"No, no," Tessa said, "but thank you."

"I adore your book." Graciela leaned in, looking conspiratorial. "Working here—" she gestured, encompassing the entire hotel. "There's such a hierarchy, you know? I can't quit, like you did, or . . ." She paused, maybe worrying about who might be listening. Then smiled. "Do what Annabelle did. But it gave me courage."

"That's so kind of you," Tessa said. Her phone buzzed in the pocket of her trench coat. She needed to check in. Call home. Get food. Try to sleep. "I love hearing that."

"And there's a package for you in your room," Graciela went on, tapping at her computer keyboard. "Let us know if there's anything else you need." She selected a black key card, put it through some machine, tucked it into a cardboard flap, handed it to Tessa. "The room number is on the flap. We don't like to say the numbers out loud."

"Thanks. A package? Do you know who from?"

"I don't. It came on the last shift. Is there a problem?"

"No, not at all." It was probably a gift from the bookstore. She put the key card in her jacket pocket. "And thank you for the kind words."

"Thank *you*," Graciela said. "And all my friends feel the same. You totally rock."

Tessa paused, then handed Graciela the peonies. "You know, I can't keep these, an early plane tomorrow. Would you like to take them home?"

"Oh my goodness." The clerk accepted the bouquet, the pink blossoms cradled in her arms. "I'll treasure them. You're even more amazing than I thought. If that's even possible."

"My pleasure." Tessa's phone buzzed again as she walked toward the bank of elevators. She dug it out of her coat pocket. *Linny?*

She stopped at the elevators, accepted her daughter's call before she pressed the up button.

"Sweetheart?" she said as the call connected. "Are you okay? Is everything okay?" A torrent of words flooded in from the other end; Tessa imagined Linny's tousled blond hair tamed into a ballerina bun, her rainbow-striped shirt, her face animated in preteen outrage. For the past three weeks, she'd seen the kids and Henry only on FaceTime. Her life evolved as a series of tiny pixelated squares, sometimes a thousand miles away. Dreams coming true had a price.

"Linny? Honey?" Tessa tried to interrupt. "Use your careful words." Linny had called on her own. Where was Henry? "I'm here. I'm listening. You don't have to raise your voice. I'm hearing that Zack is *superly* annoying you. But you know how to deal with that. Right? But where's your father?"

"Mom. I cannot take it. Zack always gets first dibs, like on *every*thing, and Dad's all about that, like they're a team, and even though I'm *so much* older, I'm like . . ."

A frazzled-looking mom cooing to a bleary-eyed, pink-bonneted infant in a strapped-on carrier and pulling a battered roller bag stepped to the elevator button, and looked at Tessa, questioning. "Don't tell me this is broken?"

"No, I'm on the phone. With my own daughter. Go ahead, I'll wait for the next one."

As the elevator doors opened and closed and left Tessa alone again, Linny's stream of complaints continued, condemning her impossible brother and bemoaning the doomed unfairness of her eleven-year-old life.

Meanwhile, precious hours of potential sleep time before her crack-of-dawn flight were ticking away. She was starving. And handling Linny's mini-meltdowns should be Henry's job.

Where was he? At least Indiana and Massachusetts were in the same time zone, but it was pushing ten in Rockport. Linny should be long asleep. And, bitter icing on the cake, this needy phone call proved Tessa had no idea what was happening in her own home.

"Linny? Sweetie? Maybe read a book instead of fighting with Zack? He teases you on purpose, you know that. He's a *boy.* Practice ignoring him. Can you get your dad?"

"Mom. He's—"

"Look, honey? I have to go up to my room. If we try to talk on the elevator, we'll get disconnected. So get your dad, have him call me in five minutes. We'll all figure it out. 'Kay?"

"'Kay. But it still sucks."

"Linny!"

"Bye-ee."

Tessa had to laugh as her daughter hung up. That age, somewhere between *Harriet the Spy* and *Twilight,* Linny not quite certain of who she was or what she would turn out to be. *Eleven years old,* Tessa thought, as the elevator carried her upward. Eleven could go either way. Tessa knew that, firsthand. But that was long ago. And forgotten. She hoped.

The long hotel corridor stretched out in front of her, jewel-toned paisley carpeting in some only-in-hotels pattern, lily-shaped sconces casting a dim glow onto the row of numbered doors. She found hers, 3016, and patted her pockets for her room key card.

She tapped the card against the metal square. The light blinked insolently red. She tried the card's other side. Red.

"Kidding me?" She tried again. Red.

Her phone buzzed in her pocket.

"Tessa?" Henry. Finally.

"Hey, honey. Hang on. My key card isn't working," she interrupted his greeting.

"Did you put it against your phone again?"

"No. I didn't." Though possibly she had. "Sometimes they're cranky. So about Linny—"

"How'd it go tonight? They loved you, right? Tessa Calloway, instant best-selling author. Inspirer of women. Bringer of power. The darling of social media. Hang on, Tesser," Henry said. "I think I heard something. A sound. I'll call you back in ten minutes. Fix your key."

"What's wrong? What sound? Is it Linny?" *The kids. Henry. Their brand-new house.* But there was only the flat white noise of nothing. He'd hung up.

Footsteps behind her. A man carrying a grease-spotted paper bag from Panera glanced at her as he walked by; he seemed to be taking in her face, her whisper, her bag, her suitcase, her phone call. She smiled at him, the wan acknowledgment of a fellow traveler, telegraphing *all good, nothing to see here, waiting for my husband to check on a strange sound in our new house.*

The man paused, assessed her again, opened his door. At least Panera Guy had a key that worked.

It'd be easy for someone like him to pretend to be a registered guest, the thought occurred to her. While, in reality, be lurking, scouting, targeting. Using the built-in anonymity and accepted proximity as cover. As disguise.

But that was her writer-mind at work. These days, with a deadline for an unwritten second book looming, everything became a potential plot element.

She examined her card again, front and back, trying to discover what was wrong. *Oh.* She patted the pockets of her new book-tour trench coat; knee-length, black, suitable for airplane, rain, and substitute bathrobe. In the right-side pocket, her fingers closed over another hard plastic rectangle. She'd been using a key card from her previous hotel. "Idiot," she whispered.

She tapped, and her keypad light went green. She opened the door, then paused. Looked, ridiculously, for Panera Guy.

But the corridor was silent, empty, only an anonymous row of identical closed doors.

She deadbolted her own door. Chained it. She was Tessa Calloway now, and safe.

4

She'd barely unzipped her suitcase when two sharp knocks on the door made her flinch. *Who?* Her imagination accelerated into high gear. *Panera Guy?* But the peephole revealed it was Graciela from the registration desk, carrying a cellophane-wrapped and beribboned plate of cheese and crackers and glistening red grapes.

"I am so sorry, Ms. Calloway," she said, as Tessa opened the door. "I thought this was already in your room, but it was still in the kitchen fridge. I hope I didn't—"

"How gorgeous!" Tessa took the chilled white platter, heavier than it looked. "From the hotel? Thank you. Again."

As the door closed, Tessa put the cheese on the desk under the wall-mounted television, untied the periwinkle satin ribbon, then peeled the cellophane from the plate, revealing thin triangles of golden cheddar and white squares dotted with caraway seeds surrounded by an array of multishaped crackers. Picking up the top piece of cheddar with her fingers, she took a bite, almost swooning with the rich, sharp creaminess. A white notecard was tucked underneath the black linen napkin.

Call me the minute you get this, the typed note said. *No matter how late. XO, Olivette.*

Not from the hotel. From her editor. But Ollie wasn't much of a talk-on-the-phone kind of person. So what was this about?

Bestseller list. Tessa had been trying all day not to think about it. She knew, everyone knew, that the all-important Sunday *New York Times* best-seller list was released on Wednesdays. This was Wednesday.

And Ollie wanted her to call. *Please let me make the list,* Tessa prayed to whatever muse might be listening, the gods on writing Olympus. Making a deal. *I'll never complain again.* She thought of their new and shocking mortgage payments, and of the precious family back home relying on her, only her, to keep the Calloway engines running.

"Guess what?" Olivette answered on the first ring.

"Don't make me guess, Olivette Iketa. Is everything okay?"

"More than okay. You made the list again, superstar. Holding at number two. Two weeks in a row. Only 'she who will not be named' is ahead of you."

"That's—"

"Put on FaceTime," Olivette interrupted. "I want to show you something."

Tessa smoothed her ponytail, knowing she must look frazzled, but she was too delighted to care. She touched the icon and Olivette appeared, chopped dark hair and enormous, black-framed glasses. She was at her desk at Waverly, Tessa recognized her big black chair.

"Ready for this?" Olivette said.

"For what?"

Olivette turned the phone and panned it across a row of smiling faces, each person lofting a champagne flute. "It's your team," she was saying. "Team Tessa. We're all here, wildly celebrating."

Tessa heard a chorus of praise and cheering, individual words unintelligible, but the support and joy wrapped around her, and her exhaustion vanished. All this could be hers—no, it already was. Team Tessa.

"We ordered the cheese this morning, by the way." Olivette's voice. "That's how certain we were. We stayed late so we could toast you. And see? Carol's here."

Olivette was protecting her, making sure she noticed publisher Carol McClintock, in Chanel as always, and publicist Djamila Parekh, and Tessa's agent, Sadie Bailey; all names in the acknowledgments of her book, all real people, all drinking champagne and applauding her. *Her.* She'd wanted to write a novel since she was . . . since the first time she'd read one. She scrawled her hopes in her precious pink diary in her loopy handwriting, and revealed her dreams to her mother, and to her best friend, and some nights, alone, she'd whispered them to the universe. *I'll give anything*, she'd promised.

"Thank you," was all she could think to say. Her face on the minuscule phone screen was distorted by the hotel room lighting, but she recognized her own joy. "This is—because of you."

"And you, Tessa. And your fabulous Annabelle." Carol, low-voiced but commanding, raised her glass, then touched it to the rim of Olivette's.

"And Olivette," Tessa said. "She plucked *All This* from the submissions and called Sadie and—"

"The rest is history," Olivette said. "As long as you keep selling those books, you can have all the cheese you want."

All the cheese. Tessa let herself fall backward onto the voluptuous row of pillows piled against the bed's headboard, and stared at the stucco ceiling. Her colleagues were laughing and toasting, miles away, and her book had changed their lives. And hers. It would all be fine. It would.

"You okay, darling? Getting enough sleep?" Sadie asked. "Any issues at your events, anyone being too pushy?"

Tessa sat up at that question, seemingly out of nowhere. Was Sadie warning her of something? She remembered the probing questions at the bookstore.

"Why would you ask that? Is something wrong?"

"Of course not," her agent said. "But I know you don't like discussing your personal life. And—"

"In fact, yeah, we're monitoring your socials," Ollie interrupted. "People can be jerks, frankly. Even . . . unpleasant. They're jealous, or bitter. Or feel you unfairly got some success that they didn't. Or maybe they love you—but maybe *too* devotedly. We'll keep that from you, though. Delete it. Best we can. That's our job. But be aware."

Aware? Tessa thought. *Jerks?* "Seriously. Did something happen?"

"Early flight tomorrow, Tessa, remember, doing my publicist duty here." Djamila, who seemed to be changing the subject, flapped a white paper at her. Tessa recognized her itinerary. Tessa was married to that schedule, with its dates and times and cities and flights. Her own printed version was in a green file folder, with an electronic backup copy in a Google doc, and if all else failed, her public signing schedule was on her website. Her agent, Sadie, had access to the doc, and Henry's copy was printed out; she'd magneted it to the fridge. Theirs had hotel phone numbers and specific airplane flights.

"Yeah, how well I know. Six a.m. departure." She looked at the glowing green digits of the clock on her nightstand, her sleep time relentlessly disappearing. "Yikes, DJ. I might as well just stay up until then."

Team Tessa—she thought of them like that now, hoped she always would—chorused "no" in unison. She laughed, relishing how it felt to be the center of attention—impossible, once you had kids. And it had been so long since she was anything but Mom, or honey, or Mrs. Calloway. Not that there was anything wrong with that; she'd adored it. There were trade-offs for everything, no one knew that better than she did.

"Seriously, no," DJ said. "Do not stay up. Get some food, have a glass of wine, go to sleep. The car will come for you at four in the morning. It's brutal, but you can sleep all the way to Phoenix."

"I'll be fine. See?" Tessa stood, turning her phone camera lens to show her room. "I'm looking for the carryout menu now." She opened the drawers of the dresser. All of them empty, pungent with cedar and disuse. "I love the cheese. And I love you. Thank you for everything."

She clicked off to another chorus of cheering and raised glasses, reluctant to let them go. She'd visited a different city every day, inhabited different but similar hotel rooms, raced through different but similar airports. She wore an Apple watch on one wrist, showing book-tour time, and a regular watch on the other wrist, set to the time at home. After the initial tour euphoria, Tessa sometimes felt as if she were never really anywhere, spending less than twenty-four hours in any one place. And her connection to her family, only virtual, felt infinitely fragile. Her reality filtered through screens.

But it was the internet, she couldn't forget, that had changed her life. Her live social media broadcast of her "my one life" departure from her job had engendered a groundswell of support, and she'd continued to post weekly about her journey—its joys and its treacheries, its perseverance and sacrifices, through Linny's first chapter book and Zackie's last day of kindergarten, eventually revealing her tentative early writing, and her rejections and disappointments and finally, triumphs. She wore sunglasses, sometimes, and floppy hats, on the days she felt nervous about who might be watching.

Her followers had shared their hopes, too, and Tessa's socials grew a supportive following, and #MomsWithDreams became the virtual hub for her journey. Someone crafted a My One Life T-shirt with colored markers. Another a stretchy friendship bracelet with #MomsWithDreams in blue beads. A woman in Tucson sent Tessa those periwinkle "sky's the limit" earrings. Tessa still wondered how the woman had gotten her home address, but now she wore blue earrings every day. And her followers copied her; found their own blue jewelry, and traded bracelets with the book's title, like their badges of solidarity.

Tessa had shared the book auction, the sale, the glowing reviews and the buzzy publicity, with her social media followers cheering every victory. "We made the cover blue, periwinkle blue, just for you, #MomsWithDreams," Tessa had told them.

Then the social media fairy dust landed on her. A soon-viral photo showed Hollywood's it girl cradling an advance copy of Tessa's book. **MAKE IT *YOURS*!** she'd urged her millions of followers, captioning the photo in huge font embellished with a spiral of animated hearts. **WE ARE ALL ANNABELLE**. Overnight, every reader and bookstore and library demanded copies of *All This Could Be Yours*. And clamored to see Tessa Calloway in person. Her wildest dreams had come true.

To keep them, she simply had to be Zoom Mom and Zoom Wife for a while longer.

And she had to stay lucky.

True, Annabelle said. And stay careful.

But where was Henry? He'd call back in ten minutes, he'd said. It had been longer than that.

Henry had heard "a sound." And then hung up. She felt the thousand miles gaping between them, as excruciatingly unconquerably distant as if her family lived in another galaxy. Anything—*anything*—could be happening at home. And not a thing she could do about it.

5

"I'm back. It was nothing," Henry was saying now. He hadn't apologized for keeping her waiting, but his delay had given her time to talk to her team, so she let it go, their connection reassuring her. "This house is always full of sounds. I guess we're not used to them yet. And the kids are fine. Zachary and Linnea were in an apocalyptic struggle over the rules of some game. I hope you're in your room now."

"Yeah, well. Turns out I was using the key from *yesterday's* hotel."

"You're tired, hon. We're good. Let's say goodnight so you can sleep. Safe safe."

"Love love." She recited her part of their nightly call and response and paused. But Henry did not answer. "Hen? You there?"

Safe safe, love love, always always. How many times had they repeated that to each other?

They'd first said it, spontaneously, when Henry left her tiny apartment that day so many years ago, all makeshift bookshelves and Marimekko pillows and piles of *New Yorker*s, and headed to some sales conference in Montpelier. The sales conference had been—disappointing. But their nightly mantra became the bedrock of their relationship. They'd whispered it to each other, the secret two of them, on their wedding day. And every night since.

But only once in their *new* home. Where she'd spent just one night before her book tour began.

All because of Henry.

After that first check from her publisher, Henry, euphoric, had promised her a surprise. Then a few days later, he'd driven them for miles, pulled up to the curb on an unfamiliar street, opened Tessa's passenger-side door, and guided her onto a crushed-clamshell driveway.

"All this could be yours. See what I did there?" He'd pointed at a three-story buttercream Victorian, spackled and shadowed with the sunshine coming through lofty leafed-out maples. Rows of windows with pristine white shutters faced them, and a bank of pink-and-white peonies lined the pillared front porch. "All you have to do is sign."

"Sign what?" Turned out he had already put in an offer on the house. It was absurd, him making this unilateral decision. And, she'd calculated, the mortgage payments would devour her book money. But she had to admit, after all those years cramped and budgeting in their tired split-level in suburban Boston, the seaside Rockport house felt like another step in their destiny. The air here smelled of salt, and sun, and it felt like she could hear the ocean. She was either delighted or outraged.

"*You've* made this happen, Tesser." He'd led her up the steps to the porch, flats of aging white wood, the fading paint revealing the gray underneath. "Selling the old house gives us the down payment, and then with my severance and your royalties? We're good. It needs some fixing, and the kitchen sucks. But the rest is epic. You go on tour, sell a million books, the kids and I will survive. I promise."

"You can't do it on your own, honey," she'd protested. "All the home stuff. Kid stuff."

At that, Henry had crossed his arms over his chest, and given her a look. "Gotcha," he said. "So I take that to mean a man can't do what a woman can? I'd never say 'you can't do it on your own' to you, Tessa. Not if it was something you wanted to do. Now *I* want to. I stay home, you go succeed, everyone wins. You gonna double-standard me? What would Annabelle say?"

She'd had to laugh. Henry had a point.

"And look." Once inside, Henry had guided her through a warren of cozy rooms, two with fireplaces and pocket doors, and around a corner. "Ta-*da*. Your writing room."

"A built-in window seat," she'd whispered. As if on cue, the sun had beamed through a multipaned window, casting stripes of light on the flowered cushions. A dogwood—slick green leaves and a chaos of flowers—had bloomed like delicate fireworks in the yard beyond. She'd fallen in love, in one beat of her heart, and her resistance had vanished.

It was lucky, ironically, that Henry now was once again "between jobs," as he always put it, so he could stay home with the kids. Now, alone in her hotel room, her phone had gone silent. "Henry? You there?"

The distance between them yawned open again, she could almost feel the vast darkness. *Where had he gone now?* Was something wrong with the kids? It was impossible to know, it dawned on her, she could only see what he decided to show her on-screen. Her view of her entire home life—in a house she'd only stayed in one night—was proscribed by Henry's laptop angles. His decisions about exactly what to show her. And what to hide?

"Hen?"

"I'm here."

She tried to picture him, pushing up his tortoiseshell glasses, maybe wearing that ratty polo shirt she always threatened to toss away. She'd said *love love*, and he had one more line, and silly as it was, she couldn't relax until he said it.

"Where were you? What's going on?"

"Huh? Always always," he said. "Now your turn."

"Always always." She said her own final line, from habit and from marital superstition, yearning to talk just a little longer, keep connected for another minute.

But Henry hung up, leaving her alone in another almost unsettlingly familiar place. The humming air conditioner, the plastic-wrapped TV remote, the elaborately folded white towels, and her suitcase, open on the folding stand. And strangers behind every door.

She shook it off. Life was good, even fabulous, her kids were individuals, curious, with agency and intent, and Henry, for all his foibles, was at least reliably and relentlessly optimistic. They were a good team. So far.

And now, finally, time for food. She yanked open the nightstand drawer, expecting a carryout menu. And stared at what was there instead.

6

Tessa blinked, as if what was in the hotel nightstand drawer might be an illusion, or imagined. But there it was. An ordinary item, in an ordinary place, but certainly not the place it was supposed to be. Tessa picked up the necklace. A locket. A slim rose gold heart, engraved with curlicues and flowers. Weightier than it looked at first. Not a trinket. A treasure. Someone's left-behind treasure.

Some poor traveling mom, somewhere, was certainly distraught. Tessa almost felt guilty as she edged a fingernail between the sides. The locket popped open. Narrowing her eyes, she held it under the nightstand light. Inside, a tiny photograph, of . . . what? She held it closer to the bulb, squinting. Frowning. Then, feeling Nancy Drewish, she grabbed her phone and took a photo of it. Expanded the photo.

It was hard to tell, it was so small. But . . . parents? And a child. In front of some cabin-like structure at water's edge.

Mother, father, daughter, in blue jeans—she guessed they were blue, the picture was black and white—and similar striped T-shirts. How old was this? Impossible to tell with the father's haircut, military, maybe. Their T-shirts were timeless, as easily from a Sears catalog as from J.Crew. The setting could even be a fake backdrop. Black and white to look "vintage," when it wasn't.

Some copy editor at Waverly had flagged the word "nondescript" when Tessa used it in an early draft of *All This*, informing her that everything was describable. But that's the first word that came to mind; ordinary, standard-issue. Three expressionless faces staring into someone's camera.

It was no mystery what had happened, Tessa thought, creating a story about the picture, imagining the—wife? Who had left this locket behind. A tenderhearted nostalgic mom who had carried it for memories of home, to wake up in the morning and see her daughter and husband first thing and remind herself that her sacrifice was important because she was doing something necessary.

Or perhaps that wasn't the true story at all. The only certainty was that someone had left it behind. Someone would miss it. Had probably already missed it.

Tessa frowned, feeling her forehead crease. Her own phone camera held hundreds of photos of the kids, a modern version of the locket. Was she a bad mom for not also wearing their family photo? And didn't that make this even more important, even more precious, for its eccentricity?

She picked up the landline on the nightstand, ignored the inexplicable buttons, pushed zero.

"May I help you, Ms. Calloway?"

"Has anyone called about something they left behind in room 3016? I found a—"

"One moment, please," the voice, not Graciela, turned brusque, interrupting. "I'll connect you to lost and found."

"No, no, I—" But Tessa was already in transfer limbo. She hung up, stashing her guilt, and called room service for her salad. The usual, Caesar with grilled chicken.

That 4:00 a.m. pickup loomed ominously closer, and Tessa could almost hear the clock ticking.

The people in the photograph didn't look happy or unhappy, just . . . there. But this tiny photo was the representation of someone's memory, a memory they considered worthy of documenting. Important enough to be kept close to their heart.

Still. It shouldn't be difficult to get the locket returned to its rightful owner. The hotel certainly knew who had occupied this room right before Tessa, and it was unlikely that it had been left behind before that, because certainly the housekeeper would have discovered it. Though they hadn't this time.

She picked up the house phone again. This time she knew the process. "Lost and found, please," she said.

"I'm sorry, Ms. Calloway, lost and found is closed until tomorrow."

How can lost and found be closed? "I found something in my room, I mean, someone left it. How can I—" she began.

"I'll connect you to voicemail," the clerk said. "They'll return your call tomorrow at nine. Around nine."

"But I won't be here tomorrow. I have to leave early, before they'd—is there someone I can talk to tonight?" But the line had gone dead again.

She jammed her feet into her airplane shoes, made sure she had her key and the locket, and headed down to the lobby. On a mission. She was about to make someone happy, and that seemed nicely karmic. The world was making *her* happy, and she could pay it forward.

No Panera Guy in the hall, she reassured herself as she trotted toward the elevator and jabbed the button. It slid open, empty, and deposited her in the marble-floored lobby, still bustling at this time of night, with a pack of almost out of control wild-haired kids scampering and chattering in front of a man and woman in Disney T-shirts, clearly parents, clearly defeated.

She and Henry could not afford to take Linnea and Zack on trips "before the book"—that's how she and Henry both thought of it, "before the book"—but as soon as she got home from this trip, they'd do it up big. She'd let Linnea choose their destination, give her some power. Or have a family meeting about it. She calculated their future happiness as she walked to the registration desk. *All this could be yours*, she whispered cross-country to Zack and Linny. *I will make it happen.*

"May I help you?" The desk clerk's voice interrupted her thoughts. Her name tag said Darleen.

"Hi, Darleen, I'm Tessa Calloway," she said, enunciating her full name, semi-hoping the woman might recognize her, like Graciela, and be extra helpful.

"And?"

Okay, then. "I think the last guest left something in my room, 3016? And I'm wondering—"

"Sure. Give it to me, thank you so much, that's kind of you." Darleen moused open her computer. "Lost and found is closed," she said, as she typed, "but I'll put it somewhere safe until morning." She held out her hand. "Okay?"

It was almost as if the locket family was speaking to her, saying *please don't do this. We'll be lost again.* Tessa smiled at her sentimental storytelling. But the imaginary theoretical family was right, handing this left-behind treasure to a harried hotel clerk was certain to end unhappily.

"Listen, I'll bring it down in the morning." Tessa nodded, earnest. "Make it easier on you."

She watched the clerk decide whether to let her leave with someone else's property. Behind Tessa, a silver-haired epauletted pilot, obviously the leader of the uniformed airline pack trailing him, edged closer to the desk. He moved his roller bag closer to Tessa, encroaching on her space.

"Sure," Darleen was saying. "Tomorrow's good." She turned to the pilot, instantly congenial. "Welcome, Captain. May I help you?"

Any other time, Tessa might have been annoyed, but in this case, his entitlement had worked in Tessa's favor.

She scurried away, and with the necklace safely back in her pocket, clicked open her hotel room door again. Twenty minutes until her salad would arrive. The lights were still on, as she'd left them, and the streaming news channel chattering, voices of video strangers filling the silence. She muted it, considering what to do next. Then took another cell phone snapshot of the photograph, pursing her lips, perplexed. It seemed an invasion of privacy to post the whole thing. Zooming in on the husband only—she already thought of him as "the husband"—she then clicked another picture of him alone at the water's edge. Then one of the mom, then the girl.

She popped her husband snapshot into Google Images, but the search brought up nothing as a match. Or even intriguingly close. And not for the mom, nor for the daughter. Time for a better search engine. Humans.

The lighting would be gruesome, but she had to try. She propped the phone against the nightstand lamp, clicked on to her live feed, watched the countdown, and began to talk.

TESSA LIVE

"Hey, you all, it's me, Tessa. It's been a while, I know, but we need to chat. Tonight I have a mystery for you to solve—and I think we can do it together. Anyone out there?"

Instantly the counter numbers in the upper left of her screen began to climb. Ten, then thirty-five, then so swiftly past fifty that she stopped checking.

"Here I am in fabulous Indianapolis, and what an amazing time at Excelsior Books for *All This Could Be Yours*. Loved seeing you all, and even a few moms with dreams! And I am so grateful for how much you are loving Annabelle."

Hold up the book, she could imagine her agent's voice, instructing. But she didn't have a copy next to her.

"So you all, I'm on book tour, which is magical and fabulous and I truly adore it. But tonight, something happened, and I need your help."

Tessa watched the "we can help!" comments appear on the phone screen, so unremitting she could barely read them. She held up the locket, dangling it from her fingers.

"Could this be yours? I found it in my hotel room. Someone left what must be a treasured family heirloom—it even has a photo inside, a photo of what looks like a family, a mother and father and daughter. And I'm crossing fingers you all can help me return it to its rightful owner."

She saw herself on the screen, realized how impossible it would be to recognize the filigreed necklace. And no way to show the photos inside.

"I'll only post a bit of the photo, since I don't want to invade any-one's privacy, and I'll put up the locket, too. But isn't this tragic?"

She paused, looking at the heart-shaped jewelry in her palm, and the story behind the locket spooled into reality, as vividly as if she were watching a movie.

"We can all visualize some woman, probably a mom, a mom with dreams, harried and hassled and running as fast as she can, like we all do, don't we? And in the midst of maybe a crazy-early plane, or some personal pressure we cannot even imagine, she leaves behind the most precious thing in her life."

Tessa held up the locket again, the heart twisting at the end of the delicate chain, and watched the comments streaming in, the list racing by, emblazoned with heart emojis, crying faces, and hugs and puppies and flowers.

"We have to help her, dear readers. I know how it feels to be on the road, to be doing your best, and missing your family, and torn apart because you have no choice, no matter how happy you are, even if your dreams are coming true, that you are so tired, and so wrung out, and trying to juggle, and . . ."

Tessa paused, her eyes misting. Her heart twisted, just like the chain of the locket. She had a cell phone full of photos, sure, but what if Henry and the kids had given her something like this, to keep them close to her? What if she lost it? Their book-tour keepsake, their magical connection? She'd be inconsolable. And this woman, wherever she was, must be, too.

"And oh, all of you, you get it, don't you? You're out there, too, doing what you need to do, and what have you sacrificed for it? What bargains have you made for it? When all you want to do is go home . . ."

And then the tears were wet on her cheeks and there was no way to stop them. She wiped them away with two fingers. Linny, elfin and sassy, who knows what was happening in her little head? And Zack, who'd revered Henry since he was an infant, or Henry himself, who existed through his unwavering belief that everything was always for the best. Her sweet family. Their ties were infinitely tenuous; a spiderweb, strong but vulnerable. So very, very vulnerable.

"Oh my goodness, you all. You have made me cry with your comments, and how wonderful you are, and how brave, and let's find this Locket Mom, okay? We need to help her. We need to be there for her. Do you know anyone who wears this? Have you seen this? Could this even be *yours*?"

She held it up again, the burnished gold catching the glow of the lamplight.

"For her sake, for all of our sakes, we need to be in this together."

She sobbed outright, her voice catching. *Poor Locket Mom,* she thought. Sometimes the world was so unfair.

"I know how you all feel, dear ones, and I am so embarrassed to cry, but you understand how I feel, and again, could this be yours?

Locket Mom, are you out there? I am here for you, and we are all here for you, and we need to take care of each other and . . ."

As her voice trailed off, the comments blurred to an unending stream.

7

The lights of downtown Indianapolis still glowed in nighttime neon, and not a ray of dawn broke the endlessly dark sky as Tessa revolved out of the hotel's heavy front door. Airplanes weren't the only ones running on autopilot, she realized, now barely able to put one foot in front of the other. She'd dismissed any idea of makeup this morning as she yanked her hair back into its ponytail and put on her airplane clothes, black T-shirt, big silky scarf, black leggings, white sneakers, and her trusty black coat, and now managed to laugh at her own exhaustion as she slid into the back of the sleek white town car that idled at the curb. A uniformed driver with a name placard, CALLOWAY, had been standing at the ready.

A car with her name on it. She let that sink in, too. No more jouncing taxis. No more unreliable rental cars with exorbitant fees. All because she wrote a book. *Thank you, Annabelle*, she thought.

You deserve it all, Annabelle said.

"You settled in?" the driver asked.

Her schedule reminded her the driver's name was Geneva, and Geneva had not only brought her an ambrosial cup of coffee in a mug labeled Beans, she'd also hoisted Tessa's bag into the trunk of the car, and installed Tessa into the puffy black leather back seat. "I can do it myself," Tessa had begun, but Geneva had tutted her away.

"You have your job, I have mine," Geneva said, buckling in, then twisting over the front seat to look at Tessa, "although I've been doing mine for twenty-five years, and from what I read in the papers"—she pushed on the ignition—"you're a newbie on the road."

"True," Tessa said, taking a sip of coffee, thought of the travel-heavy job she'd walked out on three years before. "In this role, at least."

"Did you find Locket Mom?" Geneva asked.

Tessa stopped with her seat belt halfway on. "You saw that?"

"And you crying, for all the world to see. Surprised your phone hasn't blown up. You're probably used to it, but you see how many views you have?"

"Oh no, my phone's on silent. Let me look." She clicked it on and bell after bell pinged, signaling message after message.

"Tolja," Geneva said.

Locket Mom was hitting the comment stratosphere, and shares climbed way past her usual live chats. She scrolled through the comments, eyes widening. "I see what you mean," Tessa said, as the car eased away from the hotel. *Locket Mom.* She'd debated with herself, all through her hasty dinner and her fretful sleep, about whether to take the locket with her or leave it at the front desk.

If she took it, she was stealing. Although not exactly stealing, she argued with herself, someone had left it behind. Could be they had abandoned it. Discarded it. Decided they never wanted to see it again. But couldn't bear to throw it away.

She rolled her eyes at her own imagination as the Indianapolis skyline diminished behind them. If she left it at the front desk, it would be lost forever. In the hustle-bustle of a hotel, the possibility of it getting into the hands of someone who really cared seemed remote.

Plus, if social media worked, she would reunite photo and owner in a twinkling. Done and done, and even more good karma.

Waverly Publishing's page now featured her periwinkle book cover— the sleek chignoned businesswoman with tortoiseshell glasses—with a banner saying *New York Times Bestseller—Second Week!* In bright yellow, *almost like crime scene tape,* she had to think. She looked at it, falling in love with it, thanking her lucky everything that this had happened.

Her new career was all a trade-off, though, an incalculable and unpredictable financial return on infinite emotional investment. She pictured Linny and Zack asleep now, Linny with her stuffed animals lined up on her shelves instead of with her in bed, the first break with childhood. *I'm basically a teenager,* she'd pronounced in her newly authoritative eleven-year-old's voice.

And Zack, sprawled and gangly as a marionette on a bed that would all too soon be all too small. Henry, too, she pictured him atop the mound of pillows he insisted on, flopped on his back in his flappy black shorts, the sheets twisted and cast aside, dead to the world. And, maybe, his arm embracing the empty space beside him. Her empty space.

But wait. She was picturing their old house. The rooms they'd all left behind. How they looked *now*—where they slept, what was on their shelves, whether they were smiling—she had no idea. Her own kids, her own husband; living such a separate life that she couldn't even picture them. Was she doing the right thing?

She smiled, reassuring herself. She'd be back soon enough. This would all be worth it. Plus, she had to pay the mortgage on those imaginary bedrooms. And now she'd been lost in her thoughts so long her phone screen had gone dark. She touched it to wake it up. And scrolled down her Insta page. **Could this be yours?** already showed hundreds of comments. At four in the morning.

"Great," she whispered, hopeful. Someone had to know this person. Everyone was on social. Everyone wanted to help. Everyone loved a mystery, yearned to get the viral acclaim as the one to solve it.

"You all right back there, Ms. Calloway?" Geneva asked. "We're close."

"I'm good whenever anyone gives me coffee," she said. "And it's Tessa."

"Might I say? Your book is the bomb." Geneva gave a thumbs-up in the rearview mirror. "I'm a big reader. Lots of waiting time." She held up her cell. "I read 'em on my phone."

Tessa saw the signs for the airport, the snaky twisting arrows. She'd scan the posts after she got through security. Maybe someone had found Locket Mom.

"My family will be so impressed." Geneva handed her a business card. "I drove that funny dog-book guy. And that gorgeous woman from Nantucket. But your Annabelle, she got to me. I've had to make lots of deals in my life. Trade-offs. I love how Annabelle never felt guilty. My kids are boys. Only boys. They've been making deals since they were born. Women—well, that's why you wrote the book. You tell the truth. Or at least, Annabelle does."

"You're so kind," Tessa said as they pulled up to the curb. In the pinkening dawn, Tessa lofted her too-heavy carryall onto her shoulder while Geneva pulled her roller bag out of the trunk and swiveled it onto the sidewalk.

"Look." Geneva began scrolling through her phone. "Here they are."

Geneva held up a snapshot, showing herself cuddled against a man in a starched khaki army uniform and mirrored sunglasses. In front of them, an array of boys, stair-stepped from teenager to toddler.

"Adorable," Tessa said.

"They're a handful." Geneva clicked the photo away. "That's why I hope you find Locket Mom. I know she's missing her family, too. Good that you took a picture. What'd you do with the original? Leave it there? Whoever's it is, they'll probably call the hotel."

Now she had to decide on her story. Did she tell the truth—reveal her questionable decision to take the photo with her?

"Listen," Tessa said, "big favor. I was going to leave it in lost and found, but lost and found wasn't open when I left. So I stashed it in my suitcase. Do you think you could . . . return it for me? Give it to lost and found?"

Geneva pursed her lips, looking dubious.

"Never mind. It's okay," Tessa said. Geneva didn't want to get involved. Made sense. It was a complicated and unusual story, Tessa swiping someone else's property, then asking a driver to return it. It seemed fishy in every way. Geneva might even get in trouble.

"Gotta tell you, that lost and found is a black hole," Geneva was saying. "I know that hotel. They should call it lost and *more* lost. You did the right thing, Ms. Calloway. You take care of that necklace. You take care of that family. I shared it on my socials, too. We'll find 'em. Nothing more important than family."

"That's what I thought, too." Tessa felt less guilty after Geneva's approval. *Nothing more important than family.* "And yes, we'll find them. We'll take control."

"You're exactly like Annabelle." Geneva waved at an approaching police officer, pantomimed "just leaving," and opened her car door. "Got everything?"

Tessa patted her tote bag. "Set."

"Then safe travels, Ms. Calloway. Thanks for the book. I'll treasure it. My husband says I'm not the same since I read it."

"I hope that's a good thing."

"*All* good." Geneva raised an eyebrow. "As you have Annabelle say in the book. And I'm crossing fingers for Locket Mom."

"Thanks, Geneva. Me, too." Tessa turned, headed for the terminal's wide sliding door. She heard the rumble of Geneva driving away, and pulled her suitcase toward her next journey.

8

There was no possible way anyone portrayed in the locket photograph could be in the Indianapolis airport, but Tessa couldn't help scanning every face as she made it through security. She wrote "book club books," as they called them, and her writer brain kicked in, too, searching for a potential plot wherever she went. Sadie Bailey had negotiated a two-book deal, and soon Tessa would have to type chapter one of a whole new novel. As yet unnamed, unplotted, and unknown. But there was a story around every corner. She simply had to be open to find it. Maybe it would even be Locket Mom.

On the concourse, the airport was still in overnight mode. The protective metal grate over the front window of Bursaw's Bookstore was down and locked, but she peered through the silver slats at the front table, unable to resist. And there, next to the World War II spy book, and the Nantucket book, and the newest Dan Brown, was the periwinkle blue of *All This Could Be Yours*. She paused, not another person in sight, and took it all in, hearing the persistent voice of Djamila Parekh in her head. "Social media, girl," DJ would remind her. "Post, post, post. Or they'll all forget about you."

Taking out her phone, she snapped a picture through the grate. She popped it on Instagram. ***Can you believe it? So early the bookstore isn't even open! Oh no!*** She added the *Home Alone* emoji, palms clapped

to cheeks. And then typed, ***But on my way to gate B42 and you, Phoe-***
nix! And hit Enter.

She heard the beeping of an airport jitney and watched it race by, its
uniformed driver zooming down the center of the wide aisle. The beeps
faded as it barreled toward the far gates, and she was alone again. But, it
dawned on her, not really. She had just pointed an unmistakable arrow
at herself, as specific as those You Are Here notices on the airport maps.

Because now, at five in the morning, anyone who looked on Instagram would know where she was. If they were in this airport, they'd
know *precisely* where she was. And because of what she herself had posted,
they'd also know exactly where she was going. Even what gate she was
headed for.

"Snap out of it," she muttered. "No one cares where you are. Gate
B42. Go."

A stream of likes for her airport post had already popped onto her Insta
screen. ***I'll be seeing you in phoenix!***, Superreader77 had posted. Then
added a heart, then a book, then praying hands. How could they have
seen this post so quickly? Social media was blowing up over Locket Mom.

The whole thing was either creepy or fabulous. Tessa speed-walked
past the still-closed stores; flowered handbags, yoga pants, peanut brittle.
The minute she got to the gate she'd call the hotel, see if anyone had in-
quired. She laughed at herself—now she had *another* family to be responsible for.

B42. Marked for Phoenix, on time. She sat, swiveled her suitcase in
front of her, plugged in her phone. A soft ping announced a text.

DJ.

> You are a publicist's dream. Could this be yours? Kidding me? ☺
> If this writing thing doesn't work out, girl, come work with me
> in publicity.

It took Tessa a beat to realize what DJ meant. Tessa typed back.

> No no, it's real:) I found the locket in my hotel room.

DJ's words appeared on the screen.

> Sure. Course you did. Wonderful wonderful you. Maybe in Phoenix you could find something else. Let me know if you get any responses. Where did you get that locket anyway?

Whoa, Tessa thought.

> Ha ha, I know u r kidding. Anything new?

> Confirming you're at airport. Let me know when you get to Phoenix. Good news coming, but can't tell you now.

> What?

> Safe travels talk soon big love xx

> What?

But DJ was gone. So silly, her publicist had thought she'd posted as a publicity stunt, and not out of real concern. Which was a metaphor for something, though Tessa wasn't sure what. Especially not at this hour.

What good news? she wondered. A second printing, that would be fabulous. Or another powerful influencer had been spotted with the book. Or foreign rights sales. Maybe it was a book club pick. Sadie would know, but Sadie's early morning workouts were sacrosanct, and Tessa knew never to contact her agent during running hours. She'd wait for Phoenix. Good was good, and good could wait.

She popped open her socials again. The Love counter on her #Locket-Mom post clicked up and up, and comments still appeared with blurring speed. Didn't anyone sleep anymore?

OMG, this post is so Annabelle, y'all. She's tough, but super kind. IDK this guy, though. ☹ But love you Tessa! Good luck!!!!!

Who would leave a necklace in their hotel room? IDK who it is tho.

You should put it in lost and found, Tessa. That person will be looking for it.

You ever put something in lost and found? Forget about it. Those people take everything home.

Those people? What do you mean by that? I worked at a hotel, you don't know how hard it is.

Love you Tessa! See you in Phoenix! You'll recognize me by my earrings ha ha. IDK the family either.

It looks like Maine to me. Isn't Tessa from Maine?

You should not put pictures of people you don't know on Facebook. I'm surprised at you, Tessa.

She's trying to help. Leave Tessa alone.

Go, Tessa!!! Come to Portland.

Maine or Oregon?

Tessa knows about Maine.

Where did the Maine thing come from? Tessa's chest clenched, just a beat.

The waiting area began to fill with passengers, one eating a smelly egg sandwich and another with oregano pizza, the aisles between the chairs barely wide enough to allow roller bags to avoid hitting every seated passenger's shoes or possessions.

In her peripheral vision, she saw someone take a seat across the narrow aisle from her. She saw the man settle in, pull out a book, open it, and hold it up in front of his face.

Periwinkle blue. And her own photographed face, makeupped and flatteringly lighted, stared back at her.

9

"Attention, all passengers for Phoenix," the amplified voice stilled the waiting area into silence, then Tessa saw every passenger go into action; stashing phones, closing laptops, hoisting totes onto roller bag handles, edging toward the gate. Dozens of people with one goal, to get on the plane as soon as they could. "We request that you stay seated until your boarding group is called."

No one obeyed.

Tessa felt the vibe of the surging group and yanked her charging cord from the wall. The man across from her, the one reading her book, hadn't seemed to notice her. Good.

The first-class passengers boarded, privileged and brisk, Tessa creating stories about each of them. The kid with the shock of khaki hair and earbuds was an affluent teen coming home from boarding school. Two hand-holding gray-haired lovebirds, standing as close together as they possibly could, maybe a honeymoon? Several frowning executives, brief-cased and self-absorbed. They were headed for meetings, their careers at stake.

She'd made up stories since she was an only child growing up in the "middle of nowhere," as her mother had always dismissed Ohio, with her chronic wheedling to convince her father to move them somewhere "more appropriate." They'd fought bitterly, with every conversation a negotiation, every element of their existence part of an ongoing bargain, until her father had bargained his way out of their lives, basically, as her mother archly explained later, purchasing his freedom from their "unendurable" family situation, and left them behind. By then Tessa had retreated into her imagination, where there was no such place as nowhere. And no one could be left behind.

When The Bad Thing happened—how her mother always referred to it, as if clarity were too unbearable—Tessa, Theresa Mattigan, back then, had been younger than Linny. But the fallout from her catastrophic decision that afternoon, plus the outrage from her mother's horrified and heartbroken boyfriend, and vengeful, whispered scorn from judgmental neighbors, impelled her mother to flee their hometown and move the two of them east to Massachusetts. Her mother had changed their names, too, eradicating the past. What could not be erased: Even her preteen self knew her mother blamed her, hated her, for "ruining"—her mother's word—her mother's life.

Theresa, newly and legally "Tessa Danforth," had lived even more profoundly in her own imagination then, stashing the bad thing, burying it, as if time and desire could erase it.

When Tessa was fourteen, her mother revealed that Daddy—Tessa had no idea where he lived—had made a "killing" in the stock market, a term that Tessa conjured into a dark story of greed and power. But as a result, even more money arrived from her father, and Tessa learned the terms *alimony* and *child support* and *investment funds.* Tessa's mother moved them again, to a fancier town closer to Boston. Mom's complaining stopped. Her investments and new real estate company flourished. Tessa buried herself in books, existing in other people's lives.

The next two summers, though, during high school vacation, they'd rented a cabin—that's what Mother called it, but it had been far from rustic—in Blytheton, in upstate Maine. Her still-single mother had insisted it was good for her "social connections," and Tessa had no choice but to go. Turned out, Mount Desert Island and its charming villages seemed almost a fairy tale come to life, with freedom, finally, and miraculously, a friend. A summer friend, sure, but an instant friend, a passionate, book-loving, soul-baring friend. Emily.

This is the forest primeval, one of them would say. And the response, from Longfellow's "Evangeline"—they'd both cried over it, the romantic tragedy set in this very place—*the murmuring pines and the hemlocks.* And the two of them knew they were special.

That second summer unfolded, with boys, sometimes, and clandestine beer, sometimes, and pestering greenflies, and rum raisin ice cream at the counter. Tessa had told Emily, one shimmering summer afternoon, legs hanging over the town pier, about the bad thing.

She did not say she'd been Theresa Mattigan back then, or where it happened.

"That's why we moved," Tessa had said.

Emily had taken her hand. "Because you were still scared?"

Tessa had felt the warmth of Emily's touch, seen her chipped bright-pink fingernails. Emily's mom had died the summer before, and her father quickly remarried. Emily had her own troubles, but she looked at Tessa that night as if she were the only person in the world. Soulmates, and sixteen, all their dreams ahead of them.

"Well, no. We moved because everyone blamed me." In the distance, a fish leaped from the water, or maybe it was a mermaid. "Hated me. Everyone. Even my mother."

Emily had frowned, considering. "That seems unfair. It wasn't really your fault, was it? What happened to the other girl?"

"We still don't know," she'd said. Back then it had still been a mystery. "She was such a cool person, you know? I still remember how kind she was to me, geeky, dumb me. I know she had her own stuff to do but she'd always be, like, you can do it, you can accomplish whatever you want. She even wanted to be the mayor, like her father. I still think about her. All the time. The mayor's daughter, you know? Is probably dead. And all because I . . ."

"How old were you? Like, ten? It wasn't your fault. You were like, a baby."

"Didn't matter." Their silence had surrounded them. "Like I said, everyone hated me. They still do, I bet. My mother def does."

She'd turned to Emily, beseeching. "Don't tell. Not ever. Not anyone." She still remembered the inherent power of her revelation. The danger. "Promise. And promise you don't hate me, too."

"This is the forest primeval." Emily had invoked their private mantra. "I promise."

"The whispering pines and the hemlocks." Tessa believed Emily. Her best friend would never tell.

Later that night, it all changed.

They never went to Maine again. And Emily vanished from her life. Tessa had commandeered her imagination to handle that, too, childhood's end, editing and reshaping that bewildering series of events into a story she could live with. The story she lived now.

And solidifying her core belief that revealing her past would ruin her future. She'd told Emily. Emily was gone. She could never tell anyone again.

"Group two passengers are welcome to board." The voice over the PA system incited another mini-stampede toward the gate.

The man in the airport carrying her book was focused on his phone, pale blue Oxford shirt and effortless jeans, her book tucked into an outside pocket of his carry-on. Advertising exec, she theorized, reading *All This* and trying to plumb the female psyche.

Or, imagine, he could be simply reading it, Annabelle said.

Tessa approached the gate, showing her boarding pass.

"Welcome," the agent said. Her bright red lipstick was flawless, eyelashes extravagant.

Tessa placed her barcode over the reader, but the agent was tapping on her computer. Tessa heard a whir, and a paper boarding pass popped up. The agent handed it to her, leaning closer. "We've upgraded you to 3B, Ms. Calloway. We're all massive fans."

"Well, thank you." Tessa felt her eyes widen with this unexpected treat. "That's—wonderful."

"So are you," the agent whispered. "Have the champagne."

Tessa, conscious that people were in line behind her, touched a palm to her heart. "You have completely made my day," she said, as she wheeled her suitcase away.

A few clicks of a mouse, and this agent had given her a seat worth hundreds of dollars. All because Tessa wrote a book.

She yanked her bag over the gap between jetway and plane, seeing her new seat steps away, 3B, the aisle. The window seat was empty.

Tessa dumped her tote bag on her seat, and hoisted her suitcase to the compartment above. First class, *and* room for her suitcase *and* a row by herself? Sometimes early morning flying was a good thing. She stowed her bag under the seat in front, then slid the phone from the pocket.

"Sweetheart? It's me." She kept her voice low as she heard Henry's groggy hello. "Did I wake you?"

Six o'clock at home, and the kids would be up, Linny at least, and looking for breakfast. If Henry didn't take charge, it'd be a disaster of sugary cereal and spilled milk. She pictured their kitchen-in-progress, the Swedish dishwasher Henry insisted "she" have, and remembered the fancy cabinets with glassed-in doors. "Is everything okay?"

"Everything is always okay, honey." Tessa heard Henry's voice change, maybe he was sitting up, blinking, regrouping from sleep. She had seen him do that so many times, his hair spiking up on one side, eyes not quite focusing. "It's early. Where are you?"

"Guess. Let's FaceTime." It would be fun to show him first class. The plush navy-blue leather seats, the voluptuous headrests, her full view of the still-open cockpit.

"Too early for FaceTime. What's—"

"I'm upgraded. First class. They're about to bring me champagne. How about *that*?" Tessa was aware she was whispering; she didn't want to seem goofy, or gloating to passengers headed to the back of the plane. But she was allowed to be happy. "And guess what else I'm celebrating?"

"It's too early to guess."

Passengers were still filing by her, a twentysomething in ripped jeans and an Indy 500 T-shirt, a man carrying a creature in a screened cage.

"Ma'am?" A voice at her shoulder.

She looked up. And of course. If she were writing the story, it's exactly what would have happened.

"I'm 3A." The man with her book gestured toward the empty seat beside her.

"Oh, I'm—" Tessa stood, and bumped her head on the still-open overhead compartment. "Ow."

"Careful." He slid past her, stashed his carry-on. "Those bins can be predatory."

"True," she said, and then, somehow, dropped her phone onto the thin carpeting of the narrow aisle.

"Tessa?" Henry's voice came from the floor.

"You all right?" The man was about her age, Tessa calculated. Older.

"Sure," she said, stooping to pick up the phone. "Hang on," she said to Henry. "I needed to—"

"Ms. Calloway?" The flight attendant had come up beside her, holding a stack of napkins and a ballpoint pen. "Something to drink? And you, sir?" She looked at 3A as Tessa, phone in hand and Henry's tinny voice coming from the speaker, attempted to gracefully sit down again.

"Oh, nothing, thank you," Tessa said, clicking on her seat belt. She wished the attendant hadn't said her name so distinctly, but too late for that now.

"You sure?" the man said. "I was thinking of champagne. And it's way too early to drink it alone."

10

She quickly said goodbye to Henry, promising to tell her news later. Then, as the plane's engine hummed, and they moved forward in the emerging glints of sunlight, the man leaned forward and pulled her book from his bag.

"So, yeah," he said, holding up the back cover. "I wondered if that was you. But I didn't want to say anything. It's a good photo, by the way."

"It's all about the lighting." *Shush, Annabelle said. Say thank you.* "But thanks."

"I know you must be inundated, Ms. Calloway. And probably looking forward to some private time."

"It's all good," she said. "I'm Tessa."

"Sam. And I promise to leave you alone," he was saying. "Not be the pesky seatmate. For someone like you, flying can be a juggle."

She shrugged, smiling, not sure what to make of that. "Someone like you" meant he'd categorized her, created a story for her. He thought he knew what she was.

"But could you sign it to my daughter?" Sam went on. "She'll be so impressed I met you. Her name is Anna." He paused. "Short for Savannah."

Tessa nodded, flipping the phone over and over in her hand. Savannah. Anna. Every time she heard a new person's name, her writer brain tested it, imagining it as a name for a character, wondering if it would work. But Anna, short for Savannah, no. Definitely no. Savannah was her own middle name, like her mother's. Theresa Savannah Mattigan, her birth name. Very few people, *maybe no one, come to think of it*, knew that now. Thank goodness.

"Sure," she said. "After we get underway? It's about four hours to Phoenix, plenty of time. Okay?" If *she* stopped talking now, he would stop, and then she could close her eyes and finally sleep. "But I thought I saw *you* reading it," she said, disobeying herself.

"I was flipping through." He'd tucked the book into the seat-back pocket, only Tessa's eyes, mascaraed to the hilt for the photo shoot and photoshopped even bluer, showing over the nylon pouch. "Anna was dying to read it, so I picked it up as a gift. Figured I would see what she was so enthusiastic about."

"Crossing fingers you agree." Tessa felt the gravity change as the front wheels lifted off. *Fly, fly, fly*, she instructed the plane.

Sam had lifted the plastic cover over the window beside him. "I love looking at this. This moment of slipping the bonds." He gestured at the clear, thick pane. "Can you see?"

She looked across him, the wide armrest between them, as the concrete runway and scrubby trees in the distance gave way to the vastness of clouded sky, and saw a patchwork quilt of green and brown beneath them. A pattern that could only be seen from above. A few swimming pools twinkled in the backyards of a scatter of houses, and then it was only clouds and they were on their way to Phoenix.

"Physics," she said. "Always reassuring. When I was a kid, I thought it was magic." *Shut up*, she ordered herself.

But Sam simply looked out the window. *Good*, she thought. *We're done.* She closed her eyes, leaned into the leather. Four hours. And maybe even now someone was recognizing their beloved and lost family photo, and the locket, and messaging her. Maybe that *could* be her next book. She could make "Sam in 3A" a main character, and have his daughter be pictured in the found photo. Maybe she was dead.

But no. She didn't want to write about that. She wrote about confident people. People with goals. People finding happiness.

She opened her eyes a fraction, checking. Sam was still staring out the window. She'd often vetted books for her own daughter, an inquisitive and indiscriminate reader, who'd pick up any book Tessa had left within reach. Tessa's reading childhood had been centered in the town library, a boxy building with a children's reading room downstairs where Tessa had curled up in a big red leather chair. She was allowed to take home ten books at a time, which she'd tucked into her Buffy tote bag.

But she could never go back there. Never.

Her author photo watched her from Sam's seat-back pocket. Judging by his age, Anna-like-Savannah could be fifteen or so? The plot and themes of *All This* might be a bit too old for her—not that that there was anything graphically inappropriate, but corporate intrigue and cutthroat dealmaking and women's empowerment might seem—well, never too soon, Tessa decided, for young women to get the Annabelle message. And she admired parents who cared about what their children read.

She barely remembered her own parents reading books, they'd been all about newspapers. But her mother had once pulled out an old trunk from their dank basement, and inside were musty-smelling Nancy Drews and Trixie Beldens with plastic-laminated cardboard covers. Tessa had known they were anachronistic, and old-fashioned, but she'd admired how Nancy and Trixie took control of their lives, and solved problems grown-ups could not.

She'd gotten hooked when she and Emily had checked out a Mary Higgins Clark from the local library. They'd obsessed over it, looking up unfamiliar words, dissecting the story. And they'd vowed, stationed on ratty beach blankets and smelling of parentally enforced Coppertone, that they'd be writers when they grew up. Only Tessa had fulfilled that dream.

That she knew of, at least.

She must have closed her eyes, she didn't remember when, but she did remember opening them, her body feeling the atmosphere shift as the plane began its descent. Two soft bells pinged, and the flight attendant was at her side, checking for seat belts, smiling maternally.

"Almost to Phoenix," she said. "May I get you some water? Ice? Sir, how about you? Your tray table needs to be up, sir, but the cups will fit in your armrest cupholders."

"I'd love some," Tessa said. "Sure, ice."

"Same," Sam said, and turned to her as the flight attendant stepped away.

"You were out. Totally out. I guess on book tour you have to sleep while you can. Your family must miss you. What do they think about all this?"

"They're fine, it's fine. It's—I'm grateful, mostly," Tessa said. Had she told him she was on book tour? "It's exciting. But yes, exhausting. But worth it." She blinked, trying to regain her equilibrium. Her sleep schedule was out of whack, and she hadn't napped since the days the kids were little. Now, on the road, her schedule had gone from settled to scattered, and her brain felt like that, too. *I'm a* New York Times *bestseller,* she remembered, *again.* "*Ha,*" she whispered, wrapping herself in the unlikely joy.

"Something funny?" Sam asked.

"No, no, just waking up." She looked at her Rockport watch. Eleven a.m. at home. Nine a.m. in Phoenix. She would never get this straight, whether the kids were awake or asleep, whether she herself was supposed to be tired or hungry. Her body clock was overwound, or running down, she could never be sure.

Sam had pulled the book from its place in the seat-back pouch.

"Still okay to sign this? We can sneak down your tray table for a minute."

"My pleasure." Tessa unhooked the table, and it fell into her lap. She accepted his expensive pen. "To Anna?"

"Well . . ." Sam's face had changed. "Why not sign it to me? Sam. Maybe put seat 3A. That'll be funny."

"Sure," Tessa said. People were always asking her to sign her books in certain ways, like Happy Reading, or Enjoy! It didn't matter, she knew Henry would tell her a sale is a sale. *To Sam, my seatmate in 3A,* Tessa wrote. *Safe travels.* And then signed it, *Tessa Calloway.* She made sure it was legible. If people wanted her to sign a book, it seemed disrespectful to leave a scrawl.

Signing her own book to a stranger. A childhood dream, and now true. *Nothing is promised,* someone had once told her, *but everything is up for grabs. Just take it.* She'd had Annabelle say those same words in chapter 1.

"Your daughter can borrow it," Tessa said, handing the signed book across the leather console.

"Right," Sam said, tucking it into his briefcase. "But maybe I'll get one for her tonight at your event. At ReadRunner Bookstore, right? At seven?"

11

"And I'm so honored that you all came tonight to share it with me." Tessa let the applause wash over her as she finished her speech. She customized it for every venue, even though no one would come to hear her in two different cities, but she kept the bones the same: who, what, when, where, and a bit of why. She'd noticed, with delight, the bobbing heads in her audience, and their *don't you love it* nudges. They held their books against their chests, almost hugging them.

Sam from 3A wasn't there. *See?* she reassured herself. He wasn't one of those "jerks" Djamila had warned her about. And Team Tessa was watching out for her.

"Let's take a class photo." Tessa spread her arms to encompass the group. "And if you have the book, hold it up. I'll post it on social, if you promise to share. Will you?" At the murmur of agreement, Tessa took her phone from the podium, positioned it—then put it down.

"Hey, don't cover your faces with the book, okay? I want to remember *you*. I'm saving every one of these."

The audience became a sea of smiling faces and blue rectangles, and Tessa snapped a few shots. Then put down the phone.

"Now. Shall I read to you? Then take some more questions?" She always gave her audiences a choice. Olivette worried that if you read the beginning of the book, people would skip it when they held the actual book in their hands. But Tessa couldn't read anything from the middle, everything was a clue and a hint and foreshadowing. The middle was when the book turned darker, and after that grew terrifyingly unsettling. And that hard-won ending, a surprise even to her.

"Chapter one, pages one and two. Okay?" She paused. "And you read the rest when you buy the book."

The audience laughed, appreciative. They understood, Tessa hoped, she was honestly acknowledging their participation in her life, accepting that their decisions and actions dictated her future.

"Here we go," she said, and heard the rustle of pages as her audience opened their books to read along. She took a breath, then prepared to alter her voice, make it more formal, like her audiobook. In her reading mind she *became* Annabelle—thirty-two years old, smart, driven, cagey, ambitious, relentless. Sexy. Brave. And with so many dark and ugly secrets. But those wouldn't be revealed until later in the book. She wouldn't read those parts here. "Ready?"

The audience sat, faces upturned, eyes widened in expectation, every one of them nodding. *Yes.*

The audience listened, rapt, until she read the final lines of page 2: "'But no one sees Annabelle coming. Not until it's too late. Now he's about to have a lesson in the Annabelle rules.'"

She closed the book. Set it on the lectern. "The rest you'll have to read for yourselves."

"We already have!" someone called out.

"We love the Annabelle rules!"

Her laughter, genuine, joined with the audience in a common understanding. Tessa knew the perils of the corporate world; the impossible balance between self-confidence and self-preservation, how difficult it was to stand up for yourself in the face of a system that was designed to perpetuate the old ways, not to grow. How innovation, even simply questioning, was disdained and dismissed. Especially if a woman offered it. She didn't need to remain in the corporate world to recognize that. She just needed to be alive.

"Now, who has a question?" Tessa asked. Every time Tessa had to call on someone for a question, there was a moment, a tiny interstitial moment, carrying the sinister possibility that a stranger in the audience would ask something life-changing. Something probing. Or disturbing.

A woman in the second row stood. "You've said you hear Annabelle's voice. I mean, how does that work?"

"I'm not sure." Tessa smiled, and soft laughter rippled through the audience. "There's something mysterious about a writer's imagination—it still feels surprising to call myself a writer—but I guess this book is proof that I am."

"You are!" someone called out.

"Well, thank you," Tessa said. She glanced at store owner Heather Guthrie, who looked as contented as Tessa felt. A full house at a book signing could assure the week's profits and keep the store in business. A precarious and exhausting job, Tessa understood that. Be good to your independent bookstores, DJ had reminded her. You exist because of them.

"Yes?" She pointed at a mop-haired woman a few rows away from the podium. Her blue earrings sparkled through the curls.

"Does Annabelle's experience come from anything in your real life? Did you ever make a Faustian bargain like she did?"

Another common question, as if a story could not simply be imagined. Maybe it couldn't be. But she had prepared her careful answer.

"Well, every novel comes from a writer's personal experience, and then again, it doesn't. I wrote the book when I was pushing forty, because that's when the time was right. We need to discover our strengths and come into our power however and whenever it works for us. Like Annabelle does. And it would be a spoiler to say more, okay?"

Annabelle's bargain was definitely not the same as her own, but everyone made bargains, and Tessa was no different. She thought of it every day, the bargain she'd made so very long ago, and now she was here, and Henry and the kids were home. Bargains relied on stasis; that once you made a deal, none of the elements of the deal could ever change. But that was impossible—the infinite opportunities of life ensured no modern Faustian bargain could ever be unbreakable. Still. Its inevitable and sinister requirements could not be forgotten.

She only hoped they could be avoided.

Tessa pointed to a woman in the back. "Yes?"

"Where did you grow up, and how do you think that affected what you write?"

That question again. She tried not to frown. Be question-adjacent, Sadie had instructed. "I grew up in a small town, nothing exciting, not even a bookstore, can you imagine? I lived at the library. How that affected my writing? It made me love stories, the kind that carry you away. The fictional escape books give us can also be an education, can't it? It can take us places we never dreamed we could go." Tessa pointed to a blue-earringed woman in the front row. "Thank you for sitting in the front, brave soul," she said. "Do you have a question?"

"Yes, but exactly where?" The woman in the back had remained standing, her torso now higher than the other attendees' heads. In jeans, Tessa saw, and a white T-shirt with a navy blazer. "Exactly where did you grow up?"

Some heads had turned to look at the questioner.

Uh-oh, Annabelle said. *Watch out.*

Heather had edged closer to the podium, and glanced at Tessa, telegraphing *you okay?*

Tessa nodded. *I'm fine.* "It's a privacy thing," she said. "My family doesn't like attention, and I try to protect their personal space—everything is so shared these days, isn't it? I love to share my novel and my philosophy of life, but—"

A sound came from in front of her, the lectern vibrating. Tessa laughed, acknowledging the buzz of her silenced phone, and held it up again. "See? They're messaging me now," she joked. "Telling me to go on to the next question."

The audience laughed in approval, and the woman in the blazer lowered herself into her chair, slowly disappearing behind the heads of the people in front of her.

Tessa glanced at the caller ID.

Henry.

Call me. Linny.

12

There was no way out of it. Only one choice to make. She could hide making the call, or not hide. There'd be no reason for Henry to contact her during an event, not unless it was an irretrievable disaster. He had her complete schedule, city by city and almost hour by hour, printed out and posted on the fridge. He had to know she'd be in the midst of speaking. Dire possibilities flashed through her mind at the speed of fear. But she could not let this audience know.

"My husband. Back home." She tried to keep her face calm. "Give me a second? It's fine, I'm sure. Never a dull moment, huh?"

She turned her back to the audience, away from the microphone. Hearing their concerned whispers, feeling her breath shorten. She typed back, panicking.

> Linny what? I'm in event. What?

The fear descended, the avalanche of horribles; her daughter sobbing or injured or kidnapped or dying. Or dead. Three dots meant Henry was typing his answer, three excruciating dots.

> Oh no, sorry. Time zones. Linny was throwing up.

Tessa closed her eyes, imagining her daughter, fragile and hurting and no matter what she said, a needy child longing for her absent mother. What the hell was Henry doing with them? Linny hardly ever threw up, except, hideously, if she ate bananas. But bananas weren't hard to avoid, and Henry would not be that careless. She hadn't brought bananas into their house for years.

> What did she eat? Did you give her something with bananas?

> Of course not. She's fine. Go be famous. Sell books. Talk later.

Tessa stared through the screen across two time zones and transported herself into her little girl's bedroom, her new bedroom, so new the walls weren't even freshly painted yet. Tessa pictured the menagerie of watchful plushies on Linny's wall. At least *they* were there for her.

"Time zone error, my husband says," Tessa said as she clicked off and turned back to the audience. "Husbands, right? He wanted to say hello." She held up the phone, playing the amused and patient spouse. "Shall we call him back and *all* say hello?"

The chorus of women's voices answered her, supportive and sympathetic. "Now. Where were we?" Her heart was still beating too fast. She settled her shoulders, regaining her equilibrium. Henry was well aware of time zones. He must have been so upset by Linny that he'd spaced. She'd rather know, of course, than find out later.

"So. Back to reality. Questions." She pointed to the woman in the front row.

"I'm Winnie Chun," she said. "And so honored to meet you. Um. Did you ever find out about that locket?"

"Yes, did you find Locket Mom?" Someone else stood. "So sad, isn't it? But *everyone* reads your page."

Everyone, Tessa thought. She'd found a mysterious locket in Indianapolis, made one post, and now it was a hot topic in Phoenix. No time zones on social media—everything was all the time.

"So, no news yet," she said, "If you don't know, someone left a locket in the nightstand at my hotel yesterday. I'm calling her Locket Mom. And I will confess, between us . . ." She paused, teasing them. "I looked in the drawers of the nightstand table of my hotel when I arrived here in Phoenix, too, wondering if anyone left a treasure there."

"Did they?" someone called out.

"Do you have it with you now?" The voice came from the back. "The actual locket?"

"No, I don't." Tessa leaned forward, squinting a bit, to see who had asked that—and why the tone seemed odd. But it wasn't the "exactly where you lived" woman, unless she'd changed seats.

You're still on edge, Annabelle told her. Chill.

"Hey." She tried to change the subject. "That could be my new book." Tessa clapped her hands together, as if imagining it. "Someone leaves mysterious things in hotel rooms?"

"Can't wait!" someone called out.

Store owner Heather had materialized at her side. "And now we're running out of time, so . . . I am incredibly grateful you all came tonight. Thank you. Thank you so much."

No matter how often this happened, Tessa thought, watching the standing ovation, she would never get used to it. She, an ordinary suburban woman who'd juggled kids and husband and money and fear and the ghosts of her own decision-making, and—

Something she ate? Henry's message almost physically poked her in the ribs. Linny threw up? Why? And what did Henry know, anyway, about anything even close to that realm? Their children's health, their nutrition, their personal quirks, this was Tessa's territory. That Linny could not eat bananas—*it's the texture,* she could almost hear Lin's reedy voice, but in truth she knew she was allergic to them—and would only eat cucumbers cut into rounds, not strips, and that Zack needed his grape jam on both pieces of bread, with creamy peanut butter in the middle. Those kids would eat pancakes or mac and cheese for every meal if she let them—she wouldn't be surprised if that's what Henry was doing.

"You can buy your books at the register," Heather instructed, as chairs squeaked and people stood, "then Tessa will be at our signing table. Line starts at the left."

And now two hundred people wanted to buy her book and have her sign it. Two hundred times three minutes per person was—forever. Forever.

Throwing up? She had to get out of here, had to FaceTime. Pixelated or not, she'd understand the situation the minute she saw her baby girl. Keeping her face composed as the applause ended, she risked a glance at her Rockport watch. Ten p.m. at home. Linny throwing up.

She cared about both things so passionately . . . how could she choose? Why did she have to choose?

"Ha ha," Annabelle said.

Women swarmed into position, forming one line at the register and another at the signing table, as Heather took Tessa's arm, pulling her close, guiding her to the signing table. "I'm sorry about that pushy hometown question, though, there's no way to avoid—"

"No worries," Tessa said.

"Everything okay at home? Do you need a minute?" Heather whispered. The line of blue already stretched almost to the farthest bookcased wall of the event space, with an equally long line at the cash register. "I don't think anyone will leave." She paused, seemed to be assessing. "At least, I hope not. But go, call, if you need to."

"I'm good." Tessa hoped. What could she do from two thousand miles away? For a sleeping child? She took a deep breath, sent up a working mother's prayer, *be well, my darling girl.*

She could feel the women's anticipation, even their reluctance to move aside for her; one of them, someone, touched her on the back, almost caressing. Tessa tried not to flinch, took a step back, bumped into someone else. Everyone was so close, these strangers, and even though they all looked at her with—whatever emotion it was, devotion, or admiration, Tessa suddenly felt—*no.* She had to tough it out. Linny would recover. This was her dream, and she would embrace it. One thing at a time.

She sat, picked up a felt-tip pen, ready for the woman who was first in line.

Navy blazer. White T-shirt. Jeans.

"I hope I didn't upset you," the woman said. "With that question about your hometown."

13

How had that woman gotten to the front of the signing line so quickly? "Not at all," Tessa said.

Watch out, Annabelle said.

"Who shall I sign this to?"

"How about . . ." The woman paused. "To a hometown girl."

The woman was now still as a photograph, motionless, waiting.

Often bookstores used yellow stickies with purchasers' names; to make it easier for the author, and to prevent the embarrassing situation when a purchaser said "oh, just sign it to me" and the author had no idea who they were. In the rush and crush and pressure, Tessa thought, sometimes she wouldn't recognize her own husband. This woman had no yellow sticky.

"I'm so sorry." Tessa held the pen away from the book, breaking the spell, and looked up at the woman's face. "Do I . . . do I know you?"

"Know me? Oh, I'm sure not," the woman said.

Tessa felt the time ticking away, pictured Linny, pale and abandoned, on her pink Hello Kitty sheets, pictured Henry clueless, and Zack playing video games when he should have been asleep; pictured two time zones of impossibility, and the line of women, now murmuring and speculating as they cradled their books. A few looked at their watches.

"Okay," Tessa said, so agreeable. Whatever I write in this book, she realized, however I sign it, cannot be changed. But it has no context. This person could explain it in any way she wanted. Make it mean anything she wanted. As if Tessa were agreeing, acknowledging some relationship or a shared past. It could be ammunition. Or bait. Or an alibi. "How about 'Wonderful to see you in Phoenix.'" Tessa began writing it even as she spoke. "What's your name?"

"Just sign it," the woman said. "Is Calloway your husband's name? What's your birth name?"

Yikes, Annabelle said.

"Everything good?" Heather, interrupting, was at her side. "Let's keep the line going, ladies. Tessa would chat all night, but we have to let her get some sleep."

The hometown woman—that's how Tessa thought of her—took her book and walked away, her blue jeans and black boots disappearing behind a bookcase. Why would she have wondered about Tessa's birth name? Now her brain raced, scouring the dark places in her own history. This could not be random. This could not be meaningless.

But she was Tessa Calloway now, and safe.

Still. Tessa had asked the customer's own name, and she had refused. Even more suspicious.

The next customer stepped toward the table, clutching her book like a treasure. Winnie, Tessa remembered, and said so.

"I can't believe I'm here. And you even remembered my name," she whispered, opening her book to the title page. "Sign to me, okay? And may I take your picture?"

Tessa looked up at her, grateful for the normalcy. Noted her beaded *All This* friendship bracelet. "My pleasure."

Her heart still filled every time she touched the book's suede-like cover, her name embossed in burnished gold, the graphic of the elegant businesswoman in tortoiseshell glasses who oozed self-confidence. This book had a sticky, she noticed. She signed "To Winnie" as the woman took a photo. "I hope you enjoyed the event."

Whoa. Look who's here, Annabelle said.

Tessa heard staccato footsteps. Black boots and jeans, she saw, were coming toward her. Sam. The man in seat 3A. He stopped, half the store away. Not looking at her. She could feel his intent though, as strongly as if he'd aimed a spotlight on her. She could almost feel the light. And the heat. He wanted something. From *her*.

Tessa watched him, heart racing, stealing glances, as she tried, intently, to focus on the customers, signing their books, each opened to the title page and ready for her inscription. Marjorie, Alta, Logan, Kym, which she almost misspelled. *Cindy with a* y *or* i, she asked. *Michelle with one* l *or two?* Through it all, wearing out one Sharpie pen and starting another, she felt torn by her tug-of-warring responsibilities to her job and to her home, and now, also trying stay calm as Sam stepped closer, closer, closer.

It was her imagination that had gotten her here, she knew that, her ability to make up stories. But now that imagination was emotional quicksand. Why was Sam here? She wished, sometimes, she could turn her brain off and calmly be present in the real world, not speculate and embellish and make everything a better story. Or a worse one.

"Can you give me one second?" she asked the next customer. Her sticky said Larysa. She held up her phone. "I need to—one second." She turned in her chair, looking down, thumbing in the number. Then typing, one word.

> Linny?

Three dots instantly appeared.

> She's all good stop texting.

Henry had added a smiley face.

> Missing you

> U2 Go work text when finished

> xo

Part of her knew Henry had a point—if their positions were reversed, she'd have been annoyed with Henry's hovering. She should trust him.

"Sorry," she said, clicking off. And then fumbled the spelling of Larysa. "Oh, let me get another book," she apologized. "I—"

"No, no," Larysa quickly refused. "This book is even more special now. It means you're a real person, just like us."

As Larysa turned to go, Tessa saw Sam, now three people away. It was silly to be anything but flattered—he'd mentioned the signing to her on the plane, and that's what publicity was for, to entice the public to attend. He already had her book, but it had been for his daughter—Anna like Savannah—and since he'd had her sign to him, he needed another. Nothing sinister, nothing creepy.

He told you he'd be here, Annabelle said. *Didn't hide it. Let's see how this goes.*

Clara. Mycene. And there he was. She could almost feel his shadow.

"Great speech," he said, looking down at her.

She accepted his book, saw the laugh lines around his eyes, the scattering of gray in his once-dark hair. "Such a surprise to see you."

"Is it? I told you I was coming."

"You did, true." Just another reader, she told herself. "Sign it to you, um—?"

"Sam." He paused, the briefest of pauses. "As I've said. And you did that on the plane. So sign this one to Anna. Like Savannah."

Heather had inched closer, and Tessa wondered if she had picked up on the edgy difference in Tessa's tone. Or the apprehension that must be radiating from her.

"How's *your* family?" he went on.

Tessa kept her eyes on the title page. "To Anna," she wrote, careful as a third grader perfecting her cursive. "All best wishes . . ." Tessa knew what her own best wish was. That this man would go away. "Everything is wonderful." She handed him the book. Big smile. *Go away.*

He didn't.

"Single parenting can be tough," Sam said.

Tessa glanced behind him, hoping another customer had materialized. But Sam was the last. Which was surely intentional. He'd strategized to be last in line. But why?

"Time to sign stock, dear."

Heather had wheeled in a gray metal library cart filled with the blue spines of *All This*. "Look." She swiveled the cart. "Books on both sides. We'll sell every one, I'm positive."

"Great," Tessa said.

"Great," Sam said at the same time.

Tessa capped her pen, the click of plastic unusually loud in the sudden silence. "The shelves call," she said, hearing her awkward attempt to sound casual. "I hope your daughter loves the book."

"She will. Seems like everyone does." Sam pointed to the metal cart. "That's a lot of books. I could hang out, then drive you back to the hotel. Where are you staying?"

Not her imagination, then. Her family, his single parent role, her distance from home, a woman on the road; carefree, up for a good time. *Not a chance*, Tessa thought.

"We're handling Tessa's transportation." Heather inserted herself between Tessa and Sam. "If you're all set, sir, I'm afraid the store is closing." She paused. "Unless you'd like to buy another book or two?"

"I'm good." Sam did not look dismissed. "Good luck, Ms. Calloway. Safe travels."

"Do you know him?" Heather whispered even before the sound of Sam's footsteps disappeared.

"I was going to ask you the same thing." Tessa tested her Sharpie on a leftover sticky. "He was on my plane here, had the seat next to mine. And had my book. Which was—nice at the time. Now . . ."

"Welcome to the big time." Heather pointed to an endcap display of one author's works, top to bottom, the author's name bigger than her foil-embossed titles. "*She* came for a signing, couple of weeks ago. With two bodyguards. Seriously. Armed."

"Armed?" Tessa stopped mid-signature, left a blot on the *o* in Calloway.

"So they said."

"What's she afraid of?"

"You heard of parasocial relationships?"

Tessa kept signing. "Para . . . ?"

"Parasocial." Heather placed more books on the checked tablecloth.

"People truly believe the celebrities they follow on social are their friends. Because they admire them or agree with them, or the person has touched them in some way." Heather flapped open the books, piled them with title pages showing. "You ever have people cry when they talk to you? Wear what you do, copy you? Mimic Annabelle? I saw a lot of blue earrings tonight."

Tessa closed her eyes for a beat. "I've had people cry, yes. And quit their jobs or dump their boyfriend, and tell me they were inspired by Annabelle. Like I said to my husband—oh. May I—"

"Sure, I know you need to call home. But let me finish. These parasocial relationships—they can go wrong. And you can never predict when. Someone who considers you a friend assumes, in turn, that you think of *them* as a friend. And when you don't give them everything they want— social media attention, instant response, constant shout-outs—they can go sour. And that . . . disappointment? Is as intense as the admiration. They feel you've failed them. Sorry to sound lectury."

"But I haven't done anything." Tessa frowned.

"That's the problem." Heather placed another periwinkle-blue stack on the table. "That's the last of them. But be careful, Anna—oh, I almost called you Annabelle."

"Happens all the time," Tessa said.

"That's what I mean." Heather crossed her arms over her chest. "The imagination is a dangerous thing."

14

Heather was right about imagination. Tessa settled herself into the Uber's black upholstery. It was a writer's most valuable professional tool, and their most destructive enemy. The same imagination that fueled 385 pages of a book could also escalate coincidence into conspiracy, and interest into intrigue. *That's why they call them strangers, because some of them are strange.* She laughed out loud.

"You okay, ma'am?" the driver asked.

"Oh sure," she told her. "Working too hard, I guess."

She tried to relax, adrenaline high and brain racing, searching for normal as the driver navigated the gridded streets of Phoenix, which at this time of night still felt like being inside a hairdryer.

Now, in the deepening darkness, she could be anywhere. Anywhere but home. Where now her new peonies would be out, and the hydrangea, too, which Linny had breathlessly reported bore pink flowers on one part of the bush, and blue ones on another. Oh. *Linny.*

"I'm a horrible person," she whispered. She texted Henry, as quickly as she could.

> Done w thing, what latest? How Linny?

She waited the beat or two it would take Henry to hear her message ping. She imagined him watching the news, flopped on "his" chair, the

battered and supple chocolate leather hauled to Rockport with most of
the other furniture from the old house. We'll get all new, Henry had pro-
claimed, as he'd positioned their well-worn couch, two almost threadbare
flowered chairs, and the tippy glass coffee table in front of the redbrick
fireplace, then placed a few framed family photos on the polished wooden
mantel. He'd surveyed the result, hands on hips.

"Our stuff looks different in here. Shabby."

"Shabby?" She'd scanned the room then, assessing. The double-tall
living room windows needed to be washed, and the stately rhododendrons outside were blurred through the smudged glass, the sun struggling through, softening on its way inside. "Oh, honey, it needs to settle
in. Like we do."

Why wasn't Henry answering now? A million reasons—he was in a
different room from his phone. He was in the shower. He was asleep. He
was on the phone with the doctor, describing Linny's worsening symp-
toms. He was in the car with Linny, driving her to the hospital, leaving
Zack alone. No. He was *in* an ambulance with Linny, siren screaming,
racing to the hospital, with Zack, sobbing, forced to stay behind, by himself, terrified and alone.

She was an abysmal mother. This had been the world's worst decision.
Leaving home, leaving their children, in a new house in a new neighborhood, with Henry—Henry who meant well and was certainly confident
enough, but sometimes, she knew, that confidence was . . . unwarranted.
But she wouldn't have married him if she didn't trust him. There had been
so many professional disappointments for him, and she'd always admired
his unbreakable spirit and determination. But one of them had to be the
realist, and now, she'd left her children—*their* children—home with
someone who survived on hope and positive thinking. Those had been
such admirable qualities. Until now.

Dots. Thank God.

Hey.

In an unfamiliar car in an unfamiliar city, the adrenaline high from
her event vanished like the flame in a puffed-out match. "Hey"? Like he
hadn't frightened her to death?

> What new?

She held back her annoyance. He was doing the best he could.

> All good. Linny sleeping, Z pretending. Missing u.

She shook her head. *Pitiful.* Her life, in only these few weeks, had devolved into texting her own husband, the person she'd talked to in person every day for almost fourteen years, who'd spent his days at the office—except for the times he didn't—while she juggled kids and housework and shopping and writing, they'd shared dinner-making duties, and sending the kids to their rooms, and wine afterward in front of the TV.

You worried me, she typed. Then deleted.

> I was worried.

> She's fine.

"Sorry" would have been a better answer. But Henry was doing his best.

> What eat, then?

> IDK. Neighbors dropping off stuff tho. She good.

What neighbors? What stuff? She imagined them, the strangers protected by the label "neighbors," leaving random food for her family to eat. What food?

Tessa took a deep breath, balancing her fear and her rage and her need to let Henry make his own decisions. As long as they were the safe ones.

> We need a code to let me know if something is scary bad.
> Let's try to phone more. Talking is better.

Tessa saw the lights of her hotel a block away, its bright neon logo over the now-visible trio of revolving doors.

> Nothing is bad. Nothing will be bad.

Henry was wrong, totally excruciatingly wrong, someday something *would* be bad. Lives could be ruined in an instant. She knew that, first-hand. They needed a way to warn each other. Better to be prepared.

The driver had shifted into park, engine running, at the curb. The hotel lobby glowed with warm light, maybe hoping to replicate the welcome of a faraway home.

"Here we are, ma'am," the driver said.

> For emergency put 911, okay? At hotel now.

> OK. Safe safe.

The driver was holding the back door of the car open for her. *"Ma'am? Here we are."*

> Love love.

She clicked off before she heard his reply. But he'd certainly said it, always always.

We got this, Annabelle said.

The elevator arrived, its doors sliding open.

At least she had her correct room key—*little victories*—and in the empty hallway, the door opened as it should. She hadn't said *always always* yet to Henry, so she felt at loose ends, as if some part of her life was on hold with their lucky nighttime mantra unfinished. She'd call him, first thing. And then go down and retrieve her dinner.

The door to 1205 swung open, and she popped on the light. And stepped on something.

15

Once, traveling to somewhere in Illinois for her corporate job, she'd gotten a notification under her door, a piece of paper like this one, that an insect called a corn bug was prevalent in the area, and not to be "upset or concerned" if she saw one in her motel room. From the size of the mammoth bug in the photo, and the length of its horror-movie antennae, if she had seen one in person, she might have fainted.

But this letter under her door was not mass produced. She turned it over, then over again, blank on the back—but the message on the front was written in black felt-tip pen, in spiky careful printing: *Package for you at front desk.*

Tessa frowned, holding the paper.

She looked at the chunky black house phone on the rectangular nightstand between the two double beds. The red message light was blinking. She picked up the receiver. Hit zero.

"Yes, Ms. Calloway?"

It always freaked her out that they knew what room it was, but she supposed that was prudent.

"I got a message that you have a package for me?" She set her tote bag on the bed, noting the bedspread's sage-and-amber pattern, colors of the desert. Black-and-white photos lined one wall—Ansel Adams—she recognized the light. And the Georgia O'Keeffe cactus flowers, probably the same print in every room. And it didn't matter, did it, each visitor, like her, only saw one of the rooms. No way to know—for better or for worse— what amenities someone else had.

"One moment, ma'am. I'll check."

Probably bookmarks. Waverly had an efficient system; sometimes they shipped her handouts to her destinations so she didn't have to carry dozens of cardboard rectangles.

"Hello?" The clerk's voice.

"Yes?"

"No. We have no package for you."

Tessa stared at the note, heard white noise on the other end of the line.

"I got a note under my door," she finally said. "It said a package."

"I'll check again," the clerk said.

It was not unimaginable that there had been confusion. A big hotel and one small package of blue bookmarks.

"Thanks. Call me when you find it. Okay?"

Her stomach was rumbling. She had to get food. Text Henry. Check on Linny. Try to sleep. She had to wake up horrifically early to get to the airport on time. Every single thing, and every single moment, was always the highest stress level it could possibly be, even when everything went right. Welcome to book tour. But most of her adored it.

"Certainly," the hotel clerk was saying.

Her unzipped roller bag was spread like a flapped-open book on the webbed luggage carrier by the dresser. The locket, padded in tissues and two gray plastic wastebasket liners from her previous hotel, was zipped into the front pocket. She'd never found anything in a hotel room before. But certainly people left things all the time.

Their heirloom jewelry? Annabelle asked.

Tessa ignored her, ordered a carryout salad and wine from the bar, then pulled out her laptop. Nothing new on her pages on #LocketMom; only more speculation, most comments tinged with sympathy, some with suspicion.

On ReadRunner Bookstore's page they'd already tagged her, showing a wide shot of the backs of attendees' heads, and Tessa at the podium, holding her book, smiling beatifically. It already had dozens of comments.

She was the best, wasn't she? ♥ Annabelle

Did you see cool guy who came at the end?

Friend of Tessa? He waited for her, did you see? #romance

She's married, come on. And kids.

Two. And husband Henry. #married

#happily

Ha ha. #HomeAlone

In novels, she knew, too much backstory, too much history and explanation, made readers stop reading. *Forget the backstory,* her agent Sadie
had ordered her, as she'd struggled through a revision. *Your book is about
forward motion. What happens next. Keeping your readers turning the pages.*

She hoped her own life would be like that, too, forward motion from
now on. Her backstory—the one she'd spent her life trying to avoid—
fading into the past, and forgotten.

Stop worrying, Annabelle said. *It's over.*

Even more comments now, popping up one by one.

Did she ever find #LocketMom?

Publicity stunt, IMO. #salesploy

Tessa would not do that.

Annabelle would. Ha ha. #AnnabelleRules

Do you think that's her real name?

Go away.

How come she won't tell her hometown?

How about privacy, moron. #Jealousy #getalife

Tessa stared at the screen, trying to balance what mattered and what didn't.

His name is Sam, I heard him say it.

Who Sam?

Hot guy at the bookstore. #loveinterest?

She flapped the computer closed, shutting down the gossip and rumors, marveling at how it all traveled at light speed. Nothing was stickier than speculation. Determined to turn her brain off, she slipped her laptop into its padded case and zipped it away from her consciousness.

People were trading theories, and conjecture, making up stories about *her*. People knowing nothing.

Or everything.

But she could not let strangers with wild imaginations or ulterior motives or relentless curiosity control her life.

No one had called about the package. She'd go down to the front desk and check for the bookmarks. Pick up her dinner. Sleep. And move on to her next day as a bestseller.

The only stories that mattered were the ones *she* told.

16

Tessa stepped forward in the line at the hotel's concierge desk, one transaction closer to her bookmarks.

What had been her random thought in the bookstore? A thriller about someone who finds weird things in hotel rooms. She thought of the locket again, the family photo. Who was missing it? Who was #LocketMom? What poor mom was now devastated, worried, guilty?

She knew the feeling, she had to admit. Poor, sick Linny. Her mom had deserted her.

Henry had said Zack was pretending to sleep, a nightly occurrence, so she had to assume that meant everything was okay with him at least. But—she frowned at the enormity of it—it was all because she'd left her family *alone*. Something Linny ate, Henry had said. But what? And if she'd gotten sick on their dinner, why weren't the others sick as well?

"Thank you, ma'am," the clerk was saying to a weary-looking woman, and handed her a flap of thick logoed paper. Tessa had one like it, protecting her key card. "Room 1017," the clerk said.

The clerk had kept her voice low, but Tessa heard that room number perfectly. What if someone had hovered near the registration desk when Tessa arrived? Staked out her registration. Listened for her room number. And then slid that paper under her door.

The din from the sports bar grew louder, a roar of cheers and applause. Everyone in this hotel was a stranger to her, but maybe one of these people knew who she was. Maybe she was not a stranger to them.

"Yes, next, may I help you?" The clerk finally beckoned her forward.

Tessa approached, then stopped, realizing the truth. She'd already had her event in Phoenix. Whatever package was here at the desk for her was *not* bookmarks.

"I'm the one who called about the package," she began. "Tessa Calloway. 1205." She spoke softly, giving that personal information.

"You didn't talk to me," the clerk said. "I'll call the business office."

"No, no," Tessa said, "The business office told me there was no package. But see?" Tessa held up the note.

The clerk looked perplexed. "We don't leave notes, ma'am." She gestured toward the black marble countertop behind her. "Because it'd be right here." She stepped aside. "And there's nothing."

"You sure? It's not from the hotel?"

"I'm sure, ma'am. Like I said. We don't leave notes. Is there a problem?"

"No," Tessa said. Hoping that was true.

She turned away, stuffing the note into her pocket, and slowly traversed the glistening floor of the hotel lobby, stepping on the reflections of the chandeliers above.

Why would someone leave her a note telling her she had a package, when there was no package? She stopped, mid lobby. Knowing the answer. Because they figured she'd call to inquire. And when she was told there *was* no package, she'd come to the front desk and ask about it. Figuring, when no package was found, she would chalk it up to a mistake.

Which allowed them to accomplish their goal.

Get her out of her room.

So they could get in.

She dropped her shoulders in defeat. She was exhausted. She had zero adrenaline. Her imagination was roaring, and she had to tame it. She took a deep breath, convincing herself. Food, sleep, airplane. Onward.

Spying a brown paper carryout bag at the end of the lobby's Diamondback Bar, she saw her room number on it, its flap stapled shut. She grabbed it, and the plastic-covered glass of red wine next to it. No one seemed to be watching.

Parasocial relationships, Heather had called them. Maybe one of her "fans" planned to "coincidentally" run into her in the lobby.

Maybe one of her "fans" had gotten into her room while she was gone.

Ten p.m. in Phoenix now, midnight in Rockport. She set her carryout on a marble table in the elevator bay. Pulled out her phone. Texted Henry.

> Can you FaceTime?

She waited, fingers crossed. A giggling couple in matching tank tops, arms draped around each other, stood next to her, the woman whispering in the man's ear as he pushed the elevator button. The door slid open and the two left her alone again.

> Now? You ok?

> Yup. Humor me?

> One sec

Even expecting Henry's call, Tessa flinched when her silenced phone buzzed. She hit the FaceTime button, seeing her own image pop up, shadowed in the glary overhead light. Seeing Henry, hair spiking straight up, with what looked like a sheet pulled up close to his shoulders. He must be in bed.

"Sorry to call so late," Tessa began. "Is Linny okay?"

Henry dragged one hand through his hair. "Tessa. I told you not to worry. She must have eaten something."

"Yeah, but what?" Tessa could feel her own frown. "I'm worried about—"

"Honey?" Henry interrupted her. "It's late here. Time zones? Are you okay?"

"It's too long to explain, but I want you to be on the phone with me when I go to my room."

"Why? What's wrong?"

"Just—hold on."

She looped the twisted handle of the carryout bag over her wrist, picked up her wine, and pushed the button for her floor. If anything happened, if anyone was in her room, or anyone had left something, or if there was anything untoward or unexpected, at least Henry would be there with her. She'd be alone, but not alone.

The elevator doors slid shut. She felt the motion of the machinery as it carried her upward, a murmur, and an adjusting of her place in the universe. And then her phone screen went black.

17

"Honey? Henry?" Tessa didn't have enough hands to dial again, so she set her wineglass on the elevator floor and hit Recents. A booping noise indicated the call had gone through. "Hen?"

"Where'd you go?"

"We got cut off." This was a terror of her own making, and it had only taken three weeks—which felt like three months—to wear her down. Some road warrior *she* was. "It works now. I'm on the twelfth floor, so we have a minute." She paused. "Unless someone gets on."

Henry was not under a sheet anymore, Tessa noticed. The light was different, but she couldn't tell where in the house he was now. Funny how their new house still wasn't familiar to her, its corners and crannies, how the light shifted as the time went by. Even its sounds; the air conditioner, or traffic. But Henry was somewhere silent now. And it was glary there, too. The bathroom. Or kitchen. She'd awakened him, apparently, and—

"Tess?"

"So listen, when I got to the hotel after the event tonight—"

"How did it go?"

"Great. Perfect. Loved every second. But when I got to my hotel room there was a note under the door saying there was a package for me."

"Bookmarks?"

"Well, I thought so, but I called the desk, and they said there wasn't a package."

"You need to go *down* to the desk and—"

"I did." Floor ten now. "But they said there never *was* a package. Like, they don't leave notes. It's freaking me out."

"They lost your stuff, honey. Idiots."

"But what if . . ." Almost to her floor. "What if it was a trick to get me out of my room?"

Silence on Henry's end of the line. In the oddly bright light, she saw he was frowning.

"Why?" he finally said. "I mean, that's strange." He paused again. "I mean, it *could* be strange. Or a mistake."

The elevator doors opened. She stepped out, surveyed the long corridors stretching out both ways, dimly lit strips of tan-on-black carpeting, lined with numbered doors. Hers was about halfway down to the right. Tessa heard some kind of noise wherever Henry was.

"Hey. Sweetheart." Henry was scratching behind one ear. "You want to call security to go in with you?"

There was a house phone on the long wooden table beside her.

She shook her head, gauging Henry's reaction. "It's too—I'm not sure too what. Embarrassing. Just stay on the line with me until I'm safely inside."

"Okay, but how's that gonna help?"

She had to laugh. "I know, if the crazed author-murderer is lying in wait, it won't be that fabulous for either of us. You *or* me. But I feel better having you with me." A wave of affection washed over her. "I always do. Always always."

"Can you record our FaceTime?" Henry asked.

"Record—oh, no idea." Tessa had to put down her wine to take her key card from her pocket, dumb not to have done it sooner. "It'll be fine. We can laugh in about two seconds."

She'd lowered her voice, she realized. And now she was three doors away. Light leaked out from under each of them, but none from under 1205. Which was strange, because she often left all the lights on, and the TV, too, so it wouldn't be dark when she returned. But had she done that this time?

"I'm here," Henry said. "Point the screen forward. So I can see the room, not you."

"I don't think the lights are on." She was stalling, she knew it.

"Did you leave them on?"

"I don't remember."

"Look. Call security, or let's do this. You don't have to go in. Just open the door."

"Right." She heard the noises in Rockport again. "What's that?"

"What's what?"

"I heard a noise. Are you okay?"

"Tess? Honey?"

She detected a flare of annoyance. And rightly so, it was pushing one in the morning for him, she had awakened him, and this was going to be nothing.

"Okay. I'm going in."

She tapped the key card on the pad. The light went green. Her carryout bag flapped against the doorjamb as she turned the knob and swung open the door. She held up her phone, like a camera with Henry as the lens.

"It's dark," she whispered. A glowing night-light on a bathroom wall offered only feeble illumination to the rest of the square and shadowy space. She could see the outline of the two beds, her flapped-open suitcase, the bendy aluminum lamp in the corner, the linen curtains, open to the Phoenix skyline. The white-louvered closet doors were closed.

"Turn on the light," Henry said.

His voice was lowered, too, she noticed. Now she'd succeeded in frightening him as well. There was not a sound, not a movement, not a rustle. The curtains were dead still.

She felt for the switch, pushed it. Only the light in the entryway came on.

"I have to go in to turn on the other lights."

"You see anything? I don't. Is that a closet?"

"I'm gonna open it. This is silly. There's no bad guy in the closet." She took a deep breath. Did it. Held up the phone. "See? No one in the closet. The beds have those wooden panels, you can't get underneath."

She panned the phone to the bathroom. The shower curtain was open, the tub empty.

"Never a dull moment," she said. "Thank you, honey."

"Look around again. I want you to be sure. Leave the door open as you do."

She put down her bag, one twisty handle catching on her wedding ring. The wine was still in the hall. Holding the phone as her sentry, she went from light to light, turned on everything. Flapped at the curtains, kicked the boards under the beds.

"There's nowhere else to hide," she said.

"Did they take anything?"

They. Her laptop was still in its pouch on the desk. And she had logged out and turned it off when she left, she was religious about that. Her wallet? Before she'd gone to the lobby, she'd draped her handbag handle over a hanger in the closet and covered it with a coat, as if that would protect her from burglars. She put down the phone on one of the beds, giving Henry a look at the stucco ceiling, and pawed through her handbag. Wallet, credit cards, makeup, everything. All there.

"No. Unless I missed—no," she said again. "Wallet, laptop, all my stuff, all here. It looks exactly like when I left it. I think."

Her heart had slowed now, she only noticed it as it eased back to normal.

"Close the door?" Henry suggested. "I can't see you now, only ceiling."

"Sorry." She leaned over the phone, waved at her husband in apology. She retrieved her wine, set down the phone, closed the door, locked the dead bolt and drew the chain. And picked up the phone again. "You have a crazy wife," she said.

"I have a wonderful wife," Henry whispered. "An imaginative wife. A story-creating wife. A brilliant wife."

"Aw, thank you—"

"And tomorrow you can yell at them about the lost package. They probably ran out of official paper, or someone didn't know the no-note system."

She was so relieved to see his face. So relieved.

"Get some sleep, honey." Henry yawned. "That's what I'm about to do. Again."

"I will," she said. "And tomorrow, I want to FaceTime the kids. I need—"

"And, honey?" Henry interrupted. "I am always here for you. *Always always.*"

Tessa almost burst into tears; with the tension and the speculation and the ridiculousness, and with the insistent weight of her imagination.

18

The brittle plastic clamshell holding her salad cracked as she opened it, so tightly snapped together she almost cut her finger on one edge. Sitting on her bed with a towel across her lap, Tessa squeezed a packet of generic vinaigrette across the weary-looking tomatoes arrayed on the top. Plastic fork, plastic knife, one flimsy paper napkin. The book-tour life; watching cooking shows and drinking wine from a plastic glass, dinner at 11:00 p.m. One a.m. in Rockport, she reminded herself. Poor Henry.

She thought about that note again. It had her name on it.

Maybe there's a fan who didn't want her evening with you to end, Annabelle said. Or his. Heather said that other author brought bodyguards. You only have Henry, two thousand miles away.

Weren't fans supposed to be—benevolent? Heather's admonition had thoroughly disconcerted her, and probably had her seeing danger where there was only book-tour reality.

With the television on mute, she watched the flickering video of a commercial, too riled up to sleep, too weary to stay awake.

She wondered how Linny was, wondered if Zack missed her. She closed her eyes, trying to identify the noises she'd heard on Henry's FaceTime, and wondered again about those white sheets. Henry did not like white sheets. White is for hospitals, he'd told her once. Sheets should be fun.

"What a random conversation to remember," she said out loud. So why had he purchased white sheets?

Good question, Annabelle said. *And now you have another mystery to solve. Long-distance.*

It had been complicated to get used to, Annabelle talking to her, unbidden. Once, she'd been at the grocery store, Zack balanced on one hip and vising his legs around Tessa's thigh, and Linny in the child seat of the grocery cart, banging her strappy sandals on the metal rungs and demanding every item as they walked by. *Fwuit,* she'd say. *Nanas. Pitches. Stwawbrees.*

"Yes, fruit," Tessa had tried to make it an educational experience. "Bana-nas," she enunciated each syllable. "Peaches. Strawberries."

She'd known she'd be sad when Linny grew out of her baby talk, but at that moment, with the constant Muzak, and the chittering kids, and the rumble of the unaligned wheels of the cart that yanked it left no matter how she steered, all she'd wanted was quiet.

She had peeled a banana as they walked, figuring if the kids' mouths were busy with banana, they couldn't talk. Zack had poked his and played with it with one finger; she'd given him the part with the peel. Linny had popped her whole piece into her mouth, and chewed, with an expression that morphed from skepticism to curiosity to bliss.

And then she'd thrown up. Her banana, and her oatmeal breakfast, and other unidentifiable things, all over Zack and all over Tessa, and time had stopped, and the world had stopped, and it seemed as if every single person in the grocery had stopped, and focused their attention on bad mother Tessa, who selfishly had brought a sick child to the grocery store, and now all of their children would get sick, too, and the whole thing would be Tessa's fault.

She'd heard a voice then, she thought it was someone in the grocery store. *It could happen to anyone,* the voice had said.

You're doing the best you can, the voice went on. *Eff them.*

Tessa had turned toward it, she remembered, smiling, grateful for the support. But no one had been there. She'd blinked, clearing her head, knowing she and her children smelled disgusting, that Linny was sobbing and Zack was wailing, and that she should *do* something, and someone, at least, understood her. Was reassuring her. But no one was there.

And then Tessa had realized what she'd heard. She'd said it out loud, talking to herself, right there in the grocery. She'd said, "Annabelle?"

And you're not losing it. It's just life. Linny may be allergic to bananas, and now you know. And you don't need to take any grief from any of these people.

Annabelle. Gunk-covered Tessa had burst out laughing at that moment. The cleanup crew arrived, for the floor and for her kids, then she'd popped Linny and Zack into the car, driven them home, and whisked them into the shower, all three of them. Peeled off their clothes under the rush of warm water. Linny recovered, and Zack was clueless, and Tessa had made it all work.

She'd "heard," that's how she thought of it, Annabelle daily since then. "Heard" her commentary, and finally created a whole fictional life for her. Somedays, she wasn't sure whether the book was mostly her or mostly Annabelle-as-writer-muse, but it didn't matter. It was simply that her imagination had a name. She predicted successful authors, the lucky ones at least, had characters who talked to them.

She hoped.

Now she slid into her slippers and dumped the remnants of her dinner into a wastebasket. *Other authors.* She'd had no time to connect with other authors—she'd known about conferences and conventions, but how could she take that time from the kids? And social media was no place to make real friends, let alone find a writer colleague to bare her soul to.

It was time to sleep. She had to sleep.

Wait. Had she set her alarm? What time had she decided to get up, to leave, when did she have to be at the airport? She unzipped the pocket of her suitcase and pulled out her green book-tour itinerary folder.

"Get organized," she muttered, half expecting a snarky comment from Annabelle, but it did not come.

The green file folder, already fraying around the edges—*like I am,* Tessa thought—was right where it should be. But she stopped. Envisioning. Remembering. She jammed her hand all the way into the suitcase pocket, searching and patting as if it would make a difference, as if the laws of physics had reversed, and created matter from nothing.

The rose-gold locket with the photo of the T-shirted family, the one she'd double-wrapped in hotel plastic bags, was not there.

19

Staring at an empty pocket was not going to make that necklace appear. Tessa pawed, frantic, through the rest of her suitcase, pulling out sheets of wrinkled tissue paper and two shoe bags that held her event pumps. She had unpacked when she arrived, because living out of a suitcase felt like the first step in personal travel defeat. So right now she was clawing through an essentially empty roller bag, looking for something that was not there.

She stood, not taking her eyes off the suitcase, hands on hips, and she imagined a slideshow of possibilities. Had she not packed it? Had she left it in—wherever she was before? Indianapolis? No, she definitely hadn't forgotten it. Taking it had been a Rubicon moment. Had she shown it to Geneva, that driver? Handed it to her, forgotten to take it back? No. She'd shown her the picture on her cell phone. She had not let the suitcase out of her sight as it went through luggage screening, and she herself had lifted it into the overhead compartment on the plane. And she remembered, distinctly, seeing its lumpy outline, concerned it might make her suitcase too thick for the overhead compartment. And no one could have taken it on the plane, impossible, she would have noticed.

So she hadn't been crazy. She hadn't been wrong. She lowered herself to the side of the bed, sticking out her slippered feet and staring at the toes.

Someone had been in this room, and they had taken the locket. *Only* the locket.

And what's more, and she was certain of it, that was the purpose of the note. As she'd suspected. Getting her out of the way to give them the opening to steal it. But who? And why?

She flopped back onto her pillow, slippers on top of the duvet. What was she supposed to do? Call the desk and say someone had been in her room? And, she realized in a wave of distress, she wasn't even supposed to possess that locket. She herself had stolen it from her Indianapolis hotel room.

Now, if someone on social media recognized it, and claimed it, and wanted it back, she didn't have it.

She puffed out a dismayed breath, imagining what would happen next. Calling DJ, and reporting to her publicist that someone had stolen #LocketMom's necklace from her room. *That* would be a conversation. She should never have taken it in the first place. When would she learn not to get involved in other people's lives?

"I was only trying to help," Tessa said out loud.

She stared at the ceiling, unseeing. She had to go to sleep, she had to get up for her plane tomorrow, it was now past one in the morning and there was no one to call. No one to ask. No way to figure this out.

Her door was chained closed; she could see the lock. Fans were supposed to be good people. Weren't they? Loving and supportive? She adored hers, relied on them, and could not bear the idea that someone had weaponized the personal connections of her book tour. She'd always scoffed when celebrities complained about people loving them, but now . . . She was beginning to understand how having a world of strangers know your every move could be frightening.

She grabbed her phone and googled *how to get into someone's hotel room*. When an array of answers popped up, she realized it didn't matter. It didn't matter how someone got in. They had.

Tessa brushed her teeth—*good girl*, she reassured herself, *everything will be fine*—assessed her weary face in the unforgiving bathroom mirror, then turned off all the lights except for the one in the entryway, and slid under the covers, punching her pillow into shape. She closed her eyes, and they stayed closed for, she estimated, approximately ten seconds. She reached to the nightstand for her plugged-in phone, opened her Facebook.

The ReadRunner Bookstore page had accumulated an even longer list of comments. She skimmed them for clues or personal questions or negative remarks, even knowing she'd be better off going to sleep. Did one of those people—one of the people she had signed a book for—carry some seething animosity toward her?

"Stop," she ordered herself. And then went to her own Facebook page. There was her crying, and dangling the now-missing locket, with thousands of likes, and now, hundreds of comments. Nine hundred and fifty-three comments. How could 953 people possibly have something to say about that locket? Or the man in the photo?

The locket you no longer have.

"Go to sleep," she said out loud.

But she could not resist reading the new comments.

Did you see her in Phoenix? So beyond.

I wore my blue earrings #periwinkle

So what about this photo? Who did she cut out of it?

Weird that no one knows that man

Told you #salesploy

Go away.

She wouldn't talk about her hometown, notice that?

This is supposed to be about the man in the picture.

Agree with ^^ Why doesn't anyone know him?

Maybe he's dead.

Not everyone is on social. Tessa is trying to help. #supernice

All these people, talking about her. She'd embraced it, and certainly the support from her #MomsWithDreams friends had changed her life, but now the chatter felt unsettling. Personal. Invasive. She'd taken a photo of the attendees tonight, a wide shot from the podium, her standard "class photo." She could compare it with the ones from her other events. See if anyone looked out of place. Or, even more disconcerting, familiar.

Tessa paused. Footsteps. In the hallway. She closed her eyes, derisive. *It's a hallway. People walk in hallways.*

She waited. The footsteps came closer.

But they did not pause outside her door, and continued into silence.

20

Tessa awoke five minutes before the alarm would go off. And did her first mental math of the day. Almost 7:00 a.m. in Phoenix. Almost nine in Rockport. She grabbed her phone, propped herself against pillows, checked her messages. Nothing. Henry knew from the fridge schedule that she didn't have an early flight, so maybe he didn't want to disturb her. Like she had disturbed him last night.

Happy Friday, she typed. How is everyone?

> In car, Linny recovered, Zack good, headed to fun thing, talk later LY

What fun thing? A Friday in June, she supposed there were lots of "fun" possibilities.

> Hold on Driving

She took a deep breath, engulfed, for that moment, by the life passages she was missing. Like getting used to their new house. The sales transaction had been complicated, and after the closing finally went through, she'd only gotten to spend one night there—the night before book tour began. Henry, sated with new possessions, had toasted Tessa's six-week tour with too much too expensive champagne. Tessa had been too nervous to have more than a sip, fearful of even the hint of a hangover, and sleepless with the unfamiliar atmosphere and the anticipation of the unknown.

The next morning, almost at sunrise, she'd kissed a blearily congratulatory Henry goodbye, and wheeled her suitcase toward the new front door, the Uber idling at the end of her new driveway at the curb of their new street. She'd walked by their possessions, still mostly in taped brown cardboard boxes, labeled room by room and distributed throughout their new home. Henry and the kids would put things away, she knew, and that would leave her as the newcomer when she finally returned, opening drawers and cabinets to discover where someone had stashed the cooking utensils, stacked the pans, shelved her books. Henry and the kids would have searched out the nearest grocery, and sampled pizza places, and discovered the best ice cream. Her family would be happily exploring, sharing, bonding.

Her family would be entering a new life. One without her. And where the only view she had, the only participation, was virtual. A virtual mom.

She adjusted her hotel pillow, thinking about that. She'd quit her job to be with her family and follow her dreams, but turned out, her dreams were taking her away from her family.

Irony, Annabelle said. Very literary.

And now—without her—they were doing a fun thing. Zack would want an arcade, and Linny would want to see the library. She loved the summer reading programs, exactly like Tessa had.

Driving talk later LY

Tessa stared at the phone. "Love you, too," she said out loud to no one. "Have fun." But that was good news, she guessed, they were not sleeping in or watching junk TV, they were already out doing the fun thing. Henry was not texting and driving. Linny was not throwing up. All was right with the world.

She flinched when the grating buzzer of her alarm went off. It always took her a moment, in that liminal precipice between then and now, to make sure she was on track. *Phoenix. Friday, Headed for Denver.* She whapped off the alarm. "Hush," she instructed it. "I'm awake."

The green schedule folder was open on her nightstand. She was on book-tour time, with book-tour metabolism, book-tour energy, and book-tour stress. One missed connection, one delayed flight, and the whole house of cards would topple. If an event got canceled, the travel people at Waverley would have to regroup and rebook and reschedule and it would be an expensive mess. Her responsibility was to get where she was supposed to be, on time, and sell books and make friends. Every time she felt like complaining, she reminded herself she was the luckiest person ever. A double *New York Times* bestseller does not complain. Everything was wonderful.

Got that right, Annabelle said. Except for that one pesky thing.

The locket. It was still not in her suitcase, though she had attempted to manifest it to magically return. It wasn't anywhere in the room. She showered, packed, picked up the phone to call her Uber.

Except. Her heart sank, feeling the unintended consequences of her own actions. She should call the Indianapolis hotel about the locket. See if anyone had asked for it.

At least no one on social media had claimed it. Or recognized the family. That would be a disaster, someone asking for it back, and Tessa forced to say, "oh, sorry, I don't have it anymore. And I have no idea where it is." Now her wish was opposite from yesterday.

Now, she hoped no one recognized it.

She checked the nightstand table for anything she herself had left behind, gave one last sweep of the bathroom and the closet. Made sure she was wearing both watches and her wedding ring, checked that both periwinkle earrings dangled from her ears.

"Goodbye, Phoenix," she told the room, and tucked five dollars under the TV remote for the housekeepers.

Her suitcase wheels rumbled across the lobby floor, and she slipped her room key card into the checkout box. "I'm out of 1205," she told the desk clerk, waving thanks-and-goodbye as she spun her suitcase in the opposite direction.

"Oh, ma'am? Ms. Calloway?" the clerk called after her.

She turned, frowning. "Yes?"

"Hold on a sec," he said. "We have a package for you."

"What?" Her brain crashed, trying to reconcile this. Had Henry been right?

"Is this the one you all couldn't find yesterday?" As soon as she said it, she knew Henry had been wrong. There was no real package. That was only bait. The locket was gone. Yesterday's note, still in her pocket, had been a fake, to lure her from the room.

"Yesterday? Huh?" The clerk, dapper in an almost-too-small jacket and leather string tie, had opened a cabinet in the counter behind him. He pulled out a brown paper bag, like the one the hotel restaurant used for her last night's carryout. "Here you go."

She stared at it.

"It's yours, isn't it?" the clerk said again. "It has your name on it. Calloway. And 1205. Wasn't your red message light on?"

Had it been? Tessa tried to remember.

Parasocial relationships, Annabelle said.

If it were a gift from a fan—earrings, or a friendship bracelet, or another unpackable ceramic mug—she'd stash it in her tote bag and figure out how to deal with it at the airport. She accepted the bag from the clerk, and pulled apart the handles.

And saw the package inside.

21

"You okay, ma'am?" The desk clerk's voice came across muddled, as if Tessa's fear had muted the sounds of the hotel and the entire world outside her head.

"Um, sure," Tessa managed to answer. Still standing at the counter, she removed the package from the paper bag. It was wrapped in gray plastic, with stretchy black closures tied in a tight knot.

Her heart clenched. Her brain caught fire. This was no longer irony or coincidence or a mistake.

She picked at the stubborn black knot, fumbling, pulling at the unyielding plastic, frustrated, impatient. The drawstring finally came loose, and revealed another gray plastic bag.

As she knew it would.

It was all she could do not to rip it apart.

She whirled, but no one was in line behind her. She scanned the hotel lobby for anyone watching her, or pretending *not* to watch her. A massive cactus in a huge red lacquer pot stood sentinel over three women perched on their taupe leather club chairs, but each seemed intent on their phone screens. A florid-faced man with a suitcase was yelling at the concierge, leaning halfway across his wooden desk and focused on his outrage. And the Diamondback Bar was empty, a metal gate drawn around its perimeter. Except for the clueless clerk, no one was paying attention to Tessa and her bags.

She picked at the plastic ties of the second bag, her face feeling flushed and her chest tight. Hoping, and bargaining, and trying to explain an impossible thing.

When the final drawstring loosened, she pulled the plastic open, and there, exactly as she had left it, in these very same bags, with the very same knots, was the locket.

"You have no idea where this came from?" She had to ask, though she knew it was futile.

"It had your name on it," the clerk said. "I mean, is it not yours?"

An impossible question.

"Is it a mistake?" the clerk persisted.

Another impossible question. Not a mistake on *their* part. But seemed as if somehow it was a mistake on hers.

Tucking the package into her tote bag as if it belonged there, she skirted the clerk's inquiries. "No, just checking."

She turned away, heart still racing, wondering what acting normal would look like. Then turned back to the clerk.

"I wonder if my husband was trying to surprise me with this. Cowboy boots, sandy hair?" She pantomimed *big guy, broad shoulders*, testing, on a gut instinct, to see if it might be Sam from seat 3A. "Like I told the other clerk when I asked about the package last night."

"Huh?" the clerk said.

Any second now, her heart would explode.

"Can you find out who left this for me?" She hoped she didn't look as terrified as she was.

"'Fraid not." He shrugged, the silver metal ends of his bolo tie moving with the motion. "It didn't come on my shift. We could find out tonight, maybe? Midnight shift?"

Her phone pinged. Her Uber was one minute away. The guy behind the desk was not going to be helpful. There was no one who could be helpful.

Had someone—the housekeeping staff—taken it by accident? Then returned it?

Taken it by accident from your suitcase? Annabelle asked.

At least now if someone recognized it, she could give it back, and have this monkey paw—wasn't that the story? Or hot potato?—out of her life.

That was the good news.

The bad news was that the "housekeeper mistake" story could not be true. Someone was toying with her. Taunting her. Proving she was findable. Vulnerable.

In a daze, she managed to get a cup of coffee from the lobby dispenser. She had to leave. She had to catch her plane. And someone—someone unknown—knew her timing, and her plans, and exactly where she'd be.

"Tessa?" The Uber driver greeted her at the open back door of a crimson Charger. A woman wearing a denim midi skirt and a cowboy hat. She blinked, a double take, pointed a long Charger-red fingernail. "It *is* you, isn't it?"

"Yes, good morning." Tessa tried to focus. Someone was playing a game with her. A nasty game. An upsetting game. And she had no idea what the game was, or who else was playing. Which made it impossible to win. Tessa put on her face-the-fan expression. "Tessa, yes. Calloway."

"Oh, I'da sold my soul for this. Died and gone to heaven. Will you sign my—" The woman stopped, grimaced. "Sorry. Not very professional. Airport?"

"Airport. Thanks, yes."

"Your book is on my front seat," the driver went on. "And you won't believe this. My name is Annabelle, too." She handed the book over the front seat, then shifted into drive. "Can you sign it 'To the real Annabelle'?"

Tessa uncapped a pen and waited for a steady moment when the car wasn't accelerating or changing lanes.

"For . . ." She paused, pen in midair, considering what she was about to write. This stranger, this "Annabelle," or so she said, would be able to tell people that she truly *was* the inspiration for Annabelle. And Tessa might never know, at least not until it was too late.

The cactus-dotted Arizona landscape whizzed by her window. The woman could say she and Tessa had known each other for years, that Tessa had adored her, and named a character after her. Who wouldn't believe it? It would be right there in black Sharpie, written by Tessa herself.

Thank you for everything. Tessa wrote that at every book signing without a second thought. But someone could present that as meaning anything they wanted. "She was thanking me for—" and then make up a lie. And Tessa's inscription became incontrovertible evidence.

Even the innocuous "So nice to meet you at the Burlington Barnes & Noble" and the date—what was that but a perfect alibi?

Good one, Annabelle said. You could use that.

"For another Annabelle," Tessa finally wrote. She handed the book to the driver as they stopped in a crowded line of cars in the departure drop-off lane. "So glad you enjoyed this."

"Well, yeah, Annabelle's my total role model." The driver had come around to open Tessa's door. "Screw 'em, right? And go after what you want, even if you have to sell your soul to get it. Because deals are made to be broken. She rocks. And you do, too. Since you made her up, right?"

The book is fiction, Tessa didn't say. It would never fail to astonish her, how one decision could change your life. Or change someone else's life. Or ruin it. "Thank you. You made my day."

Tessa stepped out into oven-like heat, the sun glaring on the airport's hot-as-hell white sidewalks. Thinking about selling one's soul. What was destined to happen if you did.

"Wow," Tessa said. "Brutal."

The driver took Tessa's suitcase from the trunk. "It'll be better in Denver. Not as hot."

"Denver?" How did this random driver know her destination?

"I googled your website when I was driving," Annabelle said.

"Oh," Tessa said. She needed to rein in her paranoia. That was the purpose of her events page. So people would know about her events.

"And can I ask . . ." The driver almost touched her on the arm, then pulled back. "Did you ever find Locket Mom?"

Locket Mom. Tessa's heart sank, as the terror and confusion of the morning washed over her again. There was no way to fight back if she didn't know who she was fighting. Or why.

"Not yet," Tessa said. "But I know she's out there."

22

She slid into a green pleather booth in an airport diner called Avocados, directly across from her gate, which offered a nichey menu with varieties of avocado toast and "artisanal" coffee. Tessa ordered a Desert Dark Roast and set up her FaceTime, putting her back to the arriving customers so no one would recognize her. She propped her phone against a ketchup bottle, and held it in place with a sugar shaker. She needed to call Henry. In the midst of his "fun thing" or not, she had to talk to him.

"They found it?" Henry's expression, in miniature on the FaceTime, was a portrait of skepticism. He'd said he and the kids were on the town center green, getting ice cream for "breakfast dessert" after having waffles at some place called DeMarco's. She had a pang of worry about Linny's tummy, but hey, if Henry wanted to be in charge, he could be in charge. She'd kill him if anything happened to her daughter. Their daughter.

But he'd assured her Linny was fine. They'd even met some of the "terrific" new neighbors. And a cool—"Linny's word," Henry assured her—dog walker.

"That's totally hotel CYA, honey," Henry was saying now.

The sun was bleaching out the video, and sometimes all Tessa could see on the FaceTime was a burst of light, or trees. She heard laughter in the background, music from a band, or a carousel.

"Someone took the thing by mistake," he went on, "when they left the chocolate on your pillow. They had to get it back to you without having to admit someone stole it. And thereby avoid potentially crippling liability."

"They don't leave chocolates anymore." The restaurant smelled like salsa, and it was stomach-churningly too early for that. "But that's not the point."

"Honey—"

The shot shifted, and Tessa could see Henry was not looking at the camera lens. His attention was elsewhere, but she could not see what had distracted him. He was living an entirely separate life, and she could only view the tiny fraction of it that he allowed her to.

"Hey. Hen? You with me here? The point is the thing was *in* my suitcase, wrapped up and *zipped* in the pocket, like I said, so it's not like someone thought it was trash, and then discovered later that it wasn't, and had to create a face-saving cover-up to return it. Believe me, I tried to get myself to buy into that. But—"

"Wrapped?" Henry interrupted. "Like a gift? What was it wrapped in?"

Tessa paused, took a sip of coffee.

"Trash bags," she muttered. "But it—"

Henry's laugh was so loud Tessa flinched, and lowered the volume on her phone.

"You must be so tired, hon. Look, possibly you didn't actually put it into the pocket. There's got to be an explanation."

"There sure does." Tessa heard the hiss in her own voice. "But I don't have any idea what it is. It didn't look like trash. It was *in* my suitcase. Someone wanted to prove they could get into my room, and get into my stuff, and why would they only take that? And give it back?"

"That's pretty complicated," Henry said. "You and your imagination, Tesser."

He's wrong, Annabelle said. *You know that.*

"I'm not imagining anything," she said.

23

Tessa scanned the boarding area, looking for the people in the locket photograph, or someone from the book signing. A fan, tracking her. But there was no one suspicious, no one unsettling. She'd gotten a few flickers of recognition, but not from anyone she'd seen before. She'd ignored them, politely, staying small in her molded plastic chair, keeping to herself. She wrapped her phone power cord into a careful loop, preparing.

They'd be boarding any minute, and she looked forward to the small pleasure of her solitude on the plane as they made their way to Denver. She'd watch for the Rocky Mountains. Take a picture for the kids.

Henry, after dismissing her concern entirely in the airport coffee shop, had changed the FaceTime subject to the many moving boxes that still needed to be unpacked, and Zack's discovery of a pull-down door in the ceiling of his closet that led to a "sick" attic space above.

"We could make it into an office for me," he'd said. "Put in a skylight. It wouldn't be that expensive."

"Maybe unpack first?" Tessa had tried to keep her voice pleasant. An office for him. For the job he didn't have. "Speaking of which. Have you put up the family photos? Can we wait until I get there? Make it a family project?"

"Crap, honey." Henry had seemed contrite, at least it appeared so in the FaceTime. "That was one of the first things I did. To make the place feel like home. They go up the stairs in a row. First that one of all of us in front of our old house, and then all the way to the second-floor landing. Linny got a huge kick out of hammering nails into the wall, and Zack took photos and made a stop-action video."

Tessa paused now, trying to remember exactly what that unfamiliar staircase looked like, envisioning that uniquely personal project. Her family, without her, making their home feel like their home. Making once-in-a-lifetime memories. Without her.

"But that reminds me, Tessie," Henry had said. "I can't find any old pictures of you. Nothing of you as a kid. I'm thinking I've never seen your family album—where'd you pack it? I could take some of the pictures out of it for a family history–like thing. We could make room on the stairway."

We could make room.

"Family means our family, yours and mine," she had told him. "My family wasn't much on saving pictures. If they had some . . ." She'd tried to think about it and not think about it at the same time. "They didn't give me any of them."

"I know your father was—gone. But didn't you inherit that stuff when your mother died?"

Tessa had wished her departure time was sooner. "Why are you suddenly interested in this? The pictures you put up are perfect, I'm sure."

She had no recollection of her mother taking photos, not in any of the places they'd lived. Even when Daddy was still with them. Photos were memories, and memories could be dangerous.

"Photos are memories," she had said out loud. "And memories should be good. Let's just use our own."

"I'll send you a video of it. Okay? So you can tell us what we did wrong."

"Ha ha. My plane is about to—"

"So you don't have any photos at all? Of where you lived as a kid, or anything like that?"

"Henry." She'd taken a deep breath, for some reason she remembered her heart beating just then, as if she were getting ready to pose a difficult question. "What's this about?"

"Curiosity," he had said. "No reason."

An electronic crackle came over the public address system now, stopping her mental replay of her husband's nonanswers.

Boarding, Tessa thought. *Good.* Her heart gave a preflight flutter, her imagination's acknowledgment that she was about to be in a metal tube going six hundred miles an hour at thirty-three thousand feet, and nothing would go wrong.

"For passengers flying on flight 141 to Denver," a well-modulated and sincere-sounding voice was saying.

Tessa looked up, as if acknowledging the gate agent was the polite thing to do.

"We are experiencing a slight delay in our departure," the voice went on. "Please remain in the waiting area. We do not anticipate the delay being extensive. Thank you so much for your patience."

The very air went out of the place, replaced by murmurs of frustration and annoyance instead of patience. Tessa could feel the negative energy, and watched the predictable rush of passengers swarming the gate desk.

So frustrating. She had specifically asked for this later flight to Denver, devoutly wishing to avoid another 4:00 a.m. wake-up call. And look what that had gotten her, a delay. And the possible first domino in a disastrous chain, a chain that could cause her to miss her event in Denver. A ticketed big-deal signing that had been highly promoted. If Tessa's plane was delayed too long, the whole thing might be canceled.

It also proved what a tightrope she was walking. At every single moment of her life. Tessa Calloway, high-wire artist.

She needed to let DJ know about delays, but it was too soon to panic the publicist. Ten a.m. in Phoenix (*noon in Rockport,* she automatically added, and in New York where DJ was) and that meant she had some leeway. If she worried, or if she didn't, it wouldn't matter. She'd worry when the time came.

Smart, Annabelle said. *But tick tick.*

24

The outline of the wrapped locket package still showed through the exterior pocket of her roller bag, and she stared at it as she sat at the airport gate, replaying the whole here-again, gone-again, here-again episode. The plane was delayed, that's all they'd heard. The timing would be tight, but so far, she was still on schedule.

She pulled out her phone, and examined her pictures of the locket photograph. Was there something she hadn't noticed before? Man, woman, girl. A cabin by a lake, because the water was calm, not like the ocean. Deciduous trees, not pine trees or palms. She was trying to be a detective on a case where she didn't know the crime.

Her phone pinged a message. Area code 602. Phoenix. The first green text bubble popped out.

> Hi Tessa.

The hotel, with some news about the package? Or even Sam, who had somehow tracked her down? She was making up stories again, she couldn't help it; like every author, trying to create the most worrisome, disastrous, conflict-filled plot development to crash into the main character. But you had to hope that wasn't what happened in real life.

> It's Heather. At ReadRunner. Can u call me? No rush.

"*That* could go either way," Tessa muttered. She looked at the gate agent, who was studiously avoiding eye contact with the waiting passengers. Some were dramatically checking their watches. Others paced, radiating frustration. But for her it was a benefit. She dialed quickly. If she had to hang up, Heather would understand.

"ReadRunner," a cordial voice answered on the first ring.

"Good morning, it's Tessa Calloway. Returning a call from, I mean a message from—"

"Oh, Tessa, terrific. This is Heather. How are you?"

"Good. Good. Sorry if I talk fast. My plane was delayed, but they told us not to leave the waiting area."

"So frustrating. I'd commiserate more, but I know you need to hurry."

"I hope so."

A blue-uniformed flight attendant had opened the gate to the jetway, and some of the passengers stood, expectant, hoping. The door closed again.

"Listen," Heather went on. "A customer from your event last night wants to send you a present. Wants to know where to send it. I promised them I'd ask, so I'm asking. Your fans do love you so much."

Tessa heard a sigh.

"If you know what I mean," Heather went on. "*So* much."

"What kind of a present?" That wasn't exactly the right question, she thought, as she stared at the outline in her suitcase pocket.

"They didn't tell me. And to be clear, I'm at the store. *So* many people around, if you get my drift."

"Sure. . . ." Had Tessa heard something in her voice?

"She said she had friends in Denver, and hoped they'd have the fun of seeing you, too. But she was insistent about your address."

Definitely something in her voice.

"Well, I don't give out my home address, of course. But tell her—because I'm on the road, send it to Djamila Parekh, my publicist at Waverly? Put it to my attention. And tell her I'm so grateful."

"Yeah. I suggested that, but she insisted I ask you directly. Um. Tessa? You remember our conversation about, well . . . remember?"

"Yes, I remember." *Parasocial relationships.* "All too well. So—" The crackle came from the PA system again, and Tessa stood. "Oh, I have to go. I hope."

"Safe travels. But quickly. Can you hear me?" Heather's voice had dropped to a whisper.

"Yes, I can hear you." Tessa hunched her shoulders to block out the activity around her. Why did Heather need to whisper?

"The woman who wanted your address. She's the one who asked about your hometown at the event. Remember? Navy blazer, white T-shirt, jeans? And no, before you ask. I don't know her name. I did all I could to get her to tell me. But she wouldn't. In fact, she absolutely refused."

"Attention, passengers on flight 141 to Denver. An update now on our schedule," the voice on the PA system began. "We—"

"Is everything okay, Tessa?" Heather asked at the same time. "You okay?"

Say yes, Annabelle said.

"Yes," Tessa said. "Of course. Completely fine."

25

Finally, finally, *finally*. Tessa yanked her roller bag over the gap between jetway and plane, an hour late boarding, crossing that two-inch chasm from having her feet on the ground into relying on physics and lift and the skills of whoever was in the cockpit. She remembered a book she'd read, long ago, where the writer considered the fragility of flight, and how much depended on whether the mechanics circling the plane before take-off had a hangover, or were angry in a relationship, or whether they had skipped class on rudder-bolt day.

"Welcome, Ms. Calloway," the flight attendant greeted her at the entrance to the plane, the galley door behind her open for the catering carts. Her name tag said Maddalyn. "We're big fans, and thrilled to have you. We tried to finagle you into first class, but there's no room. I can upgrade your suitcase though, and put it in the first-class overheads. Okay? And I see you have your name tag on it, good for you. It'll be easy for you to retrieve on the way out."

"That's so kind of you."

"Do you need anything from your bag first?"

"Nope," Tessa said. "I'm fine. Thank you."

She buckled herself into 10C, and in the brief interim while she still had Wi-Fi, she pulled up her socials, checking if anyone had recognized the man in the locket photo, or whether there was more reaction to last night's event. It already seemed like a long time ago, and so far away; that standing-room-only bookstore, the signing line, Sam. The "hometown" woman haunted her, concerned her, perplexed her, even more now that she'd come back to the store, pushing for personal information. That woman had some agenda. First her questions about Tessa's hometown. And now "a gift."

Tessa did not even want to think about her hometown. And certainly did not want to discuss it.

Would she recognize that woman if she saw her again? She opened her phone to her camera roll, searching for the wide shot of the attendees she took from the ReadRunner podium. She used two fingers to zoom in across the faces, scouting for the woman.

It was Where's Waldo, the sinister version. She almost laughed as she scanned the faces. They all appeared to be expectant, and happy, and everyone was looking at the camera. Hometown woman had been in the back. Tessa closed her eyes briefly, envisioning it. Way in the back, on the right. She pinched the photo to that part of the room, and it was almost as if . . . almost as if the woman had ducked down. There was a definite space for a person.

Tessa stared at the spot where the woman should have been, balancing coincidence and connection. Just because something *seemed* connected didn't mean it *was* connected. Tessa was good at finding connections—that's what successful storytelling was all about, how in a novel one thing related to another, and how one thing happened *because* of another thing.

Causation.

But sometimes, in real life, things were coincidence.

She flipped her cell into airplane mode, feeling guilty as the flight attendant, not her pal Maddalyn, tapped her on the shoulder, pointing to the phone. At least she'd ordered the guy in front of her to put his seat back upright.

Simply because she had wrapped the locket in trash can liners didn't mean it was trash. It looked like trash, *maybe*, but it wasn't trash. And if this woman was a fan of Tessa and her book, where else would she be but at the signing? She'd looked like a fan. But maybe she wasn't a fan.

As she felt the jounce of the landing gear hitting the ground, Tessa realized she'd missed the Rockies. She'd slept the entire flight. *Denver,* she thought, yawning to clear her head. The landscape zoomed by as the airplane sped down the runway. The Mile High City, she remembered, and worried about altitude sickness. She lived at sea level, and hoped her body could adjust. All she needed, to disappoint her fans by being woozy. Incredible, she thought, that people spent money to hear her talk about her book. She'd never disappoint them, altitude or not.

Two dings from the cockpit, and Tessa stood, eager to get underway. They'd stashed her suitcase ahead in first class, which was nicely convenient.

She scanned right to left as she walked through the first-class cabin, seeing nothing but empty baggage compartments. As she got to the cockpit door, she frowned, and turned, searching again.

"Um," she began. The flight attendant who had taken her bag wasn't there, but a different one was. Karine. "The other flight attendant put my bag up here? Maddalyn? I'm in 10C, and there wasn't room, so she put it in first class." She kept eyeing the empty overheads, as if her bag would appear. Her bag with all her stuff. "But it's not here."

Many suitcases looked alike, but her name tag was on hers. She thought about that, for a fraction of a second, picturing that it was marked with her entire name, Tessa Calloway. Her email. *And* her phone number. And address. She could have put any name she wanted on her suitcase, since she would recognize it, and other passengers would only think "not mine." But now her tag revealed exactly who it belonged to. And where she now lived. Her name tag was basically a billboard saying, "Here's all you need to know to find Tessa Calloway."

There could be a novel about someone getting the wrong suitcase, Annabelle offered. *Or, taking one. A suitcase can't simply vanish.*

Shush, Tessa thought. *This is real life.*

The flight attendant had opened a curtained closet at the front of the plane.

"Not here either, but I'm sure we'll find it," Karine said. "Can you step into the galley and let the other passengers go out while I look?"

Tessa eyed each passenger, examining the bags they carried, as everyone else exited the plane. She mentally catalogued the contents of her suitcase. Everything was replaceable. She never put anything valuable in there.

Except . . . the locket.

"Come *on*," she muttered. That locket. It meant something to someone, that was for sure. But, increasingly, it appeared to be more than simply a missing keepsake.

Karine had returned, looking perplexed. "Let's go to the gate. I'll bet someone turned it in. Suitcases look so much alike. Someone took the wrong one by mistake."

"True," Tessa said out loud, trying to convince herself that's what happened. And then she stopped, scanning the almost empty plane. That's when she realized why it *wasn't* true.

"But there are no other suitcases left." She gestured, wearily, toward the luggage bins, every white plastic lid flipped open, every space empty. "Someone took mine. And they did it on purpose."

26

The jetway had never seemed longer. Tessa followed behind Karine, matching her hurried footsteps, as they strode down the ramp toward the gate. Deplaning passengers moved aside to let them pass, probably assuming Tessa was getting VIP treatment. When quite the opposite was true.

Don't check a bag, DJ had warned her, *the airlines will certainly lose it. Only take a carry-on.*

She'd obeyed that sound advice, but it wasn't the airlines she was worried about now. It was who else had been on her plane.

The jetway dog-legged to the left and Tessa struggled to catch her breath, wondering if that was the result of fast walking or altitude sickness or fear or all of the above. What was in that bag? Her laptop was with her in her carryall, and her wallet and phone and schedule in her purse. Her suitcase had her jewelry, which would be sad to lose. And her oh-so-replaceable clothes.

Oh. And her engagement ring from Henry. A silly glass "diamond," set in tin and nickel so tarnished it stained her finger to wear it. *All this could be yours,* he'd said, expansively, selecting it, with utmost gravity, from the Halloween costumes at their college bookstore. And offering himself, and his life, to her.

He'd replaced the ring later with a real one, but she could not bear the thought of losing it. It meant nothing, *nothing*, to anyone but her and Henry. No one would keep such a trinket if it weren't massively meaningfully sentimental.

Also inside the suitcase, of course, that millstone of a locket.

And outside, that revealing luggage tag—a beacon that would lead someone right to her address in Rockport. And, it struck her with a heartstopping realization, right to her vulnerable family.

But who? She had absolutely no answers.

You sure? Annabelle asked.

Her suitcase had been on the plane. For the entire journey, it had been out of her sight, closed off in the first-class cabin. Thirty-five thousand feet in the air. No one but first-class passengers were allowed to be there.

The jetway took a final jog and revealed an arc of Denver daylight. Without question, someone in the first-class cabin had taken her suitcase. And the airline company could discover who that was.

Her temper simmering and her fear at the boiling point, she tried to steady herself as she hurried down the jetway. Someone had known she was on the plane. Someone had taken her bag. On purpose. If she had only looked, she might have recognized them. She had been on that inescapable plane for hours with a person who was obviously targeting her. And she had slept through it all, unaware.

Her chest tightened, remembering her engagement ring. Silly and cheap and one of the most valuable things in her life. She'd tucked it, a talisman of joy, into her book-tour suitcase. She'd die if it was gone.

Her mother had tried to teach her to make loss of possessions less devastating. Like the time she'd left her beloved stuffed Teddy in the park. Six-year-old Tessa, wailing, had discovered the disaster hours later, right before bedtime.

"It's not this *particular* bear that was important," her mother had reassured her, back when her mother did things like that. "It's what you made the bear mean. If you get another bear—and you will—tell yourself it's the real Teddy, and soon you won't even think about the other one. I promise."

"But—" Tessa, weak from sobbing, had not believed that. She had not relied on her mother's promises, not even then.

"You can make your mind decide whatever it wants to be true." Her mother had tucked Tessa's hair behind her ear, then, whispering, "You won't even remember the bear that used to be."

Her mother had been right, and her new Teddy had succeeded in its remaining brief shelf life as a childhood necessity.

But her mother had been wrong, too. When bad things happened, whatever circumstance ripped her from peaceful equilibrium and into despair—those things were always remembered. She was simply good at hiding them. "Compartmentalization," her long-ago therapist had man-splained the term to her. He'd assured her it was useful. Valuable. Necessary. The way people got through life. "Storytelling keeps us safe," he'd said. "We can believe in the comfort of our stories."

She arrived at the gate one step behind Karine. Saw the look on Karine's face.

"Look, Ms. Calloway." Karine leaned behind the agent's desk, and rolled out Tessa's suitcase. "Apparently, someone—an embarrassed someone"—Karine glanced at the gate agent, who nodded in confirmation—"inadvertently took it off the plane."

"She was totally mortified, ma'am." The gate agent, a romance novel cover model whose name tag said Lex, came up beside Karine, looking sympathetic. "She said she couldn't face you. She was so ashamed, and left it for us to give back."

"So all's well that ends well," Karine added, double-teaming. "I'm sorry we both had such a fright."

Tessa reached out, grabbed the extended handle, spun her suitcase toward her. She looked for the outline of the padded locket. And it was there, exactly as she had left it. So *was* all well? The ring, and everything?

"Well, first, thank you." Tess turned toward the crowded concourse, teeming with fast-moving travelers, striped with moving metal walkways, a highway of beeping golf carts. "What did she look like? Do you have her name? Could you tell from the flight manifest?"

Karine and Lex exchanged glances; with Tessa watching, they were unable to confer. After a beat of silent decision-making, Lex stepped back behind the desk. "I'm so sorry, ma'am," he said, looking contrite. "It's a privacy thing. We cannot reveal the names of any passengers, you understand that. And frankly, there's no way for us to get in touch with that passenger."

Tessa felt her fear battle with her relief. "But—"

"There are lots of passengers and lots of luggage, and . . ." Lex pointed. "Yours is black, like everyone else's. It's found, ma'am. Is something else wrong?"

Don't let anyone else have your bag, everybody knew that warning. And there were scary reasons for that. But she had put her own bag on the plane. Someone else had taken it off.

"Where's *her* suitcase, then?" Tessa asked. "If she took mine by mistake, where's *hers*? The one she didn't take?"

This time Lex looked happy. "Oh, ma'am, I asked her that. She told me she usually travels with a bag identical to that, but this time she only needed an under-seat bag, she'd only be here in Denver briefly? But in her haste, she grabbed yours. By mistake. Since she was so used to having a suitcase." He stopped, maybe waiting for her reaction. "See?"

Tessa pictured it, the exodus from the plane, the hands reaching up and yanking down identical-looking black suitcases. If she had only been looking, she would have seen who took hers. Someone who was in this airport right now. Someone who had taken her bag, her clearly marked name-tagged bag, on purpose.

"Calloway," Lex said then, pointing to her luggage tag. "Are you the author? With the . . ." He two-finger pantomimed drawing a rectangle over his face, like a book cover. "Book?"

Tessa imagined them regaling all of their airline friends with the story of the day. "Guess who I met," they'd gossip. "That author? Listen, she's absolutely a bitch, even when we *found* her suitcase, which she hadn't even put over her own seat, can you believe it?, she was still annoyed. Celebrities, they're all impossible."

If it hit the socials, there'd be an instantaneous cancellation, with sneery dismissive hashtags like #celebrityprivilege, or #pushyauthors. #TerribleTessa. Social media had fueled her dreams. It could blow them up just as quickly. "I'm so sorry." Tessa placed her hands together at her lips, as if praying for forgiveness. "I'm incredibly appreciative of your efforts, safe travels to you all, and thank you for all you do."

"No problem," Lex said.

"Doing our job," Karine said. "Hope to see you on the return."

The two waved at her as she pivoted, bag in hand, to hurry down the airport concourse. But as she hustled away, dodging the window shoppers and parents corralling rambunctious children and panic-faced backpacked teenagers running for their gate, she had a major decision to make. Should she grab a stall in the nearest bathroom and open the suitcase now? Or should she wait till she got to the hotel? She had to get out of this airport, though. Whoever was targeting her might still be watching.

Her agent had once instructed her that "What does someone want, and why?" was the key question in every novel. When she wrote her books, Tessa knew everyone's motive. But in this particular disturbing circumstance, she had no idea.

Like I said earlier. You sure about that? Annabelle asked.

27

"I'm not convinced about this, Zackie." She couldn't remember the last time she'd talked to her son on the phone, and never at his instigation. But Zack, on his own, had called, just as her cab was arriving at the Denver hotel. She'd watched out the back window all the way into town, looking for she didn't know what, but no one seemed to be following.

When she heard the phone's VIP ping and saw "home" on the caller ID, she'd assumed it was Henry. Then gasped when she heard Zackie's voice, wondering if her reaction was fear of bad news or that her heart was so full of love for him that it was hard to breathe. Now, as she wheeled her suitcase into the lobby, she'd happily listened to him prattle with small talk, but then heard his voice change as he got to the point.

"Overnight." Tessa went on. "At *whose* house?"

Leaving the airport, Tessa had hurried her suitcase along the concourse, looking both ways, every way, scanning for unusual attention, trying not to feel that she was transporting something alien, or contagious. If someone wanted to steal her suitcase, they could've easily walked away with it. But to take it out of the luggage compartment, and then put it back, that was a message. Like—*I know where you are. I know where your stuff is. And I can take it if I want. Or give it back if I want.*

Her imagination had taken over as she headed to the cab stand, playing out what might be inside. What if someone had replaced her possessions with wadded-up newspapers. Or drugs. Or stacks of money. Soon she had to open it.

Plus she'd read that Stephen King book, scary as hell, about the kidnapped writer. Tessa's full name was emblazoned on that suitcase. Even if they—*they?*—had taken it spontaneously, they would have realized she was on the plane. And would discover her loss instantly.

When the cab driver put the suitcase in the trunk, she almost stopped him. Almost.

And then, as she'd buckled herself into the cab's back seat—she was always buckling in, it seemed, in every part of her life—she'd decided she was an idiot. Making a thriller out of an ordinary occurrence. A mix-up with a suitcase at an airport, where everyone had a suitcase? It probably happened every minute of every day.

They'd arrived at the hotel, sleek with shiny windows, onyx trim, polished brass. The suitcase was hers again. In a few minutes she would open it. But she'd deal with Zack first.

"You never let me do anything," Zack was saying now, his dramatic tone just this edge of whine, his words extending into extra syllables. Tessa pictured the pout on his face, lower lip pooching, eyes like a baby seal. "Dad says it's only okay with him if it's okay with you, and it's summer, and they only live two houses away, Dad can practically *see* me there, and I am old enough, I am, nine going on ten, and Tris is so cool, and his mom is so cool, and it's summer!"

Zack had expended his entire stash of ammunition in one breath. And Henry, probably listening, had foisted this on her. *Dad says it's okay with him if it's okay with you.* A classic fun-Dad strategy. Which exiled her to the island of mean mothers.

"I hear you, darling, and I agree with everything you say." Tessa had stopped by a shoulder-high potted rubber plant in the middle of the hotel lobby; calculating how much time she had to register, take a shower, and get dressed. Calculating what would happen when she opened her suitcase. Meanwhile, in the happily mundane world of real life, Zack wanted to stay overnight at a new friend's house. As normal a request as there could possibly be. What new friend? What cool mom?

"And Mommy, I'm missing you," Zack said.

The hubbub of the hotel seemed to evaporate, as if she and Zack were the only two in their particular world. Her little Zack, her little precocious Zack, she had never been away from him for this long. Here in the middle of another strange hotel, her baby boy was saying he loved her. Could she remember the last time he'd said so? At least without being forced to?

She had to go home. "I'm missing you too, my darling baby." She talked faster, remembering Zack's anathema about being the baby. "I know I seem far away, but I am never far from you, my honey, I am as close as—"

"I know, Mom. I'm fine, I really am, I just want to go to Tristan's house, they have a pool too. And a *dog*." Zack, now back into full persuasion mode, had apparently recovered from his embarrassing preteen misstep into emotion. Boys of that age, she knew, were trying to pull away from their moms. Much as the moms try to wrap their arms around them and hold them forever. But Zack had to fly, and this was the moment. This was the moment, and like everything else, she was missing it.

She had five minutes. After that, she was behind schedule.

"Tell me more about Tristan." She pulled her suitcase—Schrödinger's suitcase, empty and full at the same time—a few inches closer, and sat on the arm of a black vinyl sofa at the edge of the hotel lobby. "And about his cool mom." She was trying to keep her voice light and carefree. It was taking some effort.

Henry had never given her cause to worry about cool moms or cool women of any kind, but their lives were different now.

Don't you trust Henry? Annabelle said. That's interesting.

Tessa rolled her eyes, as if Annabelle were right there, sitting in the snazzy hotel with her.

Sometimes Annabelle made her laugh, even reassured her, but not this time.

"Well, listen to this, Mom. You won't believe it. Tristan's mom's real first name is Annabelle. Isn't that crazy? And she knew it was like in your book, but they don't call her that, they call her Nellie."

Another Annabelle. "But she didn't ask *you* to call her 'Nellie,' honey, did she?"

"Mom. No." Zack's voice had devolved into full adolescent sarcasm, scornfully elongating the one-syllable words. "Her last name is Delaney. We call her Mrs. Delaney."

Tessa had a flare of picturing it, this Annabelle aka Nellie Delaney, no doubt the exemplar of Rockport-chic. White pants only after Memorial Day, sun-streaked hair, probably a sailboat. Plus, how many people could possibly be named Annabelle in the United States right now? She actually knew that; she had looked it up when she named Annabelle in the book, and turned out it was the 3,136th most popular name in the US, and there were more than five thousand people named Annabelle. So. One of them could live in Rockport.

And another one in Phoenix, she remembered. Who'd wanted a book signed to "the real Annabelle." So, 4,998 to go.

"Delaney," Tessa repeated. "Has your father met her?"

"Yes, a course, what are you *thinking?* They live two houses down. We all went to their pool yesterday. And *any*way Mom, so then they invited me to—"

"You all went to a pool party? Is there a Mr. Delaney?" Zack would assume this was a reasonable and routine question, and it was. Although she probably didn't need to know the answer this second. Although on the other hand, she did.

"He's like, away," Zack said. "Mom. Gimme a break. How do *I* know?"

"It's a sch—" It's a school night, Tessa had started to say, but it wasn't. And it was summer in Massachusetts, and he was nine, and what could happen on their very own street? Well, she knew what could happen. Precisely what could happen. But Zack wouldn't be alone. Not exactly.

"Okay. It's fine," she acquiesced, her words reluctant and a lie, it wasn't fine, and she stared across the hotel lobby, through the massive plate glass window, onto the busy crowded street. "If your dad really says it's okay."

"You rock, Mom."

She didn't rock. Not at all. She was in Denver, freaked out and sitting on a fake leather sofa talking to her son two thousand miles away who was about to spend his first night away from home in the care of a "cool" woman. A stranger. Called Nellie Delaney.

A stranger who'd told Zack her real name was Annabelle.

28

By the time she had yanked the zipper and flapped open her suitcase, her brain had become so teemingly full of worry about Zack and everything that went with it, including his childhood *totally* ending, that she had forgotten to be terrified.

Now she stared at it, the tissue paper precisely centered over her clothing, the mesh clicked tight to hold it in place. Heart thumping, and hearing the sound of her own breathing, she slowly flapped open the inside webbed pocket, revealing her shoes and two clear plastic zipped bags of cosmetics and toiletries. Her jewelry pouch, bulky and full, was still in its concealed outside compartment. She pawed through it. The ring was there. The locket wrapped in plastic. Everything looked exactly like it had before. Undisturbed.

She stood there, alone, in the pristine and silent box of yet another hotel room. Under the spell of uncertainty.

"Whoa," she said out loud. "Paranoid much?" She plopped down on the bed, on yet another quilted bedspread, and regretted the brain space her worry had occupied. In reality, hard-edged reality, nothing had gone wrong. Her suitcase was fine. Her life was fine.

Zack's life was fine, too. He needed friends. Henry had given his approval. For whatever that was worth, but Henry was the one in charge. *Conquer your fears*, her therapist had told her long ago. Face them, erase them. Experiences are real. But their effects are in your control.

True. But difficult.

Turning on the television for company, she sat at the funky hotel desk with its too-low chair and view of the wall, and swiveled the TV to watch an episode of *Chopped*, eating the turkey sandwich she'd bought at the airport. When she got home—soon soon soon—she could cook again. Who would have thought she'd ever miss that.

Linny's tummy, she remembered. She hadn't even asked Zack about it. But he would have mentioned a disaster, and anyway, Henry was in charge. She had to let go. Her past was not part of her family's present.

Still.

The hotel had scented soap, and fluffy towels, and blissful water pressure, but it was impossible to wash away her fears. She selected a black dress and black jacket, struggling to stay focused. Her troubles had begun with that locket, which still no one had recognized. And her not-so-brilliant idea about #LocketMom, also still a puzzle. But the locket went missing, and was returned. Then the exact same thing with her suitcase.

She was obviously meant to notice. But notice what? And what was she supposed to do?

And the questions about her hometown. And the appearance of Sam. Were those things connected?

You know they might be, Annabelle said. And if they are, you might know why.

Pulling her black velvet jewelry pouch from the zippered suitcase pocket, she eased open the drawstring top. "Go away, Annabelle," she said out loud.

Good luck with that, Annabelle said.

She'd packed inexpensive but photogenic event necklaces, and four sets of periwinkle-blue earrings. Now tangled, as always, because Tessa was always hurrying too much to wrap them properly. Impatient, she held the pouch from the bottom and dumped the entire contents onto the bedspread.

Her precious ring tumbled out. A jumble of periwinkle and gold and fake pearls, dull in the muted light of the hotel room, heaped in a pile on unfamiliar bedding. She picked up the pieces of blue, one by one, matching them as she did. Two dangly rectangles, two thin hoops, two filigreed periwinkle daisies, and the chunky periwinkle squares. Four pairs of periwinkle earrings. When she had moved her four pairs away from the jewelry chaos, there was still blue in the pile.

Another pair of earrings.

She had never seen those blue earrings before. She had not purchased them, had not worn them, had not been given them, had not packed them. Someone had put those earrings in her suitcase.

They sat, like blue kryptonite, on the bed. Periwinkle. In the shape of hearts. There was only one solution. The person who had taken her suitcase had slipped in the earrings, and then returned it. The pouch was a lucky find—they might as easily have stuffed them into her bag. Either way, the inside of the suitcase with her clothes wouldn't have been touched at all.

They hadn't taken her bag. They had *added* to it.

Someone was fast, and someone was deliberate. Someone had targeted her. Someone had found her. Someone was letting her know they had control of her belongings. And her life.

She felt her heart race, faster now. But there was no time to do anything, no one to tell, no one to explain it, no one who would even believe it.

"Nine-one-one, where's your emergency?" she imagined a dispatcher's voice answering her call. "I'm in my hotel room," she'd have to say, "and I found earrings in my suitcase that I didn't put there."

That would be super effective. Super convincing.

All she could do now was put on one of her own pairs of earrings, because her fans expected it, clasp on some pearls, and go. And leave the whole rest of the mess on the bed.

"*Take* it," she said out loud, daring the universe. She snapped up the engagement ring, tucked it into her purse. "Go ahead."

Slipping on her black suede pumps, she grabbed her tote bag, checked her hair, made sure she had her key card and phone. She had forty-five minutes to get to the bookstore. Tessa opened her hotel room door, and gave the pile of jewelry one last withering glare.

"You don't scare me," she said.

But that was not true.

29

Oil-painted portraits of ancestors, green velvet walls, and a flat green velvet pillow on each of the folding chairs; Mile High Books must have been designed to look like an opulent hunting lodge library. Now, at the podium, again, in front of a sold-out audience, again, Tessa would again play her part, and try to lose herself in her starring role as Successful Bestselling Author. If she failed, her entire family's livelihood was at stake.

Nothing like mortgage payments and healthcare premiums to distract you from mysterious earrings. Disappearing lockets. And persistent fans. *No.* Fans were good. End of story.

Was everyone here an authentically friendly face? She scanned the crowd, all women, searching for . . . for what?

You'll know, Annabelle said.

Bookstore manager Kenley Hayes—white turtleneck and jeans, tooled leather boots—recited DJ's carefully worded introduction. Tessa, settling herself and focusing on joy, had no bandwidth now for worry. Toxic earrings be damned.

"Thank you, Kenley. So wonderful to be in Denver," she began, as she stepped to the mic. "But what's the deal with that devil horse at the airport?"

Affectionate laughter rippled through the room, and Tessa felt, for now at least, she was back among her sisterhood.

"So let's start tonight with a photo, okay?" Tessa went on, holding up her cell. "You know I always take a class photo. So I can remember each and every one of you."

Before she could snap the photo, a hand shot up. Tessa pointed to a woman in the back, black jacket, long braided hair.

"Yes?" Seemed like the woman was so eager to ask her question that she wasn't willing to wait until after the photograph. *Okay*, Tessa thought. *Go with the flow.* "You have a question?"

"Have you heard anything about Locket Mom?"

"Yeah," another woman chimed in. "Someone must be missing that necklace."

"It's been like three days," a person in the front row added. "You'd think someone would know her."

Tessa watched a few women pull out their cell phones, apparently checking Tessa's socials. *Locket Mom*, Tessa thought. She'd created a monster. Or someone had.

"Well, no, not yet. And I'm surprised by that, aren't you? I'm still hoping I can return the necklace. But I'll keep trying, and hope you will, too. So let me tell you about myself, and Annabelle, and the book, and then we'll take more questions? What do you think?"

She regretted, yet again, having taken the locket from the drawer. Why had she ever decided she could fix the universe?

Got that right, Annabelle said. *Not even you.*

Another woman had raised her hand.

Tessa pointed again. The woman stood, wavy auburn hair, green T-shirt, clutching her book. She looked hesitant, maybe shy.

"But do you still have it? The locket?"

Tessa blinked at her, trying to separate her raging imagination from reality. This was a perfectly logical question.

"It's in safe hands," Tessa said. A woman in the back of the room stood, holding up her hand. So many people were in front of her, Tessa could only see black-framed glasses and a cascade of blond hair.

"Could I ask—did *you* make a deal with the devil, like Annabelle did? Not the real devil, I know, it's like a metaphor. But did you?"

What was the deal with these questions? For the past three weeks, she'd first given a speech and then done the Q and A, and everyone who attended these events knew that's how it worked. But it felt like a dark cloud had begun to lower, making Tessa suspicious of the motives behind every question.

Question-adjacent, she reminded herself. And stick to the truth when you can. "So funny, people often ask me that, and really, it's all in how you look at it. Is Annabelle's boss 'the devil'? Or is it her secret fear about own-ing her right to succeed that makes her *call* it a Faustian bargain? That's one of the main themes of the book."

"Yes, sure. But I'm asking about you." The woman stayed standing. "Did *you*?"

Some people turned to look at the questioner, others waited for Tessa's reply. Okay, then. One more try. "We all make trade-offs, don't we? Every day? I adore being here with you, even as I know my husband is probably giving the kids pizza again and I'm missing peony season at home."

The woman narrowed her eyes at her, as if deciding whether to pursue it. Luckily—Tessa hoped—another hand went up. A ponytailed woman in a Broncos sweatshirt. This time she looked at Kenley for guidance, or assistance to get the event back on track, but the bookstore owner just shrugged.

Whatever. She was here for her darling audience, and that dark cloud was of her own creation. Probably.

"Yes? From your sweatshirt, I'm thinking you're a Broncos fan. Is this about our New England teams?"

The audience laughed with her, but the woman's expression stayed serious.

"My friend heard you in Phoenix," she replied. "And she said you didn't answer her questions about where you grew up. Why not?"

My friend in Phoenix. And Heather at ReadRunner had told her that pushy customer had mentioned "friends in Denver." And now, here she was. And here was the hometown question again.

I don't like this, Annabelle said. *Move it along.*

"I'd love to tell you about that. And say hi to your friend in Phoenix, by the way. I grew up in a nobody-ever-heard-of-it town, and yes, for my fam-ily's privacy's sake, I don't like to say where. You understand, I'm sure."

Tessa went on, then, ignoring their raised hands, telling her book tour stories about the red chair in the library, and Nancy Drew, and Mary Higgins Clark, then her viral video; and as she got back into familiar speech territory, watching the women, so attentive, so affectionate, and so dear, all the hands lowered and the event clicked back into a familiar place, with Tessa in control again.

"Are any of you moms with dreams?" She began the final portion of her speech. "Whether you follow us on social media with the hashtag, or whether your dreams are your private dreams, kept safely in your own heart, I want you to know that that's why I wrote this book—to assure you that your dreams are valid, and real, and, no matter when you decide to pursue them, they can come true. Thank you, so much, for being here with me tonight."

The audience stood as one, applauding her, and Tessa almost forgot the stress of the day, her fears washed away. She was the luckiest person in the world, and Sadie and DJ had warned her that life wasn't always easy and wonderful.

As if she had to be reminded of that.

"We love you so much, Tessa." Kenley had joined her at the podium. "And Annabelle, too. One last question."

Tessa's heart sank as a flurry of hands went up.

"Nope, one question only," Kenley said. "Don't you want Tessa to sign your books?" She selected a woman in the back. "Yes, how about you? I was going to say, the one wearing periwinkle earrings. But that doesn't narrow it down much, does it?"

The woman stood.

"About the earrings," the woman said. "Do fans sometimes send them to you?"

Tessa stared at her. It sounded like an innocent question. But maybe it wasn't.

30

Salad, a bathrobe, a hotel key card that worked. The things Tessa had come to be grateful for. She saw the jumble of jewelry, untouched, on the bedspread, surprised the earrings hadn't burned a hole in the bedding. There was no other explanation but that someone had put them in her suitcase. On purpose.

But no answer about who. Or why.

The TV still flickered the news, she'd left it on with the volume loud enough to convince burglars the room was occupied. As if that would fool anyone. She put down her plastic-clamshelled salad, dumped her tote bag, and kicked off her shoes. The bookstore had sold out of *All This*, Kenley Hayes had implored her to write faster, and, equally reassuring, that final earring question had been benign. But Phoenix Woman's "friend in Denver" meant someone—someones—were coordinating their questions to her.

But again, who? And why?

You need to find out, Annabelle said. *You need to take control.*

Before she could think too much about it, she flipped open her laptop, clicked on her social, clicked on Go Live. As the computer organized itself, Tessa sat on the bedside, taking the shade off the nightstand lamp to create semi-reasonable lighting. She still had her book event hair and makeup and blazer. She selected the mysterious earrings from the jewelry pile.

Where did they come from? And why? Whenever characters in a novel avoided a question, Tessa would mentally yell at them, sometimes even said it out loud: "Why don't you just *ask* what happened?"

Now, that's exactly what she would do.

And you are live, the screen said.

TESSA LIVE

"Hello, you darling ones, it's nine fifteen in Denver, where I just finished a fantastic event at the wonderful Mile High Books, and I know it's late for some of you on the East Coast, but I am still floating from all your enthusiasm, and I wanted to make sure I thanked you all. And tonight, I have another mystery for you to solve. It's about these earrings."

Would anyone be watching? The comments began instantly. Which was wonderful. Or worrisome. Or both.

We love you.

I was there!

What happened? Tell us!

She paused as the earrings caught the soft light from the nightstand, wondering if this was about to create a problem more than solve one. People had used the hashtag "sales ploy" after she posted about the locket, their snarky and cynical suggestion that she was faking a mystery to get audience participation, and playing off her own book title.

She *had* found the locket. But those earrings—someone had put them there. On purpose.

"I know it seems unlikely, and I'm almost laughing as I tell you, but I found these in my"—should she say suitcase?—"hotel room. No, we still have not found Locket Mom, but I'm not giving up on that. Look at my other posts for more on Locket Mom if you don't already know. But so—these earrings. Are these from you?"

So pretty!

Ha ha pitiful. Told you #sales ploy

I was there tonight! #awesome #annabelle

"Have *you* ever found anything in *your* hotel room?" Tessa went on, seeming to be amused by her own coincidences. "But this time is different. Unlike the locket, I know these were left specifically for me."

She was finessing a bit, but after all, she had "found" them in her hotel. Whoever planted them knew exactly what happened, and that was the only person she was really talking to. She dangled the blue earrings, their tiny hearts swaying.

"So—are these from you? I love our periwinkle earrings, you all, this symbol of Annabelle's confidence and power, the symbol of all of our dreams coming true. Just like you have made mine come true. But my mother always told me—"

Tessa caught her breath. She hadn't meant to mention her mother. But too late to turn back now. She was broadcasting live.

"My mother always taught me to thank people properly for their gifts, and I'll feel her admonishments from heaven if I don't know who to thank."

Awww, love your mother, Tessa!

Mine, too!

Was your mother like you, Tessa?

Ignore that, Annabelle said.

"Of course I love surprises, and this was such a treat. But could you please let me know if you left these for me? I know they're meaningful to you, and I want to understand why. I'm eager to know the story behind them." *Their backstory,* she thought. A backstory someone was weaponizing to torment her. Maybe.

She held them closer to the screen, and the light from the nightstand glinted on their shiny surface. "Just send me a direct message," she said.

Where did you find them?

Have you worn them yet?

Had she worn them. Huh. Tessa did not have pierced ears, and only wore clip-on earrings. Which these were. How would someone know that? Although it was the safer choice.

"I know it's late, and I don't want to keep you up any longer . . . so thank you, Denver, and I'm off to a new city tomorrow, hurray, San Diego! Check my events page for details, and I hope to see you in person. Now all of you, moms with dreams, you get some sleep, and wake up to a wonderful tomorrow. All this could be yours. One life, you all!"

One life!

One life!

One life!

"Good night, dear ones, and let me know about these earrings. I cannot wait to thank you."

Tessa paused, watching the streams of emojis, hearts and flowers and stars. Then clicked her computer off.

She'd poked the bear now, that was certain. Sent a message. And she was unsettlingly aware that her message would be received. Someone, somewhere, had started this.

What terrified her—was how they planned to finish it.

You're Tessa Calloway now, Annabelle reminded her.

31

She was Tessa Calloway now. How many times had she reassured herself with that? She peeled off her blazer, then her dress, and hung them in the hotel's cramped closet, thinking about how being a best-selling author was essentially the same as being a traveling salesman: a happy salesman, sure, and a grateful one, but at the core, still pitching their wares while the family waited at home. Dependent on them, but living their lives without them. At least Linny and Zack had Henry, and they seemed happy and thriving, and Tessa would be home in three weeks, and normal would return.

Tessa's own father, absent most of her life, had created a blank space, and she'd filled that gap with her imagination. But she didn't want to think about him, or her mother, it didn't matter and it was long gone and her parents were long gone and everything was long gone and tonight she was so tired. Her family *now*, that's all that mattered.

A plush white bathrobe was looped over the hook of the bathroom door, and Tessa wrapped it, comfortingly, around her. And put on the white waffled slippers she'd carried with her from her first hotel.

Food first? Or Henry first? "Henry," she said out loud. She needed to tell him about the purloined suitcase. And the earrings.

And then her cell phone rang. *ESP*, she thought, Henry on FaceTime. Nine thirty in Denver, eleven thirty in Rockport. Her heart lifted with their mind-meld connection.

But it wasn't Henry's face that appeared.

"Linny?" A billion hideous possibilities chased each other through her imagination. "Honey? Are you okay? Is Daddy okay? Did he let you use his phone?" She squinted at the video of her daughter, incredibly, frustratingly too small, and the lighting impenetrable. Linny, her wisps of blond hair in a ponytail on top of her head and her bangs too long, even with the bad lighting Tessa could see that. Did she look thinner? Did she look sick? What on earth was she wearing? Did she have on *lipstick*? It was hard to tell.

"Hi, Mom."

Tessa almost burst into tears at Linny's thready voice. Yes, she was eleven, but she was her baby girl, and would never not be.

"Hi, sweetheart." Tessa held the phone up, saw her own worried face in the square at the bottom of the screen. "Where are you, honey? I can barely see you. Are you okay? Daddy said you had a tummy ache."

"I did, Mom. I don't know what happened, I didn't eat anything weird, I promise, I know what I'm not supposed to eat. I'm fine now, though, I promise."

"Do you need something? Are you all right?" Like Zack, Linny had never individually called Tessa on the road before. The kids hadn't needed cell phones in the past, but now they would, and both had been constantly lobbying for them. Tessa wasn't sure how she felt about it. On one hand, she could have so much more constant access, and they would be able to call for help. They would never be alone. On the other hand . . . it made them so vulnerable. So connected to bad things.

"I'm in the closet," Linny said.

"In the closet?" Tessa's brain raced. "What closet? Why?" Tessa realized she barely knew where the closets were in that house where she didn't live.

"It's like a pantry thing. By the kitchen. The yellow door. Anyway, Mom, I know Dad is going to call you soon, and he's . . ."

"He's what?" She'd heard the concern in her daughter's voice. Tessa held up the phone with one hand, pushed the pile of jewelry to one side, sat on the edge of the bed. "Is something wrong with your dad?"

"No, he's outside for a minute, so I—"

"Outside doing what?" Tessa tried to picture it, 11:32 at night in Rockport, and her husband outside? "Is everything okay? With Zack? Is he home? Linny, honey, you're worrying me a bit, okay? Wanna tell me what's going on?"

"I wanted to know if I could wear your periwinkle sweater. With the pockets?"

Tessa blinked, pictured the brand-new slouchy cashmere cardigan. Her one post–book sale splurge. "My periwinkle—"

"Yeah. Dad was hanging up your clothes, and I was helping, and it was there, and it's so pretty, and you're not here, and I don't have anything to wear."

"Of course, honey, but not anything to wear . . . to what?"

"Awesome, awesome, awesome. But don't tell Dad I asked you, okay? I don't want him to be mad. He told me to go ahead and wear it, but I wanted to ask you. It seemed righter. So he can't know I asked you. He'd be mad."

"It'll be our secret, baby girl," Tessa said, "and I know you hate when I call you that, but there you have it. And no one is going to be angry with you." *Not* ever, she thought, and wanted to tell Linny, *I love you so much I could faint.* But she didn't. "And I hereby present you with the sweater. It's yours now. I'll tell your father."

"You're the best, Mom, I'll let you borrow it whenever you want."

"Awesome," Tessa, smiling, tried out the word. Still holding the phone, she took the few steps to reach her glass of wine, and peeled the plastic wrap from the top. "Anyway, I was just about to call your dad," she went on. "Even though—isn't it pretty late for you?"

"It's *summer.* And you said you wouldn't be mad."

"Okay, sweetheart. I'm never going to be mad at you."

"So, um, I'm coming out of the pantry now. And I see . . . Dad is still outside. Should I go get him?"

"What's he doing?" Tessa took another sip.

"Oh my *God,* Mom, how do I—"

"Linny." Her pet peeve, one of them, the *Oh my God* thing. It sounded so coarse.

"OMG? Is *that* any different?" Linny's voice had the teenage back in it.

"Truce," Tessa said. "Go on."

"He's—we're—like, meeting the neighbors. They're coming over, and bringing us stuff—muffins, and mac and cheese, and it's delicious. I can't eat it much, because you know, carbs, but Dad really likes it. Because he doesn't have to cook. Hardly at all."

"You can eat carbs, Linny. Everything in moderation. Except bananas."

"Mom. I know. I'm not a child."

So wrong. "But go on about the neighbors. So your father is outside talking to the neighbors?"

"And some of them are so cool, there's like—"

"Like Nellie Delaney?" Tessa couldn't resist. She could see Linny was in the kitchen now, which seemed to be yellow. Hadn't it been white before? "Isn't Zack at their house this evening?" Tessa frowned. "And if Zack is at her house, what is she doing at *our* house?"

"Mom. Mom. Let me talk." Even the minuscule picture could not hide the eye roll. "Mrs. Delaney, yeah, she's super cool, although her son is kind of nerdy so of *course* he hangs out with Zack—"

"Linny."

"*Okay.* Anyway, though no, it's not Mrs. Delaney. There's a dog walker, like on the other side of the street? Remember the big white house, it has red flowers in the front, and a big lawn?"

"A dog walker? She walks people's dogs?"

"She *has* dogs, I don't know, she walks them. Her name is Barbara, and so funny, she looks like Barbie, isn't that so weird? But she totally does look like Barbie. And Dad is out talking to her."

"Barbie. I see. Isn't it pretty late? I mean, I know it's summer, but . . ."

"I guess," Linny said. "I better get off the phone. And if Dad sees that someone used it to call you, can we say I missed you, and I wanted to call? Not about the sweater. It would be so much better if I had my own phone, Mom, it *would*, I'm old enough now. And all my friends back at home, I mean in our other house—they're gonna totally forget me."

"Honey, they're not going to forget you. We'll talk about it when I get home, sweetheart. I promise. And *do* you miss me?" Tessa pictured Barbie on their front porch as she considered it.

"Mom. You've only been gone for like three weeks, and we're totally fine. And listen, so cool, you'll love this, there's a bookstore in town, and we went, I did, at least, and I saw your books, they had a whole stack of them. And when Dad came in to get me, he told everyone who you were. And that we live here now."

"He did?" Tessa paused, picturing that.

"Yeah. He said we live in the peony house on Algonquin Street. And that you're away on book tour."

32

So Henry had told the people in the bookstore where they lived. "In the peony house." They'd find out eventually, Tessa figured, but it should have been up to her to make the decision to relinquish her privacy. Their privacy. Or at least they could have discussed it, decided it together. As Linny prattled, Tessa imagined Henry, lording it around the place, using her for bragging rights, which, okay, was a mean thing to imagine, and unfair.

But she'd *told* him about her new fears about her increasingly inquisitive readers, and what she'd learned about bodyguards and overzealous fans and loss of privacy. The warnings from Sadie about "bitter people" and DJ's vigilant monitoring of her socials. In any world, though, you don't tell strangers where you live. And Tessa wasn't even home now. For better or worse.

"Will you have your father call me when he gets back, after he finishes with . . . the dog walker?" Tessa tried to keep the frustration out of her voice. "Tell him, let's FaceTime. And it's fine to say that you and I chatted. We'll just leave out the sweater part," Tessa went on, wincing as she lured her own daughter into deception.

"You're a good kid," Tessa went on, "taking care of your dad. That's called emotional intelligence."

"I'm not a kid, Mom."

"You're *my* kid. No matter how grown up you are."

Tessa watched her daughter, reality from two thousand miles away, watched her face change.

"I—I really do miss you, Mom," Linny finally said. "I miss your stories. It's super weird here without you."

Tessa was dying. She was. How did anyone ever do this? Bestseller or not? But she couldn't let Linny know she was homesick. Linny had to believe Tessa was happy, that she loved her, and being her mom, but that a career was a good thing. And that women could balance a career and a family, and everyone would be the better for it.

Tessa knew she herself did not *quite* believe that. It was Tessa's own deal with the devil, this was, trading her family for fame. But when did the contract come due? She knew the stories. Knew the myths about the devastatingly irresistible bargain. It always came due when you least expected it. Just when you thought you were safe. And it was irrevocable.

If you believe the stories, Annabelle said. Which I do not.

"It's super weird here, too," Tessa said. "But you have your new house, and a room of your very own. Are you getting it set up the way you want? How do you like it? How do the stuffies like it? Are your books on the shelves?"

"Mom, I have to go. Dad's coming back inside. Thank you about the sweater. You rock. It's awesome. Bye-eee."

Her daughter's face disappeared, and Tessa was holding only a black rectangle.

Tessa stared at the blank screen, imagining what she was not seeing; Linny, and the inside of the home where she'd never lived, and her husband and a dog walker who looked like Barbie. Tomorrow at this time she'll be in San Diego, seeing the ocean on the exact opposite coast of the United States from where she was supposed to be.

A sound.

Was someone knocking at her door? She flinched, willing the sound away. At *her* door? She was finished with surprises. Putting down the wine, wrapping her white robe closer around her, then tying the belt protectively tight, Tessa padded to the door and peered through the peephole.

On the other side, an owl-faced young woman, a hotel employee, it appeared, head to toe in a hotel uniform, khaki pants, khaki shirt, hotel name tag that said—Tessa could not read it.

She left the chain on as she opened the door and peered through the two-inch space. "Yes?"

"We have a package for you, ma'am."

Come on, Tessa thought. *You have* got *to be freaking kidding me.* She glanced at her suitcase, where the outline of the locket was still evident. And at the bed, where the blue earrings waited. A package?

Tessa saw it, then, the woman held a book-sized parcel wrapped in gold foil. With a red bow on top.

"It's chocolates," the woman said, offering it. "Seems like."

"How nice," Tessa lied. "Who are they from?"

"I don't know, ma'am," the woman said. "I guess someone dropped them off."

Tessa could now see her name tag.

"Sorry to keep asking questions, Yunis," Tessa said, "but do you know who dropped them off? I'm trying to figure out who knows I'm here."

Waverly Publishing, for one, Tessa thought, answering her own question. DJ, Olivette, anyone with access to the master schedule. Her agent. The bookstore. Her husband. Anyone who looked at their refrigerator door. Waverly's travel agent. The entire travel agency, if they bothered to check the records. Or, someone who had followed her from the bookstore.

You are the only person who could make chocolates a problem, Annabelle said. You have got *to chill.*

"I don't know, ma'am. The desk told me to bring them."

Tessa opened the hotel room door. The chain clanked as it fell against the metal. She took the gold box. The chocolate fragrance was unmistakable. "Thank you," she said. "I wish I knew who sent them."

"There's a card on them, see?"

"Oh, right. I guess—"

"Whatever, ma'am," the woman said.

As Tessa closed the door, she wondered what Yunis would tell her colleagues about the goofy lady in 1032 who was freaked out over expensive candy.

Indeed, under the red ribbon, a flat white envelope. She ripped it open.

In navy fountain pen, in elaborate cursive, someone had written *Sorry about the luggage mix-up, hope you fly with us again.* It was signed, too. *Your flight attendants.*

"Oh. Well. That was sweet," she said out loud. "Ha ha." And for an instant, she was embarrassed at her unwarranted fear. Then it vanished.

How did those flight attendants know where she was staying?

She felt her heart drop, but turned the card over. *We called the bookstore to find your hotel*, it said in navy-blue ink, as if anticipating her question. *Safe travels.*

Tessa could not think about it, could not worry about this one more minute. It was easy enough for Karine and Maddalyn to know she had an event, and where. Easy enough to call the bookstore, then the candy shop. It was, possibly, how the generous and thoughtful world worked if you were not neurotic and paranoid and tired. And hungry. And having to get up at six the next morning to catch another flight.

She slid the chain back into place, hearing the drone of the television voices. She was good, she was safe, and she had chocolate. "Time for dinner," she said out loud. "Time to stop worrying."

The aroma of balsamic vinaigrette hit her as she opened the lid of her salad, and she plucked out a golden-brown crouton and popped it into her mouth. This was all about low blood sugar, it *was*, and making something out of nothing. Except for the earrings. And the suitcase. And the chocolates? She'd feel better when she had food. And when she had an explanation.

Her phone pinged. A message from Henry. Facetime?

33

"Did you paint the kitchen?" Tessa surprised herself with that first question, it wasn't what she'd planned, but Henry had set up the laptop in a place with the refrigerator behind him, so she knew it was the kitchen. And it was yellow. Completely, saturatedly, sunshine buttercup daffodil you-name-it yellow. So very yellow.

"Yes. It's sick, as Zack insists on saying." Henry swiveled the laptop screen, swishing by a bank of white cabinets, past the sink and a back door that led to . . . Where again? And then past the refrigerator, and then another group of white cabinets, now ringed in creamy, American-cheese yellow.

"Is the paint color called Velveeta?"

The video screen snapped back to Henry's face. "What's that supposed to mean?"

"Well, it's just, yellow. Superly yellow. I didn't know you were painting the kitchen. I've only been gone three weeks or whatever, and that nice white kitchen, I think I remember it was white, now it looks like somebody dumped egg yolks on the walls. Where'd you even get the idea for yellow?"

"Don't you know that yellow is the new taupe? Hey, Tesser. Have you had dinner? Do you have low blood sugar?"

Henry looked sympathetic, and he was right about the low blood sugar, but that wasn't what she cared about now. He was painting the house without her. Her house. Her kitchen. *Their* kitchen. He was making the house his instead of theirs. *Yellow is the new taupe?* What kind of a ridiculous . . .

"This is not about my blood sugar. This is about . . . about . . ." Tessa stopped herself mid rant. Took a deep breath. She adjusted the screen on her own laptop, showing the headboard behind her, the bad hotel art of buffaloes on the plains, and pulled her bathrobe high around her neck. "It seems like a lot is going on at home, and I don't feel part of it."

"You'll be home soon, babe," Henry said. "I'm only trying to make it nice for you. So did you sell a lot of books tonight?"

"We did, yeah." Tessa tried to convince herself to feel normal, what-ever normal was. "But . . ." She remembered that woman, the "friend in Denver." "People are weird, that's all I can say. Sometimes they ask oddly personal questions. Where's my hometown. And have *I* made a Faustian bargain. Who even says that?"

"They're showing how much they love you." Henry put both hands over his face, rubbing it the way he did when he was trying to think. "And the deal with the devil is in your book, sweetheart. Everybody thinks the main characters of books are the authors. Don't you? Like when you read that book about the podcaster, you told me you pictured the author. And wondered if that happened to her. Remember?"

"I suppose so." Tessa heard the edge in her voice. Henry was trying to help, but it wasn't working. She should tell him about the suitcase mix-up, and the earrings but didn't have the energy for it. The more she was away, the more things became wearying to share, things that probably didn't matter in the long run, it all took too long.

She saw her own face in the screen, noticed her lanky hair and weary eyes. *She* did not look like Barbie, not at all.

"Let's change the subject," she said, brightening her voice. "I'm miss-ing you all. How was your day?"

Henry turned to his right, lifted his chin as if he were looking for someone. Or listening. "Well, Zack is on his big overnight, and so far no frantic calls to retrieve him. This Tristan kid seems reasonably sane for a nine-year-old boy. Tris's mother is there, too. Linny is up and around somewhere, I'll go get her. But remember it's summer, and it's not that late. Don't be mad, sweetheart."

"I get mad?" Tessa didn't think of herself as a person who got mad, she thought of herself as a person who understood things. Talked them through. "But isn't it almost midnight there?"

Henry's face had disappeared from the screen, leaving only a view of the refrigerator. And his stubby glass with ice and some clear liquid. Tessa turned her screen to look at the rest of the room, and laughed—but the unsettling reality was that it wasn't *her* screen that mattered. Her screen was only showing her the background Henry had set up for her to see.

On the other side of the camera, anything could be going on, totally invisible to her. Henry had absolute control over her perspective on his life. Without having talked to Linny, Tessa would not know anything about the dog walker lady, or the bookstore, or Barbie. Or that Henry had been outside, after dark, "talking" to someone. All Henry had to do was decide not to tell her something, like why the kitchen was yellow, or not to show her something, and she would never know.

Although she was the one who had told her daughter not to say anything.

"Hi, Mom." Linny had changed her hair since their last conversation, now two ponytails danced over her ears, and she wore her precious vintage *I Missed Taylor Swift* T-shirt. Henry was on-screen next to her, their two heads close together, Henry with his arm around his daughter. Their daughter.

"Hey, sweetie." Tessa squinted at the screen. "What's that on your T-shirt?"

Linny looked down, and used two fingers to pull the front of her T-shirt into her line of vision. She sighed, and Tessa saw her shoulders drop.

"Paint," she said. "The gross yellow paint from the kitchen. I *hate* this. How did it get on my T-shirt?" Her voice had tightened into that Linny voice, the voice of confusion and disappointment that often led to tears. "We all had to paint the kitchen. It was gross. And now my T-shirt is totally ruined."

"Just you and Dad? And Zack? Painted the whole kitchen? Today?" Tessa tried to calculate how that could happen. The taping and primer and prep. Someone had to choose the paint. Buy the paint and brushes and rollers. Tape the trim. Prime the walls. Before rolling on the "new taupe." Henry and the kids had done all that?

"How do I get the yellow stuff out of my T-shirt?"

"We'll get you a new T-shirt." Henry ruffled Linny's hair, and the little girl pulled away.

"Dad. You know nothing. These are like impossible to get. This is the only one. I'll never have another one and you ruined it." A tear rolled down Linny's face, and she swiped it away. "You ruined it! You made me paint. You and, and, everybody."

Tessa almost started crying herself, not only because she wasn't there to understand and comfort her daughter, but because she knew that feeling, that teenage feeling of doom and pressure and loss. Of the supreme importance of whatever it was at the time, the panic to hold on to it.

"Sweetie, depending on what type of paint it is"—Tessa risked a glare at her husband—"I can get that out for you. Put that special T-shirt aside, and we will make it as good as new as soon as I get home. I promise. Don't fuss with it, okay? Don't put water on it or wash it or anything like that. Leave it. Put it in your mind's worry pile." She wanted to make Linny feel secure; she had taught her daughter to stash things in the "worry pile" for later, and, as a result, she would learn that when she did that, the worries would disappear. "And hey"—Tessa hoped she was not stepping over a parental line—"how about I give you my new periwinkle sweater? The one you love so much? Keep it for yours."

"Awesome, awesome, awesome." Linny's face changed, briefly, the sun coming out. "Thank—"

"Just tell your father not to let you paint wearing it."

"Huh? Sure. Good night, Mom." Linny was still examining her T-shirt, pulling it away from her thin body, frowning. "I'm suddenly really tired."

"I bet you are, darling," Tessa said. "It's way too late to be awake. Even in the summer."

Linny's face left the screen, and left Tessa's world entirely.

Henry appeared. Frowning. "What is wrong with you, Tessa? It's like you're picking a fight."

"I'm not picking a fight. I'm not picking anything." She lifted her wine-glass, surprised that it was empty. "I—it's hard. I'm happy, yada yada, but I miss home and I miss you and I miss the kids and I miss everything that's going on because I'm out here doing this."

Henry sighed, she watched his broad chest move up and down, saw him run his fingers through his hair.

"Come home then," he said. "Come home."

34

"And if I come home," Tessa said—she heard the tone in her voice, it didn't even sound like her, she felt like someone else, but then wasn't she someone else? She was, had been for the past several weeks, and, actually, longer, and would continue to be, someone totally else. "If I come home, then I can meet Barbie, can't I?"

"Barbie?" Henry took a sip from his stubby glass.

"Yes, the beautiful Barbie, who lives across the street, and has irresistible dogs, and apparently"—she took a chance with this one—"talks to married men late at night when their wives are out of town."

"Yeah." Henry drew the word out.

Tessa swiveled in her desk chair, saw the light from the television news make patterns across her face. She should say goodnight, eat her salad, go to sleep. Things would be better in the morning.

"Something's going on, Tessa. What are you not telling me?"

"What am I not telling you? I? Not telling *you*? That's pretty funny."

Stop, Annabelle said. Stop, stop, stop.

"There's nothing that's funny," Henry said. "You made a decision, you and I made a decision. You got your dream. You got what you wanted. You wrote a terrific book, sweetheart, and this is the price of that. I know you're tired, I know you're exhausted, I know you're overworked. But don't take it out on me. I'm holding down the fort while you're gone."

"Holding it down? Holding it *down*? By letting Zack spend the night with a complete *stranger*? By leaving Linny in the bookstore alone? By telling the bookstore people, when you *finally* got there, where we lived? That's holding it down?" Tessa wished the internet would go out or some divine intervention would stop her from escalating this. It wasn't simply the schedule, it was everything about that mysterious locket, and the earrings, and Sam on the airplane, and the nasty woman about the hometown, and the contentious probing questions about her deal with the devil.

And it wasn't coincidence. Something was going on. Here, and at home, too.

So she had to go home. She simply had to go home.

"You're right," she finally answered. "I'll come home. I will."

"Terrific," Henry said. "Tell me your flight, and I'll pick you up at the airport. We'll have margaritas. We'll celebrate."

"I'd have to call DJ. Tell the publisher. And Sadie Bailey."

"Yep," Henry said.

"And tomorrow I'm supposed to be in San Diego. At a big influential bookstore. If I canceled now, it would be terrible. Incredibly rude. Two hundred people have signed up for it."

"Yeah, that would not be good for your career. But," Henry went on, "maybe being on the road is not good for your life. Our life."

"What if I was sick or something? Then I could cancel."

"Yep."

Tessa paused, imagined emailing her editor. Her publicist. Her agent. She'd have to call them, she couldn't do a thing like this by email.

"Maybe I should at least go to San Diego," she said. "One more event."

"Your call." Henry lifted a palm, giving her permission.

Permission? His assumption of the power role, as if he were in charge, made her angry all over again. "But why did you tell the bookstore where we lived? It's so—"

"How did you know what I did in the bookstore?"

"Linny told me." Was she ratting out her own daughter? No. Henry had relinquished their privacy in front of everyone. It was already public.

"She did, huh? When?"

"We FaceTimed. When you were out talking to dog walker Barbie."

"Her name is Barbara. She is not a dog walker. She has dogs. She just moved in, renting, I think. And she's, well, nosy."

"Nosy?"

"Who knows, I guess she's a fan. But this is not about nosy Barbara and her dogs, honey. I don't like the way you sound. I think you should come home."

Out of the corner of her eye she saw a commercial on TV showing faces of starving dogs, sad-eyed and pitiful, asking for money. With that song about angels. Even though it was muted, it would be in her head all night.

"Seriously. You should." Henry had put on his own puppy face, Tessa realized, and it was equally persuasive. Or heavy-handed. "You can meet Barbara. I bet she'll go away, once the wifey is home. To protect her sexy, irresistible husband from the predatory seductive dog walker."

"Shut up, Henry. Goofball."

They sat, each silent, for a moment, staring across thousands of miles and into each other's heads, looking into each other's eyes, but not really, only the pixelated reproduction of each other, with no real connection, only light and sound waves being carried by satellites, up thousands of miles and down thousands of miles, with human emotions diminishing in the process.

"I have to keep doing this, don't I," Tessa said.

"Your call. We'll work out something."

"If I come home, that's the end of my career. And the house."

"We'll manage."

"My reputation will be ruined. And I do love writing."

"And it certainly loves you," Henry said. "But if you're—exhausted? Come home. Write your books and be a recluse and that'll work for you. I'll love you no matter what."

"That won't pay the mortgage," she said.

"We'll figure something out." Henry toasted her with whatever was in his glass.

She kept hearing noises, but maybe it was Linny. Or the television. *Figure something out*, Henry had said. For how many years had she heard that? She'd adored him, from moment one, his relentless optimism and positivity—but sometimes Tessa needed him to face reality. The time he'd had the "best job ever" that allowed her to quit her own hellish one had been all too short. On the other hand, now he could be at home. When she couldn't.

"I guess I . . . I guess I do have low blood sugar," she admitted, eyeing the box of chocolates. Eyeing the locket in her suitcase. Those earrings.

"Come home, come home, come home," Henry chanted.

"Are you trying reverse psychology on me?"

Good luck with that question, Annabelle said.

"I guess I can't win, can I." Henry blew out a breath, flickered his attention away from the screen for a beat, then faced her, as if defeated. "I'm trying to make you happy."

She looked at him, tried to see him through the screen, *more* than see him, but it was impossible. There was utterly no way to know his motives. Or if he had motives. "I can't come home. I can't. I'm sorry I freaked out. I'm tired."

"Look. Do what you think is best. We have a terrific new home and sometimes-adorable kids waiting for you, and you have a kick-ass career on the road. Family and love and fame and money. All this could be yours, right?"

"Ha ha," she said.

Later, after they'd said *always always*, and now tucked under the hotel-issue comforter, she held her cell phone in front of her face, the only light glowing in the darkened unfamiliar hotel room. After considering whether she should encase the disconcerting earrings in toilet paper and stuff them in the wastebasket, Tessa had wrapped them in a tissue and stuck them into a corner of her tote bag. Out of sight, but not out of mind.

She should sleep. It was crazy, she had to get up so early, but she opened her socials. Mile High Books had posted photos of the event, and Tessa scanned for the woman who'd asked about the deal with the devil. But she wasn't there. Tessa two-finger zoomed to bring the photo closer. Maybe. Maybe she was there.

A string of comments dropped down below, tantalizing. She was tempted to read them, respond to them all, put hearts by the nicest ones. "Go to sleep," she instructed herself out loud. "Go to sleep."

But she couldn't resist. Her entire existence, her family's complete livelihood, depended on what people thought of her.

This was her life. She opened her laptop. And began to scroll.

35

The light from her laptop, white and glowing, revealed the pronounce-ments of strangers, the select group of people who had shared tonight's event with her, but were now sharing their reactions to the whole online world. As long as they were positive, Tessa's career would continue.

It's fab when an author lives up to your expectations. Tessa= incredible

LOVE her. See me? Blue shirt and blue earrings? #Annabelle

Kenley Hayes had posted Tessa standing in the aisle between the two sections of seats. Two hundred people, all smiling, all holding her book, and Tessa herself cradling one in her arms. It seemed the picture of success, but someone out there was a potential villain in the story. She looked, again, for the auburn-haired woman. But the person who'd questioned her so intently was definitely not in the shot.

Don't you need to sleep? Annabelle asked.
Tessa continued to scroll.

It's weird, IMO, she never talks about her childhood.

Someone tonite even asked, she totally dodged.

She's trying to keep things pri, OK? Everyone deserves privacy.

She's famous. We get to know about her. #thedeal

#wrong

Did she find out who was in that photo thing? #LocketMom

I think it's in Maine. Looks like Maine to me.

Maine, Tessa thought. She pursed her lips, remembering Maine. Picturing it. Maine in the daylight, Maine at night, unfamiliar and rural,
the pine trees higher than she'd ever seen, the nighttime sounds. She'd
learned to recognize crickets and cicadas and katydids, different than at
home. Lightning bugs, magical and impossible, carrying their personal
luminescence. Even the blackflies, so viciously predatory, seemed born
of a fairy-tale forest. The sky seemed farther away there, and the earth
denser. Emily still inhabited every mental image she created of those days.
The two of them whispering, sharing, laughing, promising. Crying, once.
Long ago, and not ever forgotten.

Did the photo look like Maine? Impossible to tell from that shot. Unless
there was some unique native foliage, trees or flowers, or a lighthouse in
the distance, something she had failed to recognize.

Part of her wanted to check the locket right now. *Was it Maine?* Was
there something she'd missed? But she was so tired, and the locket would
be in her suitcase tomorrow, and she'd look then.

Her yawn encompassed her entire body, and the screen blurred in
front of her. She flapped it down, and too tired even to get up, she put the
laptop beside her on the king-sized bed. Sleeping with her laptop. That had
to be some kind of metaphor.

She stopped herself from wondering what—or who—*Henry* was sleeping with. Sometimes her own zero-to-sixty imagination led her down unnecessarily distressing paths. Barbie. Nellie. The nosy neighbor and the
beautiful mom with an out-of-town husband. She could write about that
stuff, but that was not her life. Her book was not her life, no matter what
her readers conjectured.

She'd apologize to Henry tomorrow. Having a pessimistic imagination doesn't mean something isn't wrong. But no way to know tonight.

Her alarm was set, but she set another one for fifteen minutes after that. She could not miss a plane. She could not be late. *Everyone gets one hundred percent*, that's what she'd told a newspaper interviewer recently. And she'd meant it. Some days, though, it felt like her one hundred percent was not what it used to be.

The sound vibrated against the shiny wood of her nightstand, insistent, and though she tried to ignore it, the message buzzed again. She opened her eyes, barely, saw the glowing green numbers on the nightstand clock. Fifteen minutes after midnight. Two fifteen in Rockport and New York. Way too late for news that was anything but bad.

Scrabbling for the phone, trying to make her eyes focus, swimming out of her half sleep, she squinted at the screen.

> Is it too late?

A 303 area code. Denver. Someone who'd messaged her before. She zip-scrolled up. Kenley Hayes. From the bookstore. Tessa typed back.

> All good, I'm up.

It was easy to lie on a text. No one could see your expression.

> You okay?

> What? Sure yes. Why?

Three dots meant Kenley was typing. Stay awake, Tessa ordered herself. Why would Kenley be asking if she was okay?

> I feel horrible. I know it's too late to text. But forgot to tell you I had customers. Wanting to send you gift.

The dots paused, and Tessa, propped on unfamiliar pillows, typed back quickly.

> Yes, candy. I got it. They told me you told them where I was staying.

Tessa typed again, yearning for sleep.

> Okay?

> No! I didn't. Tell them.

> Call me?

Tessa's phone buzzed almost instantly.

"I'm so sorry." Kenley's voice was a whisper. "I *didn't* tell them. And you say they said I did?"

"They said—well, it was on a card that came with the chocolates. From Hammond's?"

"Yes, Hammond's, delicious, very Denver. But . . . I'm concerned. Someone said *I* told your hotel? No. I didn't. I would never."

"I know." Tessa closed her eyes, opened them again. "I'm sure it's fine, Kenley, and you're so kind to call. But the customers—did you recognize them from the event?"

Tessa heard footsteps in the hallway, then laughter, then silence. How many people were in this hotel? Hundreds, maybe thousands. She was alone, in this anonymous room, where only a select handful of people knew where she was. But also someone who was *not* in that handful. Someone who was not supposed to know.

"Recognize? I don't think so. A man and a woman. They looked like . . ." She paused, and Tessa could almost hear her thinking. "People who would go into a bookstore. In fact, that was their deal. They said they'd have to miss the signing, but were massive fans, and wanted you to know they were 'thinking of you.' So no. They weren't at the event."

"Handsome guy?" Tessa pictured Sam in 3A. A man and a woman. His daughter, Anna, like Savannah? Not two female flight attendants. "Kinda cowboy?"

"That's like fifty percent of the male population in Denver, Tessa."

The phone went silent, white noise from Kenley's end. Tessa pictured her in some Denver-looking house, broad windows, stark mountains in the background, the ghostly moon high above, Kenley wrapped in an earth-toned quilt, surrounded by stacks of books. Again, making reality into fiction. But those two people in the bookstore were not fiction.

"Want me to call the police?" Kenley asked.

"And tell them what?"

"Yeah, I hear you."

"You have security video?"

"Nope."

"And on *this* end, what am *I* supposed to do? Call 911? And when they say what's your emergency, I would have to say 'someone sent me chocolates'?"

At that, Kenley burst out laughing, and then Tessa did, too, and Tessa could tell both of them were trying to stop but could not.

"Whew," Tessa finally managed to say, wiping her eyes with the edge of a pillowcase. "I'm tired, and I guess you are, too. Seems like we're both used to fans."

"True. But fan comes from the word 'fanatic,' doesn't it?"

"Does it?"

"Let's hope it comes from 'fantastic,'" Kenley said. "Or 'fantasy.' Look, it's late. I'm sure you're right, but . . ."

"Who knows." Tessa couldn't ignore the troubling reality. Had they followed her from the bookstore to the hotel? *They.*

"Yeah." Another silence.

"People are funny," Tessa lied. "But we won't solve it tonight, and I'm grateful you called." She remembered her author etiquette; what DJ would want her to say. "I had a terrific time, and hope you'll invite me back."

"Well, of course, rock star. We sold more of your books than any other so far this year. So yeah, Ms. Bestseller, come anytime you want. Bring Annabelle, too, ha ha. Keep in touch, okay? And sweet dreams." Kenley laughed again. "Oh, I'm sorry. Reflex. That's what I say to my kids."

Tessa added "kids" to her mental picture of Kenley. And as she said goodnight to the bookseller, she thought of her own two children, and hoped they would have sweet dreams as well. She herself—would not.

Because whoever sent the chocolates would know what they claimed in their note could easily be proven untrue.

Which meant whoever sent it wanted Tessa to realize that. Wanted Tessa to know they could find her. Get to her. No matter where she was.

36

Tessa sat bolt upright, sleep-baffled and supremely confused. The sound, the sound, *the sound,* and the flashing red light strobing on the white ceiling above her. Heart pounding, she leaped from her bed, smelled for smoke, tried to decide what to do.

Her bleary brain tried to clear itself, to reset, to comprehend it was not a dream. This was *certainly* a false alarm, but what if it wasn't? Someone pounded on her door—*"fire alarm!"*—and a voice blared over the public address system, disconcertingly robotic.

"This is the fire alarm," the voice was saying. "Message 173. All guests and staff must exit the building. Immediately. Please follow the signs on your door and in the hall. Message 173."

"What do I take?" She said the words out loud. Her laptop. Her schedule. Her handbag, yes yes yes, and her phone. Her jewelry pouch with the engagement ring. She stashed it all in her tote bag, threw her coat over her nightgown, shoved her feet into her boots. The chocolates, the gold-wrapped chocolates, sat on the dresser.

Let's go, Annabelle said.

The robot voice continued. Every word meant *get out of here.* She grabbed her hotel key card, said goodbye to her suitcase, and followed the line of people, all bathrobed and complaining and fearful, down the carpeted hall and through the metal door of the fire exit and onto the crowded stairway.

"These things are always false alarms," a man in a white T-shirt complained. "If this happens again . . ."

"It's happened before? Here?" Tessa couldn't help but ask as she stepped down, down, down.

"Hotels in general, I mean." The man in front of her wore a sweatshirt with a Dodgers logo on the back, jeans, bare feet. "I travel all the time. It's never anything."

"Sometimes it is," someone else said.

At every floor, more people entered the stairway, the pace deliberate, constant, unstopping. At one point she heard laughter, which was quickly shushed.

"What time is it anyway?"

"Ten after four," a woman said.

"Why do these things happen in the middle of the night?" The voice came from behind Tessa. "There's never a fire alarm in the daytime."

But through the complaining and the derision and the fretting, everyone moved relentlessly downward; all the random hotel guests, all away from home, maybe thinking of home, walking with focused determination. Maybe tamping down panic, maybe praying or bargaining or simply hoping. Maybe some of them weren't supposed to be here, she speculated as she took the turn to floor eight. Might that be a plot for her next book? A fire alarm forces clandestine lovers into the street, and someone sees them?

Keep walking, Annabelle said. *Let's get ourselves to safety.*

Tessa clutched the bag with her laptop and phone and schedule to her chest, her thoughts racing. Many flights of stairs to go. She didn't smell smoke, but the public address system voice was insistent, repeating, punctuated with the *whoop whoop whoop* of the fire alarm. Her priorities crystallized—even if all of her other possessions burned, she herself would be safe. *Keep going.* Get *out.*

It crossed her mind to call Henry, to dial as she continued walking. But it would only upset him, and she had no news, simply that she was following the rules in a fire alarm where there did not seem to be smoke and there did not seem to be fire and there did not seem to be anyone in firefighting gear rushing up the stairs. Yet.

One gaunt-faced woman clutched a tawny fur coat, and had thrown it over a slinky undergarment. A husky man in a Lions Club jersey cradled a swaddled infant in his arms, sound asleep. Clomping behind him, a tow-headed boy wearing untied running shoes and a striped T-shirt.

A striped T-shirt, Tessa thought. Like the girl in that locket. Which was still in her room. She wanted to jam her fingers into her ears, but the insistent warnings were too piercing to be silenced.

She pictured Zack and Linny, home in their beds—*Zack's not in his own bed,* she reminded herself. And her children, in blissful dreamland, she hoped, had no idea their mother was in this kind of danger. If she were killed in a fire, how much would they miss her? What would they remember?

A famous author who had died because she left her children behind. If she'd stayed home, she would not be in this potential jeopardy. If she died, on the road . . . Did Henry have life insurance for her? She had no idea.

The quality of the sound changed. As she turned the corner, the stairwell widened. A bright red number one was stenciled on the wall. Beyond, the sprawling lobby of the hotel, the gray relief of almost daylight coming through the broad front windows, punctuated by swirling red lights, painting hotel guests' faces crimson as they came out of the stairway, refugees from a still-hypothetical danger.

Two hotel employees in navy-blue uniforms flanked the open stairwell doors, guiding the emerging guests.

"Let's move outside, ladies and gentlemen," one of them said, "until the firefighters give us the all clear."

The other employee held a stack of folded blue fabric. "If anyone needs a blanket, please let me know, plenty of them right here," she said.

"Is there a real fire?" Tessa couldn't help asking.

"Yeah, can someone tell us what the hell is going on?" The voice of a man behind her, sharp with anger, rolled over Tessa's question. "I have valuable documents in my room."

"We are waiting for the firefighters to give the all clear, sir," the clerk said again. "Please keep moving."

Firefighters in tan canvas turnout gear and red back-billed helmets stood in the lobby, cigarette pack–sized radios clipped to their shoulders. The doors on either side of the massive revolving front door were propped wide open and the inner partitions of the revolving door flattened so people could leave without delay.

Tessa marched obediently toward the front door, and into the not-quite-warm-enough Denver morning. The June sky had not yet turned pink, but the pulsating swath of emergency lights turned the buildings on both sides of the block into a red-and-blue light show.

"Keep moving, folks," a stocky man in a blue suit repeated, gesturing people to go ahead. "Get away from the building."

Some of the hotel guests, standing in the middle of the street now, panned their phone cameras across the clumps of people and the hotel and the fire engines, at the police who were cordoning off the street with yellow tape, at the hotel employees, some of them uniformed, others in overalls and black jumpsuits. One gangly man wore a white chef's hat and apron, and carried a spatula as if that were his prized possession.

This would be on social media in a heartbeat, an Instagram-worthy occasion, an evacuation, a danger, an adventure. But for her, it was an invitation to exhaustion. She would be miserable at the event tomorrow.

Today, Annabelle said.

"Have you heard anything?" The woman next to Tessa clutched her arm, her voice soft and Southern. Smudges of mascara streaked under her eyes, and her mass of dark hair was scrunched in a ponytail. "Do you smell smoke?"

"No," Tessa said.

"Oh, y'all," the woman whispered. Pointed. "Look who's here."

37

Tessa saw the microphone, a black stick covered with a red windscreen, and a bright red logo with the number eleven in white, before she saw the person holding it. The reporter was much taller than Tessa, she had to look up to see his dark eyes and close-cropped hair. He altered his expression to one of concern.

"May I ask if you are all right, ma'am? Can you tell us what happened?"

"Me?" Tessa saw the lens of a video camera behind the guy, reflecting the swirls of red emergency lights. Police cars had moved closer, too, their lights strobing blue.

Dawn, relentless, was also arriving, with the growing impossibility of Tessa getting any sleep. She would have to race upstairs, take a shower, change clothes and go to the airport. If her suitcase wasn't incinerated. If this took any longer, or if everything in the hotel was destroyed, what would she do? What would she actually *do?*

"Yes, ma'am," the reporter said. "I'm Morgan Hurtado, Channel 11? Can you tell us if you ever saw fire? Is anyone hurt?"

All Tessa needed, to be on TV. "I, um . . ." She must look awful. Disheveled and rumpled, and wearing her coat over a nightgown.

The blue-blanketed woman was still beside her. "I didn't see any fire," she began. *Fy-uh*, with her accent. "We just heard . . ."

Thank you, Tessa thought, and tried to edge away from being the center of attention. One exhausted clueless bystander was as good as another. Then she saw the mic logo again.

"And how about you, ma'am?" The reporter—Morgan something?—had moved his microphone back to Tessa. "Were you terrified?"

"I'd rather not say anything." Tessa held up a palm and backed away, but was blocked by the front window of a closed Starbucks.

"Look, ma'am? I have a live shot in five minutes, the five a.m. news," the reporter said, entreating. "I need one more sound bite, or my news director, um, my boss, will kill me."

Tessa had to laugh. Every job had its travails, and this poor guy, out here at the crack of dawn, was trying to make a story out of nothing. And wasn't that what she did, every day at the computer? Tried to make something out of nothing but her own imagination? She felt a twinge of empathy. She could make his day, and why not.

"It was terrifying," she began, her voice dramatic. "We were all awakened in the middle of the night by the horrible wailing alarms, and everyone raced into the corridor, in all manner of dress, bathrobes and coats, some barefoot, and there were babies and children, so scary, we had to get down all those stairs, as fast as we could, and no one knew what was going on. All I wanted to do was get out of there. I'm on business, and so glad my family wasn't with me." She paused, watching the reporter's eyes grow wider, victorious. The videographer—Tessa could see her chaotic blond hair, her black Broncos T-shirt and black jeans—moved closer, maybe zooming in her lens. "Ten floors of fear," Tessa added. "What a nightmare."

Take that, news director, she thought. *Ten floors of fear, there's a headline.*

She could read the relief in the reporter's eyes. The community of storytellers had to stick together.

"Thank you," the reporter said. "Now, could you say your name, and spell it for me? And tell me where you're from?"

The sky had changed color, now a downy lavender, and what had been shadowy undifferentiated clumps of hotel guests and employees began to resolve into individuals. Still no smoke or fire. Not even a marginal frenzy of activity. She felt sorry for the news team, who spent their days hoping for disasters. This nonstory, a dud, would probably never see a minute of airtime after that 5:00 a.m. live shot.

"That's okay," Tessa said. "I'd rather not."

She thought Morgan was about to cry.

"So, ma'am?" he began. "If you don't tell us your name, we can't—"

"Tessa Calloway," the blanket woman said.

"Her? Or you?" The reporter looked confused.

"Her." The woman pointed. "The famous—"

"Whoa." The videographer lowered her camera, stepped closer to them. "Really?" She pointed to her blue earrings. "Tessa fricking Calloway? I'm Ronnie. *Such* a—" She stopped, dropped her shoulders, looked embarrassed. "Sorry to fangirl, Ms. Calloway. Morgan, know who this is?"

"I don't give a . . . I mean, great. Tell me all about it later." Morgan looked at his chunky watch. "But we need to get the show on the road now. So—"

"We could say your name is Annabelle Brown," Ronnie said.

Not a good plan, Annabelle said.

"We need to use her real name." Morgan had lost his congenial tone. "And fast. Ms. . . . . Calloway, is it? Okay?"

38

The elevators were back in service, and Tessa had to wait two cycles to crowd onto one of them, crammed beside weary and cranky hotel guests heading back to their floors. The aluminum rectangle smelled of sweat and shampoo and marijuana.

"So that's it?" someone complained. "'Sorry for your inconvenience, we've gotten the all clear'? Like we're supposed to say, oh, no problem."

"Better to be safe," someone said.

"Better to get a good night's sleep."

A woman in a flowered flannel nightgown reached past her to poke the elevator button for her floor, and Tessa saw the whole bank of numbers now lighted green. They were going to stop on every floor, releasing the false-alarm hostages one by one, back to what was left of their night. Not much of it, at now past five in the morning, and if she went to sleep—the doors closed her into the shoulder-to-shoulder elevator—she'd be beyond groggy and hopelessly disoriented, and no amount of caffeine or adrenaline could make up for it.

"They should give us our money back," Harvard T-shirt said.

"They should give us our two hours back," Flannel Nightgown retorted.

Tessa remembered a TV show she used to watch with her parents, she might have been eight, younger than Linny certainly, where performers

would spin china plates on tall wooden sticks, one plate on each stick, a
dozen plates at a time, racing back and forth to keep the fragile dishes
from crashing to the ground. Tessa had tried it once, using one saucer on
a pencil, with no success, and was sent to her room. Now she was better
at it, metaphorically at least. She watched the numbers on the elevator
climb. But today might be the day all her plates crashed to the floor.

The doors finally opened on floor ten, and Tessa scrabbled for her room
card. Why did they make these things small and flat and losable? But she
found it, first try, and clicked open the door to her room.

Everything was as it had been before. She consulted her watch, trying
to do math. Her plane to San Diego was at nine forty-five, she had to be
at the airport at seven forty-five. It might take an hour in the Uber, but to
be safe, she should leave at 6:00 a.m. Which meant get ready at 5:00 a.m.
Which meant she was, as of now, late.

She pulled open the gauzy curtains of the window, watching the glare
of the rising sun on a tall mirrored building outside, saw the battalions of
emergency vehicles, lights off now, still gathered ten floors below. But she
had to get ready.

"I know, I know, 'you can sleep on the plane,'" she replied out loud as
if to everyone who would surely advise her of that. Those people, DJ and
Olivette and even Henry, still cozy in their East Coast beds, weren't the
ones who had to do it.

And now she had no idea how the shower worked, a twist of mysterious chrome and spigot on the white tile wall. She envisioned water
spewing, dousing her hair. She yanked the handle, and stepped out of
the way.

Out the corner of her eye she noticed a reflection in the bathroom
mirror.

A flash of metal.

Of gold . . . what?

The metallic box of Hammond's candy was now on the bathroom
drainboard. The red ribbon was missing. The top was off, and upside down
on the counter. Printed inside was an annotated diagram of where each
piece was located in the box. Cream, caramel, toffee, nougat. Chocolate-
covered cherries; their fragrance unmistakable.

She stared at the candies, the water spraying out behind her, and felt her back get wet, but did not move.

Every one of the chocolates had been stabbed. Or smashed. Or pounded, as if someone had taken a knife or a fist or a hammer and intentionally, intently, destroyed them all. Ruined them, one by one.

And left them for her to see.

There were moments, Tessa knew they happened, pivotal moments, when some line was crossed, those never-going-back, indelible, life-altering moments when choices were offered and decisions were made, and the road she'd travel by was selected. She knew that now. But not back then. So long ago, but always so nearby.

The two girls had been alone in the house that afternoon. Even then, Tessa understood her mother was trying to bond them; to connect Theresa, her "misfit," with the only daughter of her mother's newest boyfriend.

Make her like you, Tessa's mother had instructed, leaning toward her lighted mirror, applying her mascara. *If she likes you and her father likes me, our future is secure again. He needs a wife now, remember.* It had felt wrong, that kind of adult talk, but even then Tessa had felt her mother's loneliness and fear, her antipathy to being a single woman struggling with the burden of a preteen child. And Tessa did honestly admire the mayor's daughter, a high school sophomore, who didn't complain about babysitting for her, who seemed fearless and brave and beautiful, and was kind, even to the younger awkward Tessa.

That day, she'd left Tessa downstairs to read on the living room couch while she went up to her room, silver Walkman in her ears; to plan her high school's Women's Equality Day, she'd explained. "We can be whatever we want," she'd pronounced. "Never forget it." Tessa hadn't really understood that, but had pretended to, because she so yearned to be just like her someday. But even right then, on their own but together in the mayor's unfamiliar house, she felt like she'd been given the gift of a perfect older sister. Tessa was a little hungry, because her mother had forgotten about lunch. But Black Beauty, in her book, was hungry, too.

When the doorbell rang at the mayor's house, Tessa, startled, had looked up from her reading. Poor Ginger the mare had been telling Beauty how men are cruel and have no feeling, and "there is nothing that we can do, but just bear it." And it seemed so real, like a movie, and so very sad. She'd hesitated, waiting, but no footsteps came from upstairs. She remembered the Walkman. Tessa trotted to the door, she remembered it so profoundly now that it made her heart clench to relive this, understanding the freedom she was about to lose.

Don't open the door to strangers, how many times had her mother told her that? And this wasn't even Tessa's own house. But as she looked through the peephole, she saw the man, in a tie and a suit, looking like somebody important. She pulled open the door, but left the chain. And then didn't know what to say. She could almost hear her own tentative voice.

"Hi." She'd been holding her book, one finger marking the page.

"Hi," the man said. "You must be Theresa. Your mother told me you'd be here. And that you were reading *Black Beauty*."

"Do I know you?"

"Of course," the man said. "I work with your mother's boyfriend. I'm what they call an advance man. I arrange events. Like the one the mayor is attending right now. With your mother? Did she tell you?"

"Yes," Tessa had said. That seemed right.

"Good, good, good," the man had said, nodding approval. He pointed past her. "I need to run upstairs," he went on, "to the mayor's desk, and get his folder with his speech in it. You can't believe how angry he is at me, Theresa. I forgot his speech. So two seconds. I'll go get it."

Don't open the door to strangers, her mother's voice, so loud in her head. But this wasn't a stranger. "I'm not supposed to open the door to strangers."

"Of course," the man said. "Absolutely true. Smart girl. But then, I'm not a stranger."

Tessa had paused, considering this. That's exactly what she'd thought, too. She heard an ice-cream truck go by, the ice cream man, jingling out what she now recognized was ragtime. She remembered the bright pink rhododendrons blooming in the mayor's front yard, and on Buckeye Street a boy riding no-hands on a bicycle toward the ice cream man. She remembered the birds, too—pretty-pretty-pretty, one was singing. Pretty-pretty-pretty.

That day had ruined cardinals for her.

"I . . . I suppose," she'd said. But hadn't opened the door. And was gratified when the man's face seemed so approving. He looked nice, and had a briefcase.

"You're so helpful," he said. "You are such a good helper, Theresa. Thank you so much for helping me, because you know, it's not good when the mayor is angry."

Tessa didn't, but she remembered how she felt when her mother was angry with her, and that was not good.

"In fact, why don't you run and get a Popsicle," he said, reaching into his pocket. "And then come right back, and by then I'll be gone. If you let me in, I'll give you the money to buy it."

Was it okay, to let him in? But she was a little hungry. And all she wanted in the world was that Popsicle. She could imagine it, she could taste the sweet, cherry-red deliciousness, pretending that her Popsicle was lipstick, staining her lips and making her pretty-pretty-pretty, too.

The man pointed to the ice-cream truck. "Uh-oh. He's getting ready to leave," the man said. "Here. Better run."

And he had given her five whole dollars. She remembered that; the smooth promising touch of the crisp bill, and the clink of the chain as she opened the door, how she'd dropped *Black Beauty* onto the checkerboard hallway floor, and how the sun had hit her face as she ran down the front steps toward the tinkling music.

She'd returned, with half of her cherry Popsicle eaten and the rest melting, sticky red dripping on one tanned hand; her other hand holding a second Popsicle, an orange one, the one she'd bought for the mayor's brilliant daughter.

But Annabelle—and the man—were gone.

39

Now Tessa felt her back get wetter and wetter, the sounds of the spraying shower a white noise behind her, the steam from the too-hot water condensing on the hotel's fogging mirror.

The chocolates on the bathroom counter taunted her with their telegraphed backstory. Their unsubtle reference to violence.

She picked up the box with two careful fingers, looking underneath. *From your flight attendants*, it had said. It had said the bookstore told them the name of Tessa's hotel. But the card was gone.

"Personality is revealed in the choices a character makes"—she remembered an early conversation with her editor, in Olivette's aerie of a Manhattan office, sunlight glowing through its thirtieth-floor windows, the skyscrapers of the city beyond. Stacks of books on the floor and double-rowed on the shelves, and a glistening jade plant elegant in one corner, the one bit of green in a room full of paper and pages. "And I love how you've shown us," Olivette had said, "through Annabelle's clear motivations, why she does the things she does. Even if we don't always agree with them."

Olivette had patted Tessa's printed-out manuscript, almost with affection. "A good book is about causation. Remember that. Something happens *because* of something else."

Tessa had nodded, thinking how wise Olivette was, and how she herself had never thought of it that way.

"And the reason that works in a novel," Olivette had continued, "is because that's how life works. We make a decision, and as a result, something happens. And then as a result of that, something else happens. And that's a story."

"And that's a story," Tessa now said it out loud, her back soaked and the chocolates destroyed and her emotions swirling as red and hot as those fire engine lights with the fear that she *had* done something to deserve this. That it was causation, exactly as Olivette said. And until she knew what had caused it and until she knew who had reacted with this insidious chocolate message—a message saying *I know where you are, I can get to you, even in a locked hotel room where no one is allowed even to be inside the building, and I can destroy you as easily as a fancy box of candy*—she'd never be able to stop it.

In a novel, her tormentor would have been Annabelle, Tessa knew, returning from the past, bitter and haunted and vengeful. Or Annabelle's father, bent on ugly retribution, some twisted payback for Tessa's childhood deal with the devil. But neither could be true.

Soon after the humiliating headline—Mayor's Daughter Abducted After "Friend" Goes For Ice Cream, one headline sneered—Tessa's mother had come home, eyes puffy and hair disheveled, clutching her coat. Tessa's name had not been mentioned in the articles, since she was a "juvenile," but everyone in town knew. *Everyone.* Back then Tessa felt as if she walked with a force field around her. No one came close, no one made eye contact, and the whispers grew. The contempt. The narrow-eyed accusations. Where was Annabelle? Why was Tessa free, and not the mayor's beautiful Annabelle?

That day, Tessa's mother had retreated to her bedroom and locked the door, eventually coming down only to drink coffee as bitterly dark as her words, and staring at the silent wall phone in the kitchen.

"He's gone," her mother said. "He told me he cannot bear the sight of you, or even the *thought* of you, he told me that, and I don't blame him. You traded her for five dollars and a Popsicle? A *Popsicle?* What are you doing? Trying to ruin my life?"

As if Tessa had caused it. But she hadn't disobeyed, she hadn't let in a stranger, he'd said she knew him. He had a briefcase, and . . . but no one cared what she said.

Tessa's mother had hustled them out of town, creating their new identities and new lives.

"You must never *ever* speak of it. You must never *ever* tell." She'd repeated that, a spell or an incantation, in the car on the way to she didn't know where. "If you do, your life will be ruined. You are Tessa Danforth. Say it."

"Tessa Danforth," she tried the name.

"Again."

"Tessa Danforth."

"Your future depends on it, Tessa. And mine, too."

It was easy to be Tessa, in their new home in Massachusetts, where no one cared who they were, or about the new bookish kid in fourth grade. Her mother tried selling real estate, and lost herself in work. It wasn't until teenager Tessa dared to check the then-newish Google that she learned the "mayor's aide"—actually an embittered former city employee who'd gotten caught picking up the ransom money—had confessed to taking Annabelle. But in his hatred for the mayor, he refused to reveal what happened to her.

He was murdered, that same week, in prison. Annabelle's father, the article reported, had died of cancer and grief, never knowing.

Annabelle's remains were found years after that, tangled in the debris of the Maumee River. This time, Tessa's mother called her at college with the news, and, Tessa remembered, sounded happy.

"So *that's* over." In one phrase, Tessa's mother personally obliterated the entire episode. "They suspect he'd killed her, or something happened while he was waiting for the ransom. Anyway, now we know. Don't ever think of it again."

"Impossible," Tessa had told her. "I could never, ever, forget." And for a while, Annabelle's voice, a gift, remained in Tessa's mind. *You're fine,* Annabelle would reassure her, every time Tessa felt close to the edge. *I'm fine, too. Don't worry. It was not your fault.*

Eventually, though, Annabelle's comforting voice vanished, and Tessa wondered if she'd lost something fundamental. Imagination—or childhood—replaced by her first true love, then by the roller coaster of Henry Calloway's sporadic employment, by the necessity of her new job, by terrific but demanding kids, and school and camp and laundry and mortgage payments.

Until that day in the grocery store. And then so powerfully, so almost materially, when Tessa walked out of Swain and Woodworth. And then the day she typed "Chapter One."

Finally, Annabelle had said that day. *And, yes, of course, use my name. It means I can have more than one life, Tessa. And you can give it to me.*

Tessa had burst into tears. Still, she'd changed Annabelle's last name a bit. To protect everyone.

Now Tessa heard another noise, shrill and close and in her hotel room. She froze.

Then realized it was her phone, her alarm ringing, telling her it was time to wake up and get ready for another day on book tour.

But now it was clear—Tessa was not on tour alone.

Go, Annabelle said. *We can't be late.*

40

Tessa leaned her head against the back seat of her Uber and stared out the sunroof at the Denver dawn. The moon hung like a lingering guest, its time expired, but refusing to leave. The highway to the airport, featureless and flat, tempted her to sleep, but she had to stay awake. She had to power through security and onto a train and find her gate and get on that plane before she could fall asleep. It would take all of her willpower and determination to do it.

In the far distance, the mountains she had not had time to see, in another city she had not had time to see. She sighed, out loud. Those chocolates. She'd left them on the counter, and felt guilty about the mess. And terrified of their message.

Everything happens *because* of something. Was it the bad thing? Preteen Tessa was vilified for opening the door to a stranger. Annabelle's powerful father heartbroken. Her own mother humiliated. The town had simmered with animosity and accusations. And now, twenty-five years later, people in bookstores were asking about her hometown.

She had to talk to Henry. She kept meaning to, but she'd never told him about the bad thing. Or much about her childhood at all. *Never ever tell,* she could still hear her mother's brittle voice. *It will ruin you.* Now it might be too late. Would a decision she made when she was ten brand her forever? She'd told Emily, and look what happened then.

It wouldn't be easy to connect Tessa with that tragedy—she'd googled her Tessa Calloway self, too, when the book sold, apprehensive and terrified, but infinitely relieved when the search engine also discovered no matches between Tessa Danforth *or* Theresa Mattigan and Mayor Browning's murdered daughter, Annabelle. But a determined investigator who knew their stuff . . .

She winced, playing it out.

"Moral turpitude," the phrase Sadie Bailey had used. The phrase Tessa had blithely dismissed.

It didn't take a fiction writer to know that unmasking her as what one scathing, decades-old headline labeled "The Bad Friend" would reveal the truth about Annabelle's origin. And might ruin Tessa's career.

More than "might." Would definitely ruin her career. Her marriage. Her life.

That can't be what's behind this, Annabelle said. You were a child.

She dialed, and Henry's cell rang, then rang again, and again, Tessa so tangled in thought that she almost didn't calculate the delay. He might be taking a shower. *Shower.* The chocolates. She could smell those chocolates now, cloying and sweet and horrible and weaponized.

"It's early where you are," said Henry's voice, finally. "Happy Saturday."

"Is that what day it is?" Tessa was instantly comforted by the voice from home. Sort of home. "I have no idea. It's just the next day and the next day and the next day."

"You sound funny, Tesser. Tired."

Tessa heard a commotion on the other end of the line. Raised voices. The kids fighting?

"Hen? What's going on?"

"Hang on," Henry said. "Linny, what? The *what?*"

The rolling landscape outside her Uber window was invaded by aggressive signs for new homes in fancy developments, tempting buyers with drawings of ultramodern homes. Last Chance to Buy Under $399,000, one sign warned. That was less than half of what their Rockport home had cost, and then only because it had an outdated kitchen. Which was now a yellow kitchen, Tessa remembered.

The mortgage, she thought. "*You'll* pay," her agent had warned.

"Henry, are you with me here?" Tessa heard the bitterness in her voice, and tried to remember that Henry was doing exactly what she was doing, spinning plates, and his entire life could not stop because she called.

"Were you in a fire?" Henry was saying.

"No—I—wait. How do you know? It was a false alarm, anyway, so how could you *possibly* know that?"

"I have alerts for your name, don't you?" Henry asked. "Whenever your name is on the internet my phone gets pinged. Linny has it, too, on her computer, because she misses you so much. Don't tell her I told you. Hold on, I'm putting you on speaker. Anyway, apparently, you were the star of a story called Ten Floors of Fear. On some TV news in Denver?"

"Hi, Mommy." Linny's voice came over the tinny speaker. "I saw you. Was it scary?"

"Hi, sweetie. Not one bit."

"But Momma, it was a fire. And . . ."

Momma. Linny must be distressed by this, using her now-discarded nickname.

"You have fire drills in school, honey. It was like that. No biggie."

If her family had seen the story, who knows how many other people knew she was at that Denver hotel. And that she wasn't in her room. The Denver airport drew closer, its quirky roof like a caravan of white tents. She told Hen and Linny the fire alarm story as quickly as she could, portraying it as an everyday exercise in safety.

"Don't believe everything on TV, sweetheart," she went on. "Haven't your father and I told you that?"

"I guess." Linny still sounded unconvinced.

"So you didn't get any sleep," Henry was saying. "And that's why you're—whatever."

The Uber eased onto the departures ramp. Tessa yearned to tell her husband about the chocolates and the note and even the bad thing. And how yes, she was afraid. More than afraid. But there was no time, and certainly, devastatingly, the Uber driver would overhear her.

Linny was listening, too, and she refused to reveal her anxiety with her daughter there. Zack wasn't home, she remembered again.

"I'm fine," she said, trying to sound convincingly perky. "Have you heard from Zack?"

"Did you find out about Locket Mom?" Linny's voice interrupted. "Or those earrings?"

"You know about *that*?" Tessa knew she hadn't mentioned it.

"Mom." Linny was using her wannabe teenage voice, making the one word "Mom" into at least two syllables. "It's all over social. That guy in the locket picture looks like he's from another planet."

"Another planet?" Tessa envisioned the photograph through Linny's eyes. "Because?"

"Be*cause* no one dresses like that now. Zack says he's gonna do a search. If he ever decides to come home."

"Your mother has to go," Henry interrupted. "Was there a special reason you called me, sweetheart?"

"Just to say I love you," Tessa said, the song going through her mind. And lying at the same time. Her Uber pulled to the curb, stopped. "And tell Zack I already did Google Images. But I love him so much for trying. But quickly, how is he? What do you mean 'if he ever decides to come home'?"

"We're here, ma'am." The Uber driver twisted his head over his shoulder to look back at her. "You set?"

41

"Here's what worries me, Tessa." Tessa muttered the words out loud as she pulled her roller bag down yet another hotel corridor, this one the red-and-gold faux opulence of the Emperor Suites. She found her hotel room key, and tapped. "Whether you've lost your mind."

Room 715 had an only-in-California view. Outside, a massive steel-gray battleship cut silently through the sparkling water of San Diego Bay, where somewhere there were Navy SEALs, and real seals, and people laughing and eating fish tacos and drinking margaritas.

She had not slept on the plane. She'd stared out into the cotton-filled sky, wondering what Linny had meant by if Zackie "ever decides to come home." When she'd called back, after slogging through security and finding her gate, Henry's phone had gone straight to messages. She'd felt her shoulders droop. Where had he gone?

Saturday mornings they always went for bagels—but they lived in Rockport now. She had no idea where to get bagels in Rockport. Or where to get anything. Bagels, ha. She had no idea where her *family* was. Or what they were doing. The nosy Barbie woman, obviously stalking Henry. Zackie off with the glamorous Nellie.

She could not bear to think of her children alone. Before the trip, she'd told Henry, looked him in the eyes and held his shoulders—*do not leave our children by themselves. Ever.* He'd thought she was oversensitive. Or doubting him. "What could happen?" he'd asked.

She had opened her mouth to answer, then couldn't.

"Come home," Henry had urged her. He might have meant it, in a flash of impulse, until he thought about it. Until he thought about the money.

Now *she* thought about how much money there would *not* be if she panicked and took the next flight to Boston.

She hauled her suitcase onto the webbed wooden luggage stand, unzipped it. Took stock of her dilemma. Which disturbingly unusual things on this journey were connected—causation—and which were coincidence? Sam in 3A showing up at the bookstore? She hadn't gotten his last name, which now she regretted. But he could have made one up, too. Anna like Savannah? The contentious audience questions in Phoenix and Denver? DJ had even warned her, *be careful on the road. Everyone isn't always nice.* And that was certainly true.

The chocolates. The fire. Her briefly missing luggage. Those earrings.

The locket. Which was still in her suitcase.

Sheepishly, she knew it was absurd, she took the five steps to the nightstand in her new room, yanked open the drawer. Nothing. She opened all the drawers in the room, still so weary and muddled. But there was nothing in them that shouldn't be.

She clipped her black pants onto a hanger, and draped the jacket over them. The locket *had* to be a coincidence. They would have no way to make sure that she'd do anything about it.

She paused, still holding the hanger. "They."

"They" managed to get her the chocolates. "They" pulled the fire alarm. And "they" destroyed the chocolates.

"There is no 'they,' Tessa," she admonished herself. "Set the alarm, lie down, take a nap."

There might be a they, Annabelle said.

Tessa yawned, a deeply exhausted yawn, and peeled off her leggings and T-shirt and tossed them on one of the double beds. Being on the road was grueling; Sadie and Olivette and DJ, all of Team Tessa had cautioned her about that.

But secretly, she'd looked forward to some time alone. The idea of flying around the country, staying in lovely hotels, having one event each day where people lauded her and bought her books, how could that be terrible? But strange pillows and time zones and unpredictability and strangers took their toll, and now someone was trying to unsettle her. Taunt her. Stalk her. Destroy her.

She'd relied on her family for equilibrium.

And now she didn't know where they were.

42

"Were you in a fire?" Bookstore manager Rosalie McDermott, her face etched with concern, had linked her arm through Tessa's elbow, leading her into the Coronado Bookstore. Expansive windows looked toward the ocean, and an airplane flew so low over the water that Tessa flinched, fearing for the passengers on board.

"Yikes," she said, "is that plane okay?"

"We're in the flight path," Rosalie said. "But *were* you? In a fire? I saw you on the national news, some ungodly hour."

Rosalie's close-cropped blond hair was tinted purple at the edges, and she wore the world's tiniest sweatshirt emblazoned with Lit Happens. She'd finished her ensemble with an accordion-pleated midi skirt and raffia platform sandals, and now guided Tessa toward the back of the store. "Are you all right?"

"Oh, yes, sure. False alarm."

"You must be brutally tired, though. Anyway. You're here, and you look terrific. I have restorative Oreos and lemonade back in the office. And some fresh cherries."

The fragrance of bookstore-behind-the-scenes smelled familiar now; shelves of incense and ballpoint pens, scented candles and miniature soaps. Bookstores sold much more than books—had it always been this way? She had no memories of bookstores, only libraries. Her mother had never liked buying things. Things for Tessa, at least.

Rosalie opened the door to a room where three shelves full of advance reader copies lined one wall, a shiny, too-big refrigerator and an aluminum sink on the other. Four book cartons stacked up against the refrigerator's white door. Each box had lettering in thick black on the outside: **TESSA**. A round Formica table and two padded chairs tucked into a corner.

"Listen to this." Rosalie dragged a silver box cutter across the brown sealing tape on the top book box. "I have some cool news. Have a cookie. Have some cherries. Have a water."

"Cool news?" Tessa twisted open one of the Oreos. Ignored the cherries. She hated cherries. Anything cherry.

"This is stock for you to sign. 'Kay?" Rosalie sliced the side flaps of the top box, stacked the books on the table. "Anyway, someone who's coming tonight wanted me to tell you they recognized the photo in Locket Mom's necklace."

Tessa felt her eyes widen. "They did? Who?"

Rosalie put two more stacks of books on the table.

"Man or a woman?" Tessa went on.

"They texted. Here's some Sharpies, they work for you?"

"Perfect. And they're coming to tell me? Here? This locket person?"

Rosalie had opened one of the periwinkle books, flapped the paper cover to the title page, then placed another open book on top of that, making a stack of already-opened books for Tessa to sign.

"I guess so." She rubbed her palms together, greedy. "It'd be cool though, wouldn't it? If the mystery was solved here at the Coronado? We'd plaster that thing all over social. We could call the news. Reunite whoever with the locket. Happy ending. They love those on TV."

"You should be a writer." Tessa chuckled as she signed her name, over and over. "And yes, everyone loves a happy ending."

So true, Annabelle said.

"What a coincidence that *you* found it in your room, isn't it? And that you took it? I mean, anyone else might have left it, or dumped it at lost and found, but that's why everyone loves you, if I may say so. Not to mention how inspiring you were in that video. Quitting your job. Following your dreams." Rosalie put her fists on her hips, emphasizing. "You are so darn brave. And nice. I'm psyched to hear about this, aren't you?"

"Aw, thank you. And . . . yeah." Tessa stared at the next book, pen in hand. That locket had begun to feel like an albatross. She focused on signing, focused on tonight's event, focused on good things. But who would be in the audience?

"Can I ask you, before everyone does?" Rosalie was scooting another pile of books toward Tessa. "Is Annabelle based on a real person? She's so wonderful."

"I love her, too. But Annabelle is fiction."

If you say so, Annabelle said.

"Well, she's confident, like you. Goes after what she wants." Rosalie said. "I even picture her looking like you."

She felt Annabelle getting ready to say something, then she didn't.

"That's one of the pitfalls, isn't it?" Tessa signed another book. "A woman writing about a woman, readers envision the author. Hard to avoid."

A couple of taps on the door, and a young woman with a swirl of beaded braids peeked in. She had an earpiece in one ear, a cord with a flat circular mic snaking down to what looked like an intercom on her belt. Her T-shirt, tucked into skinny jeans, showed Robert McCloskey's ducklings.

"Hi, Tessa," she said, "I'm Dorrit. It's incredible to meet you."

"Dorrit is our children's section manager," Rosalie said, "but she insisted on being here tonight with you. She told me, in her job interview, that you were her inspiration."

"I was trying to be cool, Ro, thanks for outing me." Dorrit widened her eyes in clearly pretend annoyance. "But two things. One, yes, your video killed. The book, too. Life-changing."

"Well, thank you," Tessa said. "I'm glad the change was good. When readers say they made a decision because of me, sometimes I feel responsible. What's thing two?"

"Hey, Bodie." Dorrit had touched her earpiece, then looked down the corridor to her left. "They're telling me you won't believe the crowd. Bodie says every seat is full. And he wants to know, should he bring out more chairs."

"Told you," Rosalie said. "More the merrier."

"Yes on the chairs." Dorrit pulled the mic closer to her mouth. "And what?" Dorrit tilted her head, listening. "Yeah, I'm about to tell her. Tessa, thing number two. There's a person out there who says she needs to talk to you."

"She?" Tessa said.

"Who?" Rosalie said at the same time.

Dorrit blinked, seemed to be thinking about that. "She didn't say her name." She tilted her head, as if remembering. "Probably your age, ish, Tessa? Gray hair though, but in a cool way. And I probably shouldn't say this, but I think it's a wig. And big glasses."

"You think that's the person who texted, Rosalie?" Tessa had been the one to unleash this thing on social media, and now she'd have to deal with the result. In public. In front of a roomful of people. With no escape.

Rosalie set down the last stack of books. "Did she say anything about Tessa's photo? Or Locket Mom?"

"Nope. She didn't say anything about anything. Want me to get Bodie to ask?"

"Nope. I'll handle it," Rosalie said. "Keep signing, Tessa, we need to get this show on the road."

43

Tessa leaned closer to Dorrit, both of them stationed in the wings of the bookstore's event space, trying to spot the woman in the gray maybe-wig. Rosalie was finishing her introduction.

"Do you see her?" Tessa whispered. "The locket woman?"

Dorrit shook her head. "No. I don't. Ro couldn't find her, either. Weird."

"Yeah. Weird." A roar of applause interrupted them, and even in her curiosity and increasing fear, Tessa felt the audience's approval as she approached the lectern. In front of her, a patchwork quilt of periwinkle, her book on hundreds of laps in rows of taupe folding chairs.

"Aw, thank you," Tessa said into the bulky microphone, and she touched one palm to her heart. "The idea that you all came to hear me—and Annabelle, of course—"

She paused, hearing the admiring murmur. "Was not even part of my wildest dreams. So to each and every one of you, thank you." She pointedly made eye contact. Scanning the audience. It would look, she hoped, as if she was connecting. Which she honestly was. But she was also searching the rows of upturned faces for maybe-wig woman. Who did not seem to be there.

Unless she had taken the wig off. But what would be the point of that?

She buried her fears as she eased into her book talk, the themes and stories familiar, the music of her speech, chorus and verse. The moments where people cheered, and the ones where they hissed in disapproval at the villains in her life.

So far, so good, she thought. *Almost done.*

"In closing, one more thing, you all. You have the power to control your life. *Your one life*. If *I* can do it, thanks to Annabelle, you can, too." She paused, trying to telegraph her genuine gratitude. "Thank you."

Rosalie approached her, smiling, applauding, as the crowd came to its feet. The women clutched their blue books, hugging them even as they clapped, and their blue earrings bobbed and danced.

"Aw, sit, sit, sit." Tessa waved them to their seats, but nowhere in the audience was a woman in a gray wig and glasses. Where had she gone?

Rosalie was still clapping, and Dorrit, too. "Time for Q and A?" Rosalie asked.

"Sure, but—" Tessa picked up her phone. "First let's take our photo. I want to remember you all."

True. But tonight, a photo could also be evidence, if Dorrit could identify the face of the woman who'd apparently vanished. "But don't hold the books in front of your faces, okay? I want to see *you*." She positioned herself in front of the group. "Then we'll do Q and A."

The prospect of the audience questions made her more uneasy than usual, with wig woman—maybe—lurking. She felt her insides twist, even as she made sure her expression was joyful. All the blue earrings grew disconcerting now, as she imagined the ones stashed in her suitcase. Gift? Or warning?

And still no sign of the woman. Yet. Again, gift? Or warning?

Back at the podium, photos stored in her phone, she hoped the questions would be unthreatening. About her outlines, her workspace, her favorite books.

"Yes?" She pointed, stolidly smiling. "Red coat in the back?"

"Is Annabelle based on a real person?"

The audience murmured, as if that was the question they'd all hoped she'd answer.

"Well, let me put it this way." She'd thought about this, and now she had a different answer from her usual. A truer answer. "Annabelle is all of us. Our alter ego, the person we wish we were, the person whose voice remains with us, but whose words we are sometimes afraid to speak. Annabelle—the *thought* of Annabelle—allowed me to channel the hope I'd had for a better self. And if I could speak *for* Annabelle, I know what she'd hope for you. Fulfillment. Empowerment. Love. Whatever your personal happiness might be. In your one life."

For a moment, the audience was silent, so silent that Tessa feared she'd gone too far. She was too tired, or too pressured, too worried about her past. And her home. And the family she'd left three time zones away.

Then a woman in the front row stood and applauded, and even as Tessa saw she was crying, so did the woman next to her and next to her and next to her.

Yikes, Annabelle said.

"Oh my goodness." Tessa stepped from behind the lectern. "You all. You somehow asked exactly the right question at exactly the right time. I am so honored to be with you to share this."

The rest of the signing was a blur—a few reverential questions, then a rush of people buying books, readers carrying multiple copies, Rosalie's eyes wide with delight, and Dorrit rushing to retrieve the ones Tessa had already signed, supposedly their backup stash for future customers. Tessa's hand cramped and the night swirled by; teary-eyed women sharing their private dreams, their personal stories, their gratitude.

"You gave me courage," one woman whispered as she waited for her signature. "I escaped a terrible marriage. Because of you."

"And Annabelle," Tessa said. "But remember, it was really *you*, yourself, who did it. *You.*"

The right thing at the right time, Tessa had alluded to that earlier. If the bad thing hadn't happened, she wouldn't have Annabelle now. The unsettling paradox haunted her as the line continued. That bargain again. What had been lost, and what had been gained?

It was ten o'clock when the last book was signed. Wig woman had not appeared.

"Wow." Rosalie stood by Tessa's signing table as the final reader left. "What a night."

"Agreed, terrific. Thank you." Tessa sat back in her chair and capped her pen. "Let me ask you, though, d'you think it's odd that the person who wanted to talk with me about the necklace didn't show up?"

"I'm bummed, Tessa, tell you the truth. I thought we might have a big viral Locket Mom moment. But you're viral enough on your own, my dear. You made my goals for two whole weeks. I owe you. What's next for you?"

Food. Sleep. *Seattle tomorrow.*

"Flying, talking, and Zooming with my family. The writing life." Tessa tried to convey it as the most exhilarating existence imaginable. Which, often, it was.

"Ro?" Dorrit, still in her ducklings T-shirt, hurried toward them. "You guys? I was tossing out the empty book cartons. And, um—"

"Um what?" Rosalie frowned. "We have to get Tessa to her ride."

Tessa saw the concern in Dorrit's expression as she accompanied them toward the glass front door, opening it into the street-lighted evening. Tessa's stubby black Uber, its insistent hazard lights flashing, idled on the street in front of them.

"Yeah well," Dorrit said, "Look. I found this outside. Hanging on the fence."

Dorrit came closer, and in the spotlights illuminating the sidewalk, Tessa recognized what the clerk was holding.

A wig. A sleek gray wig.

"What the hell?" Rosalie took a step forward. Stopped.

"A wig?" Tessa said, unnecessarily. "Is that the one—"

"I think so," Dorrit said. "Yeah."

The Uber driver buzzed down his window. "You call an Uber, ladies?"

"Yes." Tessa held up one finger at him, *wait a minute.* "That means—"

"Yeah," Rosalie said. "She might have been there."

Tessa stared at the mop of gray. Imagining the woman who had worn it. The woman who said she had something she knew Tessa wanted. The woman who brazenly discarded her disguise—obviously hoping someone would find it.

I know exactly who you are, she might have been saying. *And I can always find you.*

44

"We always tell each other everything, right, hon?" Henry was leaning into the FaceTime screen, his face earnest or worried or both. Tessa's hair, still wet from this morning's rushed shower, dripped on the unmade hotel bed. She had fifteen minutes before she had to throw on clothes, zip her suitcase, and leave for her flight. But Henry had called, and now she was behind, and might have to go to the airport with wet hair.

But she imagined someone seeing her like that in public, taking a video, and wouldn't *that* be fun, #messyTessa trending on social media. She had to cut this discussion short. A discussion that within five seconds had devolved into the worst possible question.

"What do you mean, we tell each other everything? What's wrong?" she asked. "What're you not telling me?" Only one thing worse than that. That he was asking about something *she* hadn't told *him*. She'd wait, see what Henry meant.

Why are you waiting? Annabelle asked. Take control.

"Or do you mean you think there's something *I'm* not telling *you?*"

"Don't be mad," Henry said.

The damp white towel around her shoulders grew heavier. The ruthless air conditioning made her shiver. She drew the bedspread around her, getting that wet too, mentally apologizing to the housekeepers. "What do you want me not to be mad about?"

She pulled back her emotions. "Look. I'm not going to be mad. And yes, we tell each other everything," she lied, "so please tell me whatever it is. Okay, sweetheart?"

Henry did not answer, but was motioning someone toward him. "Come on," he said. "She's not going to be mad."

"She," Tessa thought, *"she's" not going to be mad*, as if she were some alien creature or despot who was infinitely to be feared. Henry was Fun Dad, and she was the mom who would be mad at whatever it was.

Henry's laptop moved, and Linny's face filled the screen. "Hi, Mom. How are you?"

"I'm fine, darling," she said, consciously making an I'm-not-mad face. "What's up?" She frowned, remembering. "Where's Zackie?"

"Yeah, well." Linny's face was so unnaturally close to the camera it was like a fisheye lens.

"Stand back, darling, I can't see you properly," Tessa said. "You know how to FaceTime."

When the laptop moved, Linny came into focus, head and shoulders.

Tessa blinked at the camera, trying to grasp what she saw.

"'Isn't it awesome?" Linny scrabbled her fingers through her now shaggy short hair, the ends spiked up and sticking out like a perky dandelion, or a ruffled awkward duckling.

"You cut your hair?" Tessa tried to remember being eleven, tried to remember begging for pierced ears, begging for whatever kind of shoes were cool, trying to be like everyone else. But Linny had loved her long blond hair. Loved putting it in pigtails, and braids, twisting it up into a ballerina bun. It would take years to grow back. You're only eleven once, Tessa tried to tell herself, speed of light; don't be critical, you're not home. You're not with her. Be her mom.

"Awesome," she used Linny's word, hoping to sound enthusiastic. "It'll be so easy to take care of." There was more to this story. Had to be. Yesterday her hair had been in pigtails. And now, it wasn't. "Did you . . . cut it yourself?"

"No, Mom, that would be so lame. Remember Mrs. Delaney who I told you who was so cool? She said I should get a haircut like this, and she took me to her place. It's called a salon. And Dad and Zack and Tristan went to get waffles."

The entire hotel room ceiling could have crashed down, on top of her and her wet hair and her still-not-packed suitcase, and Tessa would not have cared. She had carried her darling daughter for nine months and two days, had named her Linnea, and had then been the first person in the world to see her, and had been her best friend, she hoped, for eleven years. Linny had never had a haircut, not ever, *not ever!* without Tessa there. And now cool Nellie had swooped Linny up in her talons. Usurped the very fabric of motherhood. Stolen one of the sacred moments only mothers and daughters could share.

No mother, no *real* mother, would cut another mother's daughter's hair. Nellie was a bitch, and a little too obvious. Henry was a complete idiot. And she, Tessa, had to go home. Right now.

Whoa, Annabelle said.

"So cool, honey," Tessa said. "Yay, you. I can't wait to see it in person." Nellie Delaney was now in her sights. She just wished that woman was not in Henry's sights. Or he in hers. "I wish I could have been there with you. Did Mrs. Delaney ask your father first?"

"I'm back." Henry's face appeared. "Isn't she cute? Our own pixie child."

"Pixie," Tessa repeated. "Sure, adorable." When Henry told Nellie—she could not even say that phrase—that Tessa had been sanguine about Linnea's hair, she'd know her obvious tactics were doomed to failure.

"What else is new?" Tessa asked, obviously and bluntly changing the subject. Perhaps Henry would get the message from her icy tone. "It sounds like you all are having an *awesome* time. Any other surprises about to come my way? Especially about you and Nellie? Since as you said, we tell each other everything?"

"Lin, I'll meet you outside, okay?"

Five minutes before she had to dry her hair. Ten minutes before she had to call the Uber.

"Okay." Henry's face on the screen again. "I needed to get rid of Linny so you and I could have some privacy. Nellie seems to think I'm helpless as a father. God knows what she thinks I would do if left too long on my own."

"On your own?"

"Well, yeah, me and the kids. What did you think?"

"Nothing," Tessa said, knowing that was the placeholder for "everything." "Anyway, anything else? I have like, no minutes before I have to get to the airport."

"Yeah. One thing." Henry sat down, somewhere. "It may be nothing, but remember I told you about Barbara?"

"Yeah, Barbie the dog walker?"

"She's not a dog walker."

Tessa heard the impatience in his voice.

"Exactly what she *is*, I don't know," Henry went on. "But, honey? She's still asking about you."

"About the books?" Tessa curled her bare toes into the pile of the hotel carpeting. "Did she turn out to be a fan?"

"Yeah, must be. And man, not sure how you deal with that every day. She asked where you grew up. Who were your parents. Your mother. That kind of thing. I was vague, and I didn't have much choice, since I don't know many details anyway. They were gone before you and I even met. Your mom had a heart attack and your dad—I know they weren't sure exactly why he died. While you were at college. That's what I told her."

"Yes, all true, but why would you tell her that?"

"Because she asked. And what does it matter, it's basic new-neighbor stuff. But I started thinking about it, and it seemed . . . whatever. I thought you should know."

She had been at college, and remembered the late-night phone call. And soon after, her mother's will, when it became clear everything was gone. "I mean that's ridic—"

"No. It isn't. You're the one who told me about persistent fans, right? That's why I even told you. Do you think your family is exempt from that?"

"*No one* asks *how* someone's parents died." Tessa tried to ignore Henry's possibly correct logic.

"She didn't ask how they died. She said something like, her mother must be so proud of her. Can we not talk about this?"

"No, we can't not talk about it. So proud of me? That's not a thing people say. Unless there's an agenda. Did she ask about *your* mother?"

"Tessa, you're making way too much of this. I should never have mentioned it. She's obviously a fan. I must not be used to it like you are."

"Why not tell her the whole thing?" Tessa could not resist going on. "Tell her, oh, the last thing Tessa knew of her mother was when she was awakened by a midnight phone call from the police, on the night before she was set to come home for summer vacation, informing her she'd died of a heart attack. You could explain how that left her utterly alone, since she'd discovered her estranged father had died the year before. And oh, listen, tell her how *we* met, too, soon after. Think how fascinated she'd be."

She paused, the silence after her tirade louder than the words. The air conditioner kicked on, and Tessa saw the electronic green numbers on the nightstand clock tick ahead.

"Tessa, honey," Henry finally said. "I am so sorry. I forgot it was this time of year when it happened. June. I wish you were here."

Tessa felt her heart break; at the universe, and at the distance between them, and at the incalculable whims of providence. And at Henry, whose face seemed to have collapsed in remorse, and who was doing the best he could. New neighborhood, new neighbors, new everything. And a wife who was no help to them at all.

"Mail call, mail call!" Linny's voice came from off camera, and she then bounded into the room, brandishing what looked like letters. "You've got mail, Mom! A picture postcard of . . ."

She paused, fully on camera now, her hair like a blond porcupine, turning over a card in her hand. "Phoenix. It says Welcome to Phoenix. Like one of those old-timey ones." She held it up, reading. "It says thanks for a wonderful evening."

Henry moved into the camera shot. Tessa saw him take the postcard.

"Who is Sam?" he asked.

45

Tessa sat at gate C37, her closed laptop on her lap, her head in her hands. Eyes covered, mentally replaying the frustrating FaceTime conversation she'd had with Henry an hour ago. The now-familiar airport noises swirled around her, beeping and coughing and scratchy public address announcements, crying children and pings and chimes from scattered cell phones. "Who is Sam?" he'd asked. An unanswerable question.

Tessa had told Henry all she knew, she played it back in her head, *a guy I met on an airplane*, the lamest of beginnings, but she could not rewind to put the lingering double entendre away. He was a fan, he had the book, he was reading it, she'd said. And by chance he sat down next to me.

"By chance?" Henry had said.

Tessa had not liked the expression on his face, it was unfair and judgmental, and he was the one who was hanging out with Nellie and Barbie and who knows how many other prowling and calculating women with bouncy names.

"Airline seating is assigned," Tessa had said. "You sit where the airline tells you to sit. You couldn't possibly know where anyone else is sitting."

"Unless you convince the flight attendant to change you," Henry said. "Once you *do* know."

"Well, sure, but—" Tessa hadn't considered this, not until now, but again, wrong. "I mean, my picture is on the cover of the book he was read-ing. And there I was."

"*I've* never gotten a postcard from anyone I've sat next to on a plane." Henry had cocked his head as if he had made some massive point.

Someone sat down beside her on the adjacent blue plastic seat. Tessa looked up from behind her palms, simply to reassure them that she wasn't crying or sleeping or a problem. The woman opened a newspaper, ignor-ing her.

"Nor have I," Tessa had said, "nor have I ever, until now, had a best-selling novel, or people bringing me presents, it's all new, and I have no idea what's normal. He came to my event, and bought another book. That's exactly what I, and everyone at Waverly, and Sadie Bailey, and you, too, Henry, should be hoping for."

"You gave him your address?" Henry held the postcard between thumb and forefinger, as if it were contagious. Or evidence.

"Of course not. But who knows how people find things." Tessa had hesi-tated, wondering if she should say it. "You told the bookstore where we lived, didn't you? *You're* the one who's revealing exactly where we live. Not me."

Stop, Annabelle had said. Just stop.

"Look," she'd said. "I've got to go, Henry. I love you. Okay?"

At that, Henry had merely nodded. As if he were holding back some coup de grâce remark.

"I forgot to tell you, before you go," Henry had said then, and Tessa had seen his face change, in a way that she could not describe. "We're getting a puppy."

Tessa would never forgive herself, not for this, but she had slammed down her laptop, unplugged it, stashed it into its padded sleeve, dried her hair with mythical fury, and slammed her way into the Uber.

"A *puppy*," she'd said out loud from the back seat.

"Excuse me?" the Uber driver had said.

"Nothing, sorry," she'd replied. "Talking to myself."

And now here she was in the airport, a latte cooling in the cupholder beside her, her suitcase in front of her, and no way she was going to call Henry back. A new house. Zachary out overnight. An outrageous hair-cut. And a *puppy*. And she'd been gone, how long? Three and a half weeks?

The unmistakable click of a public address system made everyone in the waiting area lift their heads, Pavlovian, like prairie dogs coming out of the ground.

"Ladies and gentlemen," the amplified voice began, and Tessa felt the atmosphere in the room deflate. Such announcements were never good news.

"This flight to Seattle is experiencing an unexplained red light in the cockpit, and our mechanics are checking it now. We expect only a brief delay, not longer than . . ." The voice paused, and everyone in the waiting area, strangers, exchanged looks of common dismay. Tessa could almost feel them calculating how much time they'd have to wait, the complications on the other end, connections and obligations and appearances and families.

Tessa did her own calculations. San Diego and Seattle were in the same time zone, and she'd arrive in plenty of time for her 7:00 p.m. event. She tried to look at these inevitable flight delays as found time, to catch up on reading, or look at her social—*oh*. Her Facebook. It'd been days since she found that locket in her hotel room. And two days since the earrings. And still no answers. Which reminded her of wig woman. And the murdered chocolates. But worrying wasn't going to help.

Worry. *They're getting a puppy*, the thought made her seethe. And certainly, *certainly*, this was the result of their newfound life-changing experience with sexy Barbie, the dog walker. Who was coming at Henry from one side with puppies, and the other side with probing questions. Tessa had to go home. Had. To. Go. Home.

It's not the dog you're upset about, Annabelle said.

"Thirty minutes," the gate agent's voice continued. "Thank you so much for your patience."

"It's not so much patience as necessity." The woman beside her with the newspaper flapped her *New York Times* to a new page. She raised an eyebrow at Tessa. "What are we supposed to do? Walk to Seattle?"

"Never a dull moment," Tessa said.

Newspaper Woman looked at her, and Tessa saw the glimmer in her eyes. Saw her, Tessa could actually watch it happen, searching the faces stored in her imagination, trying to connect who Tessa was, where she'd seen her, and why. Tessa, polite but unengaged, picked up her tote bag and her roller bag and wheeled away, purposefully, as if she had a destination in mind. Which she did not. Recognition from Newspaper Woman, or anyone, was not what she wanted right now. Exactly the opposite. She needed to be by herself, if there were any place in the airport's bustling Brownian motion to do that.

She pulled her roller bag toward the higher-numbered gates, seeing, at the end of the corridor, a wall of wide plate glass windows. Beyond that, a vast range of concrete, and beyond that, distant and layered, gentle rolling hills dotted with rooftops. She stood at the glass, one hand on her roller bag handle, seeing into the far distance, trying to clear her mind of sorrow.

And of fear? Yes. And of fear.

46

Tessa stared out the expanse of airport window, across the tarmac and into the past. Wondering if it had come back to haunt her. "The pivotal moments of our lives cannot always be recognized when they happen," Tessa would tell her audiences. "It's not until later that your personal time bombs explode, and that's when they show you their power."

On a day like today, in the same kind of summer but so long ago, the same infinite azure sky offering the same lush promises, Tessa had ignored her mother's imprecations and told Emily, her dearest, darling Emily, about the bad thing.

Tessa lost herself now, into the green of the distant hills, the bustling airport noise going muffled and indistinct. She became sixteen again. Remembering Emily.

Emily. The only other person alive who knew about Tessa's past. Sitting on that rickety wooden pier that sunny afternoon, she'd told her trusted friend about the cherry Popsicle. The five dollars. The kidnapping.

If Emily had researched it at some point later, she'd also know about the Maumee River.

That same night, Tessa's mother had gone out to one of her events, escorted by yet another "prospect," as she secretly called them. Giggling and plotting, Tessa and Emily, soul sisters, Tessa truly believed it, had taken the car her mom rented for that summer, shared illicit beer in their "forest primeval" secret place, told stories and made promises by flashlight under the endless New England sky.

But then it was time to go home. Her mother would be returning soon.

"I want to drive." Tessa remembered Emily's voice, coaxing. "Let me."

Tessa had tried to say no. "My mother would kill me."

"No one will know." Emily had been Emily, her dearest, special friend. "It's only us."

Soon after, Tessa remembered, the approaching shadow. And the sound. And Emily's cry as she slammed on the brakes.

The impact. The instant, infinite, gasping knowledge that the road in front of them had not been empty.

How they'd been terrified to look. And there had been nothing to do, *nothing*, Emily hit the gas, and the car lurched ahead, but it made a terrible noise and finally it just stopped—*what was it they'd left behind?*—and there was nothing to do in the silence except call Emily's father from the tiny phone he made her carry and tell him the truth. Lying was impossible, what was real was real, and how could they—*change* anything? They were stranded and lost and trapped and doomed.

They waited, huddled on the narrow shoulder of the deserted dirt road, both of them sobbing, in filthy yellow flip-flops and ripped jeans. Terrified of what was to come. They would be in trouble forever.

It seemed like forever later when Emily's father arrived in his black-and-white cruiser. Played his flashlight across the murky darkness behind their broken car, then consoled them. *"Don't worry,"* he'd told them. *"You hit a deer. I'm the sheriff, and I'll handle everything."* He'd comforted Emily, too, though the two girls never got to talk about it again.

Tessa remembered—did she?—the cruiser headlights glinting on his glasses. The sheriff's blue uniform shirt, silver shield pinned to the pocket, the fabric clinging to his back with sweat or fear or power. Emily had sniffled, edged closer to her.

"Girls. Listen to me. Look at me," Emily's father said. "Emily. You should *not* have been driving this car. Tessa, that was tremendously poor judgment. An extremely irresponsible decision. You've both been drinking. I'm disappointed in you."

They'd both hung their heads. They were in so much trouble. Even now, Tessa could hear the silence.

"Look at me." He'd then pointed a forefinger at Tessa, instructing. "*You* were supposed to be driving. Emily's too young. You should never have let her. You should have protected her. Drinking teenagers and a rental car. Unacceptable. Now. Listen to me. I'll take care of this. I'll call your mother. I'll handle it."

The darkness had almost swallowed her then. She'd done another bad thing, her mother would surely declare. She *should* have protected Emily. Just like she should have protected Annabelle. She'd be grounded for the rest of her life.

She deserved it.

Emily's father had crossed his beefy arms over his chest, turned his back on them, strode away to see what was in the road. He and his new wife had never liked Tessa, Emily had divulged that about her stepmother, early on. And the Owens didn't like Tessa's mother, either. Called her "summer people." Entitled. Elite. "From away," as if that were the ultimate dismissal. Emily's stepmother, nonexistent in Tessa's world and disdained in Emily's, "bought things," Emily always said.

But that night, Emily's father had taken care of them.

She had watched him put one hand on the hood of the car, his back to them. After a minute, or an eternity, he marched back and faced them. She and Emily were arm in arm, shivering in the heat, Emily still sobbing, with no words to share.

"But I need to think of your future," he'd said. "Your future families. All of it, everything you hope for, it could still happen. But only if you erase tonight from your minds. Only if you make a new story."

Tessa had heard a night bird call then, proclaiming the darkness or looking for a lost love.

"And listen to me, both of you girls need to calm down. What you hit. What you killed. It was just a deer."

Emily's tears had glistened in the cruiser's headlights, like her father's sunglasses, like his shiny badge.

"Say it," Sheriff Owen had commanded. "Say it, girls. Each of you. It was a deer."

Her own voice had vanished, her entire body numb, and she'd listened for the night bird again. But heard Emily's quavering whisper instead.

"It was a deer."

"Again."

"It was a deer."

"And now you, Tessa. And I'll assure your mother, too, when I take you home. It was a deer."

That poor, poor deer, she remembered thinking, yearning to run back on the dirt road to see the reality, knowing if she did, if she saw it, and could not comfort it or save it, the crushing weight of it would never leave her.

"It was just a deer," she whispered, too, and it felt like a column of wild flames shot orange into the vast night sky.

In silence and darkness, he'd driven them both to Tessa's rented summer house, and must have notified her mother, because she met him at the door. Tessa had watched Sheriff Owen take Mommy aside, watched her face in the half-light as he talked, watched her mother put her head in her hands as he told the story.

"I'll bring the rental car back to you tonight," he'd said. "I'll handle it. Just turn it in whenever you leave."

Before dawn the next morning, they were heading for the airport again, in their somehow shiny rental car, with Tessa crumpled into the passenger seat and her mother stiff-backed at the wheel, red-eyed, radiating fury.

"I've done everything for you, given you everything," her mother had said. "How could you fail me again?"

"She's my *friend*," Tessa had tried to explain.

"You clearly have a problem with 'friends,'" her mother said. "And with making the right decisions. It's beyond belief that you're forcing us to leave town again. We'll have to forfeit *all* the cottage rent, and I'll miss the Atkinson gala, and—I'm appalled, Tessa. What were you thinking?"

"I'm so sorry, I didn't mean to—"

"Those *people*. That ridiculous, silly *girl*." She could hear her mother's voice, a knife's edge cutting through the awakening day. "Did you tell her about . . . oh, my God, you *did*, didn't you. Have you lost your mind? *Did* you?"

Tessa had stared at the floor of the rental car, wished she could fall through to the pavement below and be crushed and destroyed and gone, just like that poor deer.

"Don't lie to me, young lady." Her mother had not even let her answer. "You will never speak to her again. You will never contact her again. Ever. She can utterly, irrevocably, completely, ruin your life."

Now, somewhere in the far distance of the airport concourse, they were calling her plane.

47

Until she looked, until she faced it, it would haunt her. The cursor on her open laptop blinked at her, almost daring her to search again, as she sat cross-legged on the black-and-gray striped duvet on yet another king-sized bed.

Safely landed, and now in yet another hotel room, this one in Seattle, with wisps of fog out over the water, bleak and gorgeous at the same time.

Now she had to take control.

The cursor beckoned. She settled her shoulders against the head-board. Time to turn a page in her life.

Hundreds of people would applaud her tonight, but right now, she felt entirely alone. She peered out the hotel window into the gray nothing.

She typed in the words without looking at the keyboard. *Annabelle Browning. Warrenton Ohio.*

The past was not controllable, that was the dilemma. The past had its own agenda. And what was unleashed when you started to poke at it might not always be what you hoped.

But it still exists.

Okay, she thought, feeling like Pandora. *Do it.*

She hit Enter.

All the old stories came up, she'd seen them before, of course, some blurry photos of their local newspaper's front page. She knew her name had never been mentioned—the press had called them "juveniles." It was still breathtakingly tragic. Embarrassing. Humiliating. But there was nothing new. Nothing recent.

She added her real name to the search. *Theresa Savannah Mattigan.*

Nothing additional. She tried it with Tessa Danforth. Nothing.

One more try. She'd searched before the book came out, fearful and doom-plagued, but there'd been no results. What if something had changed?

Annabelle Browning. Warrenton Ohio. Tessa Calloway.

She held her breath. And clicked.

No search results match your selection, the screen reported. *See results without Tessa Calloway?*

Her phone pinged; the sound so unexpected, so in the present, that it made Tessa flinch.

Henry is asking for FaceTime, her phone screen announced.

She hit Accept, closed her laptop, turned off her memories. Henry would apologize. She'd let him.

"Hey, Hen." She saw the still-yellow kitchen walls surrounding him, the fridge behind him. "What's new?" She paused, congenial. "I almost hesitate to ask. Is Zack home? Is Linny—"

"All good, honey," Henry cut her off. "Where are you?"

Tessa blew out a breath, looking out her cottony window. He had her calendar on the fridge, why didn't he just look? "Seattle. My event's in four hours, so I'm . . ." She paused, then lied. "Working on the new book."

"You're a machine," Henry said. "What's it about?"

"Oh, too boring to tell." Tessa saw a shadow in the background, a movement. She refused to ask about a dog. If there was a dog, Henry would have to own up to it. "Are the kids with you?"

"Uh, no, they're in their rooms, doing whatever they do. Why?"

Zack is home, she thought. *Thanks for telling me.* "I thought I saw . . . someone."

"It's the afternoon shadows." Henry looked both ways. "The ocean light here is different. So, Tessie?"

Tessie. Did he have any idea how revealing a tell that was? That nickname meant he wanted something; she'd learned that early on. Here came the puppy, she bet. "What's up?"

"Um . . ."

"But first let me ask—did Zack have fun at what's-her-name's?"

"Nellie? Yeah, well, that's what I wanted to discuss."

"Discuss?" Tessa uncurled her legs, and propped a pillow behind her on the white wicker headboard.

"Stop moving the phone, you're making me dizzy," Henry said.

"Discuss?" Tessa said again. She swore there was movement, someone was there, in that house, and it wasn't the afternoon light.

"So Zack had a great time, two nights, and now he's home and he and Tris are upstairs bonding over Magic cards. I know you were worried about them making friends in a new place, and so far, so good." Henry nodded. "Nellie says she's psyched about it, too. Apparently—"

"Nellie."

"Yes," Henry went on, not reacting to the emotion iceberged under her statement. "And she's wondering—"

"Is Mr. Nellie home yet?"

"Huh? Uh, no, he's out of town, something like that." Henry tilted his head, seemed to be considering. "Is there something ominous about that? I mean—*you're* out of town."

Tessa blinked at the fog, trying to picture their new house, and their new neighborhood, and Linny's chopped-off hair.

"How long have Nellie and her out-of-town husband lived in the house next door to you? To us, I mean."

"Well, uh, I guess, years? I don't know. Anyway. She was worried about Tris making friends and here we were. She says—sometimes things just work."

"Sounds like you two are getting along." Tessa didn't mean to sound accusatory, though she could hear it in her own voice. Her family *should* be making friends, and neighbors should be neighborly, and if she were home and not exhausted and not in an emotional limbo trapped in a hotel room and waiting for showtime, she would be friends with the fabulous Nellie, too.

"Anyway, Hen." She'd change the subject. But not to the imminent dog. "What's up?"

"Like I was trying to say." Henry made a face. "Since the two boys hit it off so well, Nellie was wondering about Zack coming with them to their summer place."

"Their summer place?" She hadn't turned on the television, and stared now at the flat black rectangle across from her, picturing a summer place.

"Yeah. Is that an alien concept?"

"Hey. It's a reasonable question. Why are you acting all mad?"

"I'm not acting all mad. You're acting all mad. It's only for a week. Or two. Zack is incredibly hot for it, and really, Tessa, why not?"

Tessa chewed her lip, thinking of all the dozens and hundreds of reasons why not. Her author imagination could concoct more horrifying and gruesome stories than were probably rational in the real world, but all you needed was one bad thing. One decision with an unintended consequence. And everyone's lives could be ruined.

That she was not making up.

"We can go into 'why not' in infinite detail, if you like, Henry, but I don't think you do. So let's go on. Where is this summer place?"

"Well, that's why I called," Henry said. "Funniest thing. Barbara, you remember Barbara?"

"Barbie the dog walker. How well I remember." *She seems more interested in you than me*, Henry had told her.

"She's not a dog walker." Henry did not even attempt to hide his eye roll. "Anyway, she was there when we were discussing it."

"Sounds cozy, all of you chatting. About me. Is the dog walker going, too? To the summer place? It must be gigantic."

"Do you have low blood sugar again?"

"No, I do not have low blood sugar." Tessa had to concentrate to keep her voice even. The computer search had unnerved her, and she was taking it out on Henry. "I just feel far away from you, sweetheart," she said, conciliatory. "So yes, tell me about not-a-dog-walker Barbie and Nellie and the summer place." *Cannot wait*, she didn't say.

Henry paused, and stared into the lens at her, as if trying to decide whether to escalate the battle from three thousand miles away.

"Great," he finally said. "Anyway. Nellie's house is in Maine. And—"

"Maine."

"Yes, and so she wondered if you'd heard of a town nearby. A place called Blyton?"

The fog outside threatened to seep its smoky tendrils through the windowpane and entwine them around Tessa's entire body. Choke her with their grayness. Cloud her eyes and dull her into oblivion.

"Blyton? Are you saying—do you mean Blytheton?"

"Exactly." Henry nodded. "That must be it, so she was right, you *do* know it. Blytheton. Blytheton, Maine."

48

It was all Tessa could do not to hang up. But this day had taught her, profoundly, that hiding the truth did not make it go away.

The question was now whether to lie about it. Why would it matter if she knew Blytheton? She'd been there two summers, then made the dumb teenage decision to let Emily drive her mother's rental, and her mom refused to go back the next year. *Too embarrassing.* Mother had dismissed it, imperious. *You ruined everything.* But that was, what, twenty years ago? Why was a neighbor—Nellie? Or Barbara?—asking about Blytheton?

"Are you listening to me?" Henry was saying.

"Oh, absolutely, honey." Tessa looked at her watch, in mock surprise. "Oh, wow, I have to get ready."

"Isn't your event tonight?"

"Exactly." He could know that from the schedule. "I have to, um, talk to Sadie Bailey, and check in with DJ, and connect with the bookstore, all kinds of things. And you're right about low blood sugar . . ." She was babbling, but did not want to talk about Maine. It was so much to explain. "I need to get food. Can we talk about this tomorrow?"

"Well—"

"Safe safe, love love," she said, hurriedly invoking a short version of their nighttime mantra. She had to get off the phone.

"Always always." Henry shook his head. "Strange to say that so early."

"And it's even earlier here. But doesn't matter," Tessa said. "It's the principle."

"You're so funny," Henry said. "We miss you around here."

"Do you?" She truly wondered about that. "This is all worth it, though. Isn't it?"

Now there definitely was a shadow. And unless Henry turned the laptop to show her, there was absolutely no way she could prove it.

"Someone just came in." Tessa made it a statement rather than a question.

Henry glanced to his right. The same direction Tessa had seen the shadow. "Nope. Just me. We'll talk tomorrow then?"

"Sure."

"What's wrong now?"

"Huh?" Tessa feigned bafflement. "I said sure. Sure means okay, talk to you tomorrow. Everything doesn't have to mean something else."

"Sure," Henry said. "Bring home the bacon."

Trying to forget the miles between them. Tessa blew a kiss into the screen. And Henry pretended to catch it.

But as her husband flapped his laptop closed, her last glimpse was a slash of yellow. And a shadow.

Tessa swung her legs off the side of the bed. "There was no shadow, this is all a coincidence, you are making stuff up," Tessa said out loud. She waggled her shoulders, shaking it off. "Get food. Take a shower. Take a nap. Get your life together."

She guessed what button on the remote would turn the television on, and for background noise and video companionship, clicked to the all-news channel. Familiar-looking lipsticked and coiffed faces split-screened with muted video of a far-off war playing behind them brought her back to the troubles of the real world, far more serious than her own long-ago past.

There was a split-screen world of book tour, too; half of it gut-wrenching, high-speed activity, the other half suspended animation.

A ping on her messages. Puget Sound Books, the caller ID said. Ethan Cornish.

Got time for a call? Abt tonight?

So nice of him to check in on her.

> Sure. All okay?

Ethan's reply was the ringing phone.

A billion terrible things sprang to mind in the span of that one ring. No books had arrived, no one had registered to attend her event, the store was flooded, there was about to be a massive storm. She checked out the window; saw the fog had cleared, halfway, and the sky did not look ominous.

"Hi," she said, trying not to sound worried. "Is—?"

"Making sure you've arrived, and settled in, with no complications."

"Yes, I—"

"So listen. About tonight."

Tessa's heart plummeted. That was a real thing, not a figure of speech, she physically felt it happen. "Is everything okay?"

Ethan was silent for an excruciating second. "Why wouldn't it be?"

There were way too many answers for that, but Tessa simply agreed. "True," she said. "What's the plan?"

"Well, okay. We solicit questions in advance, online, before the audience arrives. I know you're fabulous, but sometimes authors aren't. So we always have Q and A only. I ask, and give the name of the questioner, you answer. You on board with that?"

"Sure," Tessa said, making sure she sounded like she was telling the truth.

"Again, it's not you. It's our audience," Ethan went on. "If we let the audience play a bigger role, then they feel invested."

"Okay, got it." It would be a treat not to give her speech, she'd done it so many times. "So I'll see you at about—"

"Anyway," Ethan interrupted. "We were organizing the questions, and they're . . . they're unusual."

"Unusual?"

"Yeah. We have"—he paused—"seventeen inquiries about where you spent summers as a child."

Tessa could hear a sound, a high-pitched sound of nothing, the electricity in her room, or the mechanics of the air conditioner, or the constant transmissions of the universe.

"Did you," Ethan was saying, "put something on social media about that? To elicit the question?"

"Nope, not at all," she said, her keeping her voice bright and intrigued. "I don't think I've ever mentioned summers on social."

"Huh," Ethan said.

"It's hardly sinister, though," she lied. What connected Maine to Ohio? Emily. Only Emily. That she knew of. "It's summer now, and a pretty relatable thing."

"I suppose."

"Are they all from the same person?" She scrambled for an additional explanation. "Maybe someone hit Enter too many times."

"Good point, and we aren't able to track that. So could be. There's a place to enter a name, but they were blank."

"So funny." She'd ease Ethan's mind about this. Erase it. "Okay, thanks for prepping me. I'm not worried."

"We are. Kind of." Ethan's voice had hardened.

"You are what?" She realized what he meant. "Worried? You're worried?"

Again, a beat of silence. "We don't want any trouble, Tessa. If there's a disruption in the works, you need to tell us. I can call your publicist in New York, see if they've heard anything. But—"

"No, no," Tessa interrupted, watching the dumpster fire of her life combust into roaring flame. "I agree it's odd, but I can't imagine. . . ."

Even as she spoke, she felt the doom clouds gathering. No one wanted an author who was a problem, no matter how many books she sold.

"This summer vacation thing doesn't seem random," Ethan said. "We've done this countless times, and this is new. I know fans can get— squirrelly. And we're afraid that might be happening now."

49

Squirrelly. Tessa sat on the edge of the bed. Grounded herself. She needed to handle this. "Oh, Ethan, I don't think—" she began.

"Look, Tessa," Ethan talked over her. "We have a couple of hours before the event. It's sold out. Everyone bought their books in advance, and will get them when they arrive. And they are expecting to see you. If you don't show up, we'll lose all those sales. But—"

"Okay. Summer vacation. We went to the beach, in Chatham," Tessa interrupted. This was sheer fabrication; Tessa had known someone in high school whose family went there. But she was not going to reveal any more of her personal life or past, no matter what they asked. Not one bit more. "Maybe it's someone who was there, too. And wants to reconnect. Golly, I have no idea who, but you never know what people remember." *Golly?* she thought. *I am totally losing it.*

"So you're not concerned?"

"Not at all." Tessa kept her voice as light as the fog, as if Ethan's concerns would vanish with the next ray of sun. Her career depended on this. Her livelihood. Her family. Her future. "But I bet it's a mistake, and they're all from the same person. Seriously, Ethan, sorry for giving you pause."

Silence again. She could almost hear Ethan calculating book sale profits versus potential losses, bad publicity, video clips on Insta, how many books of hers they'd have to return if they had to cancel. How to explain it to the readers who would be disappointed and blame the store and blame Tessa and spread their venom on social media. Tessa was unreliable. Inauthentic. A selfish bitch. *We hate her.*

"Chatham?"

"Yup." She had one fact, at least. "Cape Cod."

When Ethan didn't answer, she decided to push. "I mean, this seems pretty benign."

"I suppose," Ethan said. "But it's a new one."

"First time for everything, right? Just ask the debut author."

"Okay, look. We can't cancel." Ethan's voice had an edge to it. "I simply won't ask that question. We'll go from there."

"Perfect." Tessa closed her eyes. That might work. "People know I'm not big on personal stuff. See you soon, okay?"

"It's a full house, Tessa. We're counting on you."

Tessa tried to ignore the almost-threat. "Can't wait."

She'd already started a new online search as she hung up. Some article she'd seen said all a reader needed was three telling details to make a description sound authentic. She found the listing for Chatham, and tucked away enough facts to fake familiarity about a place her family had never been. There was no one alive who could refute *that* story.

Now there was no time to do anything but take a shower, get dressed, go to the bookstore, and, essentially, pray.

It was all too clear that someone was digging into her past. Someone close to her. Someone knowledgeable. Someone malevolent. Because her name was not online in connection with the bad thing, no casual search would find it. What made it more disturbing: tonight's questions were about a different part of her past. Her summer vacations.

Although they were called Danforth then, any number of people could know they'd been in Maine. Not just Emily. Her father the sheriff. Her stepmother. And the ice-cream store lady and the rental car place and the lifeguard at the lake and the librarian and who knows who else. But so what? Was the deer preservation society on her trail?

She put one hand on the top edge of her laptop, ready to close it, then couldn't stand it. She sat on the bed again, typed *Emily Owen, Blytheton Maine.*

Images.

Deep breath.

Enter.

A banker. A meteorologist. A soprano. She scanned the photos. Some were too old, others too young, no one the right age, not even close. It might simply mean she wasn't very public. Or she was dead. Or she'd gotten married and changed her name, in which case Tessa was doomed. And this search was doomed. And Tessa was, too.

And way too soon, there was no stopping it, Tessa would be in another Uber, headed to yet another bookstore, with her future as unpredictable as the weather outside.

Good simile, Annabelle said.

"This is *your* fault," Tessa snapped. Then covered her face with both hands. "Get a grip, Tessa," she whispered.

50

Tessa looked out over the audience of smilingly attentive faces. Blue earrings dotted the room like so many holiday decorations. Row after row of women, each holding that periwinkle book, elbow to elbow in matching silver folding chairs. A few days ago, Tessa would have focused on engaging her fans, meeting them, talking with them, signing their books.

Now, standing behind a weathered wood podium that matched the facade of the bookstore building, Tessa scanned for a false expression, a frowning face, a woman in a wig. She remembered Dorrit in San Diego, holding up that bobbed gray hairpiece like some sort of dead creature, and how Tessa had searched every face in her social media photographs to find who had been wearing it. How she'd failed. Every moment of tonight's book event was Where's Waldo again, this time with Waldo out to ruin her.

Her first move tonight, after her warm greeting, had been to take the "class photo" of the group—ostensibly, and truly, for her memories and her social media, but now it was even more important to get a picture of the audience. For evidence. Would she need it?

"Smile," she'd said. "Hold up the books—but don't block your faces, okay? You're the important ones."

Even with her ulterior motives, it still touched her, the smiles and the raised periwinkle rectangles. But this time there might be someone in this audience who was poised to harm her.

Now all eyes were on Ethan as he pulled another question from a crystal container embellished with hand-painted tropical fish. The Fishbowl, he'd called it, and everyone had laughed. Apparently this crowd was familiar with the Q and A routine. Tessa knew he'd trashed the vacation questions.

"This is from Nakato from Phinney Ridge. Are you here, Nakato?"

A woman in a black Nirvana T-shirt and ripped jeans stood, front row center. Blue earrings, Tessa noted.

"Nakato wants to know when Annabelle first came to you."

Tessa's heart dropped. Did she—*no*, Tessa assured herself. This was innocent. Logical. Expected. "Well, I wish I could remember. I'm sure it was before I began writing. Since she gave me the idea for the book, of course."

The audience murmured, knowing the story.

"Does she still talk to you?" Ethan asked the follow-up.

This needed to be over with. She needed to get back to the hotel, escape to another town.

Won't matter, Annabelle said. *It'll be the same wherever we go.*

"She sure does," Tessa said. "I rely on it. I'm sure you've heard from other authors who say their characters talk to them. It's a gift, isn't it?"

A soft ping from under the podium—she'd stashed her handbag there, phone in an outside pocket. It pinged again, the VIP tone.

She calculated, lightspeed, as Ethan made a show of mixing up the secretly curated questions, dramatically choosing the next, reading it out loud.

"Why don't you do your weekly live broadcasts anymore? I loved them."

It was 8:00 p.m. in Seattle, 11:00 p.m. in Rockport. And in New York. The ping could only be her agent, her editor, her publicist, or her family. Every one of them would know she was onstage. But tonight had started on shaky ground, and this event was almost over. Tessa could not risk Ethan's ire. Whoever it was would have to wait.

"Well, I promise to go back to them. And I'm so touched that you miss them. But I had to focus on writing, you know? And now I get to see you in person."

Ethan pulled the next slip of paper. "Dakota wants to know if you found Locket Mom. Or who sent the earrings."

"No, perplexingly." Tessa had posted that locket with such joy. So much for that idea. "I'm beginning to think—well, I'm not sure what to think. But who knows what'll happen."

Her cell phone pinged again. The last time this had happened, it was Henry, who'd forgotten she was at an event. *Go away*, she thought. *Be nothing.*

Question after question then, softballs. Process, dreams, her viral corporate exit. Nothing with subtext, nothing unsettling.

Except—someone in the audience was waiting to hear a question that would not be asked.

"One more, then Tessa will sign, okay?" Ethan finally said. "Marielle from Seattle asks—Marielle?"

A woman in the middle of the room raised her hand, fluttering her beringed fingers.

"Marielle wonders—do you have a dog?" Ethan asked.

A dog, Tessa thought.

"So funny." Either the most benign question in the world, or the scariest. How would someone know about the dog? She risked telling the truth. "My family's threatening to get one while I'm on tour. Can you believe it?"

Her phone remained silent while she said thank you, silent while the audience applauded, silent while Ethan escorted her through her rows of clamoring fans, some of them reaching out to touch her, one handing her a bag of macaroons, which Ethan took away. If she were in an airplane, or somewhere else inaccessible, whoever was messaging her could handle whatever it was until they could talk to her. Tessa could not control everything.

That's for sure, Annabelle said.

Ethan stood sentry next to her at the signing table, while his assistant Tara Gordon made yellow name stickies, managed the line, took photos with readers' phones. Tessa's own phone had not pinged again. Whoever it was must have figured it out on their own. Done and done.

As the line diminished, Tessa's apprehensiveness diminished, too. This had all been for nothing, their worry and their speculation. Her fragile world, her entire future, depended on what someone else did; her publisher. Her family. Her fans. Her enemies?

"Handle this for a sec, Tara, can you?" Ethan was saying. "I need another pile of books."

Tessa managed to say goodbye to an effusive customer, then welcomed the next one. Fortysomething, Tessa calculated; heavy tortoiseshell glasses and wearing too much eyeliner over hollow, weary eyes. No earrings. Blond hair so glossily perfect . . . it *might* be a wig. Tessa had a flash of fear, but there were so many reasons for wigs these days.

"Oh, there's no sticky." Tessa said. "Who should I sign it to?"

"No names. Just sign it, please." The woman had leaned closer, so close Tessa could smell the cloying fragrance of roses. "I saw what you all did." She'd lowered her voice. "Avoided my question."

"Your question?"

Tessa wrote the date, as slowly as she could. Indicating exactly when Tessa and this woman had been together. Where was Ethan? He was supposed to stay with her.

"Would you like a photo, ma'am?" Tara was holding out her hand for a phone.

"No. Thanks." The woman waved the assistant away.

"You sure?" Tessa persisted. Evidence. "I'd love to. We can use my phone."

"No pictures," the woman went on. "I mean, where your family spent your summer vacations, why would anyone avoid that question?" Her voice stayed excruciatingly, quietly, pleasantly, polite. "Unless there were some very, *very* good reasons."

Ethan had returned, a stack of periwinkle in his arms, his forehead creased with concern. He must have heard the last of what the woman said.

Tessa saw him shift professional gears, could almost see him conjuring some devastating bookstore disruption, then watched as he turned on the full-wattage charm. He put the books in front of Tessa, almost a barrier.

"Thank you so much for coming, ma'am." He stood at Tessa's shoulder, a smiling but wary guard dog. "Hope you enjoyed it."

"More than you can imagine," the woman said.

Three more women waited in the line behind her, one pretending to read her book, the other two whispering behind their hands. Probably curious about what was going on.

They weren't the only ones.

Tessa stood, put her palms on her stack of books, and faced the woman head-on. The woman looked back at her, unflinching. Lifted her chin.

Tessa was too tired, too worried, too everything. She scanned the woman's cheekbones, her eyebrows, those tired eyes behind her thick-framed glasses.

"Wait," she whispered. "Emily?"

51

But no, not Emily, it couldn't be, there was barely a resemblance, now that Tessa looked again—but the woman had locked eyes with her, with a glare of victory or confusion, Tessa never got time to decide. The woman swooped up her signed book, whirled, and trotted away, vanishing behind a stand of bookshelves.

Ethan turned his back on the three women still waiting in line. Looked at Tessa, questioning.

"Was *that* who this was all about?" He'd lowered his voice. "Are you telling me you know who that was? I heard something about summer vacation."

The disappointment in his eyes broke Tessa's heart, but it was impossible to explain. Ethan would think she'd been lying to him. Or know she had.

"Oh, well," she hurried to reassure him. "It's exactly what I predicted, our summer vacations. In Chatham," she amended. "She told me she thought she knew me, but wasn't sure, she'd been there, too, once, gosh, we were all kids . . ." Tessa knew she was talking too quickly, and sounded as guilty as she felt. "Haven't thought about those days in years."

Cut your losses, Annabelle told her. Right now.

"That was funny, wasn't it though?" Tessa changed her tone entirely, now amused and tolerant. She saw Ethan look toward the front door, saw that he was watching the woman—not Emily, definitely not Emily—walk out of the store. "I guess she *did* hit Enter too many times. Technical difficulties. But nothing sinister."

Ethan's shoulders rose, then fell, and she wondered if he was counting his blessings that the event had not imploded.

"So did she? Know you?"

Tessa shrugged. "She never said. Could be she was embarrassed, that's why she left. Who can ever tell about people."

"Huh," Ethan said.

Three women were still waiting for a signature, one of them now eyeing Tessa with concern.

"You're so patient." Tessa stepped closer to the trio, conspiratorial. "Turns out that person thought I was someone she knew from a million years ago. You never know who you'll meet on book tour."

"*Did* she know you?" one asked.

"Did you know *her*?"

"Nope," Tessa said. "Mistaken identity. Now. Who needs a book signed?"

"We *all* feel we know you." The first woman's periwinkle earrings matched the blue cardigan tied around her shoulders. "And don't worry. We would wait any amount of time for you."

Tessa could feel Ethan's demeanor relax, though their relationship would never be the same. But that summer-vacation questioner was still out there. Getting bolder. Tessa had no idea who she was. And she was baffled about her motives.

Because—why not cut to the chase, and ask about Ohio? She thought about what such a thing would mean in a novel. Maybe this was, like, setting the trap. Maybe "summer vacation" was the prologue, building up to the real story.

This is real life, Annabelle said. *Not fiction.*

When the last customer had gone, Ethan, now polite but aloof, walked her to the front door.

"We sold two hundred and three books," he said. "That's a store record."

"More than Harry Potter?" Tessa asked, relieved that he'd warmed to her again.

"Different crowd," Ethan said. "Long ago."

He held the front door, and they walked onto the wide sidewalk, the Seattle evening damply gothic, clouds snagging the moon and scudding by.

"That's probably your Uber," he said, pointing. "Look, Tessa, tonight was a success. But if something's going on with you, the best thing to do is face it. Book tour can be a lonely place, and I've seen it break some authors. The pressure, and the exhaustion. New York always on the phone. The world unpredictable and readers terrifyingly fickle."

"Thank you," Tessa said. "You're right about the loneliness. Even surrounded by people, even fans, you realize everyone is a stranger. I appreciate your concern. And truly, nothing is wrong."

Headlights flared to her left, and Tessa checked her phone, confirming the license plate. "That's me." She showed the phone screen. "Thank you for a terrific time. And your insight. I hope you'll invite me back."

Ethan lifted a hand in farewell. "Safe travels," he said.

Lucky you, Annabelle said. *That was a close one.*

Tessa scanned the sidewalks as the Uber pulled away, looking for a blond woman in a maybe-wig, in a doorway, in an alley, in a parked car. She turned once, twice, to see if they were being followed. Should she text DJ? Or call Sadie Bailey? Certainly not at this hour. And what could she say, anyway?

Her phone. No one had VIP-texted her again, she realized as she grabbed it from her bag. Which was good news, she hoped, meaning whoever it was had worked it out.

She clicked it on. *Zack?* Zack had texted? From his laptop.

> Need help.

Her heart raced, and a twist of guilt tightened in her chest.

> The new dishwasher is overfloing, like on the floor.
> Dad not home. I don't no what to do.

Ten p.m. now in Seattle, which meant one o'clock in Rockport. One in the morning. Need help? The dishwasher? Where was Henry? He'd left them *alone?*

Tessa tapped frantically at her phone, heart on fire, as the Uber turned a corner. Zack's message had pinged in at nine thirty Seattle time, twelve thirty in Rockport.

She pictured him sitting in a flooded kitchen with his laptop, with his father gone—gone? gone where? at that time of night?—waiting for her to call. He'd left them alone.

"Stupid, stupid, *stupid*," Tessa said out loud. *"Idiot."*

"Talking to me?" the Uber driver asked.

"Sorry, no," she said. "Sorry." She was losing it. The bookstore woman had unnerved her, and now this thing from Zack. The dishwasher. And her absent husband.

Her emotional upheaval had hit earthquake level. And her personal Richter scale was off the charts.

52

The lights of Seattle flashed by, a misty blur of color and neon design, but Tessa saw it only from her peripheral vision. Strapped into the back seat of the Uber, she focused on her phone screen, tapping as fast as she could.

She almost collapsed with relief when Zack's face appeared on the FaceTime screen. He wore his favorite Dungeonmaster T-shirt, his version of a security blanket, and his wire-rimmed glasses sat crooked on his nose. He was tired, she could tell, and his anxiety emanated from the laptop screen as if it had pixels of its own.

But he wasn't hurt or kidnapped or dead.

"Are you okay, honey? I'm so sorry I didn't answer your text, but I couldn't. And I figured if anything was wrong at home, your father would—where is he, honey, is he home now?" She tried to keep her voice even. No reason to scare him even more. "Did he tell you he was . . . going out? Are you two alone? Where's Linny?"

She had no idea how to phrase these questions, this was new territory, and angry and concerned as she was, she did not want to telegraph that to her son.

"I'm okay," he said. "The kitchen floor is kind of screwed up. Sorry, Mom. I just, like, turned it off and I put towels."

"And you're fine? And Linny? She's fine? I don't care about the dishwasher, we can get that fixed. You did exactly the right thing."

"Okay. It was scary though, it made a noise."

"They'll do that." The hotel was nearby, but she had a few minutes. "Sounds like you handled it beautifully. Thank you."

"It's okay, now, I think, But I didn't break it, I promise."

"Oh, honey, I know. So, your dad, sweetheart. Ah, is he okay, too?" Tessa tried to tamp down her rage, her blazing anger that her husband would leave their two children alone at this hour of the night. Or any time. He knew how she felt about that. *Never leave the kids alone*, how many times had she said that? The only conceivable explanation was that something was wrong.

"He said he had to go out, and that we should go to sleep, and he would come make sure we were okay. And so we did. Linny was asleep, I guess, but I was kind of reading, and that's when I heard the clunk, and I had to come downstairs and see what it was. Luckily, Mom, because it was totally gushing."

"Out? Where? Did you call your dad? Or text?"

"I did, but no answer. He might have it on silent."

Tessa's entire head exploded, so violently that she was surprised Zack didn't notice. If he weren't already dead, *she* would kill him. *Kill* Henry. What a total idiot. She took a deep breath. Zack did not need to see her upset. He needed reassurance.

"Well, you fixed it, you're the best, and we can FaceTime till your dad gets home, okay? Hang on, let me get out of the car. Look. Here's my hotel, I'm in Seattle. How many miles away do you think that is?"

"Mom, I'm not a little kid. I'm fine."

"I know sweetheart, but here, look." She turned the phone, and showed him the glittering façade of the hotel, water fountains reaching two stories, illuminated by dancing lights in shades of red and purple. "Isn't that cool? I only get to stay in these places for one night at a time. I'll show you the inside now. Ready for the cool lobby?"

"I don't need to see the hotel, Mom," Zack said. "I'm really, really tired, can I just leave the FaceTime on and go to sleep?"

"Sure, honey." Poor little kid, just trying to be good. "Listen, one more thing, though." She paused, calculating how to get her son to rat out his own father. "Who picked the yellow color for the kitchen? It's so pretty," she lied.

"The kitchen?" Zack blinked at her, obviously trying to stay awake. "Oh, I guess Mrs. Delaney, she does stuff like that. I guess. She came over to help paint, too. We all helped. Even Tris."

"Mrs. Delaney. How nice." Tessa imagined her own Pinocchio nose extending to infinity. "And did you get a dog yet? Was Barbara—what's her last name, anyway, do you know?—working on that?" She paused. Zackie was exhausted. "Honey? Do you have any idea where your father is? And when he's coming back?"

Zack pushed his glasses back up on his nose, a gesture so familiar it almost broke Tessa's heart. She was talking to her nine-year-old, in the middle of the night, three thousand miles away, on freaking FaceTime, and the fancy Swedish dishwasher was already broken and their new kitchen flooded and her husband was "out."

"If Dad tells me not to tell you something, do I have to tell you? Like if Dad says it's a secret, is it a secret from you, too?"

53

Kill me now, Tessa thought, *this is the bargain coming due*. Giving up motherhood for money. That's all it was, flat out, giving up motherhood and wifehood and family and home, whatever those things meant now, for fame and money. Tessa nodded at the uniformed hotel doorman and pushed through the glass revolving doors, trying to make them go faster, but they had turned to molasses.

And your own dreams? Annabelle asked. How about that? Doesn't that count? How is this your fault, and not Henry's fault?

He'd left the kids alone. They had never done that. Not ever. Even when both of them had jobs, they'd had sitters. A big chunk of Tessa's salary, to her frustration, had gone to that.

"Did your dad tell you specifically not to tell me something?" Tessa began, carefully. "Or are you talking theoretically? Like—*if* that ever happened."

"I know what theoretically means, Mom."

The glare of the hotel lobby and some supposedly inviting fragrance hit her, dark blue leather benches snaked across black-and-white marble floors, and in the center, a circular bar of black leather and burnished steel displayed racks of glittering bottles.

"I know you do, honey. So are you asking me theoretically? Your dad and I know the same things, we have no secrets from each other." She lied outrageously now, but needed to reassure her son. From three thousand miles away. "If it's a good thing, like a surprise birthday party, or something you'd think I'd be happy about, or even a present your father is getting for me that he wants to be a special treat, then"—she paused, warming to her own argument—"well, secrets can be good things. But if it's something scary, or bad, or that someone is trying to hide, for a bad reason? Zackie, are you awake?"

She'd watched his eyes flutter, it was way too late for him, and here she was making up parental guidelines. "Honey?" He had his head on his Minecraft pillow, and had put the laptop next to him in bed. She only saw half of his face, but that was enough. "Are you awake?"

"I'm awake, Mom, I'm awake. So if it's a good thing I don't tell you, if it's a bad thing I tell you?"

Kids needed rules, and Zack had just created one, and she wasn't sure if her son's rule about secrets was even true.

"If it scares you, you tell me," Tessa said, deciding as she did. "Or if it worries you." She hoped this was right. How was she supposed to know? If she'd been home, none of this would have happened. Whatever it was.

"And then you won't tell him I told you? You promise?"

This was dangerous territory, Tessa knew it. "If it's scary or bad, honey, you can tell me. I promise. Your father and I will work it out. But our goal is to make sure you're safe and secure. We love you, honey. You can tell us anything."

But she could see Zack was asleep now, eyelashes against the pillow, and she had no idea if he'd heard one word she'd said. She could not bear to wake him up to grill him about secrets.

But now she knew there were secrets.

"Ms. Calloway?"

She heard her name, coming from behind her as she crossed the lobby, headed for the elevator bank, heels clacking on the marble floor. She stopped, turned, inquisitive. An elegant woman, in a sprayed chignon and sensible flats, wore the severe dark uniform of the hotel's desk clerks. Her name tag said Min Liao.

"I was going to leave a message on your phone, but I saw you walking across the lobby." The woman paused, took a breath. "I'm such a fan,

Ms. Calloway. I wish I could have gone to the bookstore tonight. But . . . anyway, there's a message for you." She handed Tessa a sealed white envelope, blank except for the embossed return address of the hotel.

"Thank you." Tessa held up her phone. "I'm on FaceTime with my son, but he's sleeping."

"That's so adorable," the woman whispered now, held a palm to her chest as if to keep her emotions inside. "You are such a good mom. How do you do it?"

"Oh dear," Tessa said, glancing at her phone screen. Zack was still asleep, eyes closed, motionless. "We do the best we can, all of us, don't we?" She smiled in solidarity. "I'm sorry you had to work tonight, and thank you for giving me the message. And for your kind words. I wish I had a signed book for you."

"That's so sweet of you. And—Ms. Calloway? You're exactly like I thought you would be."

"Aw. And it's Tessa." Tessa checked the phone screen again. Out like a light. Then she held up the hotel envelope, heart pounding, trying to stay calm. At least, to appear so. She needed to open this. "May I ask, did someone drop off this message? And you put it in the envelope? Or . . ."

"She asked for the envelope. She sealed it." A flare of concern crossed Min's face. "Oh. Is there a problem?"

"Oh dear, no. No." Tessa waved off her concern. "I get notes all the time. I'm sure you understand. But tonight I had a friend who was going to meet me . . ." Tessa stopped. "About my height? My age? Chopped-off hair like this?" She gestured, demonstrating. "Blond? Perfect hair?" Tessa tried to appear as if she were reminiscing. "She always had perfect hair."

"I'm sorry," Min said. "It could be, I guess, but I was kind of hurrying. I'm so sorry. I hope it doesn't matter?"

"Not at all. Don't give it another thought."

"Mom?" The reedy voice came from the phone.

Min clasped her hands to her chest again. "So sweet," she whispered, and fluttered a wave goodbye as she backed away.

"I'm here, honey." The note could wait. It had to.

"I was resting my eyes."

"I saw that," Tessa said.

"It's supposed to be a secret, Mom," Zack said. "But if I tell you, then can I go to Maine with Tris and his mom? I really want to, Mom, I really do. And I saved the kitchen, didn't I?"

"This is not a negotiation, Zackie." This whole thing was out of hand, was what it was, but at least she knew there *was* a secret. And she did not need to pressure Zack to tell her. Not right now at least.

Tessa pushed the up button on the elevator. "So, does Tris have a dad? Have you met him?"

"He's out of town, Tris says. He's like always gone out of town. Tris doesn't care. He says it's easier to get stuff from his mom when his father is gone."

Tessa hoped Zack did not hear the irony in his own statement. Then the sound in Zack's bedroom changed. Footsteps.

"I heard you talking. Is Dad home?"

Linny's voice.

"Where is he? Why didn't he come to my room first?" Linny went on. "Why are you on FaceTime? I'm going to tell."

"It's Mom," Zack said.

"This late?"

"It's not late where she is, stupid."

"Zachary. Linnea." This was truly otherworldly, disciplining her children over FaceTime.

"You're the stupid one," Linny said, ignoring her.

"Hey!" Tessa called out. "Linny, come show me your adorable self, and stop tormenting your brother."

"O-*kay*."

The laptop video swished, and Linny had aimed the camera at herself.

"Hi, Mom."

Her new haircut, even spikier after hours on a pillow, almost looked cute, Tessa had to admit. Her T-shirt, which she still wore, showed the splotch of yellow paint.

"Hi, swee—"

"Are you getting little soaps for me, Mom? I love those cute hotel soaps."

"You are infinite-level dumb," Zack said, off camera. "Soaps. So lame."

"See, Mom?" Linny said. "Zack is the lame one. He's super lame. You are *infinite* to infinity lame."

"You two? Can we be civilized? I'm missing you like crazy, and I—"

"What are you two doing awake?" Henry's angry voice came from down the hall, and Tessa heard his footsteps get closer. "And what happened to the dishwasher? The whole kitchen is—"

"It's Mom on the phone," Linny said.

And as Linny turned the screen toward him, Tessa saw the expression on Henry's face.

54

Tessa waited. Her silence, she knew, said more than any words. It screamed louder than any rage, and rumbled darker than any thunderstorm. Henry wasn't dead. And that was the only excuse that she would have accepted.

From the look on his face, he might be wishing he *were* dead.

She waited. Imagining Linny holding up Zack's laptop, imagined her seeing Zack's shredded Pikachu sticker on the back of its case, imagined the chaos of explanatory sentences that must be tumbling through her husband's mind.

In the silence of the distance, and the distance of the silence, Tessa kept waiting; waiting him out. What Henry said next might change their lives, and what *she* said after that might do the same thing, and right now, standing on the thick jewel-toned paisley carpeting of the hotel elevator bank, aluminum sliding doors on either side of her, and with a mysterious message in a sealed envelope tucked into her purse, her world was on the verge of collapse.

Henry was wearing his favorite black T-shirt, a thin quarter-zip pullover on top, his hair tousled and his face bristly and unshaven. Clinically, technically, empirically, any person would think Henry was a fortysomething knockout, and Tessa was not surprised that some predatory and bored suburban housewives had set him in their sights.

Whoa, Annabelle said. Really?

Fine. She was being unfair and wrongheaded in every way, and yet Tessa could not decide whether she was being tormented by rage or by sorrow.

"Hi, sweetheart," Henry finally said.

Her two children were in the room, hanging on every word just as she was, assessing their father, and assessing their mother, and assessing the ruined kitchen and Henry's unexplained disappearance. She would not be the one to incite that battle. She would not.

"Hi back," she said. Waiting. "What's new?"

She could see Henry evaluate; watched his brain computing whether possibly Zack had not told her he'd been "out." That extravagant dishwasher had been Henry's undoing. And now he would have to own it. But she had control of how that would happen.

"You were right about the too-expensive dishwasher, honey," Henry began.

"How so?" She longed to see the expressions on her children's faces, but Linny was stolidly aiming the camera toward Henry.

Henry ran both hands through his hair, mussing it even more, which made him even *more* attractive. "Well," he said, "apparently it was running, and God knows what went wrong but water is . . . was . . . It's totally screwed up. It might be the hose connection."

And here was the moment when she could pull the rug out from under him. She could confront him, right now, about the omission that he had not been home.

Henry had secrets, all right. Exactly like Zack said. And he was clearly in the midst of covering them up. But she couldn't force the issue with her children in the room. Whatever he had done, wherever he had been, whoever he had seen or been with or whatever he had been sneaking around doing while he left their children alone—it had already happened. It could not be erased. But it did not have to be faced at one in the morning when her poor kids were exhausted and confused and afraid.

"What a mess," Tessa said, meaning every word of it.

"We'll handle it." Henry waved off her concerns. "Don't worry about a thing. But the kids are bushed, it's late for them, but I'm glad they got to say hello to you—I didn't hear the phone ring though." He looked past her, apparently at Zack and Linny. "I thought you guys were sleeping."

"Long story." Tessa interrupted his obvious testing to see whether he could suss out the extent of her previous conversation with Zack and Linny. "Let me say goodnight to kid one and kid two," she went on, "and you and I will talk in the morning, Henry."

Linny turned the laptop to put herself on camera. "Don't forget the soaps, Mom. I love the soaps."

"Bring me something, too," Zack called from off camera.

A whir of machinery in the background announced the arrival of an elevator, and if it carried curious and eavesdropping passengers, Tessa did not want to have extra company for this conversation.

"My elevator is here," she said. "I've got an early plane, so good night, you all, and—"

"To Des Moines? According to your website?" Henry had turned the phone screen back to himself. "So did you sell books tonight? Did you find Locket Mom?"

"We'll talk about it tomorrow." She took a step toward the elevator, feeling more like she was walking a fraying rope bridge stretched precariously across a bottomless abyss. "I'm getting in the elevator, and I know the call will get cut off as soon as I do."

"Safe safe," Henry said.

The elevator doors opened, revealing no one inside. Tessa stared at the phone screen, where Henry's face looked back at her, expectant.

Waiting.

Tessa walked into the empty square mahogany and mirror cube and the doors slid closed. And she hung up.

55

After her hotel room door closed behind her, Tessa flapped the security bolt and slid the chain, wondering what Henry was thinking. She had never ever not said "love love" in response to his "safe safe." Not ever in their fourteen years of marriage. Neither dead bolt lock nor steely chain could make her feel safe; not here, and not anywhere.

Tonight Henry had gone somewhere and had not told her about it, not before and not after. And before that, Nellie and Barbara—"not a dog-walker," Henry had said—had grilled Henry about Blytheton, and Tessa had avoided talking about it, because how could she not? Their marriage contract did not have "disclosure of material fact" clauses like her publishing contract did, but transgressions were equally devastating.

Some contracts don't have to be signed, Annabelle said.

Zack had a secret. And she had a sealed envelope. It crossed her mind, as she examined the flat white thing—and even, so silly, held it up to the light—to tear it into sixty billion pieces and flush it down the toilet. Whoever had left it for her had no way of confirming whether Tessa had received it. Maybe the hotel had never given it to her. Maybe someone forgot. Maybe they'd lost it. Maybe they didn't care.

She sat on the edge of one of the beds, exhaling, staring at the envelope as if that would reveal some answer.

Like Henry, she could pretend that whatever had happened that evening at home had not happened. Three thousand miles apart, she could simply pretend this envelope had not arrived.

The necklace. Sam's postcard. The stolen suitcase. The earrings. The destroyed chocolates. The woman at the bookstore.

And now this note.

Connected or not, those were not "nothing."

"Whatever," she said out loud, and in one motion, before she could rethink her decision, she slid one fingernail under the flap of the envelope, peeled away the stubborn glue, ripped the envelope, and pulled out a piece of paper, not hotel stationery but anonymously white. And in careful felt pen, black superfine point, someone had written in meticulous penmanship:

San Diego was fun. Seattle, too. See you in Des Moines.

"Do you want us to send someone to be with you?" Olivette asked. The editor's face, framed in the Zoom screen, was etched with concern.

Tessa's suitcase was packed and zipped, but after she'd rolled it to her hotel room door this morning, she'd stopped. Was it safer in her room or in the lobby surrounded by people? Paralyzed by the *See you in Des Moines* note, she'd called her editor for advice. Seven a.m. in Seattle, ten in New York.

"And do not apologize, Tessa," Olivette was saying. "You did exactly the right thing, telling me about the note. I'll patch DJ into our call, and we'll find an escort for you."

"Like a bodyguard?" Tessa had an hour before she had to leave for the airport—and now sat in a lumpy brown chair in her hotel room, look-ing out the window at another fog-shrouded Seattle day. The night before had passed, with her pillow uncooperative and her brain reduced to smol-dering ash, as if all time had stopped and each minute that ticked by on the green-numbered bedside clock lasted an eternity. "I don't think that's necessary, Ollie."

But half of her yearned for a bodyguard. She wondered if there was such a thing as an emotional bodyguard, too. Henry, at home, was still only showing her the virtual views that revealed his curated reality—keeping the rest of his world a mystery. *A secret*, Zack had said.

Zack had not gotten to tell his secret last night. So it was still a secret. From her.

"Tessa? A bodyguard? Well, no, you don't need *that*, do you?" Olivette sat in her office chair, talking via her laptop, stacks of books piled against the dramatic hunter-green wall behind her. Tessa saw a stripe of periwinkle blue in one pile, and wondered whether Olivette would someday regret that she had chosen to publish *All This Could Be Yours*.

"But no," Olivette went on. "There's a thing called an author escort, they have them in every big city. They'll drive you, take you to the event, wait for you, make sure you have food, and back to the hotel. You don't have to chat with them if you don't want to, but they're always knowledgeable about stuff. They take you to the airport, too, meet you at the hotel, so you're never alone. We use one in Seattle, Evelyn Wickwire. I'll see if I can get her. And then we'll find someone in Des Moines. Don't worry. Price of success, kiddo. Better than no one coming to your events, remember that."

Tessa watched Olivette pick up her cell phone, tap in numbers, then give Tessa a thumbs-up. "Ringing. But other than that, you're okay? I'm so sorry, Tessa, rabid fans are part of the—oh, hang on. Here she is."

Tessa stared into the Zoom screen. The only way to beat this was to face it head-on. Face her. Him. Them. Whoever. She would not be a victim.

Someone was coming to Des Moines. Coming for *her*. Okay, then. Bring it on. If social media was supposed to connect people, then that's exactly how she would use it. She'd examine the photos on her phone, try to find the same images in Phoenix and San Diego and Seattle. Burn that image into her brain, and when that person appeared in the audience, Tessa would corral her, and face her. Or him. Or them. Because running from a problem gave someone else the power. She had done nothing wrong. She'd been a kid.

Tessa sighed, and mourned her unexpected consequences. Because of her success, she'd lost control of her life. How could such a good thing lead to such darkness? But the door to darkness had been opened long ago, and Tessa had been forced to cross the threshold, and now she knew, in this random hotel room on the edge of the world, that no one had the power to go back. There was only forward.

I'm so sorry, Annabelle. She almost said it out loud.

"Hold on a second, Tessa, DJ is getting Evelyn, the escort. Don't worry. Team Tessa is on it. You're our girl."

She wondered what Henry was doing right now, maybe putting soggy towels in the still-working dryer, and she bitterly hoped he was haunted by her calculated withholding of their special mantra. She had actively tried to hurt him. But what had he done to her? How much had he hurt *her*, doing something so inappropriate that he had to keep it secret? She would not be a victim there, either.

But though Olivette and DJ and Team Tessa—she almost teared up at the thought, the cadre of people who loved and supported her, for now at least—could call in an author escort to protect her, Henry was the one designated to protect her children.

What if a bad thing happened to them?

But if anything happened to *her*, she dared not imagine it, it would be only Henry who could take care of them. If someone came to . . . She could not face it.

You know it'll all work out, Annabelle said.

"I *don't* know that, Annabelle!"

Olivette turned back to her, quizzical. "I'm sorry, Tessa, are you talking to . . . me?"

"Just thinking out loud." Tessa took a deep breath. "I'm pretty tired. And I truly hate to bother you. But we sold lots of books last night, and that's a good thing. The bookstore seemed pleased."

"Oh, def. Yes. DJ already forwarded me an effusive email she got from them. Hold on though, getting Evelyn."

Tessa rocked her suitcase in front of her, pulling it back and forth in the contained space where she sat. The motion recalled the afternoons she had rocked a tiny Linnea and a squally Zack in their strollers, comforting her precious and unpredictable charges, with Annabelle whispering in her head. Some days she brought a notebook with her to the park, but when Annabelle began to speak so fast that she could not write it down anymore, Tessa had taken to dictating Annabelle's story into her phone. Almost as if she were channeling another person.

She'd never questioned, not consciously, how she knew it was Annabelle. Or how this worked. The voice felt comforting, and benevolent, like Annabelle's reassurance that she knew the bad thing had been out of Tessa's control, and that Annabelle forgave her.

"Evelyn Wickwire will meet you in the lobby in thirty minutes." Olivette's voice interrupted her thoughts. She was holding her phone to her ear, as if someone on the other end was telling her what to say. "She'll drive you to the airport, go with you inside as far as she can. I hate that she can't go all the way to the gate, but we can do what we can do." Olivette paused, held up one finger to Tessa as she listened to the person on the phone. "I'll tell her," Olivette said into the phone, nodding. "Thanks. You're the best."

Olivette tapped off the call, then looked at Tessa, satisfied, as if everything was done and dusted. "Listen, Evelyn appears to be one of the classic ladies who lunch. But don't judge. She's super tough. And ready to protect you. She wants you to know that."

"But she doesn't have a . . . I mean she's not going to carry a—"

"Of course not. But it'll be like having a really savvy aunt. You're important to us, Tessa, and we don't want you wasting brain cells on worrying. You don't have to pay her or tip her, it's all taken care of. You'll recognize her not only because I'm sure she'll be impeccably dressed, but because—and don't tell her I said this—because her blond hair is always perfect."

"Perfect? Hair? Like a . . . a wig?" She remembered how Dorrit had described the woman at the bookstore, and what she herself had said to Min in the lobby, using those exact words. "Perfect hair." And now this Evelyn Wickwire, too?

56

"Back or front?" Evelyn Wickwire wore ladylike low heels and a possibly-Chanel suit, and her blond hair in a severe French twist. Not a wig, at least not today. She'd insisted on wheeling Tessa's suitcase to her gray Volvo, where she popped the trunk and with one motion hefted Tessa's bag inside. "I'm hoping you'll hop in the front seat and confess everything."

Tessa tried to calm the flare of alarm.

Evelyn slammed the trunk. "Or you can sit in the front seat and tell me nothing. Or grab forty winks in the back. No pressure. It'll take at least half an hour on I-5 this time of the morning."

"Front is good, thank you," Tessa said. She'd wait and see. What might have been a boring ride in a random hired car was now, potentially, part of some bigger game. "I've been in about fifty thousand Ubers over the past several days, and all I see is the back of people's heads."

"I hear you." Evelyn opened the passenger door, gestured Tessa onto the saddle-colored leather. "There's a bottle of Evian for you, and coffee with milk in the cupholder."

"Coffee. Fabulous," Tessa said. "First time I've smiled all day."

"Oh dear." Evelyn drew on her seat belt, pushed the ignition. "Olivette indicated you were—unsettled."

"Yeah," Tessa said. "Long story. Boring."

"Oh, I've heard them all." Evelyn pulled out of the curved hotel parking lane. "I had an author, a while ago, readers came to her house. With gifts, expecting to be invited in. She actually had to move, leave town. I'm telling you"—Evelyn stopped at a light—"nothing induces passion like the passion for a book."

Had to move, Tessa thought. *Leave town.* "Have you ever heard of anything dangerous happening?"

"Not . . . really. Most do not act out their fantasies—"

"Fantasies?"

"Hopes is perhaps a better word. A book can be an all-consuming thing. Remember the ones that obsessed you when you were a child— *Black Beauty*, for instance?"

Tessa's eyes widened. *Coincidence*, she thought. Coincidence.

"*Anne of Green Gables?* The Edward Eager books?" Evelyn continued. "Sometimes kids literally *become* Katniss Everdeen, or a Scottish Highlander. Cosplay, when readers dress up as their favorite characters, can be wonderfully entertaining and a shared community, or it can be—how do I put this. Delusional. I'm not criticizing, necessarily, I'm simply observing. And if you've created one of those icons, then your very existence, in your fans' minds at least, becomes a center of worship."

"Oh, come on." Tessa took a sip of coffee, that welcoming bite of caffeine.

"Believe me or not." Evelyn glanced at her, raised a carefully tended eyebrow. "And the authors can also become objects of scrutiny, dissected and discussed, and, not to alarm you, but easily toppled from that created Olympus."

Tessa pictured that, and all it included.

Evelyn glanced in the rearview, signaled, steered into the fast lane. "And they'll dig, too," she continued, "into your personal life, and your past. It's not intentionally destructive, but your privacy can vanish. I'm sure your editor and agent have warned you." The car purred, accelerating, tires silent on the smooth highway pavement. "That's why publishing contracts have those moral turpitude clauses, where the authors hold the publisher harmless if something devastating is revealed. But why are we talking about this? You should be riding high on your success."

"Oh, I am." Tessa reassured herself at the same time. "I'm homesick, sometimes, though, two kids, and I always think of them. And my husband, too, doing God knows what."

"What would Annabelle say about that?" Evelyn turned to her and winked.

"I wish I were more like Annabelle in the book. She has her fictional life all figured out. The rest of us mortals . . ." Tessa took another sip of coffee. "As an author, I can make stories turn out the way I want, most of the time at least. But in real life, that doesn't happen."

"You want to tell me about it?"

"About what?"

"Your editor and publicist called me this morning, as you know, worried about you, and said you were upset about some note you'd received? You haven't mentioned that."

Can of worms. "It's nothing," Tessa said.

"They're paying me four hundred dollars an hour because of your nothing?" Evelyn kept her eyes on the traffic ahead.

"I did get a note," Tessa admitted, since Evelyn already knew about it. "I'll read it to you." Tessa pulled the envelope from her bag. Read it out loud. "That's all it says, see you in Des Moines. So it's either from someone enthusiastic, or someone scary."

"And you don't have *any* idea who? Have you noticed the same person in several of your audiences?"

Tessa again replayed the past few days. "It all goes by in a blur, but I take pictures of every audience. On the plane I'll compare them, see if anyone repeats. But that's not all." She took a deep breath, then told Evelyn about the wig. And then, because it all seemed to pour out of her, about the woman who'd questioned her about summer vacation.

"This is what you're calling nothing?"

Evelyn had eased the car to the right, toward a green arrow pointing to Sea-Tac airport.

Tessa hadn't even told Evelyn the whole story. And now there was almost no time.

"It all started, I *think*, with a locket I found." Tessa spoke faster as they turned onto the exit, hoping Evelyn was someone she could rely on. "Could this be yours," Tessa finished the story. "I thought I was so clever, and that the necklace would be claimed right away. But no."

"Yes, I saw your Locket Mom hashtag. But no one's recognized the man in the photo?"

"No one."

"Did you Google Image reverse-search the picture? And the necklace?"

"Yup. Nothing."

"Well, someone left that necklace there. Question is—why. Did someone call lost and found to claim it? Does the hotel know you took it? It's possible that person is not on social media. And when they call the hotel, their necklace is not there. Because you have it."

"You think I should—"

"Tessa?" Evelyn shifted into park, and pointed to a sign that warned drop-off time was three minutes only. "Some poor forgetful hotel guest may be facing a dead end."

"A dead end that I caused." Because she'd wanted a good social media story. As a result she'd created a monster, and now she was fretting about it, and complaining, when in reality, the situation was her own fault. She'd stolen someone's property—even worse, someone's *privacy*—and exploited it to get attention from readers.

She certainly had gotten attention. But not the kind she'd wanted.

And even *worse*, hideous to admit, the massive public attention she'd brought to Locket Mom's life was exactly what she'd worried someone would do to her.

"I'll take it, if you like." Evelyn turned toward her, palm extended. "I can handle it for you."

57

It couldn't possibly be true that her suitcase was lighter, but it felt that way as she hoisted it onto the conveyor belt at security screening. The wave of guilt that had washed over her when Evelyn essentially called her a thief—and the realization of her own selfish appropriation of some poor woman's personal life—made her frantic to extricate herself from this potentially embarrassing situation. She still had her phone snapshots, so she wasn't totally separated from the locket. Evelyn had promised to send it back to the hotel, offering some explanation, and would report the results to Tessa.

"Maybe someone wanted to get rid of it," Evelyn had said, as she popped the Volvo's trunk and hefted Tessa's suitcase onto the sidewalk. "Maybe it was a hated memory. Or a painful one. You could make up all kinds of stories." She had paused. "You, especially, Tessa, that's what you do, correct? Make up stories?"

Tessa tried to gauge whether Evelyn's tone carried an undercurrent of sarcasm. Or accusation.

"I do, sure," Tessa decided to accept it at face value. "An author's life is full of stories. If we're lucky."

"You've certainly told a good one."

At that Tessa had swiveled her suitcase to face Evelyn again, questioning. "A good one?"

"A *New York Times* bestseller, Tessa, is all I mean."

"Thank you." Tessa's mind was too full to calculate nuance, and her own fears—about Zack and his secret, and the dishwasher episode, and Henry's mysterious whereabouts, not to mention the personal scrutiny that seemed to be following her—were coloring everything this morning. When she got the truth about what was happening at home, she could focus on what was happening on the road. But she was not making stuff up. She was not paranoid. That unmistakably real threat was in her handbag right now: *See you in Des Moines.*

"Safe travels, Tessa." Evelyn had given her a quick hug goodbye. "I'll be in touch if I hear anything. And I'll tell your team you're safely at the airport. They told me, by the way, that someone was meeting you at DSM. Des Moines airport. I'm sure they'll carry a sign, you'll see it."

"Oh, no," Tessa said, "I don't need anybody to—"

"It's simply in case more of your 'nothing' happens." Evelyn had tucked the plastic-wrapped necklace into her brown leather tote. And raised a hand in goodbye. "Be careful out there, Tessa."

Careful. Of what? She'd wanted to ask. But Evelyn—who could not have given a satisfactory answer anyway—had driven away.

Careful? Annabelle said. That was weird.

Tessa pulled her roller bag toward gate B19, looking out the bank of windows onto the dark asphalt tarmac as she walked.

Her phone buzzed in her pocket, the VIP sound. Home, or Sadie Bailey, or DJ.

DJ. Her publicist was the best, keeping track of her. Of all the lovely perks she'd imagined about being an author, she hadn't realized she'd be blessed with such a supportive team. *All the cheese.* When she got home, when this was over, she'd send *them* cheese. And champagne.

Tessa stepped into the lee of a Hudson News, passengers lugging suitcases and corralling squally children bustling around her, and a public address system squawking unintelligible announcements. She'd sign books in the store later, if there was time, and she tapped the button to accept the call, scanning the bookstore for periwinkle. As the connection was made, she faced the polished tile wall to block out distractions.

"Hey, DJ," she began, "thank you so much for Evelyn, everything's—"

"Are you okay?" DJ interrupted.

"Sure," Tessa said, "thanks. Like I said, uneventful, and—"

"But you canceled."

Tessa tried to figure out the meaning of the word "canceled." Canceled what? "Canceled what? I didn't cancel . . ." She tried to remember if there was anything DJ might be talking about. No. "I didn't cancel anything."

"Well, the bookstore thinks you did."

"What bookstore?"

"The Des Moines bookstore, Tessa. Oakdale Books. They just called me, frantic, half worried and half enraged, about why we would cancel your appearance. They'd sold however many tickets, they're—"

"I didn't cancel, Deej. I didn't."

"Nevertheless. They say you did. They put out an email blast to everyone who registered, saying you had called and canceled without explanation. Now they have to return all the money. And the books. Do you understand that? That's—unacceptable. I was terrified something was wrong, but you sound fine. So what's going on?"

"I *am* fine. Well, I mean, I'm not fine now, I'm mystified. Wait. They did that without talking to you?" Tessa touched her forehead to the coolness of the tiled wall. Pulled her suitcase closer to her. The public address system announcements grew louder, or possibly that was the ringing in her ears. "Or checking with me? No one called me, no one contacted me, or you, no one confirmed that it was a real phone call—*wait*. They said it was *me* on the phone?"

"How long until your plane, Tessa?" DJ's voice had turned abrupt, clipped. "I could not tell the bookstore that you hadn't canceled, because I didn't know. So you're telling me you did not, one hundred percent, you did not cancel your event."

"Of course not!" Tessa tried to keep the wail from her voice. "Why would I do that?"

"You're saying someone *else* called? Who?"

"How do I know? I only know it wasn't me. It wasn't."

"Did you get another note? Are you afraid of whoever is coming to Des Moines? Why?"

"No. I can't imagine who such a person would be." She actually could imagine a whole spectrum of horribles, but that's all they would be, imaginary adversaries. The better question was could she *understand* it, which she could not.

"Should we bring you home? Is something going on?"

"Oh, no, no. I'm so sorry—"

"Tessa. You can't cancel an event. You have a plane ticket to Des Moines. Your next plane leaves tomorrow *from* Des Moines. You can't break a tour in the middle. You can't change the schedule without calling me. We're your team, Tessa. We can't operate any other way."

"I would never—I didn't—"

"Look, Tessa, you told me about some sinister note. We sent Evelyn to take care of you, and she just told me you were upset, and moreover, that you had *taken* that necklace from the hotel room. I did not know you had *stolen* it. I thought you had taken a *photo* of it. Thank goodness no one has claimed it."

"Oh my God," Tessa said, "no, that's—no. No. I can tell you all about that, but can we talk about the bookstore?" She squinted toward the glowing electronic numbers on the schedule board across the crowded corridor. People hurrying, fulfilling travel plans, people whose book tours were not upended by forces unknown. "My plane boards in half an hour. Should I still go?"

"You *have* to go, Tessa, if you don't, the airline could cancel your future flights, and the whole thing will be a mess. I'll try to put out the fire on this end, but what am I supposed to say to the bookstore?"

"I don't know." Tessa felt her voice tighten. "I'm as confused as you are. I would never do such a thing, DJ. You know that."

Silence on the other end. Tessa filled it with every catastrophe her brain could conjure. Henry, the kids, the house. Her career. Their livelihood. Nellie Delaney, with her summer house in Maine. Her eyes throbbed, nothing stayed in focus. She had to face it. Someone or someones was deliberately trying to ruin her tour. And they definitely understood what would be most destructive—to disrupt events, cause thousands of dollars in financial distress, disappoint and alienate her fans and bookstores. Enrage her publisher.

And make it look like it was all *her* fault.

See you in Des Moines. The note in her purse felt radioactive. Deadly.

"Maybe tell the bookstore the truth?" Tessa suggested, before DJ could answer.

"Which is *what*, Tessa? We have no idea," DJ replied. "They'll think I'm covering up some diva move on your part. Or that someone's deliberately sabotaging your appearance. They don't want any security situations. Better to blame some imaginary intern who screwed up and canceled the wrong event."

"Really?"

"It's what I do," DJ said. "And bigger picture, it means we'll have to— look, get your plane. I'll get with the powers that be. Figure out what to do. Now *and* later."

"I'm so sorry, I don't—"

"We don't have time for that. I need to get these sales back, and these people back, and help the store figure out how not to look like idiots. And for us not to look like idiots. I'm gonna get nailed for this. Totally nailed. Luckily nonexistent interns can't complain."

"Listen. About Des Moines. I really don't need an escort."

"Whatever. I have to go, Tessa. Call me when you get to your hotel."

"Do you want *me* to call the bookstore?"

"No. Stay out of it. We'll post on your socials. Saying how much you're looking forward to it. I'll call the store. We'll make this work. Just—go."

58

Of course there was no Wi-Fi on the plane, and of course she had a middle seat, because this was obviously one of those days when nothing would work. She relinquished the armrests to the passengers who sat on either side, and stared at the seat back in front of her, trying to make sense of what was going on thirty thousand feet beneath her.

If there had been even fifteen minutes before Tessa boarded, she could have called Henry. She'd been so involved with Evelyn that she'd neglected her phone altogether. As a result, her life was full of loose ends. Unknown and menacing loose ends that felt like they were strangling her. Now, buckled in, and with a moribund internet, hulking seatmates, and suspended by physics and geography, she was absolutely and totally helpless.

Tessa tried to look toward the rear of the plane, rows of tops of heads, everyone on the way to Des Moines. Was anyone going to Des Moines because *she* was?

Someone was meeting her at the airport, and she was awash with gratitude about that. DJ could be prickly, but she was doing her job, and would work this out. By the time Tessa got to the bookstore, she would have been filled in on the fictional explanation DJ had given. DJ would be happy again. Team Tessa would be back.

It doesn't make that note go away, though, Annabelle said. "See you in Des Moines." *Wonder who you'll see?*

Did all authors have a Greek chorus in their imaginations? A personal narrator who would weigh in, unbidden, with sarcasm or criticism? As a teenager, Tessa had imagined the muse as a benevolent goddess, an apparition who visited lucky people and transformed them into authors. Now she thought maybe the muse had a dark side. And you could not accept her gift of craft without also receiving her burden of insidious doubt.

But the voice of Annabelle, she knew, was trying to help.

She must have slept, since a raspy, unintelligible voice over the plane's public address system startled her into consciousness. Out the window, the plane was descending through puffs of white, breaking the thick barrier into blue and revealing, beneath, a geometric landscape slashed with the dark curves of a river.

Okay, onward. She was a happy best-selling author, on a successful book tour. She'll be met by a friendly escort, get more coffee and even some food, and be driven through the Iowa sunshine to a comfortable hotel and a convivial bookstore.

And as she pulled her suitcase toward the terminal exit, what she was seeing now proved it. A smiling, blue-suited woman with graying hair and oversized black-framed glasses displayed a book-sized whiteboard with **CALLOWAY** carefully printed in thick black marker.

Tessa waved, thankful that she had not had the opportunity to cancel— that word again—her personal escort.

The woman, rail thin, reached out a gloved hand, claiming Tessa's suitcase, which Tessa gratefully relinquished, leaving her tote bag attached to the extended handle.

"Wonderful to meet you, Ms. Calloway," the woman said. "I'm Emily."

Holy crap, Annabelle said.

"Are you all right, Ms. Calloway?" Emily said. "Did you have a rough flight? Do you need some water? Or a bathroom?"

"Yes, no, really, I'm good." Tessa tried to regroup, this was not *her* Emily, beyond impossible, but this day was doomed to be a roiling disaster. Three bad things, her mother had taught her once, three bad things would happen at a time. Had Tessa already had her three today? Or was the universe poised to hit her with one more?

"Second thought, yes, bathroom," Tessa said, reassessing. "Can I leave my stuff with you?"

"My pleasure." Emily pulled the suitcase closer to her. "I'll take care of it all."

"Wait." Tessa reached out, retrieved her roller bag. "I might need something, and my tote has my phone. I'll meet you right here. Two minutes."

"I'm here for you," Emily said. "No rush. There's plenty of time to get to the hotel."

She opened the door to the bathroom stall and wrangled her bag inside, relieved that the door lock worked. Her phone pinged, from deep inside the zipped-up canvas. A VIP sound. Maybe DJ, having solved tonight's worrisome cancellation.

But who would have tried to sabotage that appearance? Why? Tessa wondered for the ten millionth time as she unzipped her bag and foraged to find the phone. In that fitful half sleep on the plane, she'd dreamed of people chasing her. And now, awake and in a strange bathroom at a strange airport, she realized that was not entirely a dream. Someone really *was* chasing her.

At random bookstores, customers were asking about her hometown. She went over her confounding list again—the locket, the chocolates, the fire alarm, the earrings. Did it all connect? The picture in the locket was not Annabelle, or her family, Tessa knew that. But someone was taunting her about the bad thing. Someone knew about her past. Who? The only person she'd told was Emily. Emily. But Emily would never tell.

She found the pinging phone in a side pocket. *Henry.* And turned it off. Henry could wait.

But she stood in the metal cubicle, staring at the door. There was no way to ignore this. Although DJ and Team Tessa could smooth over tonight's mysterious disruption, there was a bigger problem. Now, Tessa calculated, she had three hours until the bookstore event to figure out who was causing it. And stop them.

Because if she didn't, it would keep happening. And everything she cared about would be taken from her.

59

"No one is certain what 'Des Moines' means," Emily was saying from the driver's seat. "It might be the traditional name for what's now the Des Moines River, or it could mean 'from the monks,' or it could mean 'in the middle,' since we're between the Missouri and the Mississippi Rivers. So I've read."

She'd opened the door to the back seat, showing Tessa two bottles of water in the center console, with a wicker basket of chips and pretzels on the seat. Then she'd stashed Tessa's roller bag in the trunk, and tried to stow her tote bag there, too, but Tessa had retrieved it. She needed her stuff. Her schedule, her laptop, her phone.

"Interesting." Tessa, buckled in, wished Emily would stop her tour-guide prattle and let her think. *Emily.* It was way too strange to call her that. Even though Tessa knew from her research that in the US, Emily was consistently one of the most common names. This Emily appeared to be much older than Tessa. But this was not Emily Owen. Not *her* Emily. Or anyone she'd ever seen before.

"I need to call my husband, forgive me, okay?" Tessa hoped Emily would understand the shorthand for *I don't want to talk right now.*

"Take your time," Emily said. "Although it's not far from the airport to your hotel. Oh good grief." They'd stopped at a red light.

"Everything okay?"

"I'm an idiot. I forgot my entire itinerary, and it was so last minute this morning that I was assigned to this, and I didn't have time to put it on my phone. But you're at the Midlands, correct? The Midlands Hotel? If I remember correctly?"

"Yes, right, and I completely understand." Tessa attempted to be congenial. "If I didn't have that typed-up schedule, I'd have no idea where I was."

"So many authors say that." Emily adjusted her rearview, caught Tessa's eye. "The Midlands it is. Lovely place. Expensive, though. You must be valuable to your publishers."

"Thanks." Tessa tried to tune her out. Her brain was too full for small talk. She had already turned her attention to her phone, but not to calling Henry. He'd texted "call me," but she didn't feel like talking to him. He could handle whatever it was. Just ask him. Or maybe Barbara could help. Or Cool Nellie. As, she couldn't help thinking, they both apparently already had. Henry would 911 her if there was a real problem, they'd discussed that.

Don't you want to find out where he was last night? Annabelle asked. Why he left the kids alone?

Tessa did not trust herself to be civil to him. Trying to juggle his fatherly decision-making with her maternal fears, it was all she could do to avoid emotional land mines.

"Where do you go from here?" Emily asked. "On a plane again tomorrow?"

"Ahh . . ." Tessa said, half listening as she pulled up Google on her phone. "Nashville, I think? It's on my website."

"Are you having a good tour? Good turnouts? Selling lots of books?"

You have to stop talking, Tessa thought. "So far, so fabulous," she said. "I'm reluctant to say much about it. Feels like it'll jinx it."

"And you have family at home?"

Tessa saw the green highway signs for downtown, arrows pointing to exits on the right. Her driver passed the first one.

"Um, yes." *Emily Owen, Blytheton,* Tessa was typing in the Google search. At home, people were asking Henry about Maine. On the road, readers were asking *her* about summer vacations. Emily, from her Maine summers, was the only living person who was connected to both. And the only living person who knew about Tessa's connection to the bad thing.

And now, because the universe was perverse, "Emily" was driving her.

"Lovely," Emily went on. "They must be so proud of you."

They must be so proud of you. Tessa almost laughed out loud, remembering how she had been suspicious of that exact phrase in Barbara-the-dog-walker's small talk with Henry. People who said things like that were fishing for information. Or maybe this was simply a chatty book-tour escort trying to be pleasant.

"Well, I figure they're all living it up while I'm gone, you know, pizza every night, probably for breakfast. But I'll be home soon. And we'll be back to kale and Brussels sprouts."

There. That was funny. See, she was having a conversation.

"How old are the kids? Is your husband taking off work to stay with them? How does he feel about that?"

"It's fine," Tessa said, "but thank you for reminding me, I should call them now before I get caught up at the hotel. They love to know that I've safely arrived, that's part of our ritual."

"You always tell them when you arrive? They expect that?"

"Yeah, they do." Tessa relaxed a bit when she saw the green-and-white Exit To Downtown Des Moines highway sign coming nearer. She knew Emily was supposed to be a companion, but right now she felt like she was being chatted to death. "My publisher, too," Tessa added. "They're all about knowing where I am at every moment. In case they need to make a change in the schedule, I suppose."

Someone had canceled her Des Moines appearance, the thought came crashing back. Maybe by now DJ and Olivette had figured out who.

Emily was staying in the middle lane, not moving toward the exit ramp.

"They're spending a lot on you, I can tell from your website," Emily said. "Publishers don't do many extensive book tours anymore."

"I'm always grateful," Tessa said. And she would be even more grateful if Emily steered to the right, and onto the exit. It was seconds away.

"Isn't that our exit?" Tessa couldn't resist asking. She pointed to the right.

"Oh dear," Emily said. "It was. Plot twist."

60

"What?"

Tessa felt the car accelerate. But Emily was not steering onto the exit for Des Moines.

"Plot twist. Like in your book," Emily said. "So. Now, while I have you—"

"Have me?" Other cars peeled off, headed for downtown. Emily's car did not. "What are you—"

"Don't worry, Tessa, we won't interrupt your precious book tour. Although I do hear there was an annoying glitch in today's event, I hope they can remedy that. The more books you sell, the more money your publisher makes and, as a result, the more money *you* make. And money is extremely important to us. You wouldn't want your events—or your hotel stays—to get interrupted again. Silly old fire alarms, they do go off at the slightest touch, especially in those mid-century hotels."

"We? What we? I don't understand what you're talking about, and I certainly don't understand what you're doing, and I need you to take me to the hotel now. You're making me very uncomfortable. Please get off at the next exit. And take me to the hotel, as my publishers arranged."

"I should tell you, I suppose, your publishers did not arrange this particular ride. But I'm still happy to take you to your hotel. The Midlands, as you yourself told me. But we need to chat first."

"Chat about what?" The car was going faster now; the architecture of downtown Des Moines, off to her right, silhouetted in the glaring sun. Tessa, buckled into the back seat, with her suitcase locked in the trunk, and a stranger at the wheel, was suddenly a passenger on her way, at more than sixty miles an hour, to whereabouts unknown.

The necklace, the chocolates, the cancellation. And now this. Someone was trying to ruin her life.

Henry. Linny. Zack.

Henry had *texted* her, not half an hour ago, and she'd ignored it. What if he'd been calling for help?

Please be safe. She willed her family to hear her thoughts. *Please be safe.*

"I asked you, chat about what?" Tessa tried to keep her voice from quavering. "And how did you know where I was?"

"Yes, well, your schedule is not difficult to find, again, as you yourself told me, it's on your website. Since you were flying from Seattle for an event tonight in Des Moines, there were only two flights you could have taken. And you came right up to me, expecting a driver. Exactly what I hoped would happen."

Tessa held up her phone. "I'm calling the police."

"Do," Emily said. "I'm not sure missing an exit is illegal, but call if you must."

"You pretended to be my driver. This is kidnapping."

"I *am* your driver. And you came with me willingly, didn't you? You even, at one point, offered to relinquish your suitcase."

"But the publisher—"

"Yes, call them, too. Tell them you got into the car with a stranger. Had they mentioned they were sending a driver? *I* didn't see one."

"You just told me you set off the fire alarm in Denver and canceled my event here in Des Moines. Did you put a locket in my room, too?"

"*I* most certainly did no such thing." Emily shot her an over-the-shoulder glance. "That locket was on all your socials, and the fire was on national TV, and everyone who signed up for your event tonight got an apologetic last-minute email from the bookstore. I was simply commenting on your string of disruptions."

"What is it that you want?" Tessa could not falter here. "Tell me. Now."

This was The Bad Thing, exactly as she'd feared, coming back to haunt her. It would taint her forever. Follow her. A grotesque and indelible tattoo she had not asked for. Now she'd have to deal with it. And the knowledge that the real Emily had certainly betrayed her. This person had chosen that name on purpose. "And Emily—that's not your real name."

"Oh. Very wise. Cutting to the chase. Just like in your book." Emily checked her side mirror, then looked at her in the rearview. "My name is not Emily, correct. But I have to say it was truly fun to see your reaction when I introduced myself as such."

The car was going faster now, Tessa could almost feel Emily, or whatever her name was, pressing the accelerator. They were not going over the speed limit, with Emily—she did not know what else to call her—inconspicuously staying in the center lane.

"Might as well call me . . . Harper. First of all, this highway is a circle around the city, we are now passing nine o'clock, if you can imagine it that way. When I make the entire circumference, we'll be right back here at nine, and I'll happily drop you at your fancy hotel so you can continue your fancy book tour. I wanted to give us a chance to talk."

Tessa fingered her phone. She could call the police, but by the time the cops arrived, this "Harper" could have taken an exit, and dumped Tessa on the side of the road somewhere. Did Tessa know the license plate of this car? No. Did she know Harper's real name? No. Was there any way for police to capture her?

No matter. Tessa was trapped. With her suitcase locked away into the trunk and her future—and her precious family's future—in the hands of a stranger.

61

"We're at twelve on the clock now," the woman—Harper—was saying, "and let me reassure you that the last thing we want to do is hurt you. Or your family, in that pricey new house. You're really raking it in with this book. Keep it up. We rely on it."

"We?" Tessa clenched her phone. Henry would figure she was still in the air. Her publishers, too. She'd told DJ she didn't need an escort. No one was expecting her to be anywhere but in transit. No one would worry that she had not arrived at the hotel. There was no way for anyone to know where she was.

"I need to call my husband and let him know I'm okay. He'll worry. Then he'll call me, and worry even more. I want him to know I'm all right."

"Are you though? All right?"

Tessa had spent so many days and nights by herself in hotel rooms, trying to get used to the solitude. Now, surrounded on all sides by cars and people and trucks and traffic, she had never felt more alone.

"Listen." She would not be a victim. "You can taunt me, or tease me, or hold me captive in a moving car, which, no matter what you say, is kidnapping. Life in prison." *I could silently take her photo,* Tessa thought. *I could record this.* But safer to commit her face to memory; her hairline, the distance between her eyebrows, the length of her earlobes. Things she could not change. There was no way to fight back using two plastic bottles of water and two bags of potato chips; she was not MacGyver or Nancy Drew. She was in real-life trouble. "Wouldn't it be easier to tell me what you want?"

Harper smoothed her hair behind one ear, and Tessa noticed her chewed fingernails. "The reason I chose the name Emily. Let's start with that. I'm sure you remember your summer friend Emily? And what you two got away with?"

"I have no—"

"And if you are about to tell me you have 'no idea' what I'm talking about, that's a lie, Tessa, and we are at one o'clock now, and if I were you, I would hurry this along."

"Tell me what you want. And who you are."

"There are consequences, *Tessa*, for your actions. When you were just another housewife, saddled with your ne'er-do-well husband, you weren't much help to us. But now our Tessa has had a publishing windfall. And instead of your *mother* paying to keep us quiet, it's *your* turn. And, if you are keeping track, we are now at three o'clock."

"My mother? Paying? Paying who? For what? No. No way. My mother lost her money in the real estate crash, if you know so much."

"Oh, please," the driver said. "I'm sure that's what she told you. But here's the hard truth. She *used* her money to pay *us*. Until it ran out. So *she* may have 'lost' it, but it was our gain. She did not want her darling daughter to be arrested. And she bankrolled the cover-up. Now it's your turn."

"What are you even talking about? Cover-up of what? Besides, both my parents died when I was in college. You're lying."

"You live in utter fiction, don't you, Tessa? Your mother was *protecting* you. And herself, I might add. Until she couldn't anymore. And she killed herself, Tessa, as a result."

"No." Tessa shook her head, refusing to believe that, her stomach hollow and her brain imploding. That was a monstrous and atrocious lie. "No. That's not true. Absolutely not true. She had a heart attack."

"Isn't it helpful to think so? You were *told* she had a heart attack. And because it's easier for you, safer for you, more palatable for you, you believed it. Your entire life is a made-up story."

"I—you—there's—wait. My mother was paying you? For what?" Tessa had to keep her head. Shift the power. The bad thing was long ago. But she would handle it now. "Let me out of this car. I'm calling the police."

"Wonderful. Make the call." The woman twisted over the seat, offering Tessa a simper of a smile. Then turned back to the highway. "But then, I'll simply . . . tell them. Tell them the truth about the dead, mangled, abandoned body they found on that back road in Maine."

"In *Maine?*" She tried to rethink. *Maine?* Annabelle had been found in *Ohio*. That meant . . . this person *wasn't* talking about Annabelle.

That meant . . . this was *not* about the bad thing.

That meant . . . Tessa had been on the trail of the wrong story. Totally wrong.

"Maine?"

"And how that body was actually a victim," the woman went on. "A victim of Tessa Savannah Danforth, the underage drunk-driving daughter of a money-grubbing mother, a social-climbing bitch who let her get away with anything, even vehicular homicide. I'd call it murder, but the legal definition will do. And the prison sentence is twenty-five to life, just so you're aware. With no statute of limitations. Think what murder would do for your career."

"Murder? What victim? Victim of *what?*"

"Do I need to replay it for you? One fine summer night, in Blytheton, you two hotshot, boozed-up teenagers took your mother's rented car . . . is it coming back to you, pray tell? The dark night of your soul?"

No. *No.* Talk about fiction. This woman had it wrong, too. She was spouting some warped, horror-movie version of the truth. Was Emily behind *this?* The . . . blackmail? If that's what this was. She gulped for air now, her heart racing faster than the cars speeding beside them.

"No. It wasn't a person. Emily hit *a deer.* And I wasn't driving."

"Again, isn't it helpful to think so?"

"No." Tessa had to call the police. "You can't do this to me."

Harper caught her eye in the rearview. And winked. "Ah. Yes, I can. And I am. And I'll let you contemplate, for a moment or two, exactly how."

62

Strapped into the back seat and speeding down an Iowa highway, Tessa felt that night in Maine summers ago wash over her in strobed flashes of disconnected sounds and scenes. Emily pleading to drive. The jangle of the keys as Tessa reluctantly relinquished them to her. The fragrance of beer and pine woods. The onyx night, the radio blaring about surfers and sunshine, Emily flipping the headlights off, head thrown back, daring the universe to stop her. The ugly sound of the rental car hitting something.

Tessa could almost feel her knees shaking now, the way they had when she'd opened her door. "Don't look," they'd whispered to each other.

Emily trembling, her skin clammy with fear and dread. Emily's father's condemnatory whisper, "*You should have protected her.*"

The sheriff told her they'd hit a deer. A *deer.*

She'd been sad, for twenty years, about that deer.

If it had been a person—she would have known. She would have.

She wrapped her arms around herself, shivering suddenly, staring at the flat Iowa highway now unspooling in front of her.

But if her mother had paid for someone's silence, to cover up something horrific and devastating, then it must have been true.

Her mother would not have paid for a deer.

If Emily had killed a *person* that night—and Tessa had been with her—the sheriff might have tried to protect them. Protect his daughter, and protect his reputation. He certainly could have made a body disappear. And—she assumed—also had the power to do it leaving no evidence, resulting in no investigations or repercussions. *He* had gone to look at it, *that* she remembered, gone to look at the deer. And then talked to her mother.

Her mother would not have paid for a lie.

Or would she? Her mother had been lying their entire lives.

Her mother. If what this person said was true—*if*—she must have known about the real victim. And that's why she'd lived in such tormented silence. She'd been protecting her daughter. Hiding her complicity. Her crime. Until she died, too. Of grief, Tessa would have to accept that now. And of disappointment. In her.

Would she be proud of Tessa now? Would she think her bargain was worth it?

Mile markers flew by, as if marking chapters of her own life, going too fast, unstoppable, unreadable, relentless. It was as if she were a fictional character. She had lived a fictional life for the past twenty years, and now her backstory had come to destroy her.

Not the bad thing she'd feared. Not her wrenching childhood decision.

But a bargain her *mother* made to protect her. A bargain Tessa hadn't even known existed.

Right now, at this moment, in a stranger's car on this dreary and cornfield-lined highway, time and history were catching up with her. It had begun the moment her book deal was announced, and then, the past had followed her. Stalked her. To Rockport, and to Seattle, and to San Diego, and in every bookstore and every hotel.

Henry did not know about that night, she'd never thought to bring such a thing up, hitting a deer almost two decades ago. Back then, she and Emily had shared two magical summers. Which ended the night of the crash.

When—could it possibly be?—the impetuous, invulnerable Emily had *not* hit a deer.

Henry. She put a palm to her heart at the thought. And the kids. How would she explain to Linny and Zack? Her life was over.

In her book she left white space for emphasis, to give her readers time to breathe. She needed that now, white space.

She had killed two people. Two.

Yes. She was responsible for what happened to Annabelle, because she could have—done something. Run upstairs and get Annabelle. But she hadn't. Or refused to open the door. But she had. And now it sounded, astonishingly, like she was liable for yet another person's death.

It didn't matter that she'd believed Sheriff Owen. What happened had happened. To a real person. Whose life she and Emily had taken. She could not pretend that away.

The crushing reality almost suffocated her, that to the thousands of people who'd loved her book, and relied on her, and admired her, Tessa would soon and inevitably become a shocking disappointment, a flash in the social media pan, a quickly fading memory, and all that would be left was conjecture and embarrassment and disgrace. It would all come out. All of it. She'd be the answer to an obscure trivia question. Fodder for the tabloids.

Now, this New York Times *best-selling author is serving a life sentence for a deadly hit-and-run, and the ensuing cover-up. The disgraced Calloway also turned out to be the little girl in the—*

Little girl. *Oh.* Her heart plummeted, free-falling.

Linny. Henry. Zackie. How would they remember her? How would their dear lives be twisted by her transgression? She understood, with stabbing brutal intensity, how her mother must have felt at the end. Police, investigating her unattended death, had reported it as a heart attack, but what if she'd—who knew what. Taken pills. Or *not* taken them. Anything to end it.

She could almost imagine doing the same thing herself, ending it. Grabbing the wheel, pulling and twisting and crashing and not caring, and no one would know anything, they would be a mangled pile of metal on the side of the road—how sad, people would say, that was the famous Tessa Calloway, her career cut so tragically short on an Iowa highway.

Or she would go to prison for life.

And never see her children again. She was a murderer. She had only one option.

In one motion she could unclick her seat belt and get to her feet and yank the wheel and make it all end.

63

Unless. Unless none of it was true. Unless Harper was a miserable, devious liar.

Exactly, Annabelle said. Good call. You gonna accept this story?

"Harper? Or whatever your name is?" Tessa began. "You've stalked me, and kidnapped me, and called me a murderer. Now you're threatening me with blackmail." She tried to keep her voice confident, channeling Annabelle. *We're all a little Annabelle,* she told her audiences. Well now, even belted into the back seat, she was a lot the hell Annabelle. "I don't care what you do, I'm calling the police. It'll be your word against mine. And *I* am Tessa Calloway."

Word, Annabelle said.

The woman flipped a dismissive palm.

"You are, indeed. But if you do, then we, in turn, will get to pose the question all over social media. Let's see. How would I phrase it?" Harper tilted her head one way, then the other. Eyes on the gray Iowa highway. "How about this? Ahem. 'Big news! Best-selling author Tessa Calloway was the privileged daughter of insolently affluent and relentlessly protective divorced parents, and, we have learned, as a drunken underage driver she killed someone in a hit-and-run, and we have proof her mother spent the rest of her life paying to keep quiet about it.'"

"Paying." Even channeling Annabelle, Tessa could not form an entire sentence about this. "Paying who?"

"Oh, you summer people," Harper said. "You breeze into town, taking up all the room and all the oxygen, with fancy parties and exclusive charity balls, and you never even notice us until we give you the wrong ice cream flavor, or dare to give you a parking ticket. Your mother thought she could *pay* her way into—or out of—anything. And one thing that's so beautifully funny." The woman held up a punctuating forefinger, still watching the road. "Turns out she was right. For a while, at least."

"No. Impossible. I asked you—paying who?"

Cars surrounded them, Tessa could see drivers' faces pass, one at a time; a young woman apparently singing at the top of her lungs, a bearded man in a red ball cap, a teenager with earbuds. She'd read somewhere there was a sign for people to give if they were in trouble, but no way she could remember that now.

"Hardly impossible, Tessa. It's precisely what happened, whether you knew it or not. Your poor mother, trying to protect you from your lies. She made a bargain, didn't she? A deal with the devil? Where do you think the expression 'there'll be the devil to pay' comes from? She paid."

"Sheriff Owen"—this person knew about him anyway, no reason to hide it—"told us it was a deer. I never saw a person in the road. It was a deer. And he told my mother it was a deer, too. I saw him do it. She told me that."

"Please. You only saw what you wanted to see. You created a story about it. And believed it."

"Of course I believed it. Because it's true." Although she'd never actually seen the deer. Or anything in the road. If Sheriff Owen had lied, that meant Tessa, on that pivotal night, had unwittingly agreed to make that her truth. If this woman was right—*could she be?* That truth would end. It would all end. Her beloved family, her shiny, brand-new career—she didn't deserve any of it. She'd bargained it away.

Bull, Annabelle said. You can't be blackmailed if you have nothing to fear.

This woman had accused her of being complicit in a murder and a cover-up. But Tessa refused to believe that story was true.

Which meant now—Tessa had to bargain again. To protect her family.

But not like this, a prisoner in some stranger's back seat.

On her own terms.

Because Tessa had recognized her best bargaining chip. She was only valuable to this person if she were successful. And alive.

64

The highway signs flashed by, names of places she didn't recognize, arrows in directions this car would not go. No one would be expecting her, or waiting for her, or concerned about her. Built into book tour were times her colleagues and family *expected* her to be unavailable—in the air, with scattershot flight delays and schedule changes, capricious ground transportation, spotty internet. No one would worry about her for hours.

She was on her own. Now she had to find the truth. Wherever it led. She prayed that would not be behind bars.

She was a main character who did not even know her own true backstory. Now, as in any good novel, the author had to discover her protagonist's past.

Harper had stayed in the middle lane, steady as if she were on cruise control. She was the only one in the car who knew where they were going.

"Listen, Harper," Tessa began. "Emily's father was the sheriff. He came. He looked. He yelled at us. He said it was a deer. He called my mother, and he told her. He was the *sheriff*. Do not try to extort me all these years later by—"

"Honey. Fast forward to the final chapter. Bottom effing line? You killed a person, and you ran. You and your mommy dearest got the hell out of town—while your victim was lying on a backcountry road, dead."

"Who?" Tessa asked, before she could stop herself or decide if she really wanted to know. "Who? Tell me."

Tessa watched the woman shake her head, her face in the rearview with an expression of pure venom.

"Fiction has served you well, hasn't it? Your mother left enough money after she died to keep things, shall we say, in balance. For a while. Did you wonder why you got nothing in her will? She left you a life-changing gift, Tessa. She bequeathed you the powerful safety of silence. And even arranged to have the money continue after she died. To cover up for you. But, alas, that money has now run out. And that is why you and I are here today, circling beautiful Des Moines. Your life of fiction is about to become a true-crime story. A story about *your* crime."

"But my mother never—" She was having difficulty making the words. "I didn't—we didn't—do anything wrong. And I *wasn't* driving."

"Fiction, fiction, fiction," Harper said. "And we are at six o'clock, I might point out, so better make your decision. We can solve this now or we can . . . keep driving. Perhaps it was a good thing that your event tonight was canceled. No one will miss you. Until it's too late."

"You're asking me for money. Why do you care, anyway? Who are you?" Tessa's fear mixed with her emerging anger, a noxious toxic concoction of uncertainty and rage. Her poor mother—she'd believed this was true. She'd thought—known?—Tessa was a killer. And must have remembered it every time she saw her. But she'd protected her, too, in stoic and tragic and ruinous silence.

In fiction, sometimes darkness had a happy ending. In real life, it often did not.

If this woman was telling the truth, she *did* live in fiction. "Are you behind this? Or are you simply a messenger? For who? At least I should know."

Tessa fingered the phone in her hand, grateful for the lifeline, relieved she had not allowed this woman to stash her tote bag in the trunk.

"*I'm* not asking for *anything*, Tessa, and certainly not demanding. I'm simply wondering." The woman paused, cleared her throat, checked the rearview. "What do you think would be the best way to keep your long-lost best friend quiet?"

"It *is* Emily? I can't believe it."

The woman burst out laughing, a disquieting incongruous sound.

"Oh, that's perfect, Tessa. *Now* there's something you *can't* believe. Imagine that."

"How much?" *I'm so sorry, Henry,* the thought came to her again. *Always always.* Linny and Zack. Sadie Bailey. DJ. Olivette. All who had trusted her. All she had failed. "How much do you want?"

"About time you asked. But right now, we simply want your acceptance. Your understanding of our mutually assured destruction. You tell *anyone* what happened in this car? We'll hear about it. And then, *we'll* tell what happened. So for now, you go sell books. Lots and lots of books. Besides, you've got your family to support. And that hefty mortgage to pay."

"Mortgage? How do you know about—"

"Tessa. You're an author. You do research. I've been researching every move you make. For years. Even have a Google Alert for you. And public records—including publishing announcements about 'significant deals'—are wonderful things. The moment you and that husband got that outrageous mortgage on that bougie house in Rockport, it went right into the Registry of Deeds, and we were back in business. *Your* success means *our* success. Isn't that a perfect bargain?"

Tessa was tired of bargains, weary of everything good depending on her agreeing to something horrific. Even her signature on that life-changing mortgage contract had engendered devastating complications. Talk about life-changing.

You're gonna give up? Annabelle asked. *Make a deal of your own.*

"How will I contact you?" She'd never learn anything if she didn't at least pretend to acquiesce. She had no facts, none, except that *she* was not a fictional character. And the story of her life was her own decision.

"I'm tempted to say 'we'll find *you,*' but that sounds like one of your made-up villains. Let's make it easy. I'll pick you up in the morning. Take you to the airport. I saw from your helpful website that you're actually headed for Philadelphia. Then we can talk further."

"Not a chance."

"Your call." The woman's face turned viperous. "And that means I do have to say my line. We'll find *you.* And that may not be fun for you. For your family, either."

"My *family?* Unless you leave them alone, I'll let the chips fall where they may. And if you think I'm getting into this car again—"

"It'll be a different car, just saying, in case you're deciding to get the plate number. But you'll recognize me. And I hope you've realized, Tessa, for now at least, we benefit when you sell as many books as possible. So. Agreed. We'll make sure your family is safe and sound. As long as you make sure *we* are."

Tessa could not come up with an accurately repulsive adjective for this person. "As long as *you* answer one more question. Emily. The real Emily. Where is she?"

Good one, Annabelle said.

"Huh. Where is Emily? Interesting question. Oh look, there's our exit. Shall we take it? Are you in agreement? Do we have a deal?"

"Yes. Agreed," Tessa lied. "Where. Is. Emily?"

The woman turned on her blinker, its ticking like a time bomb. "You know, now that I think of it, I'm not the best person to ask." The car eased toward the exit marked Downtown Des Moines. "Perhaps you should . . . ask your husband. He seems to be making a lot of new friends."

65

Ask your husband, that revolting woman had suggested. And what new friends was he making? How would she even know?

Did that mean Henry was *in* danger? Or that *he* was dangerous? Had "they" already gotten to him? She contemplated that disturbing thought as she headed toward the concierge desk at the Midlands Hotel. She *would* ask Henry, that was for sure. As soon as she figured out how to phrase it. She'd texted him, frantic and fearful at the same time, with a guarded *landed, you okay?* He hadn't replied.

Dog-walker Barbara. Cool Nellie Delaney. The new neighbors—new friends?—with the alluring summer place and the probing questions. No way either was Emily. Still. She needed to see their faces. Just to be sure.

"Ma'am?" The concierge, natty in a khaki jacket and tattersall tie, looked at her over a mahogany desk topped with a plastic rack of colorful *Des-lightful Des Moines* brochures.

"Can you point me to the library?"

"Ma'am? The hotel does not have a library," he said, looking baffled. "Do you mean gift shop? There's—"

"Oh, thank you, no," Tessa interrupted, realizing what different worlds people lived in. "I mean—a public library. The Des Moines Public Library. I'm hoping it's nearby."

"Got it. Library." He pointed toward the revolving doors. "Go out, turn left, look for the rabbit."

Now it was Tessa's turn to look baffled. She'd already had a day right out of *Through the Looking Glass,* and now this guy was talking about rabbits?

"Yes, it sounds strange," he went on, maybe reading her expression. "But the library looks like a big copper box with a rabbit in front. You'll see."

Tessa felt as if every rule in the entire world had changed, as if sinister eyes watched her, and strangers listened to her thoughts. She'd quickly stashed her roller bag in her hotel room, not opening any drawers, not opening any closets, not even unpacking. Haunted, too, by the fact that Emily, driver-Emily and the real Emily and whoever else was involved with this, were monitoring her. She had not known what "alone" meant until now. Now there was absolutely no one—no one—she could trust. No one in the world.

Ask your husband, that woman had said.

She pushed her way out the revolving door, looking for the *rabbit,* for God's sake, carrying only her phone and a credit card in her pants pocket, terrified that anything else she carried would be tainted or wired or compromised. The library had to be safe. Didn't it? She had time before her event. She'd do her work there.

Her phone pinged with a text. VIP. *DJ.*

She paused on the sidewalk, scanning. None of the pedestrians seemed to be interested in her—some with carryout bags, heads down, headed for offices, probably, sticking to routine. Probably wishing for excitement in their maybe mundane lives. If they only knew. She clicked open her message.

> Event fixed, plan as usual. Why you not meet your driver at DSM? $$$

Tessa gaped at the words. And what must have happened. She *had* met her driver at the airport, the person she *thought* was her driver. But DJ had sent someone else. The poor real driver had probably been standing out of sight, or late. And finally figured, as the last of the Seattle passengers filed by, that Tessa had stood them up. But instead, too-stupid-to-live Tessa had gone with an impostor.

And how was Tessa supposed to explain that to her publicist?

> I did not see them.

Tessa continued typing her lie, seeing her silhouette as a fidgety shadow in front of her.

> I am incredibly sorry. Thank you for making tonight OK.

She hit Send, then considered typing "I'm sorry" again. They'd think she was a complete flake. DJ probably thought she *had* canceled the event, and then avoided her driver. So much for Team Tessa.

> Talk soon.

Tessa waited for the three dots that meant DJ was replying.

The phone screen faded to black.

Like her life. Fading to black.

Nope, nope, nope, Annabelle said. Onward.

One step at a time. Tonight she'd apologize to the booksellers; *another wacky book-tour experience,* she could say. And they'd forgive her, and the audience would love her, and everything would be fine.

At least the genre fiction of her life, the glamorous adventure, would be fine. Tessa as main character, the supremely relatable best-selling author, with her book-club-worthy story of sisterhood and empowerment intact.

The nonfiction version, though, the tragedy, would relentlessly play out in secret.

Ask your husband, those three words thrummed in her mind as she strode along the petunia-lined sidewalk toward her destination. A few blocks away, she could indeed make out what looked like a big copper box, so at least she would not get lost. Physically at least. In every other realm of her life, she felt totally lost.

Ask Henry what? "Have you met anyone named Emily recently?" might be an opener. But his next answer would not be whether he had or not. He would ask why.

And for that, Tessa could not possibly provide an answer.

She tried to steady herself and quiet her heart as she kept walking, the early summer sun on her shoulders, still feeling the bondage of that seat belt. Harper had let her out in front of the hotel with a chirpy "have a successful event!" and it was all Tessa could do not to slam the door, or kick it. But she was so relieved to have her suitcase back she simply strode away. She noted the plate number of the car, though that would never matter.

She needed advice. But Henry was unreliable, her publisher already furious with her, and her agent would freak out. *All this could be yours.* That was supposed to have been such a good thing.

When reading a suspenseful book, Tessa sometimes flipped to the ending, to ease the tension and learn who was left alive and how the villain was captured. In real life, she couldn't take that shortcut. Something would happen at the end of this chapter of her life, and it was impossible to read ahead to find out what.

She thought about the chapters she had already lived. If she were writing the rest of her own story, how would her fictional heroine triumph?

Oh, Annabelle said. *Shall we write this in the next book?*

"Shush," Tessa said out loud. She pictured herself not on a Des Moines sidewalk, but at the kitchen table of their old house, typing on her beloved laptop. There were days when her fingers flew as if possessed, typing so quickly, the story pouring out of her, that afterward, rereading, she honestly didn't remember that she herself had written it.

Other days she sat staring at the screen, wordless. She had read somewhere that when you were stuck, a trick was to go back over what you'd already written, which unearthed what mistake your subconscious was trying to reveal. A story element you had forgotten. A broken link in the story chain. A hole in the plot. What were the holes in this story?

Harper had *not* mentioned Annabelle.

But Harper *had* mentioned . . . what? Her mother. Sheriff Owen. The real Emily, of course. Tessa had asked "who did I kill?" She winced, remembering. But Harper had not answered.

There. That was a critical story point. Harper had not answered that question.

She'd also brought up her mother's will. How would that woman know what it said? Back then, Tessa had gotten a call from a lawyer, whose name had irretrievably vanished from her memory, informing her she'd been left nothing in the will, because there was nothing to leave.

The lawyer had then asked if Tessa wanted a copy of the document, and Tessa had said no. She didn't want anything from her mother, the way her mother had never wanted anything from her. Tears came to her eyes now, of confusion and regret. If Harper had been telling the truth, her mother had been protecting her, and she had done so until she died. And even from beyond the grave. The lawyer must have known about that.

Could Harper be that lawyer? And that's why she knew so much?

Tessa tilted her head, considering that plot line.

The lawyer, conniving with Emily, to have the payments continue, only this time paid to her, and by Tessa.

Meh, Annabelle said. *Totally contrived.*

Annabelle was right. That was not the solution.

As a result, Tessa needed the library.

66

And there was the rabbit. Tessa laughed out loud when she saw the ten-foot plaster statue, with stiff white ears and black-dot eyes, standing sentinel in front of the copper-windowed library. Miffy, it said on the front. She remembered, for a flash of a moment, her mother reading her stories about Miffy—sweet Miffy, her mother would say—a bunny who lived in a garden. Someone had written the Miffy stories, Tessa thought now, staring at the creature.

I need to write my own story, Tessa told herself, *the best I can. With the ending I want.* Once she let someone else into the manuscript of her life, she thought as she pushed through the wide glass front doors of the library, they'd take control of the ending, too. She needed someone to trust. And who better than a librarian?

The woman at the front desk had hair the color of the library, in spiky copper waves, and emerald-green glasses perched like a headband. She looked up from her double-screened computer as Tessa approached, and Tessa saw her evaluating. She imagined what was going through the woman's mind. *Do I know her? From where? She looks like—*

She tilted her head, looking perplexed, when Tessa got closer. "May I help—" she began. The woman's lanyard ID tag said Mayzie Longworth, Research. "You know, you look exactly like—"

"Thank you." Tessa smiled. Sharing a secret. "I look more like her than anyone, I guess."

Mayzie's eyes widened in recognition. "We can't keep your book in the building," she said. "Massive waiting list. I was gonna come to your thing tonight at Oakdale Books, in fact, a bunch of us linguistics majors from Drake registered, we adore Annabelle, and you, but then we got the word you'd canceled—wait. You're here."

"Big misunderstanding." Tessa leaned forward, keeping her voice low. "Check your email."

Mayzie clicked her keyboard. Nodded. "Cool. Yeah, I see it. On again. Cool."

Tessa wondered what DJ's concocted excuse had been. Her heart fell as she remembered that the radio-silent publicist hadn't felt it necessary to tell her.

Mayzie swiveled the computer back into place. "So, yay. Hey, did you ever find out about the earrings? Or Locket Mom?"

"Nope. Seems like Locket Mom's the only one who didn't see the post." It was such a relief to have that deadweight gone. "Maybe they'll contact the hotel to retrieve it."

"I hope so. I'd love to know the story."

"Agreed. Me, too. Anyway." Tessa took a deep breath, hoping she could spin this so it made sense. "I'm at the Midlands Hotel down the street, but I'm researching my next book, you know how it goes, I have to work between my appearances. Now I need to be pointed in the right direction."

"For? To?" Mayzie had picked up a pencil, and pulled a yellow pad closer. "Ready."

Tessa looked behind her, making sure no one was eavesdropping, or watching them.

"Can a regular person access a police report?" Tessa kept her voice library low.

"Ah, it's like, local rules. If you filed a formal request, maybe, or went in person to the police department. Otherwise"—she shrugged—"could be a dead end."

Tessa flinched at the phrase. "Okay. How about . . . oh, never mind. Thank you. And I hope to see you tonight."

Mayzie looked at the chunky white plastic watch on her thin wrist. "'How about' what?"

Here you go, Annabelle said.

"How do I look up a will?"

"Public records. If it's old enough. And probated." Mayzie waggled her palm. *Fifty-fifty.* "*If* you know what state, county, and the person's name, and a kind of date, then . . . *ma*ybe?"

"You're amazing."

"I try. How can I be a research librarian if I don't know where to research?" She pointed. "Records. Upstairs, second door on the left. Hope you find what you're looking for."

67

"Are you in the bathroom?" Henry's voice and face came from Tessa's cell phone, now propped on top of a tissue box in the cramped and frustratingly dim bathroom of her room at the Midlands Hotel.

"I have to put on makeup. Get ready for tonight," Tessa said, dragging down one eyelid to swipe her charcoal eyeliner. She wished she could blame the lighting, but she knew it was guilt, and fear, and the specter of her life irretrievably crashing that made her look so haggard. Being accused of participating in the cover-up of a hit-and-run murder could do that to you. And even if she knew it wasn't true—and it wasn't true, *could it be?*—even the hint of such a catastrophe could ruin them all. The truth might even send her to prison.

But she could not tell Henry. The fear battered at her, a trapped creature demanding to escape.

"When last we spoke," Henry began. "If I remember correctly, and I do. You hung up on me. And did *not* say always always."

"If *I* remember correctly, and I do, you were *out*, and had left the children home. Alone. You know how much I hate—"

"If *I* remember correctly, and I do"—Henry's face was so small she could barely read his expression—"you have no idea where I was. Or why."

"On that point, at least, we agree."

"I was not 'out.' I was outside."

Tessa unscrewed her black mascara and leaned forward, talking into the mirror instead of the phone. "With your phone off. Did you figure you would simply hear the children screaming?"

"Tessa, I was outside the front door. I had turned my phone off because I kept getting spam messages."

"Oh yes," Tessa said. "So annoying. And when all hell was breaking loose in the kitchen, what were you doing, 'outside'? Were you 'outside' by yourself, pray tell?"

"*Pray tell?* Tessa, what's going on with you? I was out front, talking to the neighbors, like people do. Would you rather everyone ignored us? And the dishwasher broke, what can I tell you. I don't control the universe. I know you hate the dishwasher, you haven't even seen the dishwasher, but you hated it from moment one. I refused to argue with you over a broken dishwasher, that's insane. What is wrong with you?"

"What neighbors?" Tessa had applied makeup thousands of times with Henry watching. Now, inured to the road, Henry on the phone seemed almost as real as if he were physically standing beside her. She smoothed her eye shadow into submission, pulled out a lip pencil. Fifteen minutes before she had to leave for the bookstore. Would Harper be there, mocking her, watching her?

And tomorrow she'd have to get back into the car with that woman. So ironic—her own success was her best protection. Talk about a Faustian bargain.

"Let me ask you, Tessa." Henry's voice sounded brittle, not like Henry. "Are you imagining some mad affair, some neighborhood fling while my successful wife is gallivanting around the country? In front of our children, perhaps, wild and bacchanalian?"

"Who told you 'yellow is the new taupe'? Let me ask you that." She'd smudged her lip liner, trying to talk and apply it at the same time. She heard the edge in her own voice, shrewish and badgering, the worst kind of stereotypical wifey character, and she didn't need Annabelle to tell her to chill. But in real life, it was hard to do. She was trying to act normal when she didn't even know what normal meant.

"Before you were a big-time writer, you weren't such a pessimist,"

Henry said. "Now everything is a sinister plot, and my life is a sordid back-street affair. Nellie is a decorator, kind of, so she must have said that. We picked the color just for you. She said all writers love the sunshine."

"That's the dumbest thing I've ever heard."

"Do you want to talk later? This is no fun."

"And on that we agree as well," Tessa said. "Was it Nellie the kind-of decorator who was in the background of your phone call the other night? I saw her shadow. Or was that Barbara?"

"Mom! Mom! Is that Mom on the phone?"

Zack's voice.

"Hey, darling one." Tessa flipped the switch to Happy Mom. The kids, what would she ever tell them? "How are you, sweetheart?"

"Did you see the thing on Facebook?" Zack's face, his glasses askew, replaced Henry's on the phone screen. "About that picture you posted?"

Tessa paused, lipstick brush in midair. "No. I haven't been on Face-book all day."

"Hang on, I'll get my laptop and pull it up," Zack said. "Dad, you talk."

"What did Zack find on Facebook?" Tessa asked, filling in her lips with Ruby Slippers.

"Not a clue."

Which gave Tessa an idea. Something she should have done days ago. She could look up Nellie on social media. Barbara, too.

"While I have you," Tessa said. She checked her makeup handiwork, which was as good as it was going to get. "Did you ever get a dog?"

"We decided—"

"Who decided? When?"

Hush, Annabelle said. Let him talk.

"Whenever. I told Zack to keep it a secret, but the kids and I, and Bar-bara, decided to wait until you got home. So you can choose, too. Okay? If you ever do come home. Which sometimes it feels like you aren't."

"You wish."

"What?"

"Nothing." Tessa picked up the phone, walked toward the bedroom. So that was Zackie's secret, the dog delay. Not some earth-shattering, marriage-ruining disaster. Now, her event clothes lay like black stripes on the beige bedspread; black dress, black jacket. Blue earrings. Not the ones from the airplane. She was pretending those didn't exist. "So, this Barbara, I keep forgetting to ask you her last name."

"Willoughby," Henry said. "Why? Are you going to call and yell at her about the dog?"

Now she had two profiles to look up.

Her phone pinged with an incoming call. *Unknown caller.* Tessa's stomach hit the floor. "We'll find *you*," Harper had threatened.

Tessa had to answer. But she needed to know what Zack found on Facebook. She could look herself, though.

"I'm getting a call, and it's probably about tonight's event. I have to go. I'll call you back. Or something. Later." She paused. "Henry?"

The phone pinged again.

"I heard you," Henry said. "You'll 'call me back or something.' Very gratifying. I'll tell Zack you're too busy to hear his discovery. He seemed pretty excited to share it with you. But he's just a kid."

"No, no, please, don't do that." Her heart was shattering, smithereens. "I'm getting a business call. I *have* to answer." No. She couldn't leave it this way. "But Henry, quickly, do you know anyone named Emily?"

"Emily who?"

"I don't know. I don't know." She hadn't planned to ask him, but how could she not? "Just Emily. Emily Owen."

"Why? Who's that supposed to be?"

"Just *do* you? Oh, Henry, I have to go. I'll call you later."

"What's wrong with you, Tessa?"

"Mom!" Zack's voice, off camera, came back on the line.

"Mom says she doesn't have any more time for you now, Zachary. She says she loves you and she'll talk to you later."

And Henry hung up.

Tessa's heart wrenched in her chest, heavy with sorrow and fear and decisions and with impossible distance. She touched the green Answer Call button and prayed.

68

"Oh, it said unknown caller. Hi, DJ." Tessa's unzipped black dress hung open in the back, her jacket still flat on the bedspread. She aimed her voice at the phone on the ruffled pillow sham, trying to sound happy and normal. Trying not to worry that her publicist was breaking her radio silence with more hideous news. "I've got you on speaker because I'm getting dressed for the event. Can you hear me?"

"Yeah," DJ said. "You cannot be late, not after all that. And I'm using my other phone. But it's about Locket Mom. And that photo."

Tessa had yanked up the back of her black dress, trying to reach the zipper pull. Now she stopped, frozen. At least DJ was talking to her again. About Locket Mom.

"Did you find her?"

"Listen, I'd thought it was a fake photo, like a computer-generated or clip art sample. But it seems to be real."

"How do you know? Did you find the person?"

"Nope." DJ was still talking. "I got a dude to check a database on the down-low, don't tell, but no matches. Which only means, though it's a good thing, the guy in the photo isn't a criminal, or wanted, or has a warrant. That they know of."

That they know of, Annabelle said.

That they know of. A phrase like that, such a land mine.

"Well, that's good, at least." Tessa tried not to gulp. Had to risk it. "Um, DJ? Might it mean he's dead? The man in the picture?"

"Dead?" DJ paused. "I guess so. Why would you ask that?"

"Just—nothing. Thanks, DJ, for thinking about me. I know it's a lot." Tessa had conquered the zipper, finally, and clasped her necklace into place. She was running on empty now, in mental overload, the clock ticking away the minutes until she had to be erudite and engaging. And sell enough books to keep her family safe.

"Well, yeah. That picture is still getting comments on Facebook," DJ was saying. "That's the other reason I called. Someone posted that they'd analyzed the shoreline behind the father."

Tessa pictured the photo. The man, the corner of a cabin, and the water's edge. The comment must have been what Zack saw.

"How?" was all she could think of to say.

"Whatever. It said it's topography, and easy to do with a computer. And they said it turns out that it's—"

"Maine." The word came out before she could stop it.

"So you saw it."

"No." She sat on the edge of the bed. Doomed. "I just guessed. Maine. Mount Desert Island, right?"

"So that means something to you." DJ's speakered judgment hung in the flat hotel room air.

Tessa stayed silent. That was unanswerable.

"Tessa? Is this place your hometown, where you told us someone was asking about?"

"No."

"The picture is on Facebook, Tessa." DJ's voice from the pillow had hardened again. "It doesn't matter who has the actual locket and photograph now. *You* posted it. It's public. If there's anything secret about it, *you're* the one who revealed it. And *we're* the ones who are gonna get buried in the blame for it."

Tessa lowered herself to the edge of the bed, stared at the dreary wallpaper. DJ had thought posting it was a great idea at the time, but this wasn't the moment to bring that up.

"I'll take it down."

"Too late for *that*, I'm afraid."

Too late for everything, Tessa thought. *And I'm afraid, too.*

"But listen," DJ was saying, "no one's tried to claim that locket. If someone wanted to get rid of it, they'd trash it. So it must have been left behind for a purpose. For you to find it."

"But why? And how would anyone know I'd be in that room?"

"A million ways. Tessa? Do we need to bring you back? Call this tour off? You have to tell me, right now."

Silence again, and Tessa pulled on her shoes. She wore her event makeup, and her book-tour outfit, but there was no way to dress up her emotions. The past was indelible, immeasurably deep, and now threatened to drown her in its reality. And drag her family down with her.

Because once her mother's money ran out, Tessa had received a locket.

And then been given an ultimatum in the back seat of a stranger's car.

They had to be connected.

Tessa could almost hear the police knocking on her door. Could almost feel the handcuffs. Watch her family disappear into the prison van's rearview.

She was the loser in a bargain she did not know she'd made.

"Tessa? Do I pull the plug? I'm about to. Even though it'll be an unmitigated disaster."

"DJ, no," Tessa began, praying in earnest now. "It's fine. All fine. I promise," she lied. "But the commenter who said it was Maine. Did they say anything else?"

"In fact, yeah, as if this whole thing isn't already enough of a debacle. They wondered if you wrote about Maine in your pink diary. Does 'pink diary' mean anything to you?"

69

"I ask myself: What does someone want and how far will they go to get it?" Tessa could not believe she was saying those words, now, in answer to a "How did you write such a page-turner?" question from the Oakdale Books audience. She'd made it through her presentation, bestseller-mode fully engaged, and now calculated how much longer she had to pretend she wasn't consumed with guilt and fear. Fifteen more minutes of Q and A, then the signing. She could do it. So many in her audiences wanted to be writers—"just like you," they'd always say, which meant a bestseller and successful and happy and on book tour, which tonight almost made her collapse with sorrow.

Had they but known that "just like you" meant terrified and black-mailed and haunted and probably a criminal. That "just like you" meant about to lose your livelihood, and your family. And your freedom.

"Does the character want love, for instance? Money? Revenge? Justice? When you know what a character wants, you understand their motivation." She gestured across the crowded audience, making eye contact, making sure they were interested. The events manager, Judith Hensle, had rolled the store's book-filled shelves behind dozens of beige chairs. Tessa stood behind a wooden podium on an elevated rectangular platform. The center of attention. Or the target. "You understand their passion. In real life, what do you do when you want something? You go after it. And that is *action*. And that's what makes a page-turner."

Tessa paused, watching the rapt faces listening to her, nodding, some even taking notes. The women, in pastel cardigans and pressed jeans, many in periwinkle earrings, dressed for a balmy June night in Des Moines and an hour's worth of entertainment and conversation about books and writing. How could the world still look so normal? How could things seem so unchanged?

"Let me ask *you* a question." She leaned in, conspiratorial. "Since I'm working on my new book, I'd love your advice. What do *you* think makes a page-turner?"

The audience laughed, appreciative.

"Secrets!"

"High stakes!"

"Good ones." Tessa nodded, smiling, pretended to write the words down. "More?"

"Increasing danger." The voice came from the back of the room.

Tessa's chin came up, alerting at that voice, and she tried to stand taller to see past the heads and shoulders that blocked it. No mistake about it. That Harper woman. And now, standing in the back of the room, half-hidden behind a rolling bookshelf, she was taunting her, brazen and fearless. Just like this morning, speaking words that sounded innocent on the surface, but carried deep and deadly subtext.

Tessa fingered her pearl necklace, thinking about secrets and high stakes and increasing danger. That woman was here. Menacing and audacious. But she could not be allowed to disrupt tonight's event.

"Do you think justice should always be done?" Tessa asked. "When you read a book, are you disappointed if the bad guys don't get what's coming to them?"

"The bad guys should always pay," the voice came back.

Tessa clutched the molded wood podium in front of her, grounding herself. There was nothing she could do about her knees, which were threatening to give out. She was trapped, surrounded by two hundred people. Trapped.

"Do you agree, everyone?" Tessa asked the room, making herself engaging, making this be a fabulous and memorable writerly conversation, one that the audience would cherish and remember. For better or for worse.

A murmur of agreement, and Tessa went on.

"Do you have to *like* the main character? Let me ask you that. If they make a mistake, can that be forgiven?"

A hand went up, a woman in a center row with tight ebony curls and periwinkle earrings.

"Yes?" Tessa felt as if she were living in a parallel universe, Happy Tessa fielding questions from an admiring audience, with Miserable Tessa cowering underneath, uncertain and terrified, every element of her life at risk. And the audience had no idea.

Except for one of them.

"Yes, you with the gorgeous earrings. Go ahead."

"Are you talking about Annabelle?" The woman stood, her neighbors on either side tilting their heads up to watch her. "Annabelle made some questionable decisions, and some dangerous bargains. But we love her all the same. She knew what she wanted, she knew her truth, and she went after it. Even when it was dangerous. And everyone makes mistakes." The woman stopped, put a French-manicured hand to her chest. "Oh. Sorry for babbling, I got carried away."

"No, that's a terrific insight," Tessa said. Everything hung in the balance. It was all she could do not to look at her watch. She was disappointed she had not heard from librarian Mayzie about the will—she'd been frustratingly unable to find it, and Mayzie had offered to search after hours, even bring it to the bookstore if she succeeded. She'd been counting on that. "Yes, everyone makes mistakes. And we try to forgive them, if we can."

"We love you, Tessa," someone called out. "And Annabelle, too."

"You're the best," Tessa said. "I am so grateful."

It was only these women who were keeping her sane. They felt she had changed their lives with her Annabelle book—and little did they know they were now saving hers. But if she failed to sell enough books tonight, or let this bookstore down, it might be the beginning of the end. The events manager would grumble, or send a testy report to Waverly: *Tessa wasn't herself. We expected better.*

But now Judith Hensle was hurrying toward her; clapping her beringed hands, her short dark-blond hair tamed behind her ears with a periwinkle headband, her face beaming with appreciation. "Tessa, thank you," she was saying. "We could talk all night, and you all would stay, wouldn't you? We're grateful the cancellation was a mistake, but as someone said, everyone can make mistakes. As long as there's a happy ending."

The audience agreed, one voice.

"Happy endings are my favorite," Tessa said.

"One more question," Judith said. "I'll choose."

Good luck, Annabelle said.

Hands shot up. Tessa searched for Harper, but she was not in sight; still hiding, or gone. And no Mayzie. She probably hadn't found anything, and was embarrassed to show up.

Judith closed her eyes, pointed back and forth across around the room like a child's game. Stopped. Opened her eyes. "Yes. You in the blue earrings."

Whew, Annabelle said.

"Tessa? Did you find Locket Mom?" A twentysomething in wire-rims, floppy fuchsia T-shirt. "Why'd you take down the photo?"

70

If there was any remaining possibility of rational thought, it had vanished. Tessa's brain felt like those schedule boards at train stations, *clack clack clack*, as the flaps switched positions, changing everything. Obliterating what had been there before. *Clack clack clack*, in Tessa's head now, as her weary brain tried to comprehend what this person in the Oakdale Books audience could possibly mean. Tessa had not touched that photo.

DJ must have done it. She'd been angry on the phone. And early on, she'd happily given DJ access to her Facebook page.

"The man by the water," the woman went on. "His photo is gone."

"Oh, right, of course. My poor, overworked book-tour mind." Tessa banged her palm to her forehead, *duh*. Get it together, kiddo, she thought. If DJ had taken the photo down, fine. But she had not told Tessa. So now she'd have to make up some reason why it wasn't there. If it really wasn't. Unless this person—who seemed straightforward and guileless—was testing to see how Tessa would respond.

"Here's a secret." Tessa leaned forward, conspiratorial. "I'm not the only one who has access. My fabulous publicist does, too. So maybe she has news. I'll check when I get back to the hotel."

Slow down, Annabelle said. *People don't need to know every single thing that might possibly have happened. They're only trying to connect with you.*

"Oh, do," the woman said. "And post it. It would be so fun to know who Locket Mom is."

"Wouldn't it?" It was all Tessa could do not to look toward the far bookshelves. Search for Harper's face. "I'm as eager to find out as you are."

"And on that note"—the store manager took a step closer—"I think we will—"

"Could I just ask?" The voice from the back, again.

Damn it, Annabelle said. *She's still here.*

"Sure," Judith said. "Quickly."

"Before—someone—took it down," Harper said, and Tessa could hear the disdain in her voice, "I saw a comment that said they thought the photo was from Maine. Did you see that? Or hear about that?"

Everyone, even the store manager, was watching Tessa, expectant.

If she lied now, Harper could make this worse. And push her and push her and push her, and who knew how far this woman would go? She had spent the last weeks, even longer, Tessa was sure, making Tessa miserable. And now, the hook set and bit between her teeth, it was impossible to control her. Talk about understanding a character's motivation. And how far they would go to get what they want.

"I *did*," Tessa said, feigning enthusiasm. "Isn't it *superly* fascinating! Yes, I've been to Maine, and I *love* it there." Oh-so-perky. Oh-so-congenial. "So—thank you so much, you all!"

The applause gave Tessa a moment to think. DJ had told her the person who posted the Maine reference had asked about her pink diary. Did that mean something to her? DJ had asked.

No, Tessa had told her.

But it did. The pink leather book with the tiny brass lock—the key long ago lost—she'd had since she was fifteen. The only people who had ever seen that diary were her mother, who had given it to her when times were different, and Emily. The real Emily. After that second summer in Maine, it became Tessa's solace, writing in her bedroom, even keeping track of how many times she'd written to Emily. How many letters went unanswered. Until she'd finally tucked it away. Tessa hadn't opened it since. But it wasn't gone. She knew right where it was.

And of course it revealed The Bad Thing. And her real name.

ALL THIS COULD BE YOURS   289

She thought about that diary as Judith pointed Tessa's fans and readers toward the signing table.

At least, in their *old* house she knew where it was.

But it had been packed and moved and was now someplace in their brand-new Rockport home.

And now, everyone in that house—including and especially Henry— might have access to it.

71

Had she forgotten to leave the lights on? When Tessa clicked open her hotel room door into dense and unfamiliar darkness, it was all she could do to cross the threshold. Strangers had gotten into her hotel rooms before, that was not her imagination. Someone might be lurking behind every closet and sliding door. Danger might be hidden in every drawer. In her suitcase. Under the bed. She clicked on all the lights, every one of them, even the ugly gooseneck by the window, and the television, too. Yanked the curtains across the windows, shutting out the street below. Changed into her jersey nightgown with the bathroom door closed and wrapped on a terry bathrobe, needing privacy, craving security. Security that had utterly vanished.

She'd made it through the event, unsettled and wary, had forced herself to focus on her readers. Signing two hundred books, and searching every face. Meanwhile, Harper had disappeared. Tessa, hyperalert, Ubered back to the hotel. Felt like a fugitive as she hurried through the hotel lobby and up to her room, apprehensive at every step, feeling watched and monitored and trapped.

Ten at night in Des Moines, and she was starving, but the front desk clerk had told her room service was closed. Now she was in her nightgown, with nothing but a bag of pretzels from the airplane and the two complimentary bottles of hotel water. If she broke down, from the fear and the guilt, it wouldn't matter. Nothing would matter. And her search for the will had been a dead end.

She yanked open the foil bag of pretzels with her teeth, spilling salt and twisted things all over the gray carpeting. *Do not cry,* she ordered herself, she did not need Annabelle to remind her.

She could foresee a day when she'd never see her husband or children again. Whatever Henry's petty transgressions had been, it didn't matter. Not when Tessa had been a part of a devastating crime. She hadn't known, she honestly hadn't, but because she didn't know didn't mean it didn't exist.

Tomorrow that woman was picking her up. Tomorrow she would know—something.

Perched on the edge of the bed, her back to the curtains, the light from the muted TV in her peripheral vision, she flipped open her laptop. And opened Facebook.

The woman at the bookstore had been right. The locket picture on Tessa's Facebook page was gone. Everything else remained; Tessa's snapshots of audiences, her airport adventures, the joyous hoopla of book tour, success and adventure. Only the photo of the man in Maine had disappeared.

Three sharp raps on her door. *Wrong room,* she wanted to yell. *Mistake. Go away.*

Three more raps. There were no packages for her. She would never accept another package. No more chocolates. If she pretended she was not here, they would go away.

It worked. The footsteps receded. She closed her computer and crept to the peephole. The padding footsteps started again. Coming closer.

Tessa pivoted. Put her back to the door, her head covering the peephole. Her heart pounding. Trying not to breathe. She heard a sound, and then a white thing came under her door, slid past her bare feet, and lay there. A single white, business-sized envelope on the gray carpeting.

She stared at the blank rectangle. Lying there, taunting her, daring her to look inside.

"What do you *want* from me?" she said out loud.

They've made that pretty clear, Annabelle said. *And more to come when she picks you up tomorrow.*

She yanked open her hotel room door, not caring about the bathrobe, and looked both ways, up and down the sconce-lighted hall. She grabbed her room key, closed the door, and raced, barefoot, toward the elevator. But the doors had already closed.

And now, she realized as she raced back to her room, the envelope was probably gone. Of *course.* Whoever was tormenting her would certainly not have missed the opportunity to screw with her one last time tonight.

She tapped her key card, opened the door.

The room was still empty. The envelope was still there.

Every ugly name in her vocabulary raced through her mind. Every bitter and hateful description of that woman in the car, the woman who'd seemed to revel in showing how much access she had, how much power over Tessa's career and family, her entire life.

Blackmail never worked for long, Tessa knew that, from movies maybe, or reading thrillers? But it seemed to be working now, that was for sure. She closed her door. Locked it. Chained it.

She swooped up the envelope, giving only a moment's thought about fingerprints—then ripped it open. Inside, white paper folded in thirds.

The paper made a crackling sound as she pulled it from the envelope. Papers, plural, it turned out, stapled at the upper left corner. She walked toward the desk, unfolding.

Copies, she could tell from the intermittent gray borders around the edges. And no mystery what this was. She recognized it instantly from the caption at the top.

THE LAST WILL AND TESTAMENT OF
SAVANNAH MATTIGAN DANFORTH

72

"Got your tickets, dear? Watch, wallet, phone, laptop? Just being your help-ful driver today." Harper had come into the bustling hotel lobby to collect her, wearing a lavender Iowa State ball cap, Jackie O sunglasses, an over-sized lavender sweatshirt, frumpy jeans, and pristine white tennis shoes. She looked more like someone's softball mom than a blackmailer. "Don't want you to miss that plane. The bookstore in Philadelphia is sold out, so I hear."

The woman reached for Tessa's roller bag, but when Tessa swiveled it out of her grasp, she fluttered a dismissive hand at her, *whatever*, and sashayed through the revolving door.

Tessa, fuming, trailed her to a white Toyota. The license plate was different from yesterday's car. Harper clicked open the doors, and Tessa tossed her suitcase into the cramped back seat. And put her tote on top of it. No trunk. Not this time.

"Whatever works for you," the woman said as she slid into the driver's seat. "Sure you don't want to sit in the front?"

"What do you want from me?" Tessa yanked on her seat belt, enraged. What was truth and what was fiction—that was still to be determined. But the dénouement was coming fast now, and where Tessa would wind up when this story was over—she had to keep that in her sights. She felt gut-twisting guilt, and heartbreaking sorrow, but she'd been as much a victim—almost as much—as whoever they'd left in the middle of that shadowy Maine dirt road.

Reading her mother's will last night had only made things worse. So. Much. Worse. It appeared—shockingly, unimaginably, devastatingly— that this woman was right. The payments existed. The will had spec- ified the amount to be paid every six months, and created the trust to receive them. Her own mother's will meant Tessa, innocently complicit in a horrible crime, was irrevocably trapped.

"Let's get out of the hotel driveway before we talk, Tessa," Harper said. "Although I'm gratified you seem eager to come to an agreement. Airport, here we come."

"Bull," Tessa murmured, making sure her voice did not carry to the front seat. The driver merrily waved to a bellhop as they rounded the curve onto the main street, took the first left. A square green sign with an arrow pointed forward—DSM Airport 10, it said. Ten miles until she could get out of this car. Ten miles to see how much she could learn. How much she could fight. Depending on traffic, that could give her twenty minutes.

But Tessa could not miss her plane. This woman knew that.

Because Tessa was only good to these people alive. And so intensely ironic, that Tessa's one superpower lay in book sales. If she stopped selling books, she was valueless to them.

Still. It was difficult enough to sell books without having someone put a metaphorical gun to your head.

Stoplights, rush hour traffic, an orange cone narrowing two lanes to one. The woman had not said a word. And Tessa was not about to start this conversation.

Last night, she'd barely slept. Mayzie had tucked a yellow sticky note inside the will: 'Found it! Sorry couldn't make it tonight, so cool to meet you.' But with the incriminating document zipped in an inside pocket of her suitcase—even if she'd burned it, the original document still existed—she'd lain awake, spiraling into irretrievable tragedy. She'd imagined walking out the door of the Des Moines hotel, with this monster to greet her. Imag- ined getting into her car, *actually getting into the car*! In a novel, no smart heroine would ever do that. Not ever.

Unless her family's safety was at stake, Tessa had reassured herself, smashing her hotel pillow into submission. Unless everything in her entire and complete life was on the line.

Highway signs whizzed by now, a blur. In her mind's eye she saw the old-fashioned typed words and the arcane legalese as plainly as if she were holding the pages of the will in her hands. Tessa needed a lawyer to untangle the details, but the wording indicated the payments were a "periodic bequest" to a trust that would continue as long as Tessa herself—who was referred to as Tessa Danforth, her post–bad thing name—was alive.

Or until the money ran out.

And the same phrase looped through her brain, over and over. Her mother would not have paid for a deer.

This was real blackmail. With an explosive secret behind it. The story of that night—*not a deer*—was all true. And that meant Tessa's entire history, everything she believed, was all a fiction. Now, exactly as this woman had threatened the day before, Tessa was a character in a true crime narrative. And what's more, she was the guilty one.

Starting now, everything she did on this tour—signing books, engaging audiences, chatting with bookstore owners, accepting the praise of her publishers—was a performance. A fake. The illusion would shatter into infinite pieces if she did not do what this woman ordered.

She closed her eyes, feeling the forward motion of the car, and tried to remember her joys; the day she met Henry, and when Linny was born, and then Zack, too, and when she'd recognized Annabelle's voice, and then the book and everything that happened. And today was Tuesday. Tomorrow the bestseller list would be out.

She would do anything, anything, to make this all go away.

Would you? Annabelle said. Now you understand how your mother felt. Now you're the parent. How far will you go to get what you want?

73

Three exits until the airport. The woman in the front seat had not spoken. Tessa had been tempted to record the whole thing on her phone, but that would simply result in creating evidence of *Tessa's* crime. The key here—the entire goal—was to keep this woman from talking about what had happened that night. Money, apparently, had accomplished that for all these years. So said her mother's will. Would money work again?

She loathed the thought of it. It sickened her to her core. But how much was her family worth? Happiness? Safety? How much would she pay for that?

"You should have *seen* your face when I asked about your Facebook post last night." The traffic had slowed, rubbernecking at some fender bender, and Harper had twisted over the front seat, maybe to gauge Tessa's reaction.

Tessa saw her carefully outlined lips, and the reflection of Tessa herself mirrored in the dark lenses of her oversized sunglasses.

Harper clicked on the turn signal as the traffic picked up, steered into the fast lane. "You were completely gobsmacked."

"I wasn't anything." Tessa put as much scorn as possible in her voice. "My publisher took it down. Exactly as I said." Tessa had texted DJ last night from the Uber, trying to sound cheery and chirpy, reporting the successful event, then mentioning the missing photo. She'd also told her, lying, that she didn't need a driver to the airport today. I'll take the hotel shuttle, she'd texted. It's easy, and only hotel guests allowed. Totally safe.

It's your tour, DJ had texted back. And stolen photo was distraction. Cld not allow. Told you we watch yr socials. We have access. TTYL.

DJ's enthusiasm had vanished. And maybe all of Team Tessa's, too. "Distraction." If only DJ knew.

"Why do you care anyway? The locket?" Tessa now asked.

"What do *you* think?"

The highway traffic surrounded them, people on their particular journeys, shifting gears, changing lanes.

"So you *did* put it there. How? Why? And who are you, anyway? Who is Locket Mom? Is it you?" The necklace had been in the nightstand in that Indianapolis hotel room. "How did you manage to get someone to stay in that room before I did?"

"Please. *Locket* Mom. Kidding me? That was the fairy tale you invented. After we learned which room you'd been given, we put it in the drawer, and waited. Not me personally, of course. We'd made a backup plan, because you might have simply turned it in. But you didn't. As a result you added our tracker to your luggage."

"A tracker?" A sinister surveillance system materialized in Tessa's mind, some electronic thing mindlessly, silently, mapping her every move for these people. "But *why?* And how did you get into my room in Denver to steal it again?"

"Tessa, you are incredibly entertaining. You write fiction, what ways could you think of that we might do that? It was one of those. Moving forward, though. We want to impress upon you that you are never really alone. We always know where you are. We can get to you. And your family. We run your life. Remember that."

"That's impossible." Tessa pushed at her suitcase, bitter. Its wheels were digging into her thigh. This was supposed to be her triumphant book tour. Not a kidnapping on a Midwestern highway.

"Hardly," the woman said. "Your website? Your social media? Your out-of-town events? Your life is pretty much—forgive me—an open book."

"No. You know more than that. And who *are* you?"

"Pass. Next question."

"Is Evelyn Wickwire working with you? Or a person named Sam?"

"Good lord. Whatever. We saw you give that woman the locket. As if that could extricate you. At least now we know where *she* is all the time. Until the tracker battery dies. And we won't need to steal it back to replace it, like we did for you."

Tessa's heart deflated like an exhausted balloon.

"But who's *in* it? The picture?" Tessa had searched the image, and came up with nothing. But DJ had told her it was a real person. Devastating as it was, she had to know. "Who's the family?"

Harper made a sound like a game show buzzer. "Nope. We're finished with the Q and A part of this ride, Tessa. And excellent timing. There's the sign for the airport."

"That's not . . . fair," Tessa said. "You're asking me to pay to keep something quiet. I don't believe what you're accusing me of is true. So, since you insist it *is* true, whose life is it that you allege I ended? If you can't tell me that, then we have nothing more to discuss."

"You're a better writer than you are a negotiator, Tessa. You have nothing to bargain with. As for the photograph. Come on. You know who it is."

Harper swerved right, crossing two lanes, narrowly missing a speeding red Jeep. Tessa braced herself against the front seat to keep her balance, and her tote bag fell onto the floor. The Jeep driver leaned on the horn. Harper barked a sharp laugh. "If only you had been as good a driver as I am."

"I was *not*—" Tessa stopped herself, mid denial. "The man," Tessa said. "The man in the photograph is the one who . . ."

And at that moment, everything she already knew rearranged itself into gasping clarity. The man in the photo was the victim. It was his family photo. Treasured by his survivors. The family who, it was immaculately clear to her now, demanded retribution for their loved one's death.

"You always were a smart girl," the woman said.

Tessa barely heard her words. How could anyone even argue with retribution? If she—and the real Emily, the one who'd been driving—had killed someone—she could barely think it—then they both *did* owe his family something. Nothing could make up for a life, but they had taken something precious, and money was the only way to try to make up for it.

Her brain raced ahead. Why hadn't they simply sued her? Or her mother? And Emily's parents? The answers came quickly. Emily's parents were not well-off; her father a county employee, and if Tessa remembered correctly, her stepmother a stay-at-home parent. But *Tessa's* mother—an outsider, aggressively affluent, prowling for status—was a perfect target. Plus, she'd already admitted, by setting up the payments to continue even after she died, that her daughter was guilty. Why argue in court if there's nothing to argue *about?*

The man in the photo was dead. Emily had killed him. Tessa was complicit. Guilty. And her mother had acknowledged it.

She was part of a Faustian bargain she'd never known she'd made. And now she'd be the one to pay. Her mother had sold her soul . . . for *her.* Now it was her turn.

That was her mother's legacy. Or her own.

"Tessa?" Harper slowed, pointing. "Airport exit dead ahead. Do we have an understanding?"

Silence in the car now, the only sound the tick-tock click of the turn signal.

"Tell me who it is. Was. Tell me."

"So we'll contact you to arrange for your mother's agreement to continue?" Harper went on, as if Tessa had not spoken. "Or will you have to miss your plane?"

"You don't win if I miss my event," Tessa said. "You need me to be a bestseller. You need me to sell books. If I fail, you lose."

"I never lose," the woman said.

74

The morning light filtered through the tall windows of the Des Moines airport, a flat, tree-spiked green expanse outside, corridors of gray carpeting and white-stanchioned waiting areas inside. The last thing Tessa had heard from that woman was a cheerful "talk to you soon!" As if she were simply some accommodating friend making an airport run. On an ordinary day, Tessa would have been looking forward to a packed bookstore in Philadelphia, then settling into another hotel with a cozy bathrobe and bad TV. And, along with her loyal Team Tessa, trying not to fret about whether she'd make the *Times* bestseller list.

But it hit her, hard, with the leaden weight of inevitability. She would never have another ordinary day. Never.

Trundling her roller bag toward the gate and seething with fear and despair and frustration, she strode by the familiar coffee shops and newsstands and trinket shops, not even tempted by the periwinkle covers at the already bustling bookstore. The one thing airports did *not* have was the one thing she needed—privacy. There was absolutely nowhere for her to make this phone call. But she had to do it. She had an hour before her flight boarded—8:30 a.m. in Des Moines, nine thirty on the East Coast. She would do it now.

Choosing a molded plastic seat close to the window of her gate, she jabbed her charger into the wall plug. She'd looked up the phone number

last night. Added it to her contacts. And now, turning her back to the airport concourse, she hit Call.

"Whittaker Law," a voice answered. "How may I direct you?"

"Bernard Whittaker, please," Tessa said.

"Are you a client?"

"My mother was. Savannah Mattigan. Um, Danforth. Savannah Danforth."

"One moment, please."

Tessa had searched Bernard Whittaker last night, calculating how old
he must be. Over seventy, but still practicing trust and estates law. Luckily
for her. She hoped.

"This is Bernard Whittaker."

"Mr. Whittaker," Tessa began. "This is—"

"I've been waiting for this call," the lawyer cut her off. "I'm afraid
there's nothing I can do."

Tessa blinked, trying to understand. "Nothing about what? Waiting . . . why?"

"The funds have been exhausted. The disbursements have stopped.
Whatever you were doing with that money, there is no more."

"Oh. Mr. Whittaker, no. I mean, no. The money wasn't—*I* wasn't getting the money. I'm her daughter, Theresa Savannah Mattigan. I mean, she
changed it to Tessa Danforth, and now I'm married, Tessa Calloway. I've
seen the will now. She didn't leave anything to me. Isn't that correct? That's
what you, or someone in your office, told me? Back then."

Tessa heard silence on the other end of the line. Then tapping, maybe
the lawyer getting into his computer.

"Ms. Danforth? Yes. Calloway. I see. Your mother told me if you ever
called, I should ask you a question to confirm you were who you said you
were. I have to say, she told me she hoped you would never call."

"I understand," Tessa said. "What question?"

"One moment," he said. "Let me open the file to make it official."

Behind her, the airport commotion that had become so familiar. An
infant crying, the laugh of a child, the rumble of roller bag wheels. Muffled announcements from across the concourse. The real world. Not hers.

"Are you there?" Whittaker's voice sounded gruff, and wary.

"I'm here." What question could her mother have relied on her to answer? They had never discussed this. They had never discussed anything. Tessa had gone to college, and the next thing she knew, her mother was dead.

"The question," he said, "is, 'What kind of animal was it?'"

"A deer," she said, without even thinking.

Tessa felt the atmosphere change.

"How may I help you, Ms. Calloway?"

Tessa explained, as quickly as she could, that she had gotten a copy of the will, and seen the payments to the Acadia Road Trust. "What is that? Who is behind that?" She paused, hesitant to ask something incriminating. "Did she tell you *why* those payments were being made?"

"Why? No. I thought you were the beneficiary, frankly. But in that type of trust, the beneficiaries are sealed. Secret. That's the point."

"No," Tessa said. "It's not me. I never got—"

"Your mother said the opposite, Ms. Calloway. Your mother indicated it *was* for your benefit. I asked about bequests to her children, and she told me this was for her sole child. That is you, correct? She and your father divorced at some point, and he is deceased as well. Correct?"

"So can I—can I find out where that money went?"

"I'm afraid not."

Tessa gazed out the window across the wide swath of grass and past the row of trees and into the blue Iowa sky. She'd thought calling her mother's lawyer would reveal who was behind this scheme. But it was another dead end. Everything was a dead end.

"I know this month is the anniversary of her death," he went on, "so I understand it's top of mind. But your mother loved you very much, Ms. Calloway." His voice had softened. "If I may tell you that. Even after all this time, it can be reassuring to hear. And I am sorry for your loss. I'm sure she told you of her . . . issues."

She heard the cautiousness in the lawyer's voice.

"Issues?"

"Your mother's illness. Chronic heart disease."

She had not thought her own heart could be any more deeply broken, but apparently sorrow and regret had no boundaries. Her life had been a complete fiction. Her personal history infinitely false. Her own mother, with "issues" she knew nothing about.

"I was dismayed, though, when the police called about the heart attack," the lawyer was saying. "One of those unforeseen things, supremely bad luck."

"Not suicide."

"Sui—no. There was no evidence of that whatsoever. Why would you think that?"

"Well, I . . ." She could not answer that.

"Tessa? If I may call you that? Every record of every unattended death is public. It's kept in the municipality where the death occurred. But you don't need to go into that. As executor of the will, I dealt with it at the time. It was a heart attack. I was fond of her, and I know how much she loved you. That's why I assumed that the trust was for you. 'This will take care of my daughter for as long as I can,' she told me."

"Take care of me," Tessa said.

"That's all she was concerned about, Tessa. She wanted you to be free to follow your dreams."

75

"Sweetheart? Honey? I'm on the plane and they're going to make me turn off my phone in a minute, but I wanted to say how much I love you. And miss you all." The flight attendant had given Tessa a baleful look, pointing to her phone. And then to the chunky watch on her wrist. Tessa nodded; *I get it.* "We're about to take off. But yes, isn't that funny that the picture was in Maine? Did you know about topography?"

"Mom?" Zack had interrupted. "Dad's trying to get the phone back, even though I told him you have to go. Can you get me a Philadelphia hat?"

"I'll get you all the hats you ever wanted. Give Linny and your father a hug for me, and I'll call you the minute I land, okay? Do you miss me?"

"Did you make the *Times* list?" Henry's voice now.

"Hen, you are too much." Tessa rolled her eyes. "I won't know until tomorrow. Got to go. I love you though, Hen, I really do. No matter what happens . . ."

"No matter what happens with the *Times*?"

The flight attendant was now flat-out glaring at her.

"No matter what happens with anything. I have to go, darling. I love you."

"Love you too. And, oh, can you send me your schedule again? It's not—"

"Ma'am?"

Tessa turned off the phone. "Done." She held it up for the flight attendant to see. "Thank you so much for your patience."

The flight attendant hustled away, leaving Tessa with her thoughts. She was grateful for the empty seat beside her: she did not need recognition, or scrutiny, or chitchat. Her future, and her family's, hung in the balance. A balance she could only regain by agreeing to a limitless, bottomless persecution. Dark thoughts tiptoed into her mind. Blackmail never ended, not until someone was arrested. Or killed.

Remember when you tried to get me to kill someone? Annabelle said. In the book?

You wouldn't do it, Tessa thought, remembering the moment in her first manuscript draft where the only option seemed to be for Annabelle to shoot someone. Tessa remembered sitting at her computer, stuck, blocked, unable to find the words. And realized she was trying to make her character do something she wouldn't have done. "Out of character," she'd said it out loud then, realizing what the phrase meant.

Exactly, Annabelle said. You thought of something else. A better idea. Now's the time to do that again.

Harper had not been on the plane, and that gave her some solace, at least, as she trotted up the steps to the Free Library of Philadelphia, still in her airplane clothes, the muggy gray sky streaked with clouds. A green-framed historical marker, emblazoned with a portrait of Benjamin Franklin, promised "free books for all" since 1891. This particular branch, according to the sign, had been open for almost one hundred years.

Harper could not possibly be here. Not immediately at least. Had that woman been the person in the gray wig in Denver? The person in Seattle who asked about her summer vacation? Tessa saw so many people every day, and Harper looked different each time she saw her. Technically, though, geographically, it could have all been the same person. If Tessa could physically get to those places, so could she.

Tessa had checked in and dumped her stuff at the boutique hotel—longing for sleep and lusting over the voluptuous four-poster bed and luxurious comforter. She had two hours to see what she could find.

The library's central room, with lofty white molded ceiling and Palladian windows and with the unmistakable fragrance of sharpened pencils and aging paper, reminded her of the power of words. And the power of history. She followed a floor plan upstairs to the room marked Reference.

"You're . . ." The woman at the desk, whose name plate said Constance, pointed to her. "Annabelle."

"In a way," Tessa said. "Thanks. Can you help me with some research?"

Constance, with a coronet of gray braids and prim Peter Pan collar, might have worked there since the beginning. Fragile, with slender fingers resting on her keyboard, reading glasses dangling from a chain around her neck.

A row of long wooden tables had a green-shaded lamp at each seat, but all were empty.

"That's my job," Constance said. "Is it for a new book?"

"It is," Tessa lied. There would probably never be another book. "I need to—well—you know how they say books are based on real life? That works for true crime or nonfiction. But in fiction, it's the opposite. We want to make sure something *didn't* happen in a certain place, so readers don't think we're referring to it."

Constance nodded. "You want the book to feel realistic, but not step on toes."

"Exactly." Tessa checked their surroundings again. Coast clear. "Can you look up deaths in general? By the specific place?"

"I can try. I mean—it's possible."

Tessa bullet-pointed place and date. "So I need to find out whether anyone was killed there then. Or died. Doesn't matter who or how."

Constance clicked her mouse.

"*Any* deaths in Blytheton on that date," Tessa went on, wondering if the now-even-more-despicable Sheriff Owen had pulled some strings to make it look like the person—Tessa's heart dropped to her feet, and she tried to ignore it—had died another way. She had to pursue this. "Or even around there. Even a few days after."

"Not a problem."

For you, Tessa thought.

"I know you have other work—"

"Hush," Constance said. "Sit."

Tessa couldn't bear to sit, so she pretended to examine the dingy oil-painted portraits on the wall. Trying to keep herself from running out the door as fast as she possibly could.

Was she about to discover the name of a person she'd killed? Not *her*, specifically, but *they*, her and Emily. In their forest primeval, they'd spun out the stories of their futures; promising to live next door to each other in someplace cool, and have careers as famous authors and smart, loving husbands and perfect children who loved to read. And then it had happened, and Tessa had never returned to Maine. Physically, at least. All of her clandestine letters to Emily had gone unanswered. But that's what always happened when you told about the bad thing. And Emily probably hated her for getting her in so much trouble.

Finally, Tessa had given up. Let Emily go.

"I'm in," Constance said. "Deaths, village of Blytheton and in the entire county, that one week in August. Starting the eighth. Okay, I'm underway."

76

"My. Will you look at that." Constance was leaning forward, face close to the computer screen.

Tessa whirled toward her. "What?"

"One last moment." Constance's fingers tapped across her keyboard, and her silver mouse clicked once. Then again. "Let me confirm."

Tessa imagined the bang of a gavel. A cosmic jury verdict. *If the answer is there, and you don't know it, the truth still exists.*

And what was impossibly gut-wrenching: at this moment in the recesses of the Philadelphia library, if she was about to hear who she'd—who had died, she'd also understand exactly who was behind all the threats. She'd know the name of the victim's family.

Her victim's family.

In which case she *did* owe them. And Emily, too. Not just money, but owed them for years of shirked responsibility and manipulated delusional thinking and covering up the death of their loved one. Tessa hadn't been driving. But that was no consolation.

"Ms. Calloway? Tessa?"

Tessa had fallen so deep into the past that she startled at Constance's voice. "Did you—"

"Nothing." Constance swiveled her chair to face Tessa. "No deaths reported. Must be sparsely populated."

"Not at all?" Tessa tried to figure out what this could mean. No meant no. None meant none. "No deaths at all?"

"Not a one. So, good for you. You can write about whatever you want. No one will think it's based on reality."

Part of her said to leave well enough alone. Jury goes home. End of story. End of guilt and end of danger and end of fear. Could that be?

No one had died that entire week in that entire county. The Rubik's cube of her memories clicked, adjusted, created a new picture. A new picture of her own life.

It *had* been a deer?

It had been *a deer*?

"Not even in an unexplained accident?" She had to ask. Had to push. Had to know, now that she was so close. If she was going to do this, it had to be no-holds-barred. "Or someone who was never identified?"

Constance looked at her from over her glasses. "Forgive me, do you *want* someone to be dead? These are the official statistics."

"No. Definitely not. Okay. Terrific." She tried to laugh, the self-deprecating author. "This is a treat, having someone do research for me. Usually I do my own. But is there another place to look?"

"One moment . . ." Constance was mouse-clicking so quickly Tessa could not follow her trail.

Tessa's reality—her memories—felt in motion, rearranging themselves.

"All right. Here." Constance gestured to the screen. "Local paper has no obits for August. In the July obits, it says a Sally-Anne LaJeunesse fell off a ladder in her apple orchard, then someone drowned at a hotel. Then nothing until September, when a Porter Harmon had a heart attack at the fish plant."

"So that means no one died there. In August."

Constance pursed her lips. "Well, not exactly. I can only show you what exists, so it simply means there's no *official* record of it. And you know how unreliable newspapers can be. And official records are only complete if everyone follows the reporting rules."

"So there still may be—"

"Well, Ms. Calloway, you know how people are about following rules."

"True." How well she knew.

Tessa looked at the stacks of cello-covered library-bound books on the floor beside her. Stories authors had spun, tales that were created to sound true, but that, in reality, were fully imagined. *This story changed my life,* people would say about a favorite book. Stories could matter, and they could have influence, but they were still only stories. But truth was truth.

But *if* no one in Blytheton had died that day, or even that week . . . *If* what Constance found was true, her mother's acquiescence, or her fear, had sentenced them all to twenty years of sorrow. Tessa had not failed her mother. By accepting a lie, her mother had failed *her*.

If the records were complete.

"Anything else?" Constance had stood. "I'm looking forward to your next book."

"Thanks, Constance." Would there even be a next book? "You've been so helpful."

"I'm a librarian," she replied.

"Lucky for me." Tessa smiled her gratitude, but as she hurried back to the hotel, she hoped it *had* been lucky. At least she had evidence. Of . . . something.

But there was no way Tessa could know what was actually true—and what she only wished was true.

77

"I hope this becomes a habit," Henry's voice came from the open Zoom on her laptop screen. "It's incredibly provocative seeing you get dressed via the internet. I'm gonna stop talking, and watch. And will you do it again tonight when you get back to the hotel? I'll send the kids away."

Henry's chuckle was so familiar, such a reminder of home and what she'd left behind. She almost didn't care about the yellow walls or the photos on the stairway. She'd told him to handle things, and he'd handled them.

Tessa wrapped the white bath towel around her and tucked it in at the top, wondering about the propriety of appearing online wearing only a precariously attached towel.

"You're an idiot, Henner," she said. "The best kind of idiot. And I'm sorry I've been . . . distracted. Lots going on. Anyway, you were saying. On the plane. About the—my schedule?"

"Let me get to the kitchen," Henry said. "Hang on a minute."

"What?" But the camera blurred, and she could hear Henry's footsteps as he walked. She grabbed the hotel's fluffy white bathrobe, tied the belt over the towel. Home seemed impossibly far away. But again, things like impetuously buying a new house paled in comparison to being blackmailed for murder.

A murder that, she was hoping as hard as she'd ever hoped for anything in her life, was imaginary. A weapon. A story.

Had *Emily* made it up? To get—Tessa shook her head, wondering. Revenge? Money? People can be jealous, DJ had warned her. Bitter. When you get something they don't.

Emily was your friend, though, Annabelle said. Wasn't she?

She'd scoured the Facebook pages for more Emilys, but no one fit the description or history. Barbara Willoughby, also nothing. But Nellie Delaney popped right up. Her entire Facebook history tracked exactly what Henry described—traveling husband, mathy son, home in Rockport. And many photos. She was not Emily. But did she have an agenda? That kind of information was never on social media.

Emily might be dead.

Wherever Emily was, in this world or departed, she was not the one who'd pretended to be "Harper," an author escort. Emily was not sixty.

Tessa took herself out of the camera's view as she waited for Henry to come back on the line, quickly tugging on her underwear and stashing the dirty stuff. She'd put those mysterious blue earrings in the laundry bag, too, not quite able to throw away potential evidence. She figured Harper had planted them during the missing-suitcase debacle. *We always know where you are*, that woman had said. Tessa still could not face the embarrassing necessity of telling Evelyn Wickwire about the tracker in the locket.

Might Harper have planted another one in the earrings? She'd think about that later. And what would she say to the audience tonight, if they asked about Locket Mom?

"So, yeah, weirdest thing about that schedule," Henry was saying now. "I put the printout, with all the contacts, on the refrigerator. But the other day I looked for it, and it was gone. See?" He turned the camera, showing the refrigerator. "The banana magnet, too. I thought it had slipped under the counter, or, who knows, but no one has seen it. Someone must have thrown it away by mistake. Can you email me another one?"

"It's on my website," Tessa called over her shoulder as she selected her dress from the closet.

"I know, but that's only the public stuff. It doesn't have the people at the bookstores, your exact flights, your hotels, that kind of thing."

Tessa stood, one hand in midair Tessa is not hovering over the hanger, her finger is hovering over the wooden hanger. She could hear the sound of the internet transmission, the soft hum of the hotel's ventilation system, the low murmur of the television. "How long has the schedule been gone?"

She turned from the closet, picked up the laptop. Held it at eye level. "Henry? How long has the schedule been gone?"

Henry scratched his forehead, made his thinking face. "Hard to tell."

"The kids?"

"They say they don't have it. Why would they? And they didn't throw it away."

"Where are the kids now? Are they okay? Who else has been in the house?"

Past five o'clock now. Time was ticking by. Tessa needed to get to the bookstore.

If no one had died that night in Maine—what was all this about? Harper certainly thought she had some blackmail-worthy ammunition. Were Henry and the kids in danger?

"Oh crap," Henry said. "Who knows who's been here."

"*You* do," Tessa said.

"It was a figure of speech, Tessie, let me think. A bunch of movers. The dishwasher installer. The dishwasher repair guy. Don't get me started on that, I'm just saying. The guy who delivered the paint. And yeah, the kids are upstairs, doing whatever they do. We're getting pizza for dinner."

"Henry? Come on. Who else was in the house?" *And why are you avoiding it?* She left that part out.

"Well, Nellie, who helped with the painting. And her son Tris, he was here with Zack. And Barbara, she's dropped off mac and cheese and all kinds of goodies almost every day, got to say, she's like the mom I never had. The kids love her."

Tessa had to get ready, she *had* to. She put the laptop on a pillow, moved out of camera range, and stepped into her dress. "A mom? Pretty young for a mom."

"Who said she was young? Tessa? Where'd you go?"

"Linny said she was Barbie. That she looked like Barbie. Barbie, at least the doll Barbie, is nobody's mom."

"Huh. That's the story about her you created, I guess. She's thin, and blondish hair, but she's older than you. Twenty years or so, I'd say. In her sixties, for sure."

Tessa tried to calculate, envisioned a calendar. "When did you last see her, Henry? Seriously."

"Umm, geez, two or three days ago?"

"Is she home? Now?"

"How do I know? I mean, I could look out the window? See if her car is in the driveway. Not that it would mean anything."

"Do."

"Why?"

"Could you just do it? Please? I'll tell you in a minute. But I have to go, I'm about to be late, just tell me if Barbara's car is in the driveway."

Tessa struggled with her zipper again, slid her feet into her pumps. She would throw this dress away when she got home. If she ever got home.

This person, this Harper, had promised—threatened—to keep in contact. To let Tessa know how much money they wanted, and how to pay it. Harper had appeared at the Des Moines airport yesterday.

She imagined Henry at their front window, peering across the street to wherever Barbara's driveway was. Harper had not seemed to care about—or even know about—the bad thing. Harper was solely focused on—and *had* known about—the *Maine* accident. Known some version of what happened. Known about *Emily*. Plus she'd known exactly where Tessa was on book tour, even things that weren't public. Who could possibly have all that information? About now, and about so long ago? Who would still care?

Was it possible that Barbara Willoughby was part of the family of the victim they'd—but no.

No.

If they had not hit anyone that night, there *was* no victim. Which meant Tessa's entire theory of the victim's family demanding retribution was completely and totally wrong.

And someone sixty-plus years old was not the real Emily.

But where *was* Emily?

And where was Barbara?

"Her car isn't there," Henry said. "For whatever that's worth."

"Okay. One more thing," she said. "Can you see if Nellie is home?"

78

What does your main character wish for? Tessa smiled with genuine gratitude as she walked to the podium at Liberty Bell Bookstore, listening to the
warm applause from the standing-room-only audience. She'd read in some
how-to-write essay that imagining what your character wished for was the
key to every scene. But if someone had asked her what she wished for now—
she adjusted the microphone, centered herself behind the wooden podium,
put her book down on the slanted surface in front of her—she would have
difficulty articulating it.

She scanned the room, keeping an appreciative expression on her
face, but looking for the woman in the car in Des Moines. Did she wish to
see her? Or did she wish she wouldn't?

What Harper didn't know was that Tessa now had potential ammunition of her own. Unless there was some research land mine that librarian
Constance had not uncovered, the gruesome hit-and-run story was not
true.

Not true.

And though the depth of her grief for her mother's tragic deception
was unfathomable, Tessa refused to be drawn into the same manipulative
trap. Question was, who had set it? And how did Tessa get out?

Since she couldn't contact her would-be blackmailer, Tessa would have
to wait.

"I'm so honored to be here," she told the bookstore audience. "And so delighted to see all your periwinkle." The supportive murmur enveloped her, a contrast to the dark tension she held inside. She wondered how many other authors were hiding a grim secret, or family drama, or fear, or disappointment. How many of them were simply pretending, as she was now, to be content and successful?

She was presenting *herself* as a fictional character, she realized. Someone whose story her audience only thought they knew.

She made it through her speech, made it through the minefield of, as it turned out, benign questions—including one about the earrings, and one about Locket Mom, both of which she answered with a baffled "it's a mystery, isn't it?," persevered through the signing and, on high alert, eased out of the bookstore and into the Uber. No one was following her. No one was watching her. That she saw, at least. When she clicked open her hotel room door, she paused, making sure. Everything was exactly as she had left it.

Except the red message light on the nightstand phone. Flashing.

"Is there a message for me?" she asked when the clerk answered.

"Yes, Ms. Calloway. It's from an Olivette Iketa. She says please call."

Tessa had dug out her cell phone even as she hung up the landline. Found her editor's contact, clicked it. 10:00 p.m. in Philadelphia, 10:00 p.m. in New York. At least they were in the same time zone. But why would Olivette call the hotel? And so late? And not text?

"Is your phone on silent?" Olivette began before she even said hello.

"I don't think so . . ." Tessa paused. Checked. "Oh. It is. I guess I . . . whatever. What's up? Why didn't you text?"

"It's not a thing I can say in a text. Only in person."

"Is it a good thing or a bad thing?" Here it came. Had to be. The bad thing.

"Well, it's the good news *and* the bad news. Which do you want first?"

Tessa could not read Olivette's tone. She sat on the edge of the four-poster bed, heart fluttering, and wondering why Olivette couldn't simply tell her instead of making it into melodrama. Outside her window, the early-summer nighttime lights of the Philadelphia skyline glowed.

"Bad news first."

"You sure?"

"Olivette. You're killing me here."

"We're canceling tomorrow's event in Pittsburgh."

"What? No. No. Completely no. I didn't cancel, Ollie. I have no idea what's going on." Which was semi-true. What would Harper have to gain from this? She sank into the white comforter, wishing she could disappear. They'd made a *deal.* So much for deals. "I would never—"

"No, no. *We* canceled. More like postponed. We're moving Saratoga, too. We're still puzzled about what happened in Des Moines, but onward."

"So why—?"

"And that's the good news. Congratulations. You made the *Times* list again! DJ finagled the word early. Holding on at number two. I'm afraid the dragon lady is invincible. But yay."

"Oh. I—fantastic," Tessa said. "I've been worrying all day."

"Yeah, my bad, I thought DJ was telling you, she thought I was telling you. And then your phone was off."

"But wait." Tessa sat up, tried to juggle. "Then why are we *canceling* Pittsburgh?"

"Because *you* are going to Boston, sweetie. Best news ever. Annabelle is a network morning show book club pick, and they're shooting you live in Boston. They want to do it at a bookstore, and we're arranging that now."

"What? Really? But I thought—it wasn't—that's not how it works. I thought."

"This is a new thing. It's incredible. You're like, the first. Annabelle is such a star."

Thank you, Annabelle said.

"Are you sure it's on the up-and-up?" Tessa paused, bit her lip, fearing the worst. "That this isn't someone messing with us? Like Des Moines?"

"Tessa?" Olivette drew out the word, wary. "Your voice is funny. If someone is—messing with you, as you say, we're not going to put you on live TV. No matter how many books it would sell. You need to tell me. Now."

What could she even say? She rolled the dice.

"No, all good, better than good, in every way. It's wonderful. So—"

"Okay, then. You'll fly out of Philadelphia tomorrow. Arriving Boston late afternoon. You can stay home overnight, if you want. And then to the bookstore by nine a.m. for the show."

"Home?" Tessa could barely say the word.

"They're teasing it on the show tomorrow, but the title of the book is not public. So don't say a word, not to anyone. We told the bookstores there's big news, and to trust us, but for now, this is a massive secret. The network's making a huge deal of it. Having a big reveal."

"Amazing. Amazing." Tessa searched for words in this new reality. "I have to tell Henry, though. If I'm coming home." She laughed. Then stopped, with a flash of imagining what she might see if she showed up unannounced. "So he and the kids can—clean up, at least. Hide all the pizza boxes."

"Would it be awkward if you waited till tomorrow? Your plane's at one fifteen, so you could call right before that. The network's revealing the title tomorrow night on their socials, because they want a crowd at the bookstore. But they told us to keep this under wraps until then."

"Sure," Tessa said before she even thought about it. "However they want. It's terrific. Thank you." She needed to talk to Henry tonight, just to say *safe safe*, and how would she avoid spilling this? Still, though, that possibly-stolen schedule would now be incorrect. Misleading. And would send someone to Pittsburgh. Where Tessa would not be.

"*All This Could Be Yours*," Olivette was saying. "Looks like that title is coming true."

"Thank you," Tessa said. "I hope so."

79

"Sorry I had to get off the phone so quickly last night." Tessa held her cell between her cheek and shoulder as she buckled her seat belt. "New York was calling, and Olivette had schedule changes, and we all needed to talk. And I was so tired."

"No problem. Zack and Linny deigned to play Super Monopoly with their 'lame' father, and Tris was here, as per usual. His mother, too. It was quite the competitive evening."

As per usual. A lot to unpack there, Tessa thought, as she adjusted her seat to the full upright position. Other passengers were still boarding. She had time. Picked the least contentious question first. "Super Monopoly?"

"Three boards at a time. Don't ask."

"With Nellie?"

"And her son, yes. He won, by the way."

"Oh, and," Tessa began, as if it were a logical next question, "what about Barbara? Is she back yet?"

"You're obsessed with this, Tessa. Okay. I'm walking. To the window. Walking, walking, walking. Looking out the window. Nope. Her car is not there. But maybe she's out to lunch. Do you want her mac and cheese recipe? Someday you'll have to tell me about this obsession. But hey—great about the *Times* list, sweetheart. You must be flying high."

"Actually, that's precisely true. At least, I'm about to. Guess to where."

"No idea," Henry said. "The itinerary is gone, remember I told you that."

Hard to forget, Tessa thought. And Barbara could have looked at that perfectly-typed schedule every time she was in Tessa's kitchen, delivering all that distracting food. Or Nellie, cynically using her son Tris as a decoy while she snooped around. Were they in it together? Either one might have snapped a picture of it on her phone, then eventually decided to swipe the whole thing.

Why would they be so blatant? Precisely because it *was* so blatant. *I know where you are*, the woman had said. *I can find you at any time. And your family.*

"Boston," she told Henry now. "I'm flying to Boston."

"What?"

"It's a long story, and a wonderfully good one, and I'll tell you when I get home. *Home.*"

"Home?"

"Yup. We're taking off soon, and I arrive in about ninety minutes. I'll Uber. Tell me the address again, ha ha."

Tessa's bad angel had suggested coming home as a surprise, to see who was there and what they were really doing, but in the end, her better nature prevailed. Plus, Henry would be worried when he saw her unexpectedly, and that moment of concern and fear was not something she could ever inflict on him. Game night with the suspiciously ever-present Nellie aside.

"We'll come pick you up!" Henry sounded authentically enthusiastic. "But are you sure everything is okay?"

"More than okay. But truly, it's easier to Uber. Then I'll tell you everything."

Well, not everything, Annabelle said.

———————

Home but not home, Tessa thought, as Henry opened the front door of the house that her family lived in without her. Enveloped in his hug, in his fragrance, she closed her eyes for a moment, then looked behind him at the galleried stairway wall, down a hallway carpeted with an unfamiliar rug, the glimmer of butter yellow from a kitchen beyond. A place she knew but didn't know. Like her life as an author. Like her own past.

But now she'd *be* here. No more Zoom. No more secret shadows. Everything in the open. For better or worse.

A stampede of footsteps down the stairs. Zack and Linny, each of whom must have grown inches in the time she'd been gone, threw themselves on top of Henry, adding themselves to her husband's hug, and wrapped their arms around them all.

"Hey, you cute baby chickens," she said into their shoulders. They were safe, and she was home. "I missed you every minute." She stepped back. "Let me look. You're so tall!"

"We are not." Linny's newly chopped hair was actually charming. "That's impossible, Mom."

"I am," Zack said. "Soon I'll be taller than lame-o Linny."

Even their sniping sounded wonderful. She grabbed her suitcase handle, but Zack took it from her.

"I'll carry it, Mom," he said. "Do you remember where your room is?"

"Good one," she said. Henry, in his ratty Red Sox T-shirt, looked as handsome as she'd ever seen. His eyes twinkled with genuine welcome. She'd been suspicious of him, but maybe he was simply a good guy who'd been manipulated by someone with ugly ulterior motives. Someone who seemed to be helping him keep his children happy. Just like her mother had done for her. Maybe Henry had not been unfaithful, just unwitting. Maybe. Either way, that didn't mean he wasn't in danger.

And *she* had put him there.

"Linny and I will make you a snack, won't we, kiddo?" Henry said.

"Yum. I can't believe I'm here. Home. Zack and I will head upstairs, and be back in a minute."

As Tessa watched her son lug her roller bag up the staircase, she scanned the house she'd barely seen before. The long upstairs corridor, the row of closed doors. The master bedroom looked over the front yard, and as she and Zack entered, the top branches of a pink-flowering tree showed through open slats of the white-shuttered window.

And then. A sound.

"What was that?" Tessa frowned, looking at the ceiling. The closet. The door. "Did you hear that?"

"Gah. This dumb old house." Zack waved her off. "It makes sounds, like all the time. It's the trees or something, or squirrels. You'll get used to it. We all did."

The sounds, Tessa thought, remembering. Her imagination had made them sinister. When they were simply sounds of home. Their home. *Her* home.

"You okay, bud? In this new place? I hear you had some delicious mac and cheese. And listen." She perched on the edge of the bed, grabbed Zack's wrists, and held him in place. "We'll talk later about going to Maine. It's a big decision, and I need to meet Mrs. Delaney. And Mrs. Willoughby. About waiting on the dog."

"Oh." Zack winced. "That was the secret, remember I asked you? We—"

"Yes, I do," Tessa had to interrupt. She didn't have much time. "Your father told me about it. And you kept that secret, honey. You're the best. But back to Mrs. Willoughby. D'you have a picture of her? It's so funny that I've never seen her."

"If I had a phone I would, Mom."

He plunked down beside her on the bed, pouting about the phone, and she draped an arm around his narrow shoulders. Her *son*. She'd do anything for him.

"Did you at least bring me hats?" he asked.

"Yes, my darling sweetheart. Hats for everyone. So, no pictures of Mrs. Willoughby?"

"Where would they even be? I don't have a phone. Remember? I really, really, really need a phone."

"We'll talk about that later, too, Zackeroo." She kissed the top of his head, and he squirmed away. "Too big for that, huh? Never. Let's go down for that snack. We'll get the hats, after, and you can tell me more about Mrs. Willoughby, and the Delaneys. Okay? I'd love to hear all about them."

Zack was looking at his feet, his chunky sneakers. "It's good you're home, Mom."

She would never let anything happen to him. No matter what she had to do. If anything good could result from her manipulated childhood, or her wrenching mistake that day with Annabelle, it was that she'd vow to be fearless. Brave. And, though she would probably have dismissed it, learn from her mother's mistakes.

And from her own.

Tessa, Annabelle said. *Give yourself some grace here. That's what life's about, learning from mistakes. And you're already fearless and brave.*

Zack looked up at her then, winsome. "I bet it's fun being famous."

"It is," she said. "But being your mom is also fun. And I cannot wait to find out what happens next."

80

"Hair and makeup are in the back, can you believe it?" Vivian Smith ushered Tessa through the front door of the Smith Bookstore. "This is the most exciting thing that's ever happened in this place. I mean, even since I was a kid and my dad ran it. We've hosted some major leaguers here, Patterson, and Oprah, that level. But I've never seen this much commotion. Lights, camera, everything." She gestured, pointing. "We had to roll back all the shelves. Remove every questionable cover. And they made us close until noon. But it's worth it."

Nine o'clock call time with the live hit at eleven thirty, Tessa had been told. She was to be interviewed by Abigail Adams, the glamorous morning anchor who hosted the network's popular book club, who'd be in the New York studio.

"This is—" Vivian pointed to the woman who was striding toward them.

"Rebecca Segura," the woman interrupted. Black jeans, black T-shirt, clipboard in hand, earpiece in her left ear, its wire plugged into a metal box on her black belt. "Producer. We'll give you an earpiece, you look into the camera, Abigail will ask you three questions, I have no idea what they are. I'm sure you can handle."

"Sure, I—"

"Good." She pursed her lips, scrutinizing Tessa. "You look good. Black jacket is good. Blue earrings good. We'll fix the hair. Pat down your face." She looked at Vivian. "Audience? Chairs? Copies of the book?"

"We blasted out to our mailing list this morning." Vivian did not seem cowed by Rebecca's staccato delivery. "You can see the big display of Tessa's book over there. Chairs up at nine thirty, attendees arrive starting ten thirty, doors close at eleven. We'll station someone outside to quiet the overflow. They'll look through the front window, of course. Can't stop that."

"I'll let New York know. Four minutes total, max. Be natural. It's a conversation. You good?"

Tessa nodded, wondering if she'd have her voice when the time came. The producer pivoted, focused on two men setting up lights on expandable metal poles.

"Full of herself, right?" Vivian whispered, raised a judging eyebrow. "But still cool."

"My family is coming," Tessa whispered back, then realized she didn't have to. "I kind of wish they weren't, it'll make me way more nervous. But they insisted."

"Kid one and kid two?" Vivian said. "And is it . . . Henry? I'll take good care of them."

"Thanks. I guess I'd better go to makeup. I wish they could do something for the butterflies in my stomach."

You got this, Annabelle said.

Fifteen minutes later, Tessa looked at her new TV self in the three-paned mirror a chatty makeup artist had propped on the linoleum table in the bookstore's back room. The fragrance of powder and hairspray almost overcame the smell of paper.

"You didn't need much," the woman said. "You'll be amazing. I love Annabelle, by the way. That's how I got this gig. I was completely petrified, but I asked myself—what would Annabelle do? And I went for it."

"That's—"

"I'll come back for final tweaks in a bit." She sprayed one open palm with hairspray, then ran it gently over Tessa's hair. "Perfection. You okay?"

"Sure. Thanks." *Terrified,* she didn't say. Tessa, sitting in a rickety aluminum chair and surrounded by shelves of upcoming books, was doing her best to stay calm, but every nerve cell in her body buzzed on high alert. She could not feel her feet. She wished she knew yoga. Or meditation. DJ and Ollie and everyone at Waverly had planned to watch from the office. *You have no trouble speaking in public*, she admonished herself, *why is this any different?*

Because it's two million people, Annabelle said. And someone uninvited might show up.

Someone tapped on the doorjamb. Vivian.

"Everything okay?" Tessa could not read the expression on the bookstore owner's face. More than an hour until showtime. "Viv?"

"Yeah, fine," Vivian said. "But, uh, there's someone outside who wants to see you."

"Who?"

"She didn't tell me her name. She just said she was an old friend."

She wouldn't. *She wouldn't.* Ghastly possibilities paraded through Tessa's mind. Harper had not contacted her, and Tessa had, possibly naively, relied on the fact that Harper, still in Philadelphia, would discover the schedule change too late to make it to Boston to disrupt this event. But Philadelphia was driving distance. And this would be a place where she could make a massive power move. Tessa, about to appear on live television. As exposed as anyone could ever be.

Henry would be here. And the kids. Clueless. Vulnerable. Helpless.

Still, if the woman wanted money, Tessa's failure or humiliation would ruin that. The woman needed Tessa to succeed. So why would she be here? *Henry*, she thought again. *The kids.*

Tessa would be on live TV. And unable to warn them, or come to their rescue.

"How old is she?" Tessa said. "What does she look like?"

"Are you expecting someone? Really short hair, kinda chic and Parisian looking."

"Parisian?"

"Like Audrey Hepburn in those old movies. But blond."

"Like Barbie?"

"Huh? Is something going on? She's quite insistent, and says she only needs two minutes. Do you want me to send her away? She got in the store when no one was looking, but I can throw her out. Nicely."

"Is there a way for me to see her without her seeing me?"

"Tessa, you're about to be on national TV. Shouldn't you stay back here?"

"Can I see her?"

"Look, I'll go out, and tell her you're in makeup. I'll stand so she has to face this way. I'll ask if I can take a message. You peek out the door."

"Thanks."

As Vivian left the room, Tessa tried to decide what she would do if this were Harper. Harper would never go away simply because she was asked. This is what happened with blackmail. The victim was eternally the victim. And Harper clearly relished her power.

Last night, in bed with Henry, Tessa almost told him the whole thing, but could never find the words. Something about this story was missing, and she couldn't put her finger on it. She still couldn't believe her mother would pay for a lie.

Which meant Harper had some piece of evidence Tessa didn't. Constance the librarian might have missed something. Maybe Sheriff Owen had successfully covered his tracks. *Their* tracks.

She'd snuggled closer to Henry, pushing away the bad thoughts. She'd seen the sheets on their queen-sized bed were white, and mentioned that. He'd laughed. "Yeah, when I bought them, the wrapping was flowers, but inside the sheets were white. Who knew they did that? Consumer fraud, no question about it."

Henry had traced the edge of her face, as he always did, and it was intoxicating to breathe the same air with him. Home was Henry, no matter if the brick and mortar was new. Even knowing the kids were sleeping down the hall felt settled, safe.

When that was the farthest thing from true.

In less than half an hour, she'd be speaking, live, to millions of people, and her future was on the line. And she could not escape the irony that at any second, she might be visited by her devastating past. Not the bad thing, the thing that had consumed her, and haunted her for years. Not *her* childhood decision.

But a devastating bargain her mother had made.

Maybe.

Because Emily was the only one alive who knew about Annabelle.

And if Emily had divulged that secret, and told Harper about the bad thing—or told Barbara, or told Nellie—it would be Emily who could still, as her mother had grimly predicted, ruin her life.

Now she gathered herself in the back room of the bookstore, not trusting her knees, and took the three steps to the closed door. She put her hand on the doorknob.

You have to do it, Annabelle said. See what she wants. Be fearless, like you promised. It's the only way to stay in control.

Tessa pulled open the door. Peeked down the bookstore hall. Risked two steps closer to the main room. Saw the network crew adjusting the boxy, black-hooded klieg lights, a video camera on a tripod with its lens aimed at a low-backed stool, black wires snaking across the bookstore floor, Rebecca and her crew drinking coffee from blue paper cups. The display of *All This Could Be Yours* under a spotlight of its own.

She saw Vivian's back. And facing her, a woman in jeans and a white shirt, gesturing, earnest and determined.

Tessa felt the blood drain from her face.

This was not Harper.

This was Emily.

81

It was all Tessa could do not to run toward her. She'd recognize Emily anywhere, she knew that tilt of her head, the way she talked with her hands, that dancer's posture.

At the same time, it was all she could do not to pivot, race back into the bookstore's office, slam the door, and hide.

Emily.

Emily. The only one who knew her secret.

Emily. Who was either her long-lost dearest friend, or a devious manipulative blackmailer.

Emily, who had come to this bookstore, knowing it was a pivotal moment in Tessa's career.

And had arrived either to celebrate it—or ruin it.

Or maybe, commiserate.

Maybe Emily was being blackmailed, too. Maybe, after all these years, they were once again together, and, once again, in unimaginable trouble.

Tessa put her hands over her eyes, despairing, then quickly pulled them away, fearing she'd smudge her makeup. She had to wait for Vivian to tell her what Emily said. All the while knowing it wasn't necessarily true. All the while knowing she could not trust a word of it. If she made the wrong decision, her life would fall apart. Her career. Her family. If she made the wrong decision, all would be lost.

She walked, backward, slowly, into the office. Eased the door almost closed. Waiting for Emily's next move.

She heard footsteps in the hall. Just one person.

Vivian opened the door. Tessa whirled, trying to keep the panic out of her expression.

"She says her name is Emily Rousseau." Vivian closed the door behind her. "And that you will know her by the name she discarded—that's how she put it—Emily Owen. Do you know her?"

Tessa nodded. She sat at the table again, the three-paned makeup mirror reflecting her uncertainty.

"She says she's thrilled for you, and happy to wait until your event is over, and doesn't want to make you nervous. She was pretty cute about it, I have to say. Seemed like a big fan. And says to tell you—in her words—'both of our dreams have come true.'"

"Discarded? Her name?"

"Yeah, that's what she said. Tessa, I think you should wait until this is over. I'll tell her that. I'll take the blame."

No. She had to know. *She had to know.* It'd be impossible to do this interview knowing a potential time bomb was ticking. If Emily was about to tell her something terrible, to threaten her, it would be better to know it than to fear it.

There was no way to avoid this.

"I'll come out," Tessa said. "I'll come out and say hello."

"You have seven minutes, I'd say." Vivian shook her head. "Seriously. This is a distraction. You should get ready for the interview, Tessa. Focus."

You're good, Annabelle said.

"I'm good," Tessa said. "I'll be quick, then come back here."

Vivian moved aside as Tessa opened the door to the office. Then, step by step, gradually erasing twenty years of distance, Tessa came closer to the woman now outlined by a burst of sunshine from beyond the bookstore window. Emily in silhouette, twenty years later, was the same Emily she'd seen in the light of that Maine summer. Even the way she held her chin was familiar. They'd shared so much back then, the wonder and the disaster. The discoveries and the dreams and the beauty and the poetry. And the pain. Which of those was about to appear now?

They finally stood a foot apart, the glow from the TV spotlights surrounding them. Tessa saw people gathering on the sidewalk, lining up to be allowed inside.

"This is the forest primeval," Emily said.

"The murmuring pines and the hemlocks," Tessa whispered.

They stood in their own silence for a moment, sharing the space between them while the bustle of the bookstore, the lights, the camera, the crew, all dissolved into background noise.

"You remembered," Emily said.

"Of course I did. Why didn't you answer my letters?" Tessa could not cry, for fear of ruining her careful mascara, but her pounding heart could not be denied.

"Letters? I never got letters." Emily shook her head, frowning. "And I never expected any. I got you in so much trouble about the car, Tessa, I am so sorry." She looked up, her face the picture of remorse. "It was all my fault. I thought you would hate me forever. My father, and his wife, *told* me you did, that you were incredibly mad, said you never wanted to hear from me again. And I understood, I still do. You already had so much upheaval in your life, and we were kids, after all. And maybe you'd even forgotten. But I couldn't resist coming today—this is all you ever wanted, and now you have it. I'm so proud of you. You don't hate me?"

"Hate you? Forgotten? I wrote you letters. For weeks. Months! I thought *you* hated *me*. Because of what happened. And your parents hated me, too."

"They did, yes, I'll admit that. But I should have stood up for you. I should have told your mother it was my fault. Instead I left home. As soon as I could."

"I did, too, and—" Tessa began. She pressed her lips together, then worried about her lipstick. The producer, Rebecca, was now sitting in what would be Tessa's chair, and the techs were adjusting the lighting. People peered through the store's front windows, gesturing and pointing at Tessa, holding up their books, waiting to get inside for the live broadcast. Vivian waved both hands to get Tessa's attention, then pointed to her watch, looking worried.

"I searched for you on Facebook, in fact." Tessa had to hurry. "Because—"

"Facebook." Emily scoffed. "Social media. Waste of time. I'm on this bookstore's mailing list. That's how I found out about this today. We live in Boston, right nearby. I'm an English teacher. I make the kids read the entire 'Evangeline.' And I think of you every time."

"Emily, I—" She thought of their shared dreams and how they'd turned out. But there was no time. "I have to go," Tessa said. "You'll wait for me?"

"Of course, superstar. I knew you would do it."

"Em." Tessa reached out, touched Emily's arm, briefly, timidly. "That night."

"I know. That poor deer." Emily made a regretful face. Rueful. Remembering. "I had nightmares about that deer for years. My father made me look at it. He was—such an awful man."

Tessa's chin came up. She narrowed her eyes. "You saw it."

"Yeah. Be glad you didn't. My father got rid of it, it was just roadkill. Later that same night. My stepmother made him do it. He's dead now. My father."

"It was a deer."

"Well, yeah. What did you think?"

"Tessa!" Rebecca now, calling for her. "Time!"

"Don't leave, Em," Tessa said.

"I'll be here," she said. "See you after."

82

"Wait." Tessa grabbed Emily's arm.

Emily turned, curious. "What?"

"Two things. Quickly." Tessa steeled herself. Had to ask. "Did you ever tell anyone about—the bad thing?"

Emily's eyes widened. "Of course not. I *promised*. Why?"

"I'll tell you. But first." Tessa took her phone from her blazer pocket. Opened her photos. Selected one. Held it out. "Do you know who this is? These people in the photograph?"

"Where did you get that?"

"So you *do* recognize them. Truly, it's important. Who is this?"

"Well, yes, okay, I've seen that photo before. At our house. That's my stepmother as a child. And her father, he died, gosh, I forget what she said. That's their cabin. On Acadia Road. Back in Maine."

"Your stepmother's family?"

Emily nodded. "Where did *you* get it, though, Tessa?"

"Where's your stepmother now?"

"No idea. And I hope I never know. She was a sleaze, forgive me, all she wanted was money. She and my father." Emily shook her head. "Quite the team. I couldn't get away fast enough. She's probably out ruining some-one else's life now."

"You'd know her if you saw her?"

"Sadly, I have no doubt. There are never enough years to wipe that face away. I wish there were."

"Tessa!" Vivian called out from across the room. More people had gathered outside the window. "Time!"

"Em. Can you do me a huge favor?"

"Sure. But you have to tell me—"

"I will. But go back behind those bookshelves." Tessa pointed. "Behind me. Kind of . . . hide. And then, when they let the audience in, see if there's anyone you recognize."

"Why? Who? Hide?"

"Can you trust me? After all these years? I'm so sorry to be vague, but as it turned out, you're about the only one I *can* trust."

"What's wrong?" Emily whispered, now leaning closer.

"I'll tell you. I promise." Tessa was deciding even as she said it. "But for now, just see what you see."

"Tessa! *Now.*" Vivian and Rebecca, a tag team, each took one of Tessa's arms, and led her toward the chair. The makeup person, brandishing a puffy brush, dabbed it across Tessa's nose and cheeks as Rebecca clipped a microphone to her black blazer.

"We're keeping the people outside," Rebecca said. "New York decided they don't want noise."

"But they can come in after," Vivian said. "We'll have a signing. And the videographer will shoot them, too, so they'll be on TV. I'm headed out to tell them. Lucky it's a nice day."

"Ten minutes," Rebecca said. "Here's your earpiece. Tuck it in your ear, let's run the wire down the back of your jacket, to the power pack . . . good." She clicked a button on her own black box. "New York, are you hearing us?" She nodded. "Test Ms. Calloway, okay?"

"One, two, three, can you hear me?"

The voice came in Tessa's ear. She clapped a hand to her earpiece, startled. "I hear you."

"Tessa." A different voice in her ear. "This is Abigail Adams in the studio. I know, the name was my parents' idea, they thought it was aspirational. But *you* call me Abby. I adored your book, and cannot wait to chat with you about it. Four minutes, tops. I'll ask you some easy-peasy questions. Our viewers already love you. Your one life. And Annabelle. Do you mind that we're keeping the audience out? Sometimes they get noisy."

"I'm so honored. Whatever works," Tessa said. "I'm a massive fan."

Vivian had gone outside, Tessa saw, and was speaking, pointing to the camera, must be explaining to the crowd about the network's change of plans.

"Back at you, Tessa," Abby was saying. "I wish you were here, but we'll do that next time. So I know they told you, but look right into the camera, pretend it's me, we'll have fun. Talk to you in a few."

"Three minutes." Another voice in her ear.

"Three minutes," Rebecca said. "We're in a commercial break now, you'll hear Abigail on the air introduce you. Just answer her as if she were here. You don't have to hold up your book, we have a graphic for that. I'll cue you, too. And when I do this"—she spiraled a forefinger—"wrap it up. You don't have to panic. Finish your thought. And Abigail will thank you and say goodbye."

Tessa nodded, pretending to be calm. "Got it."

Rebecca made a thumbs-up to the camera lens, then positioned herself beside the videographer.

Tessa twisted around to tell Emily about the change in the audience, but she'd disappeared. She had to forget about that now.

Outside, Vivian was talking with someone as the crowd adjusted position. *Henry,* Tessa realized, as he turned to face her, and the tops of Zack's and Linny's heads bobbed above the bookstore's low window displays. Next to Henry, a honey-haired woman with a sleek pageboy, and next to her, a bespectacled boy. *Tris,* Tessa thought. *And Nellie Delaney.*

She closed her eyes, briefly, blocking it all out. This was almost too much for one person. She'd read about something called Dalton's Law, which stated that individual pressures added together into one big pressure. Right now, she was the epitome of Dalton's Law. Pressure from all sides.

From her family. From her publisher. From her readers. And from her blackmailer.

And now from the arrival of Emily.

Who'd—finally—brought her the truth.

83

"You were fabulous, Tesser." Henry had thrown his arms around her, even as she still sat in the interview chair, muted microphone still attached to her lapel, and the onlookers from the sidewalk poured into the bookstore. Chairs clanked, the audience buzzed, and store owner Vivian, beaming, stood with hands clasped in delight.

The interview had been over in a heartbeat. Tessa barely remembered what she said, or what Abby Adams in New York had asked, not one word of any of it. Except the producer, who'd slashed a finger across her throat and said, "And we're clear."

"Really? Fabulous? Really?" she asked Henry now, as Rebecca unclipped her mic. "I don't remember what I said. Not at all."

And we're clear, Rebecca had said. Nothing had gone wrong. Was it over? Or just beginning?

Her cell phone pinged from her jacket pocket, then again, and again. She glanced at it, Hoping it was good news. Team Tessa loves you! I'm posting on Facebook and everywhere right now. DJ had written. You're the queen! Olivette had said. Sadie sent a string of hearts.

Great job, Annabelle said.

"You were so cool, Mom." Linny had ducked her head under Henry's arm, getting closer to Tessa. Zack had come up behind him, too. "Awesome," he said. "We watched on Dad's phone."

She drew them into hugs, and over her shoulder saw Nellie, had to be, her arm around the shoulders of her gangly Tris. No sign of Barbara. No sign of Emily.

Vivian stood facing the first row of chairs, clapped her hands, quieting the attendees.

"We'll have a signing," the store owner said. "Let us get things back into place." She pointed. "There's a rack of Tessa's books, if you don't already have one, she'll be happy to sign as many as you like. Right, Tessa?" She didn't wait for an answer. "As a souvenir of this special occasion."

"I have to do this," Tessa said to her family. "Don't leave, though. We'll go home together."

"Looks like you're about to sell some books," Henry said. "And this is Nellie Delaney, by the way, and her son, Tris."

"I've heard so much about you," Tessa said.

"You mean Linny's hair, I bet." Nellie leaned closer, whispering, gestured to one side of her own hair. "She'd gotten bubble gum in it. She was so upset. And embarrassed. I tried to make the best of it. I hope I didn't—"

"Thank you," Tessa said. "I—"

There was no time for anything more, or to hear Nellie's answer, as Tessa was hustled to her signing table. Book buyers, some carrying several periwinkle copies, had lined up, waiting, and more people were still coming through the front door. *The power of television*, Tessa thought.

The power of storytelling, Annabelle said.

She felt a presence behind her, and turned to see a woman in oversized dark glasses and a *Game of Thrones* cap pulled low over her forehead. Her heart leaped—then she almost burst out laughing. Emily.

"I got these from a display," Emily whispered. "I'll stay in back of the shelf behind you. But I don't see anyone I know."

"You're hilarious," Tessa whispered. "Keep looking. Hide. They may not come."

As Emily vanished again, and the signing line continued, there were moments when Tessa forgot her life was under siege. Women with periwinkle earrings, and earnest confessions, women with their daughters who described how sharing Tessa's book had brought them together. She lost sight of Henry and the kids, and not a sound from Emily behind her.

The store had opened for business, too, so the aisles filled with shoppers and browsers.

"Carol with an *e?*" Tessa asked the next woman in line.

"Tessa?" Rebecca, still wearing her wired earpiece and with a coiled cable hanging from one shoulder, came up beside the customer. "New York loved you. Abigail's happy. We'll send you a mug, okay?"

Tessa stood, wishing things hadn't gone by so quickly. The good parts of her life, the joy of her success, those moments seemed to vanish before she could adequately appreciate them. "Tell everyone thank you," she said. "I—"

But Rebecca was gone.

"Sorry for the interruption," Tessa told the customer. "So—Carol with an *e?*"

"Mom, Mom!" Tessa heard Zack's enthusiastic voice, and followed the sound. Her son was hurrying toward her. And Zack was leading, by the hand, a tall, thin, blond woman carrying a periwinkle book. With a face Tessa would never forget. Harper.

"Mom, Mom," Zack said. "This is—"

"I'll be right with you, honey." Tessa turned back to Carol or Carole, trying not to faint. "This has been quite the day. So, with an *e?*"

"No *e*. And I love your book so much."

"That's wonderful." Tessa handed her the book. "And I hope you'll keep in touch."

"I promise," Carol said.

"Mom. *Mom.*" Zack had brought the woman to the table. "She's my mom," he explained to the next woman in line. "This is our neighbor. She has to leave. Can we—"

"Aw, that's so cute," the customer said, stepping aside, gesturing Zack and Harper in front of her. "Please. Go ahead. You must be so proud of your mother."

"I am," Zack said. "Mom, she's the one who—"

"Yes, I know," Tessa said. No more gray wig, no more oversized baseball-mom attire, no more suited author escort. "Barbara. I've heard so much about you."

"Your interview was marvelous, Tessa," the woman said. "I bet you sold lots of books."

Tessa took one from the stack next to her. "Let me sign one for you."

"That's not necess—"

"Zackie," Tessa interrupted, "can you go get your dad? Now? Good. And yes, *Barbara*, I insist." Tessa flapped open the book. Watched Zack trot away. And wrote, *I have the money you've asked for. After the signing, meet me in back of the store. And we'll be done. Just say "that's perfect" when you read this.*

Smiling her bookstore smile, she handed the book across the table. Waited. Watched.

"That's perfect," the woman said.

84

Tessa could hardly focus on the rest of the signing. Henry and the kids were sitting with Nellie and Tris in the bookstore's coffee shop. Harper—Barbara—had positioned herself in front of the magazine rack, pretending to browse, her back to Tessa.

Emily—still in that ludicrous getup—had come out from behind the bookshelf. She bent down, close to Tessa's ear, whispered, "That's my stepmother."

Almost unable to breathe, Tessa welcomed the next person in line, then gestured toward Emily, as casually as if she hadn't just revealed something utterly shattering.

"My assistant," she explained to the customer.

"Lucky you," the woman said. She turned, looked behind her. "Wow, I'm the last person in line. Can you put it to Justine?"

"You're so patient," Tessa said as she signed. "I do appreciate it."

"What on earth is she doing *here*?" Emily stayed close, kept her voice low. "My stepmother?"

"I hope you're writing another Annabelle book," Justine said.

"In fact I am," Tessa said. "Want to hear about it? Since you were so patient?"

"Can't wait," Justine said.

"Well," Tessa began, and put a hand on Emily's arm, signaling her to stay. "It's about two teenage girls, who, on one wild night, hit a deer on a back road. But the evil sheriff told their parents they'd hit a person. *Killed* them." Tessa felt Emily flinch, and looked at her, nodding. "Isn't that horrible? And for years and years, their families were blackmailed, at least one of them was, to cover up a crime that never happened. And even when one of the girls grew up, the blackmailer continued to ask for the hush money. There's a lot more to it, but, turns out . . . Well, guess who the blackmailer was."

"Her stepmother?" Emily said.

"Yes," Tessa said. "And her father, until he died."

"Whose stepmother?" Justine looked confused.

"It's complicated," Tessa said to Justine. "I'm still working on it. But one day, listen to this. One of the girls, now an adult, and a bit of a celebrity, is essentially kidnapped by the stepmother, and pretends to agree to the blackmail. But later, they confront her in the back of, oh, I don't know, a bookstore? And little does the blackmailer know, the girl's best friend has called the police about it. So they come and arrest her. The stepmother, I mean."

"What friend? And how does the friend know?" Justine asked.

"Exactly, and there's the plot hole," Emily said. "The police couldn't just arrest her. They'd need evidence."

"Right. And I *just* figured that part out," Tessa said. "Listen to this. They *have* evidence! It's in a book she just signed."

Justine tilted her head. "Who just signed?"

"Oh, Tessa," Emily said. "Wouldn't it be cool if the friend knew a police detective?"

"Does she?" Tessa's eyebrows went up.

"No, sadly. But she might know someone who does. How about you make her husband a lawyer. Would that work?"

"Whose husband?" Justine asked.

"We'll fix that in the editing," Tessa said. "Writing a book is so hard."

85

With Emily out of sight—and, she hoped, calling her lawyer husband—
her family still in the coffee shop, and Vivian helping a customer, Tessa
knew the final confrontation was looming; she could almost hear the
soundtrack intensify and knew she could not delay the climactic conflict
much longer. Two stragglers had arrived, and Tessa had been grateful
for their conversation. She had drawn it out, stalling, chatting, needing
to give Emily all the time she could. *We live in Boston*, Emily had said.
Nearby.

Barbara had stopped pretending to browse the magazine rack, and
was now standing, arms crossed, watching her.

"I hope you enjoy it." Tessa handed over the last periwinkle book in
the store. "Keep in touch, okay?"

As the customers left, Tessa caught Barbara's eye. Cocked her head
toward the office door, held up two fingers. She capped her pen, adjusted
her blazer, and turned toward the back of the store. Anyone watching—
besides Barbara—would think Tessa was headed for the bathroom.

Tessa went all the way to the back, and found what must be a shipping area; a long table with six chairs, a huge rolling cylinder of brown
wrapping paper, and dispensers of clear tape. The shipping nook was
surrounded on three sides by rows of green metal bookshelves filled with
shiny hardcovers. She turned on the recorder of her cell phone, just in

case. Even if Emily came back alone, or not at all, that might be enough. She'd have to play it by ear.

The same way you write, Annabelle said.

Footsteps now. Tessa stepped into the hallway, putting herself in view. Barbara saw her, and held up the book, striding toward her.

Tessa nodded, held her ground. She didn't want to spook her. This woman wasn't going to hurt her, and Tessa had now, in a book inscription, agreed to her demand. Harper—Barbara—thought she had won.

As she approached, Tessa stepped back, gesturing her into the shipping area.

"I found this spot," Tessa said. "It seems private enough."

"Good for you," Barbara said. "I'm glad you've come to your senses. I may raise the price, given your success. Today must have been off the charts."

Tessa thought of the recorder running in her jacket pocket. "You've never told me an actual price," Tessa said. "I did see in my mother's will, though, she had paid you fifty thousand dollars twice a year."

"My, my," Barbara said. "You *have* done your research. But she didn't pay *me*. No one paid me. From what I understand, it went to a trust."

"And then you took it from the trust."

"Shall we talk about the future?" Barbara perched on one edge of the table, leaving Tessa halfway into the hallway.

Tessa darted a glance down the corridor.

"Expecting someone?" Barbara seemed wary.

"My family is out there," Tessa said. "Just watching for them."

"It was such a joy to get to know them," Barbara said. "And so convenient of you to post your schedule on the fridge. Did Linny tell you she found your diary when she unpacked? I asked to see it, but she told me it was locked, and she was keeping it safe for you. I wonder what I'd find inside."

"Do not talk about Linny. Do not even say her name." Tessa felt her fingertips grow cold. "How dare you try to befriend my family? When all you want to do is ruin their lives."

Barbara was looking at the inscription in her book, as if eyes on the prize. "At least Henry and Zachary loved the mac and cheese. Which I made specially, after a brief but revealing food allergy chat with Linnea. You can put bananas in it, did you know? And it's impossible to tell."

"You made her sick? She's a *child*." Tessa imagined the mind that would concoct that, offer that, embrace that depth of evil. "She could have died."

"It wouldn't have killed her, dear. It was just my shot across your bow. To let you know that no one, not you, and not your family, was safe from me. And I wouldn't have 'ruined their lives,' as you put it, unless you forced me to, Tessa. There are other things that make me happy."

"Like money," Tessa said. "But those people in bookstores, Indianapolis and Phoenix and Denver, who asked the personal questions—who were they? They couldn't have all been you—I would have recognized you when you met me in Des Moines."

"So naïve." Barbara closed the book. Cradled it like a baby. "When you pay people, anything is possible. And all they had to do was ask one innocuous question at a bookstore. Or pull an alarm. Or inquire about your past on social media. In fact, I often did *that* myself. And—how'd you like the earrings?"

"*You* took my suitcase? You were on that plane?"

"The suitcase was risky, and not my original plan, but I took the opportunity. You were so intent on your phone call, you walked right by me." She shook her head. "One of my . . . helpers, shall we say, thought you'd caught him after he placed the locket. But you were oblivious then, too. Yammering on the phone."

"Panera Guy," Tessa muttered, remembering. *Hurry up, Emily.* Tessa glanced down the hall again, couldn't help it.

"You and that locket. I adored your ludicrous search for Locket Mom," Barbara went on. "*Locket Mom.*" She raised an eyebrow. "As if such a person existed. Truly, Tessa, your imagination is boundless. But as long as you're selling books, you can perpetuate whatever myths you want."

Tessa took a step into risky waters. "What were all those questions about my hometown?"

"Pffff." Barbara waved her off. "To show you we knew all about you. You and your hoity-toity mother, lording it up in McMansion, Massachusetts. Deigning to visit the plebes in Maine."

Massachusetts, Tessa thought. Not Ohio. Barbara incredibly, amazingly, didn't know about the bad thing.

Maybe her mother *had* successfully protected her, changing their names, moving. Maybe her desperate plans had worked. She wished she could thank her.

"Lording it," Tessa repeated. "Hoity-toity. Nice."

"So, shall we get to business? Before your beloved family interferes? Since you're up to speed with the will, that makes it easier. Call that same lawyer. Tell him you'll continue to contribute to the fund. Fifty thousand, twice a year. Or, hey, you can pay by the month."

Tessa pretended to consider. She had that clear bit of evidence recorded now.

"Are you extorting Emily's family, too?"

"Emily is dead," Barbara said.

"Dead. I see." Tessa had to stall, needed more on the recording. "But did you blackmail her, too?"

"It's not Emily I care about. I never did."

"You 'never' did? So you knew her? When? Where?"

"Forget about Emily." Barbara stood, paced toward the back wall. "Like I said. Dead."

Tessa waited. And then heard footsteps. Two sets. Three. She crossed her fingers. And almost held her breath.

Barbara whirled to face her. "Do I have your answer? Or do I go to the media? They'll love this story, especially after today." She put up her fingers for air quotes. "Massive cover-up as best-selling author hides fatal hit-and-run." She shrugged, cat with canary. "Those fans of yours will simply gobble that up."

"Hi, Mom." Emily's voice came from behind her. "You've discarded the name 'Owen' too, apparently."

"Guess what, Barbara." Tessa pointed to Emily. "Not dead."

"And this is my husband, Cameron Rousseau," Emily was saying. "But more important, *this* is Boston Police Detective Jaylen McKee."

"Guess what else," Tessa said. "Emily saw the deer."

Barbara clutched the book to her chest, and though she had bookshelves on three sides and a police detective on the fourth, her eyes darted around the room, as if seeking an escape route. Then her gaze landed on Emily.

"It was your *father's* idea," Barbara said. She looked at Tessa then, leering contempt. "Summer people. You think you can have it all."

"Shall we take a seat?" McKee said. "Sounds like we have a lot to talk about."

"No." Barbara held up her periwinkle book. "I did nothing wrong. And I have proof." Her face had hardened, her eyes narrowing. She opened to the page Tessa had inscribed, showed it. "This woman agreed! It's here in writing. It's all of her own volition."

"Oh, come on," Tessa said. "You know very well I write fiction."

86

Someone had tipped off the newspapers, and now Tessa sat on a new wicker stool in their new yellow kitchen, her laptop open on the counter, reading the "breaking news" about this morning's "shocking" events. A shadow flickered in her laptop screen. She turned, surprised. *Who was that?* Everyone else was upstairs.

The flicker again. She turned. Waited. The light from outside fractured through the swaying sugar maple behind her, and in through the shutters, making an intermittent shadow.

She'd seen that shadow before. In Henry's FaceTime backgrounds. And decided it was a person. Not simply a person, but a sneaky, predatory, seductive neighbor. Usurping her place with Henry.

A tree. The shadow flickered, then disappeared.

So much for that *story line, Annabelle said. Let's not mention it again.*

A commotion from the stairway, then Henry, Zack, and Linny crowded in behind her.

"That's quite the headline." Henry pointed to the screen. "'Stranger Than Fiction: Bestseller Nabs Real-Life Blackmailer.' Has your publisher seen it?"

"Is she going to jail?" Zack asked. "She seemed nice. Her mac and cheese is awesome."

"You're an idiot," Linny said. "She's a criminal. She tried to make Mom pay for a lie. Isn't that right, Mom?"

"We'll see what the court says, honey." Tessa turned away from the computer, faced her kids. "It's very ugly, and very sad, and someday I'll tell you everything about it. But greed is an evil destructive thing, and envy is, too, and some people feel that the world has been unfair to them, and they'll do anything to get what they want."

Tessa had a moment, then, of connection with her unique and exquisite children. This was part of what parents were for, she thought, to persevere through the tough times, and teach them life lessons. Her own mother had done her best, whatever her failings, and Tessa would, too.

"Can we still get a dog?" Zack said. "And can I get a phone?"

Henry's laughter was the most comforting sound Tessa had ever heard. The newspaper had printed the whole story, mostly correct, that Barbara Willoughby and her late husband, Sheriff Malcolm Owen, had extorted Tessa's family for years, falsely accusing a teenaged Tessa of being involved in a fatal hit-and-run accident.

"Did you see your socials?" Zack put his laptop next to hers. "Everyone's going crazy. There's, like, a justice for Tessa hashtag. You've got like a million new likes."

"Your sales numbers have skyrocketed, too," Henry said.

"You looked at that?"

"What can I say? Husband of a bestseller, that's my job. King of the home front."

"The doorbell!" Linny said. "I'll get it."

"Speaking of your job, *king*. Nellie Delaney and Blytheton, what was the deal with that?" Tessa had decided Nellie was simply a congenial neighbor, and had handled Linny with compassion, not competition. And from the way they'd chatted at the bookstore coffee shop, Zack and her son Tris were apparently soulmates.

"Her family's had a summer place there forever. I told you that. She's younger than you, of course."

Tessa punched him in the arm.

"But she told me," he went on, ignoring her, "that the librarian up there recognized you on the book cover, remembered you'd once been a summer person, and put two and two together."

"Emily and I did go to the library. Back then." Tessa nodded, envisioning it. "But I was so freaked out over her. Nellie, I mean. And you. I imagined—"

"Mom! Look!" Linny's voice came from behind a massive bouquet of frothy hydrangeas. "Who're they from?"

"Let me carry that thing," Henry said, putting the flowers on the counter. "This must be all the blue flowers that ever existed."

Tessa took the card, opened it. "With massive love from Team Tessa," she read out loud. "FaceTime us when you get this. Big news!"

"What's that about?" Henry asked.

"Let's find out," Tessa said and tapped the keyboard, and DJ's face appeared. She was standing at her desk at Waverly, tall stacks of books behind her, Olivette and Sadie Bailey flanking her.

"Hey, rock star," DJ said. "We sent flowers instead of cheese. We're all here cheering you on."

"They're gorgeous, see?" Tessa turned the screen to show them. "You understand why I couldn't explain all the—"

"Totally. Difficult to tell your publicist that you have a demented blackmailing stalker from the past, I get it. We'll talk about that later, okay? But for now—Ollie, Sadie, want to do the honors?"

"What honors?" Tessa exchanged glances with Henry, and felt Zack and Linny clinging to her.

"There's someone we want you to say hello to," her editor said. "Remember we told you we had some good news that we couldn't tell you yet?"

Tessa did, vaguely, a conversation that seemed an infinity ago; a promise long since smothered by bad news.

"Um, sure."

"Well," Sadie said, "here it comes. And I'm the one who gave him your address."

"Huh?" Tessa looked at Henry, bewildered. "Address?"

The women had moved out of the camera's range, and a man's face replaced them.

"Tessa?" the man said.

Tessa leaned closer to the screen, as if that would help her see more clearly, and then sat up straight.

"Sam? From 3A?"

"You remembered." Sam's blue eyes twinkled even through the Face-Time. "I sent the postcard as kind of a joke, of course. I'm sorry to have—well, not been straightforward with you. Meeting you at the airport was a happy coincidence, because I'd only planned to come to ReadRunner to see you in action. We don't want to work with someone who isn't confident in public, or a team player."

"You've lost me," Tessa said.

"I hope not," Sam said. "We want to put Annabelle on the big screen as soon as we can. And you'll talk to Sadie here about details. If you're interested. And Annabelle approves."

I have another good book idea, too, Annabelle said. Just so you know.

"I think we can make that work," Tessa said.

Tessa heard applause and cheering in the background, and then applause and cheering in her new yellow kitchen, as the people in her digital life and the people in her real life combined into one happy glorious moment in time, a place where hard work and good luck—and love and trust—all came together. Emily, too, was back in her life. And storytelling had brought them all here.

And such a relief, too, that her nemesis hadn't been an impassioned fan or an envious rival author. Although Barbara Willoughby, who'd created her fictional story to amass fraudulent wealth, had almost succeeded in weaponizing admiration.

Hours later, snuggled under white sheets and her body pressed against Henry's, the darkness surrounding them, and with the sound of her husband's gentle breathing, Tessa envisioned her mother and tried to understand what she had sacrificed for her. In the thrall of greedy manipulation, and to her own peril, she had protected Tessa, simply out of the power of love for her. Would any mother have done the same?

I would, I promise. Tessa wished she could tell her in person. Even, strangely, thank her.

A branch battered against the side of the house, not scary, not suspicious, only the still-unfamiliar sounds of their new home.

This is my one life, she thought. So much had changed. But some things, she hoped, would never change. Stories could change lives, and stories could inspire. And Annabelle, smart, kind, innocent Annabelle—Annabelle could have more than one life now. She could thrive and succeed, and, living in readers' imaginations, could inspire them into their own power.

And you have given that to me, Annabelle said. Thank you.

And with that, Tessa could almost feel the scales of justice tilt back into balance, as her precarious world righted itself. She'd never thought about it quite that way—but Annabelle was correct. She, Tessa, had—in fiction—given Annabelle more than her one life.

Or maybe they had done it for each other.

Henry had turned over in the dim light of the almost darkness, and now traced a finger down her cheek as he'd done from the day they met.

"You're home," he whispered. "I can't believe it."

"Me either. Sweet dreams." *Moms with dreams,* she thought. Her own mom had a dream, too, that Tessa would be safe. And now she was.

"Safe safe, darling." Henry propped himself up on one elbow. "Love love."

"Always always," she said, moving closer. "Always always."

THREE WEEKS LATER

"Can I talk to you about one more thing?" Tessa stood in the doorway of Olivette's office. The skyscrapers of Manhattan, framed in wide windows, spiked through murky clouds of the waning July afternoon. Their planning meeting at Waverly had ended. Her editor had just hugged her goodbye, DJ still perched on the edge of Olivette's desk, and Sadie Bailey was wrapping a filmy silk scarf around her neck in preparation for their celebratory dinner. Henry and the kids had gone to the Delaneys' house in Maine, and Tessa would join them soon. Emily and her husband were summering in Paris, but in the fall, she and Tessa had promised, their lives would begin again. Together.

Barbara Willoughby was in custody, charged with extortion and interstate banking fraud and a raft of other charges. A judge had refused bail. The Locket Mom ruse had ended, blazing through social media, instantly making Tessa a sympathetic hero. Secretly though, Tessa had to admit, it had taught her a lesson about privacy.

All This Could be Yours went into a fourth printing, then a fifth.

All this could be yours, Tessa thought as she watched her beloved colleagues. But not yet. No good book could be satisfactorily concluded until all the loose ends were tied up.

And there was still one more loose end. One more loose end to resolve before Tessa could begin her next chapter.

And this was the moment.

"Is something wrong, Tessa?" Her agent paused, one manicured hand holding her scarf in place.

"You have a funny look on your face," Olivette said.

"What?" DJ took a step closer. "Is there a problem?"

Tessa had thought about this, mentally practiced what she'd say, but here with these three women, her career on the line, her outline had vanished. She'd told Henry last night, the whole thing, and he'd dried her tears, comforting, and they'd decided it was part of her, part of what made her who she was.

"I love you even more now, Tesser," he'd reassured her. And that reassurance gave her the courage to face today's confession. Which would definitely be the end of her bestseller journey. One that would not have a happy ending.

"When I was about ten," she began now.

"Do you need to sit down?" Olivette asked. "Are you okay?"

The whole story poured out. Her day at Annabelle's house. *Black Beauty.* The knock on the mayor's door. The man with the briefcase. The postcard-perfect Ohio afternoon.

"He said I knew him," Tessa went on. "And he said I was a good helper. He told me he needed to come in to get the mayor's speech."

The music of the Popsicle man.

"And then . . ." And then. The part that Tessa could barely manage to say. She looked at the carpeted floor, unable to meet her colleagues' eyes. "He made a deal with me. Gave me five dollars to go get a Popsicle. And when, when I got back . . ." She took a deep breath. Too late to stop now. "Annabelle was gone. He had taken her."

Olivette gasped, but Tessa went on, had to go on. She would probably never see these people again, except with a lawyer.

"We left town after that, my mother could not face it, the mortifying headlines, and the humiliation. Everyone said I had exchanged Annabelle's safety for five dollars to go buy a cherry Popsicle. My mother changed our names. She would never discuss it, only called it The Bad Thing."

Tessa watched as each woman took in the rest of the story; the capture, the years of uncertainty, and, finally, Annabelle in the Maumee

River. Sadie staring at her, Olivette with her arms crossed over her chest, DJ's eyes widening.

And then the silence, the dreaded thud of leaden silence that Tessa had feared, where she imagined all three of them assessing the extent of the damage; to their star author, to their careers, to their sales projections, to their futures. The inevitable social media firestorm. Tessa's disappointed fans outraged, betrayed, pursuing her with pitchforks and flaming torches.

"Annabelle is real?" Sadie finally asked.

Tessa took a deep breath. "She was. She *was* real."

"So she's not a fictional character," Olivette said.

"Well, she is, in fact." Tessa had planned for this question. "Because I only knew her when she was fifteen. There's no Annabelle Brown who's a confident, witty, kick-ass corporate genius. That part I made up. But I realized I was honoring Annabelle in the only way I could, by writing a story where she lives on, as a hero. An inspiration. With success and happiness."

With my help, Annabelle said. *Goes without saying.*

"You were ten?" DJ said. "Ten years old? Like, thirty years ago?"

Tessa nodded. She felt ten years old even now, her heart beating like a baby bird. "One local newspaper called me 'the bad friend.'"

Her editor leaped up, enveloped Tessa in a hug. "That's insane. That's so wrong. You poor thing." Olivette took a step back, palm to her heart. "How awful. How breathtakingly awful. You're brave and strong and wonderful. And you were a child."

"You've kept this a secret all this time?" DJ asked.

"I cannot believe you didn't tell me," her agent said. Sadie's eyes widened. "I instructed you, specifically, that you needed to disclose everything."

"I know. I know." Exactly what Tessa feared. "Is everything ruined? I'm so sorry. I'm so incredibly sorry. You explained the moral turpitude clause, but I was—"

"You were a victim, darling," Sadie said. "A child. A child in an impossible situation."

Tessa nodded. "But still—"

"And *that's* why you wrote about a bargain, isn't it?"

"You could put it like that," Tessa had to admit. "A deal with the devil. That I made."

"No. That's not true." Sadie shook her head. "You simply—"

"Wait. Are you kidding me?" DJ interrupted. "You're saying Annabelle is inspired by something that really happened to you?"

"In a way. It's sort of . . . I created the person Annabelle *should* have been. Could have been. Gave her a life she would have wanted."

I'm still here, Annabelle said.

"I mean—" Tessa tried to put her passion into words. "She saved me. So I did my best to save her. In fiction."

"Tessa Calloway." Sadie pointed a forefinger at her. "You are even more of a rock star than I thought. Ollie, DJ, you agree?"

"Got to love 'inspired by a true crime,'" Olivette said. "Cover line if I ever heard one."

"I'm writing the news release right now." DJ pulled out her cell phone, tapped the screen. "Sales will go astronomical. Can you go live on social again, Tessa? Like you did with Locket Mom? It'll be freaking viral."

Tessa frowned. "You mean—it's okay? You want me to . . ." This she had not anticipated. "This is . . . a *good* thing?"

"Hundred percent," DJ said. "Your fans will be even more wildly devoted than they are now. And think of all the affinity groups, and—"

"Your next book could be *this* story," Olivette interrupted. "The Bad Friend. About a brave and spunky preteen who sacrifices—"

"Wait." Sadie had come to Tessa's side, put her arm across her shoulders, drew her close for a beat. "Tessa, what do you think?"

"I think . . ." Tessa drew in a breath, remembering how fiction had helped her escape as a child, and helped her triumph as an adult. Novels were stories that needed to be told. In real life, though—some stories could stay private. Disguised, yes, embellished in fiction to select what was important, what was inspirational, and share it. That was the power of story.

But some stories, some real-life truths, did not need to be shared. And should not be the exploitive fodder for fiction. Annabelle was a tragic victim, and Tessa did not want to cause her family—wherever they were— any more pain.

"Sadie?" Tessa began. "I'll think of a new plot, I promise. How about a writer who's a serial killer? With misguided parents. And a theme of reconciliation. But—let's keep this *my* story. And Annabelle's. Privately. The book will keep her alive, and she can happily live in fiction world. Because of you—and you, Ollie, and you, DJ—she got to have more than one life, you know? Now everyone gets to admire her spirit, and honor what her life could have been. Like I do."

I love you, too, Annabelle said.

And for a moment, the room was silent again, each woman, maybe, considering her own private dreams, and her own dearest hopes, and her one precious life.

"*You're* like Annabelle now," Olivette whispered.

And then Tessa laughed, a real laugh, a laugh that erased years of fear and guilt and shadows. A laugh of freedom.

"No way," Tessa said. "Unless we're *all* like Annabelle."

"Totally," DJ said. "We are all Annabelle. I'll put that in your next *Library Journal* ad."

"And from now on, I'll be the one making deals," her agent said. "But only with good guys."

Tessa's phone pinged. *VIP. Henry.* Where are you? Missing you.

Now her family was waiting for her, ready to begin their next chapter. Together. Even, maybe, with a dog. Maybe. But the truth, strange as it seemed, was the opposite of what Annabelle had told her—it was *she* who had given *Tessa* more than one life. And because of Annabelle, she could continue to live it. Free, and happy, and loved, and fearless.

Live it for herself, for her husband, for her children, and for all the women who needed someone like Annabelle in their lives; needed to see her confidence and her perseverance and her possibilities the same way she did. Live it for readers—who understood they could heal themselves with fiction, and then, empowered, turn the page, and find their dreams.

Acknowledgments

Have you ever been to an author event at a library or a bookstore? I remember the very first one I attended—maybe twenty-five years ago, in a now out-of-business bookstore in Harvard Square. The author was a crime fiction writer, an acquaintance of my husband, and I absolutely remember thinking, as he walked to the podium, that if this ever happened to me, my feet would not be touching the ground. I would be so happy, I would be so thrilled, I would be so overjoyed, I would never be the same.

(I also remember asking myself: Why doesn't he look happy?)

It makes me laugh so much, now, all these years later, because now I know what's behind it. And that's one thing that inspired this book.

I know. I agree with you. It's pretty hilarious, isn't it? I'll be an author on book tour talking about a book called *All This Could Be Yours*, which you will realize is about an author on book tour talking about a book called *All This Could Be Yours*. It's about as meta as it can be, and supremely life-changing. I am so eager to chat with you about all of it.

Readers and booksellers and librarians, and all my darling friends in the publishing world: If you think you see yourself in this book—well, you may be right. I have to admit that. Oh, no one specific, no one who is created in the image of a specific person, but oh my goodness, yes. There you are. This book is—I hope—a twisty, fast-paced thriller. But it is also a love letter to you, dearest ones, to readers and booksellers and librarians and authors—and parents—and anyone who loves reading and writing and telling a good story.

(There is a truly great story about the genesis of this book, too, so ask me about it on the road.)

The cast of characters who made this book happen is completely stellar. The people on the pages you've just read are fictional, but let's talk about some real people now.

My beloved team at Minotaur Books—thank you endlessly for welcoming me so warmly into your incredible family. I am constantly impressed with your knowledge and brilliance and constant perseverance, and honored by your support and friendship.

Standing ovation to my total genius editor, Kristin Sevick. Readers, every word you read in this book, she has read two, three, and four times, always gently and brilliantly shepherding me in exactly the right direction. Without her this book would be so different, and I would be, too.

Thanks to the patient and incredibly organized editorial assistant Jill Schuck. The indefatigable and superstar team of Kayla Janas and Allison Ziegler, who will make sure everyone knows absolutely everything about *All This Could Be Yours*. I am incredibly grateful to you, amazing ones.

Copy editor Lesley Allen! Thank you for protecting me from career-ending errors, for letting me have most of the commas, and for watchdogging me through airports and time zones.

Kelley Ragland, I am so grateful for the opened door, and for your wisdom and guidance. (And for letting me have some of your french fries.) Jen Enderlin and Andy Martin, so honored to be on your team! It is a true joy.

Art designer David Rotstein: woo-hoo and thank you. Managing editor Alisa Trager, marketing VP Paul Hochman, production editor Laurie Henderson, designer Gabriel Guma, and production manager Gail Friedman. You all know there is no real book without you. Thank you.

And to my friends at Forge Books: Linda Quinton, Lucille Rettino, Alexis Saarela, Sarah Weeks, Troix Jackson, Eileen Lawrence, and Laura Pennock—I love you so much. And am forever grateful.

Agent Lisa Gallagher. Standing ovation. My dear friend, and a treasured heroine and fierce protector, you are utterly brilliant. I always say I love every decision we make.

The artistry and savvy of Madeira James, Charlie Anctil, Mary Zanor, Pamela Klinger-Horn. Christie Conlee, Stacey Looney, Nina Zagorscak, and Jon Stone. You are all so fabulous. Kathie Bennett—wow. You are such a life-changing powerhouse. Angela Melamud—you are certainly magical! Karen Bellovich and Margaret Pinard at A Mighty Blaze, you are perfection. Maxwell Gregory, I am in awe.

Sue Grafton, always. Mary Higgins Clark, ditto. You are both still with me. Nita Prose, Jeneva Rose, Ashley Elston, Jean Kwok, Riley Sager, and Elle Cosimano. Thank you for your remarkable generosity—I am honored to know you. Lisa Scottoline. Erin Mitchell. Barbara Peters, Kym Havens, and Robin Agnew. Katie Mannix. Rae Titcomb. Jeff Kinney. You are amazing. James Patterson, you are a treasure.

My dear blog sisters at Jungle Red Writers: Julia Spencer-Fleming, Hallie Ephron, Roberta Isleib/Lucy Burdette, Jenn McKinlay, Deborah Crombie, and Rhys Bowen. And my Career Authors posse: Paula Munier, Dana Isaacson, Jessica Strawser, and Brian Andrews. What would I do without you? And Ann Garvin and the Tall Poppies, you are the best. Thank you.

And my darling sister Nancy Landman.

Speaking of life-changing: Bookstagrammers! If I list you, I will forget someone, but you know who you are. I am grateful every single day.

And also life-changing: my partner in fictional crime, bestseller and treasured friend Hannah Mary McKinnon. There would be no First Chapter Fun without you, and you are brilliant in every way. And the amazing Karen Dionne—our collaboration on The Back Room is a constant joy. And to all of you, Funsters and Blazers and Back Room attendees, it is always a treat to see you. Thank you.

Jonathan is my darling perfect wonderful husband, of course. Thank you for all the driving, and carryout dinners, and your infinite patience, and your unending wisdom. (And for being my in-house counsel.) Love you so much.

Do you see your actual name in this book? Some very generous souls allowed theirs to be used in return for an auction donation to charity. To retain the magic, I will let you find yourselves.

All This Could Be Yours. The title came to me, unbidden, and I still can't believe how appropriate it is. Our lives are all hopes and dreams, trade-offs and bargains, a search for happiness and peace and joy and fulfillment. My true inspirations are you, darling readers, and those who helped this book become a reality. It's not fully realized until you read it, and I am so grateful to you for keeping it alive. And yes, indeed, tears came to my eyes writing this.

Sharp-eyed readers will notice I have tweaked Massachusetts geography a bit. It's only to protect the innocent. And I adore it when people read the acknowledgments. Keep in touch, okay?

Lynn Wayne

Hank Phillippi Ryan, *USA Today* bestselling author, has won five Agatha Awards, five Anthony Awards, the Daphne, the Macavity, and the Mary Higgins Clark Awards. As on-air investigative reporter for Boston's WHDH-TV, she's won thirty-seven Emmy Awards and many more journalism honors. A former president of national Sisters in Crime, a founder of Mystery Writers of America University, and a board member of International Thriller Writers, Ryan lives in Boston.